Pillar of Fire

Also by Joyce Hollyday

On the Heels of Freedom: The American Missionary Association's Bold Campaign to Educate Minds, Open Hearts, and Heal the Soul of a Divided Nation

Then Shall Your Light Rise: Spiritual Formation and Social Witness

Clothed with the Sun: Biblical Women, Social Justice, and Us

Turning Toward Home: A Sojourn of Hope

Clarence Jordan: Essential Writings

Forgetting the Former Things: Brain Injury's Invitation to Vulnerability and Faith
(with Tamara Puffer)

Waging Peace: Global Adventures of a Lifelong Activist
(with David Hartsough)

Held in the Light: Norman Morrison's Sacrifice for Peace and His Family's Journey of Healing (with Anne Morrison Welsh)

Faith Beyond Borders: Doing Justice in a Dangerous World and *With Our Own Eyes: A Christian Response to the Wounds of War, Racism, and Oppression*
(with Don Mosley)

Cloud of Witnesses and *Crucible of Fire: The Church Confronts Apartheid*
(with Jim Wallis)

Follow or contact the author at www.joycehollyday.com

Pillar of Fire

A Novel

Joyce Hollyday

RESOURCE *Publications* · Eugene, Oregon

PILLAR OF FIRE
A Novel

Resource Publications
An Imprint of Wipf and Stock Publishers
199 W. 8th Ave., Suite 3
Eugene, OR 97401

www.wipfandstock.com

PAPERBACK ISBN: 978-1-7252-8223-0
HARDCOVER ISBN: 978-1-7252-8224-7
EBOOK ISBN: 978-1-7252-8225-4

Manufactured in the U.S.A.   SEPTEMBER 29, 2020

Para mis queridas hermanas de Mujeres Unidas en Fe
For my dear sisters of Women United in Faith

Preface

Nestled in the charming Belgian village of Sint-Truiden is a brick chapel with a barrel-vault wood ceiling, lovingly restored to its thirteenth-century dignity. The Church of Saint Agnes is similar to many others I have visited, except for this: women permeate this holy site, not only through the haunting recorded chants that echo through it, but also in the images on its stone columns and white-plaster walls. Ancient paintings and frescoes portray biblical women and saints: pregnant Mary and Elizabeth greet each other with an embrace; Veronica dries Jesus's tears as he falls on the path to crucifixion, and Mary Magdalene gazes in grief at the cross; Agatha prays to heaven under the Inquisition's torture, and Catherine, Helena, and Agnes bear witness to centuries of courageous faith. Subtly painted in the bottom right corner of many of the frescoes is a pair, or small huddle, of women in plain gray dress and white head coverings. Observing.

The Church of Saint Agnes is at the heart of a beguinage, a cluster of simple dwellings that eight centuries ago housed two hundred of these women known as Beguines. They were part of a movement renowned for its deep devotion and compassionate works of mercy. They cared for people suffering from leprosy and those who were dying; and, in an era when child brides were common and girls were excluded from education, they provided safe haven and study. Spurning cultural dictates of the time limiting women to the roles of wives owned and subjugated by their husbands, or nuns cloistered and controlled by the church, the Beguines lived together in spiritually empowered communities, supporting themselves by spinning and weaving, making candles and lace, baking bread and brewing beer.

Thirteen Belgian beguinages, in various stages of preservation, have been designated UNESCO World Heritage Sites. I visited eight of them—from the narrow cobblestoned streets and tiny whitewashed apartments of Kortrijk to the large, walled compound encompassing a field of daffodils and surrounded by canals in Bruges. A few have small museums where visitors can sip Beguine beer, or sample an oatmeal biscuit made according to an ancient Beguine recipe with marigolds and honey.

Although the Beguines are proudly remembered in Europe, little has been written about them, and this movement that embraced a million women over several generations is virtually unknown in North America. My particular passion is to share their story with young women, who face enormous pressure to be thin in body, mind, and spirit. But I believe the bold witness of the Beguines is broadly compelling, particularly given the remarkable parallels between their era of the Crusades and our own: marked by the ideology of empire, the weight of patriarchy, a widening chasm between the well-off and those on the economic margins, and a rise in ethnic and religious intolerance. I hope that all readers will find inspiration and encouragement for these challenging days in the pages that follow.

For their courage, the Beguines eventually became targets of state and ecclesial authority. The most well-known Beguine, the mystic Marguerite Porete, was audacious enough to write a book about the feminine aspects of love and of God. *The Mirror of Simple Souls* drew the attention of the Inquisition and was burned in a public square in Paris, with the accompanying threat that, if she did not stop writing such "heresy," she would suffer the same fate.

Her story inspired the closing chapters of *Pillar of Fire*. The earlier chapters are my fictionalized account of one young woman's life in medieval England and France, and the birth of the Beguine movement, which grew organically and spread rapidly across Europe's Low Countries. Historical details about the Middle Ages, falconry and the path to knighthood, Benedictine life, the treatment of people with leprosy, the persecution of Muslims and Jews, the Crusades, church corruption and the pope's council, the heresy campaign and the Inquisition were carefully researched.

I've dedicated this book to *Mujeres Unidas en Fe* (Women United in Faith), the bilingual women's group I was blessed to be part of until my recent move from the mountains of Western North Carolina. With Rebecca Sharp and Becca Heskamp graciously offering translation when needed, our circle of two dozen women worked on improving our Spanish and English skills, educated ourselves about immigrant rights, and helped get family emergency plans in place, in the event that one of our members got targeted for deportation. It was crucial work in a frightening time.

But the most important thing I learned came as a surprise. From their daughters' festive *quinceañera* birthday parties and dear Tereza Martinez Almaras's joyful mariachi-enlivened wedding to our *Día de los Muertos* altar overflowing with colorful homemade tissue-paper flowers, these sisters have shown me how to celebrate. Even—perhaps especially—in difficult times. When we gathered around the casket of our beloved Berta Valdez García, dressed like Our Lady of Guadalupe in a bright red satin dress and green mantle adorned with gold braiding, clutching her rosary and two white flowers, we were reeling from the unexpected loss. But expressions of gratitude and stories about Berta's mischievous wit flowed as profusely as tears.

These women are among the most devout and generous people I know. They have spread their generosity into the surrounding community, cooking Mexican lunches at local churches that are always sold out, raising money for a humanitarian fund to which everyone has access. It has provided needed support during medical emergencies and job losses, for students involved in special school activities and children separated from their parents at the U.S.-Mexico border.

They are beyond courageous. Soon after the White House's terrifying January 2017 announcement of an escalation in deportations, many people living undocumented in the U.S. understandably chose to be as invisible as possible. But the *mujeres* overcame their fear and invited our county sheriff, his deputies, and the local chief of police to a special "Lunch with the Law" in order to introduce themselves and tell their stories. The sharing over a feast of tamales and empanadas, rice and beans, flan and sweet *dulce de leche* caramel cake is now an annual event.

Like the Beguines, these dear sisters remind me that we need one another in order to be brave. And we can accomplish in community far more than we can ever do alone.

Acknowledgments

Pillar of Fire is a novel about the power of community. So it seems right that I should begin my thanks with the formative faith communities of my early years: the First United Methodist Church on Chocolate Avenue in Hershey, Pennsylvania; the Bates College Christian Fellowship; Church of the Resurrection in East Harlem; and Father Henri Nouwen's weekly communion circle at Yale Divinity School.

During the fifteen years that I was part of the intensely activist ministry of *Sojourners* magazine and community in Washington, DC, I found respite from time to time at All Saints Convent in Catonsville, Maryland. On my first retreat there, I imitated what I thought was the breakfast genuflection—only to discover that an older sister had gone to her knees to rescue a dropped vitamin pill. I can only be thankful for those sisters who tolerated my inexperience, and for many things revealed and learned on my spiritual journey in the decades since.

I'm exceedingly grateful for the Benedictine Sisters of Erie, Pennsylvania, who offered me warm hospitality and writing space over the years. I especially thank Sister Joan Chittister, my first spiritual director, who at a painful and critical juncture in my life gave me guidance that enabled me to choose freedom and joy. When I discovered the Beguines, I recognized them in large part because I had already experienced a community of empowered women, devoted to prayer and service, committed to courageously confronting patriarchy and working tirelessly for peace.

The gracious Benedictine tradition continues to beckon. I made final revisions on *Pillar of Fire* while on retreat at Saint Scholastica Priory in Petersham, Massachusetts. Each evening at Compline, with candles flickering in the darkened chapel and black-robed sisters and brothers chanting in Latin, I experienced a powerful glimpse of what the mystical life of the Beguines must have been like. I have felt similarly moved by the Benedictine

Monks of Weston Priory, whose music has inspired me since my days at So-journers Community, and who, since my recent move to Vermont, now live a scenic, winding drive through pine-and-birch forest just north of home.

I'm grateful to Don Richter, Keri Liechty, and Edwin David Aponte of the Louisville Institute for awarding me a research grant that made possible my visit to Belgium. It also enabled me to enlist the help of four extraordi-nary young women in shaping the book-in-progress. Joy Siler, Anna Far-lessyost, Rachel Rasmussen, and Hillary Brown offered invaluable insights, and they continue to inspire me with the courageous choices they make with their lives.

My good friends Cathy and Jim Stentzel made a generous contribution from their family foundation to support the writing of *Pillar of Fire*. Steve and Christine Clemens have been magnanimous in offering sustaining sup-port for my writing and for many efforts toward justice and peace. Mary Cowal, who was lavish with friendship, hospitality, and prayers while she was on this earth, left me an unexpected financial gift upon her recent pass-ing that helped carry me through the last stages of preparing the manuscript for publication.

When I was a student at Emory University's Candler School of Theol-ogy, I participated in a Middle East Travel Seminar, courtesy of the Pattillo Family Foundation. Our visit to Saint Catherine's Monastery in the Egyp-tian desert, from which we launched a middle-of-the-night trek by camel up Mount Sinai, provided many of the details for the pilgrimage in chapter 14. My thanks also to the Collegeville Institute, which twice gave me the gift of quiet space to write and connection with like-minded, and like-hearted, authors—and provided an opportunity to peruse *The Saint John's Bible*, a work of sacred art handwritten in elegant calligraphy and beautifully illu-minated in the ancient Benedictine style. Good friends Beth and Joe Vogler gave me days of writing in their cozy cabin perched on a ridge in the Blue Ridge Mountains, and Beth's 95-year-old father, Bob Abernathy, has been my most ardent enthusiast.

I'm grateful for Wipf & Stock Publishers. In an increasingly corpora-tized, monopolized, and profit-driven publishing world, it is a rare gift to find a publisher that embraces progressive faith and produces fine books based on the worthiness of their content rather than the whims of the market.

Very special thanks are due to Nancy Rue, who writes beautiful books for young adults. Nancy gave countless hours reading through the manu-script, offering detailed and inspired guidance as well as constant, ebullient encouragement. Rose Marie Berger, a poet who has been a good friend since my days at *Sojourners* magazine, also applied her experienced editorial eye.

Beth Maczka shared important insights about Mary Magdalene and the women mystics, and Jenny Ire and Terri Nash offered crucial enlightenment about midwifery.

When we baptized twins a few years ago, my Circle of Mercy co-founder and co-pastor Nancy Hastings Sehested offered a moving prayer that inspired the one found in chapter 38. I'm thankful for the creativity and mutual support of our enduring friendship. And for the vision of the late Stephanie Egnotovich, an editor at Westminster/John Knox Press who invited me almost thirty years ago to write *Clothed with the Sun: Biblical Women, Social Justice, and Us.* The compelling stories I discovered then about the vulnerability, strength, and courage of women in the Bible appear throughout *Pillar of Fire.*

Lydia Wylie-Kellermann, Erinn Fahey, Denise Griebler, and Bill Wylie-Kellermann gathered round for an early reading of the manuscript in Detroit. Lucy Wylie-Kellermann invented The Onion Game described in chapter 26 when she was eight years old. She and her family had just received the news that her mother was suffering from an aggressive brain cancer, and young Lucy thought that, amid all the sadness and fear, they should have something to celebrate. Two months before Jeanie passed on New Year's Eve of 2005, we all played the game in their home, and I was moved as each one made an outlandish guess in order to make sure Jeanie won her last Onion Game. These dearly beloved friends still celebrate Onion Day on October 25 every year.

Murphy Davis, Ed Loring, and Hannah Murphy Buc also listened to an early reading, in a cabin on the edge of North Carolina's Lake Santeetlah. I am tremendously grateful for this friendship that has spanned four decades, and for all the ways they have inspired me to greater courage and deeper solidarity with people on the margins. Several other dear friends read the manuscript and encouraged me to keep believing in *Pillar of Fire,* including Ken Sehested, Elaine Enns, Ched Myers, Mahan Siler, Missy Harris, Larry Wilson, Jane Wilson, Jo Hauser, Mark Siler, Kiran Sigmon, Betsy Corner, Kate Stevens, Lynne Hinton, Lynda Weaver-Williams, and Michael McGregor.

I'm immeasurably grateful for my sisters Kay Filar and Debra Link and their families, who have been pillars of steadfast love through the decades. Thanks also to Gerri Ryons-Hudson, Wiley Dobbs, and the Ramsey clan for cheering me on. Marianne Mitchell opened my heart to the mystical power of healing. Sandra Smith, Darilyn Dealy, Sky Kramer, and the other sisters in our Asheville women's ritual group kept me grounded in story, ritual, and awe. Terri Farless regularly kept up my spirits over omelet-and-hash-brown breakfasts at The Wagon Wheel in Mars Hill, North Carolina.

I'm blessed with many wonderful and deep friendships. There's not enough space to name all of you who offered an encouraging word, a chocolate hit, a hike, a party, or a prayer—but you know who you are. I'm grateful for my connections with you through Word and World, Circle of Mercy, *Mujeres Unidas en Fe*, the ARCHES community for dying well, the Open Door Community, the Southeast Conference of the United Church of Christ, the AnamCara clergy group, the Brevard women's communion circle, the Agape Community, and the Shelburne Falls vespers group.

Loving thanks to my surprise late-in-life partner, Bill Ramsey, a creative, courageous, and compassionate soul. I'm grateful that we share a forest home, with bashful moose and boisterous owls for neighbors. Greece will always make me smile: morning writing and afternoons of reading aloud your poetry and my early book chapters; swims in the sparkling-blue Aegean Sea and bike rides through ancient olive groves; stunning sunset feasts at Limnisa with other writers from all over the world and the search for wedding rings. You were chauffeur extraordinaire when we chased down beguinages all over Belgium, driving us off onto a sheep trail only once. I look forward to whatever shared, off-the-beaten paths lie ahead.

I stood alone in the heart of a vast desert ringed by jagged mountains. Everything around me glimmered in the silvery glow of a full moon perched atop the highest peak. The moon crawled up the sky, and a piece of it disappeared, as if bitten away. As it climbed, the bite grew larger . . . and then larger still. When it was entirely swallowed, the moon blushed crimson.

Stars blinked to life, strewn like diamonds across the blue-black expanse over my head. The brightest fell to earth and flared into a flame that danced in the distance. I walked toward the light, across a broad stretch of deep and drifted sand, and came upon a rose bush. Its branches and blooms were ablaze, but the fire did not harm or consume it.

As I watched, the bush sent out tendrils. These grew into massive, gnarled roots that snaked across the ground in all directions. A voice in the center of the bush called my name. Then a single flame separated from the blaze. It burst into a towering pillar of fire that reached from the ground to heaven. When it began to move through the wilderness, I followed . . .

From *The Radiant Soul: Aflame with Love*
Swansong Bluff, near Calais, France
November 1209

One

_____

Her sister's screams pierced the velvet veil of the night. Clarissa hunched in a corner by the foot of the ancient oak bed and shuddered with each cry. "It'll be all right," whispered the midwife Beatrix, as Josselyn paused to gasp for air. Clarissa took a deep breath in sympathy with her sister and held it, afraid to move.

Thick logs blazed in the massive fireplace, filling the room with an eerie orange glow and casting shadows that danced like ghosts on the walls. A wool fleece and strips of linen lay on the hearth. Next to them sat a basin filled with creamy milk, warming up for the baby's first bath. By the bed was a jar of honey, a few drops of which would be rubbed on the newborn's palate to stimulate its appetite.

Beatrix, bent over by age and the weight of her work, encouraged Josselyn to breathe slowly. "In . . . and out. In . . . and out. Yes, that's it." Clarissa exhaled and tried to match the rhythm of her sister's breaths. A hint of lavender hovered around her in the corner, and the sweet scent prompted a cascade of pleasant memories. She allowed these to tumble through her mind, hoping they would crowd out her worry and her fear.

Readying this room in the manor that was reserved for birthing had begun a week before, when the servants swept it clean with bulrushes plucked from the edge of the lake. That afternoon Clarissa threw on her cloak and ventured out into the autumn chill with a basket to gather the last of the herbs from the garden. She could have sent a servant, but for weeks she had anticipated offering this gift to Josselyn and was determined to carry out every detail herself.

When her fingers were numb and her basket full, Clarissa headed straight for the birthing room and began scattering the sweet leaves on the floor. As she worked, the door behind her opened gently and Josselyn

walked in. "I wanted to surprise you," said Clarissa with a trace of disappointment, helping her sister onto a stool by the table that held the basket.

Josselyn smiled at her, and Clarissa moved to a corner and resumed
her delightful task. When she turned around, a fistful of herbs landed in
her face. She gave Josselyn a playful glare and then laughed. "Not exactly
proper behavior for a sixteen-year-old about to be a mother," she declared,
scooping up a pile of the leaves and tossing them into the air to shower over
Josselyn. Josselyn grabbed another fistful and, giggling, the sisters gently
pelted each other.

When the basket was empty and the herbs were strewn across the
floor, Clarissa announced, "We need to crush them." She took Josselyn's
hands in hers and helped her off the stool. They circled and spun as best they
could, a young woman ripe with pregnancy and her younger sister, dancing
awkwardly but joyfully in the sunlight that streamed through the window.
The gentle pressure of their feet released into the air the fragrant sweetness
of lavender and rosemary and mint.

When Josselyn stopped to catch her breath and rub her aching back,
Clarissa moved next to the bed. Moving slowly and deliberately, Josselyn
positioned herself on the other side. Together, beaming smiles at each other,
the sisters spread a cream-colored coverlet edged in eyelet lace, the finest
of the manor, over the feather palette on the old oak bed. Then Clarissa
stepped back and swept her eyes over the room. "It's ready," she declared
proudly.

"And so am I," murmured Josselyn, pressing her fingers into her back
again. Clarissa moved toward her with her arms extended, intending to help
rub away the soreness. But Josselyn grasped her hands and placed them
where Clarissa could feel the baby, which was moving a foot, doing its own
dance. Clarissa smiled.

"What would I do without you?" said Josselyn, returning the smile and
running her fingers tenderly through her younger sister's dark curls. Then
she added in a whisper, "Thank you for being with me." Clarissa attempted
to give her a hug, but she was barely able to reach her arms around Josselyn,
and the sisters laughed once more.

§

The next few days had been laced with anticipation. Clarissa peeked into the
birthing room at least twice each day to make sure that everything was still
in order. And then, at last, the waiting was over. The night before, sometime
in the dark middle hours, she had been awakened by the commotion of

Bickford, the livery servant, rushing out and riding off in a horse-drawn wagon. Clarissa knew it could mean only one thing: he was on his way to fetch the midwife.

She leapt off her palette and flew into the hall. She found her mother, with one arm around Josselyn, slowly ushering her older daughter toward the specially prepared space. Clarissa ran ahead. She pulled the coverlet off the bed and plumped up the feather pillows. As her sister settled into the bed with a groan, their mother moved around the room lighting candles. A servant rushed in to start the fire in the hearth. Clarissa, unsure of what to say or do next, squeezed Josselyn's hand as her sister panted in pain, feeling great relief when Beatrix and her young assistant, Emmeline, appeared.

Her mother obviously felt it, too. With a warm glance at the midwife, Thea said softly, "Thank you." Then she bolted out the door. Clarissa, shocked at the quick exit, noticed tears streaming down her mother's cheeks as she rushed past her. Both confused and concerned, Clarissa thought she should follow. But just then Josselyn let out a wail and grasped her hand with such force that she knew her place was at her sister's side.

Clarissa had watched closely as the midwife reached into her large bag, pulled out a jar, and scooped from it a sticky substance that she spread over Josselyn's swollen abdomen. It smelled both sour and sweet, and Clarissa wondered what it was. Before she could ask, the midwife explained, "It's a poultice. I gathered droppings below the nest of an eagle deep in the forest and mixed them with rose water. It'll help to ease the pain."

Clarissa was fascinated, repulsed, and doubtful in equal measure. But she noticed that Josselyn immediately relaxed at the gentle touch of the midwife. And her sister opened her mouth like a starving baby bird when Beatrix took out a crooked spoon and, with a shaking hand, lovingly fed her a potion of vinegar and sugar, pronouncing, "This will help, too." When she finished, Josselyn leaned back against the pillows, sighed, and closed her eyes.

Her curiosity overtaking her, Clarissa took advantage of the pause. "Why did you become a midwife?"

Beatrix smiled at her. "Do you know the story of Shiphrah and Puah?" Clarissa shook her head. "They were so brave," Beatrix said with a sigh. "The first ones in the Bible to stand up against bad power." She broadened her smile and looked intently at Clarissa. "Imagine," she said. "It was women that did that." Clarissa noticed the candlelight reflected in the old woman's eyes, causing them to shine.

"They were midwives," Beatrix explained, "and the powerful pharaoh in Egypt ordered them to kill all the baby boys the Hebrew women birthed. He owned the Hebrew people as slaves, and they were growing, and he was afraid they were going to rise up against him." Beatrix laughed, causing Clarissa to wonder what could possibly be amusing about this sad story.

"Shiphrah and Puah refused," the midwife continued. "And when that scary pharaoh called them into his palace threatening to kill *them*, they told him that Hebrew women were so strong they gave birth before they could get there." She chuckled and shook her head. "And he believed them."

Clarissa had spent a lot of time in church and wondered why she had never before heard this astonishing story.

"But I was a midwife long before those two brave women inspired me to it," said Beatrix. She grinned as she declared, "I was a midwife the day I was born." Clarissa saw the gleam in her eyes again and anticipated another good story as Beatrix began, "You see, I—" But just then Josselyn cried out again, her eyes now open wide, and Beatrix turned her attention to alleviating the next surge of pain.

§

At the break of dawn that morning, the rest of the manor had come to life. The kitchen servants threw open all the cupboards and drawers, and the cleaning maidens raced through the rooms untying knots and unlocking trunks, to prompt the opening of Josselyn's womb. Beatrix reached again into her bag and removed a small pouch, shook some of its powdery contents into her palm, and tenderly rubbed the herb on Josselyn's thighs. "Coriander," she said to Clarissa. "With a sweet smell to attract the baby."

The midwife then instructed Emmeline, who at fourteen was only a year older than Clarissa, to look in the bag and locate a small vial filled with rose petals steeping in olive oil. Emmeline pried it open and handed it to her. Beatrix poured out the oil and massaged it vigorously where she had applied the herb, while Emmeline waved what looked to Clarissa like the clawed white foot of a large bird, maybe a crane or a heron, over her sister's body.

Beatrix began to chant, murmuring words Clarissa couldn't understand. Then the words became a prayer, as the midwife turned her gaze upward and folded her hands: "Holy Margaret, Blessed Saint, I beseech you: Come to me, your humble servant. With the power you used to open the mouth of the dragon, open the door to this child's life."

The words surprised Clarissa. When Beatrix finished her prayer, she began to tell the miraculous story of Saint Margaret as she returned to massaging Josselyn, who was far too distracted by her anguish to appreciate the tale. "When Margaret was fifteen years old," related Beatrix, "a Roman official noticed her beauty. He wanted her so bad, he tried to force her to renounce her Christian faith and marry him. But she refused. So he had her tortured and thrown into prison. One night the Devil appeared to her in the form of a dragon. He swallowed her whole. But the cross she was holding so irritated his insides that he spat her right back out. Sort of like a baby being born."

Well, not exactly, thought Clarissa. She knew next to nothing about childbirth, but even she knew babies didn't come out of their mothers' mouths. And apparently, she was learning that day, they didn't come quickly. "And that's why Margaret is the patron saint of childbirth," declared Beatrix.

For most of the day, Clarissa had been a fixture at the midwife's side, watching every move with fascination, asking questions as each mysterious item appeared from her bag. She held tightly to her sister's hand, trying to offer Josselyn comfort as the painful hours crawled slowly by. But as the day faded and the shadows closed in again, both Josselyn's cries and Clarissa's fear escalated. Clarissa couldn't bear to witness her sister's agony so close. Reluctantly, stammering an apology, she had dropped Josselyn's hand and moved to the foot of the bed, where she now crouched in the corner.

"It'll be all right," Beatrix repeated to Josselyn, stroking her arm. Clarissa wanted desperately to believe those words. But her sister's wails, and the urgency of the midwife's tone and movements, seemed to indicate that it was not going to be all right at all. The excruciating hours had dragged on far too long, Clarissa feared, for this to end well. She hunched further down in the corner, wishing she could disappear.

§

Beatrix pulled out her last hope, placing a round stone of jasper, the color of blood, on the bed between Josselyn's knees. She turned her eyes heavenward again and repeated her prayer to Saint Margaret, this time more ardently, ending with the plea, "We need you here . . . *now*." Clarissa noticed the tears gathering in the midwife's eyes.

The logs shifted and sputtered in the grate of the fireplace. Clarissa wished that one of the servants would come and poke the fire back to life, but she knew that none of them would dare enter the room now. "The light—I need it here!" said Beatrix with urgency to Emmeline, as the last remnants of flame disappeared.

Emmeline held a torch in one hand and was gently mopping beads of sweat from Josselyn's forehead with the other. Her face held a look of terror that mirrored the laboring mother's. When Josselyn cried out again,

Emmeline removed the damp cloth from her forehead and placed it into her gaping mouth. "Bite on this," she urged, "against the pain." Then she moved quickly to the foot of the bed with the torch.

Clarissa was overcome by a powerful urge to take the girl's place. She desperately wanted to hold her beloved sister's hand again, to stroke her forehead and recite a psalm to comfort her. But her limbs were frozen, her feet unmoving, as if fastened to the floor with cobblers' nails.

"Push," Beatrix repeated over and over. Emmeline held the torch but averted her eyes. Clarissa, transfixed, could not look away. Her lips moving rapidly, she began murmuring the prayer that had been her comfort since the day she and Josselyn and their young friends who loved the church had memorized it together: "Hail Mary, full of grace . . ."

"It's coming," Beatrix announced as the baby's head crowned. Emmeline gasped and let out a deep breath. Finally.

". . . the Lord is with thee."

"Push!" Beatrix said one last time. Clarissa noted the worried look on the midwife's face as she caught the child and escalated the fervency of her prayer.

"Blessed art thou amongst women . . ."

"A girl," whispered Beatrix, barely audibly. She gave the frail creature a cursory look, shaking her head sadly and clucking her tongue softly. She set the child on the corner of the thick palette that covered the bed and quickly cut the cord that had nurtured and bound her to her mother.

". . . and blessed is the fruit of your womb."

Then Beatrix turned to the more urgent matter before her. She used the linen cloths at hand to try to stanch the bleeding, but they weren't enough. She reached up and grabbed the cloth out of Josselyn's mouth, and Josselyn cried out again. The prayer kept tumbling from Clarissa's lips.

"Holy Mary, Mother of God . . ."

Josselyn's frightened eyes darted around the room. She groped at her neck, locating the wooden cross she wore suspended on a thin strip of leather and, with a moan, brought it to her mouth and bit down hard on it.

". . . pray for us sinners . . ."

Her eyes brimming with tears, Josselyn reached out her arms toward her younger sister. Clarissa swallowed her terror and ran out of the shadows to her sister's side. With her last remnant of strength, Josselyn gripped Clarissa's hand.

". . . now and at the hour of our death."

Josselyn smiled faintly, and the cross fell back in place over her heart. "My dear sister, my beloved Clarissa," she said. "Don't forget me."

"Don't leave me!" Clarissa begged.

"Take care of my daughter," Josselyn whispered as her eyes gently closed.

"I promise," Clarissa said as she fell upon her only sister. She began to sob, repeating again and again, "Don't leave me!" She felt the faint throb of Josselyn's heart weaken and fade. And then it disappeared altogether, as a thick and suffocating silence seeped in and took up all the space in the room. Choking on tears and gasping for breath, Clarissa saw the soul of her beloved sister swell into flame, fill her heart, and then fly into the night.

"Amen."

§

"You must go. Quickly!" said Beatrix, with an edge of panic in her voice. But Clarissa could not make her feet take her away from her sister's side. She tenderly lifted Josselyn's head and removed the cross from around her neck.

Several moments passed before she was able to move to the foot of the bed. The pale bluish body lying there was still and so small that it almost disappeared in the thickness of the feathers that filled the palette. Clarissa, trembling, lifted her sister's daughter in her hands. The creature reminded her of the many broken birds she had rescued in the forest, the baby's tiny ribcage as fragile as their porous breastbones, her limbs as motionless as their fractured wings.

Clarissa's heart pounded with grief as she cradled the child to her. And then she felt a slight stirring. The faintest of heartbeats pulsed next to hers, sending a shudder through Clarissa. She held the baby in her arm, with its head in her palm, and placed two fingers gently on her soft chest. The child slowly opened her eyes and moved her lips, as if trying to form a question that had no answer. Clarissa, with tears spilling down her cheeks, began to pray again. "Live," she pleaded, her eyes fixed intently on the child's. "Please . . . *live.*"

The baby's tiny eyelids fluttered like the wings of a butterfly and then went still. Her soul flickered briefly and then followed her mother's into the night. Clarissa, sobbing, placed her lifeless niece back on the palette.

"You must hurry!" cried Beatrix.

The fire in the grate was a heap of dying embers. The wool fleece that had been spread on the hearth to receive and wrap the new life lay empty and cold. The basin of milk had also surrendered its last hint of warmth. Clutching Josselyn's cross, Clarissa fled from the room.

Beyond the walls, the shrill shriek of a screech owl skewered the silence of the night forest. The watchful bird swooped from its perch in a tall pine, pounced on a young rabbit, and carried it, trembling with fright, in its grasping talons into the sky.

Two

"Why such sadness?" the baron asked his wife. "It was only a girl."

Aldrich's words chilled the air like an early winter frost. In the silence that fell around them, he took a swallow of warm mead from the bronze goblet in his right hand.

Yes, drink it up, thought Thea bitterly from her chair by the hearth. *Perhaps it will melt the ice in your soul.* Such words would never have escaped her lips into her husband's hearing. A huge, solid oak table separated them, and Thea was grateful for the distance. She felt the rage rising from the soles of her feet up into her throat, where it lodged like a stone. She targeted her gaze on Aldrich. "Are you referring to our daughter," she asked, "or to hers?"

The baron's profile was stark against the tapestry that covered the entire wall of the dining room behind where he stood. The elegant weaving of deep greens and royal blues accented with threads of gold was of a style found only in the finest manors of medieval England. It depicted a graceful unicorn, innocently summoned by a young maiden who gently stroked its neck—encircled by men brandishing swords at its heart.

Aldrich scowled at the impertinence of his wife's question and took a step away from her. The shift placed him in the center of the tapestry, his body blocking the maiden and the unicorn, the hunters' weapons now aimed at him. Thea tried desperately to push away the savage thoughts that were crowding into her heart, shocked at her own uncharacteristic coldness.

That afternoon she had watched as the servants, under her husband's orders, hauled out the finest liquor from the storehouse and the fanciest goblets from the cupboard. Only the best was suitable for the toast to celebrate what the baron had hoped would be an heir. Aldrich's frequent pronouncements of confidence that their older daughter would please him by delivering a baby boy had become insufferable to Thea in recent weeks. She kept her distance from the bustle of activity and excitement that had attended Josselyn's return to the manor to give birth. Thea shared with no one her fear that she might drown in the deluge of memories and cascade of emotions that were swirling through her soul.

Aldrich took another swallow of the sweet mead, which had been expertly crafted weeks before from the honey contributed by the bees in the apiary in the adjacent meadow. "No use to waste it," he muttered. "It's not my fault things turned out so badly."

Thea shifted uncomfortably and began self-consciously rearranging the folds of her gown. Made of velvet brocade in a shade of deep purple, it was her favorite and the warmest in her wardrobe. But still she found it necessary to sit in the ornately carved chair closest to the fire that blazed in the hearth. She pushed back the tears that threatened to spill down her cheeks, wondering if she could ever forgive herself for not being at her daughter's side at the end. She found herself unable to push away the question that haunted her: *If this catastrophe is not Aldrich's fault, is it mine?*

§

"We've got to get rid of that midwife!" the baron thundered, slamming his goblet on the table for emphasis as he took a seat behind it, shaking Thea out of her troubling thoughts. She wanted to believe that his emotion was an indication that he was more moved than he wanted to admit by their loss. But she knew that his outrage was more likely prompted by the tragedy that had befallen the lord of a neighboring manor a few days earlier and his own dashed hopes for an heir.

The baron's angry resolve was unnecessary. In the hallway minutes before, Beatrix had passed along to Thea the heartbreaking report from the birthing room. The tear-drenched silence that dropped between them was uncomfortable, and the midwife shifted awkwardly from one foot to the other and attempted to fill it. "Birthing babies is the most dangerous job there is," she said. "Carpenters fall off ladders and blacksmiths tumble into fires and liverymen get run over by horses, but more mothers die having babies than all them rolled together." She sighed. "There's just so many things can go wrong." Keeping her eyes fixed on the floor, Beatrix continued, "About half the babies come out the way they're supposed to. Half the rest of them come out all right in the end, after a lot of work." She paused. "But the rest . . ."

Thea understood that the words were intended to comfort her, to assure her that she was not alone in her suffering. She tried to imagine a lifetime of witnessing so much tragic loss, feeling waves of both gratitude and compassion for the midwife wash over her in the midst of her own heart-wrenching sorrow.

Beatrix had looked up then into Thea's tear-rimmed eyes. "Maybe if I had done more for the baby . . ." Thea, wanting to offer reassurance but finding no words, moved forward and put her arms around the hunched, old woman. Beatrix sighed into the embrace. "I thought I could save your daughter," she said, "and I gave her all my attention." A stream of tears coursed down her face as she confessed, "I didn't baptize the baby before it died."

The church's teaching was clear: unbaptized souls, born under the curse of original sin, were damned for eternity. So many babies struggling to get into the world died before a priest could arrive that the church had authorized midwives to baptize them in an emergency, to guarantee their salvation. *But what kind of God,* Thea wondered, *would condemn a helpless child who never got to live?*

Beatrix informed her that Father Augustus had been summoned at the moment things began to go wrong in the birthing room and was on his way from the town of Gladdington at the far edge of the forest. Trembling, the midwife said, "I'm so sorry he didn't make it in time." She spilled her hope to Thea that a posthumous baptism by the priest would save her grand-daughter's soul, "even if the church doesn't believe it." She promised "I will pray for her," and then added "and for your beloved Josselyn."

"Thank you," said Thea, moved by the midwife's concern. "Let me get Bickford to take you and the girl home in the wagon."

"Please let him be," Beatrix responded. "He fetched us in the middle of the night last night. It's very late—and he's very old. He should sleep."

"But you were up all night," said Thea, choosing not to add "and you're very old, too."

"If you have a place where Emmeline and I can stay, I'm sure she would be happy for a ride in the morning. I'll walk home after I've had a bit of rest. I'd like the time to myself, and the walk through the forest will be good for my soul after . . . after this hard night."

Beatrix then confided to Thea that she had made a difficult decision in the birthing room. "I told Emmeline I'm going to move in with my daugh-ter, to live out the rest of my days in peace and leave this hard work to her." She paused for a moment. "Emmeline told me she's going to seek work as a milkmaid or shepherdess." That made both the baroness and the midwife smile for the first time that night.

"I can't blame her," said Beatrix, shaking her head. "They accuse us of being witches and collaborating with the Devil."

"Who accuses you?" Thea asked.

"The church," replied Beatrix. "When our herbs and prayers ease pain and calm mothers giving birth, they blame us for going against the will of God. They quote God's curse on Eve for her disobedience in the Garden of Eden: 'I will greatly increase your pangs in childbearing; in pain you shall bring forth children . . .'"

Thea thought about that familiar curse from the Bible's first book, which her mother had often recited to her when she was young, including the part that Beatrix had left unsaid: ". . . and your husband shall rule over you."

Beatrix continued, "And when things go wrong that we can't fix, they blame us for that, too." She focused her weary eyes intently on Thea's. "The church accuses us of having too much power," she sighed. "And of having too little."

Thea pondered Beatrix's words for a moment. "As bad as it is," she said in response, "I know that many more mothers and babies would die without the care of midwives. It's a great comfort just to know that we are in safe, kind hands we can trust." She felt tears coming again and said quickly, "Perhaps we should go find Emmeline."

Thea led the two women to an empty bedroom. "Thank you both. I wish you well," she said, as Emmeline fell into a deep sleep and Beatrix closed her eyes for a brief rest before disappearing into the night.

After leaving them, Thea walked with hesitation down the hall and gingerly opened the door to the birthing room. Beatrix had placed the baby in Josselyn's arms. Kneeling by the bed, Thea clasped her daughter's lifeless hand, kissed it, and whispered, "I'm so sorry." She stroked the smooth head of her granddaughter and offered a prayer for both of their souls, pushing back the tears that pooled in her eyes. Then she got up and walked back into the dining room.

§

Thea decided not to relay her conversation with the midwife to Aldrich. Instead, she said to her husband, "We must get word to Galorian." She wished she could spare her son-in-law this sorrow. Regularly in her prayers, Thea voiced her thanks that Galorian had rescued Josselyn and the entire family from a very grievous and vexing situation a few years earlier. Her awareness that he had done so unknowingly made her no less grateful.

Thea recalled the look in the young knight's eyes when he had first encountered her older daughter's blossoming beauty; how he had also recognized her loving spirit and fervent faith. Galorian later confided to Thea that his heart had been immediately captured, and that he would have married Josselyn even if she had been given to him without a dowry. He was stunned when Aldrich insisted on paying double the expected sum.

Before a messenger could be deployed to the knight with the tragic news, Galorian himself rushed into the dining room, clearly anxious for word about his wife and child. Thea would always remember the sound of his boots on the floor as he approached them that night. Aldrich, rising from his seat and stepping out from behind the table, hailed Galorian by name and extended his hand.

"Sir," replied Galorian, mirroring the gesture. "I came as soon as I heard. Is she . . .? "

"Gone," said Aldrich. "Both gone."

Silently lamenting her husband's blunt callousness, Thea gently told her son-in-law, "It was a girl."

The dark-haired knight, still wearing his riding cloak, went down on one knee, crushed by the weight of the tragedy. Thea's thoughts leapt to the moment six months before when, in this very room, underneath the large unicorn tapestry, Josselyn had announced to her parents that she was going to have a child. Galorian's arm was wrapped tenderly around her, his face flooded with pride and joy. Now a very different look overtook his countenance. He stared up at Thea, struggling to comprehend the loss, his face etched with grief and his eyes filled like two small, bright blue lakes. "I got here as fast as I could . . ."

He had been deep in the forest with an encampment of knights who were honing their skills for the next Holy Land Crusade. Thea pictured the messenger arriving there with the news that the baby was on its way. She imagined Galorian, driven by expectant joy, unable to keep from leaping on his horse and pointing it toward the manor, his cloak flying behind him as he raced through a forest maze of towering pines.

"My dearest love . . . gone," whispered Galorian, so softly toward the floor that Thea could barely hear him. She gazed with compassion upon this strong man who was so visibly moved by the death of his wife and the daughter she bore. At twenty-seven, Galorian was separated from her in age by only three years, but he seemed to Thea in that moment to be far younger than she.

Aldrich's voice interrupted her thoughts again. "I have a proposition," he announced to his son-in-law. Galorian rose slowly and took a seat at the table. The baron picked up a goblet that matched his own: heavy, bronze, with a ruby embedded on the side of the cup and a pattern of gold crosses around its rim. He poured another glass of mead and handed it across the table to the knight.

Thea dropped her gaze to the floor, dread ambushing her as her husband spoke. His argument was as impenetrable as a Crusader fortress. "I paid a double dowry," Aldrich reminded Galorian, "and you owe me an heir. I have another daughter. This is the way things are done."

The silence seemed interminable. But then Thea heard Galorian say "Yes." He cleared his throat. "Yes," he repeated with more confidence. "I loved one of your daughters, and I can love the other."

Thea brought her gaze up to meet her son-in-law's. In the brief moment before he averted his eyes, she observed something troubling there. It looked to her like doubt. She noted that Galorian seemed restless, nervously fingering the rim of his goblet. Thea wanted to acknowledge aloud that he must be reeling from the shock of his loss: the wife he adored, and a daughter he had never met, wrenched from him in a tragic instant, his family and hoped-for future gone forever. But she understood the tradition that bound them. And she knew that her son-in-law was the sort of knight who would, above all, do what was honorable and right.

She opened her mouth to protest the arrangement on Clarissa's behalf. But Thea had no argument to make. As her husband had frequently complained, the king and his Crusades had plunged England into such financial instability that the couple could not count on having enough money in their future to pay a suitor for the hand of their second daughter. And Clarissa was already thirteen. Girls much younger were being given in marriage. Thea herself had been handed over when she was ten to Aldrich, who was only two years younger than her father. Galorian was a good man, she assured herself, and he would treat her second daughter as well as he had her first.

§

In her bedroom, Clarissa gazed at the cross she held in her palm. Her brother-in-law had carved it from a piece of pine and given it to Josselyn on their wedding day. It was square with flared ends, the same style of cross that Galorian and the other Crusader knights had sewn onto their cloaks and emblazoned on their shields. The soft wood bore the marks where Josselyn had bit hard against her worst pain. Clarissa picked up its leather cord and placed the cross around her neck.

Carrying a candle, she snuck down the hall, back through the heavy door into the room where Josselyn lay cradling her daughter in her arms. The sight of them clasped together in death took Clarissa's breath away. She had often envied her sister's beauty, her hair the golden color of wheat and her large eyes a shade of green that matched the meadow at sunrise. Josselyn looked even more beautiful to Clarissa in death. She stood at the side of the bed and stared for a few moments, then reached out and touched her sister's forehead, finding her body as cold as the room.

Clarissa turned away and fell to her knees in front of the fireplace, now bereft of all warmth. Trembling, she reached in and scooped up a handful of ashes in her left palm. She dipped her right index finger into them and then marked her forehead with the sign of the cross. "O God, forgive me for my weakness and my fear," she cried. "And for the terrible secret I now have to bear. Have mercy on me!"

Knowing that she had left her sister's side at the critical moment caused Clarissa great distress. But what overwhelmed her with guilt was what had followed—what she alone knew. Moaning with shame, she feared that the truth would one day come to light; that her secret could not stay locked in her soul forever.

She raised her gaze to the ceiling and began to sob again. "Oh, Josselyn!" she wailed. "How can I live without you?" She felt that this anguish would go on forever; that she would never stop crying. Several minutes passed before she felt spent, as if turned inside out, with every ounce of heartache wrung out of her. She picked up the candle and walked slowly out of the room in a daze of grief.

Footsteps brought her attention back, and she was relieved to see her mother approaching from the other end of the long hallway. Clarissa ran toward her, anxious to find comfort in her arms, oblivious to the candle that sputtered with each rapid step. But when Clarissa got near, the look on Thea's face stopped her.

Her mother gave her a weak smile and then took the candle from her hand. Raising her daughter's chin, Thea held the light up to her face, reaching as if intending to stroke Clarissa's hair. But instead, spying the smudge of ash on Clarissa's forehead, she declared softly "It's dirty" and, without asking why or how it got there, rubbed it away with her sleeve.

Clarissa began to weep again as her mother spilled the details of the arrangement her father and Galorian had made. This, she realized then, was the fate that Beatrix had feared for her—though she wondered where the midwife thought she could possibly run to escape it. "But I don't love him!" Clarissa wailed, feeling panic rising in her throat.

"It's not about love," Thea retorted. "It's about duty."

"But he loves Josselyn. How could he ever love *me*?" Clarissa was stunned at her mother's insistence. She had spent many hours in the preceding months trying to convince Thea of her maturity, claiming since the day she had turned thirteen that was ready to own her own horse, to ride by herself to the village, to spend a night alone in the forest. She had lost every one of these arguments. "How can you possibly believe I'm ready for marriage?" she cried. "I haven't even begun to live yet." She looked at the ground and said under her breath, "I won't do it."

"That's enough," Thea scolded. "Consider yourself fortunate to be given to a brave and handsome man with a kind heart."

Clarissa sniffled loudly, wiped her tears on her sleeve, and wrestled her emotions under control. She looked her mother in the eye with a piercing stare. "You should have been there," she said. She knew that a daughter should not speak so disrespectfully to her mother, but she couldn't stop herself from pouring out the indicting words. "Josselyn came home to have the baby, and she needed you." Clarissa took a deep breath. "Maybe if you had been there . . ." She left the sentence unfinished.

Thea cast her eyes to the ground, away from her daughter's accusing glare. Clarissa struggled to keep her voice calm and the tears at bay. "She was only sixteen," she choked. "Isn't it enough that you lost one daughter? Do you need me to die, too?"

Thea raised her eyes slowly, the tears that had gathered there glistening in the candlelight, her gaze toward her younger daughter now tender. "Please," Clarissa begged, as she threw her arms around her mother's waist. Thea drew her in, and for a brief moment mother and daughter comforted each other.

Then Thea gently extracted herself from Clarissa's embrace. She walked slowly back to the dining room. "She will do her duty," she announced coldly to the two men, who sat with mead in hand. As the goblets of Aldrich and Galorian met across the table, Thea rushed out. When she got to her room, she threw herself on her bed, buried her head in her pillow, and sobbed.

Three

___

Clarissa shuffled sadly to the old wardrobe that held her clothes and pulled her linen nightshirt off its hook. It was halfway over her head when she threw it off and began sorting through her dresses. "This one will do," she announced to herself, pulling down a favorite: a green velvet gown, its bodice embroidered with silver thread and scores of tiny pearls in an intricate rosette pattern.

To protect her family from robbers and marauders, the manor had windows only on the inside walls, which surrounded a courtyard where the servants slept. Clarissa could not get to the door without walking through them, a risk she knew was too great to take. She pondered her options, feeling for a moment that she had none. Trapped without a stitch of hope.

But soon she was stretched out on her palette, her heart pounding with anticipation of the plan that was beginning to take shape in her mind. She assumed that Bickford had been sent on his way with the wagon to deliver Beatrix and Emmeline to their homes. She imagined her mother trying desperately to sleep, tormented by grief and remorse. She was sure that Galorian and her father would be the last to retire, one drowning his despair and the other celebrating his hope in a river of mead in the dining room.

As the minutes crept by, Clarissa lay awake rehearsing her escape in her mind. At least a dozen times she interrupted the path of her thoughts and decided she had to stay, convinced that leaving was too risky . . . and foolish . . . and sad. And then, again and again, with her heart pumping so vigorously she thought she could hear it echoing off the walls of her room, she talked herself back into running away.

As soon as she felt certain that the whole household had finally surrendered to snores and dreams, she sprang from her bed with determination. She grabbed her wool cloak, woven for her at her mother's request after the spring shearing of the ewes in the pasture, and threw it around her shoulders. Then she pulled her feather palette off the bed and crept down the hall, dragging it behind her. She headed for the winding stairs that led up a narrow passageway to the tower room perched on top of the manor.

Clarissa smiled as she stepped onto the stairway, so frightening to her and Josselyn when they were young girls. Like grand adventurers, they had held their breaths and opened the thick oak door, plunging into that dusty passageway and another world. Josselyn had conjured special evenings for Clarissa by setting a circle of candles in the tower room. Clarissa, sitting on the floor under shadows that shrank and grew menacingly in the flickering light, munched on rosemary biscuits she had wheedled out of the cook. She was riveted with suspense as her older sister regaled her with tales of scary dragons and brave knights, majestic unicorns and beautiful princesses.

It took all of Clarissa's strength to drag the palette up the twelve steps of the steep stairway. She paused halfway to catch her breath. When she reached the tower room, panting, she knelt and prayed, giving thanks for her beloved Josselyn and beseeching God for protection as she left behind all that was familiar and stepped out toward who-knew-where.

The tower room had a shuttered window that opened above the second-story roof below. With great effort, Clarissa pushed the palette through and then hoisted herself up after it. She turned herself around and held on tight as she lowered herself as far as she could. Then, shutting her eyes, she let go and dropped down. She landed on the mattress as intended but then tumbled off onto the flat roof.

She stood, pausing to listen and make sure that the noise of her fall hadn't awakened anyone in the bedrooms below. She gazed up at a clear expanse of sky and out over the pasture, which was bathed in the eerie light of a full moon. She shivered in the cold and panicked a bit when she saw how far the ground was below her. But determination pushed her forward.

She lined up the palette at the edge of the roof and then gave it a gentle push. It took an unexpected bounce off a protruding rock in the wall on the way down and landed farther away than she expected. But it was still within reach, she convinced herself. "One . . . two . . . three." She repeated her cue several times but pulled back every time from the edge, giving herself a few more minutes to build up her courage. Each time she looked down, the ground seemed farther away. She moved her gaze back to the moon high in the sky, which seemed to be smiling reassuringly at her.

"Oh, Josselyn, help me," she whispered into the wind, clutching the cross at her neck. "Mary, Mother of God, come to my aid." She took a deep breath, closed her eyes, and jumped. She spread her arms on the fall, imagining herself a songbird soaring from its cage into the vast world.

§

Clarissa hit the palette with a thud, the thick goose down cushioning the worst of the impact. She landed hard on her left shoulder, felt a jolt of pain, and knew that she would have a bruise to tend. But she was whole . . . un-broken . . . *free*. She struggled to her feet and raised her arms to the sky in triumph and laughed—softly, so as not to wake anyone on the other side of the walls. And then the laughter melted into hot tears.

She headed across the pasture toward the forest. Just before entering it, she turned and took one last, longing look at the only home she had ever known. She allowed the view to imprint itself in her mind: the tower, the distinctive double columns that marked the manor's entrance, and the flag hanging calmly between them, bearing her family's green-and-gold crest.

Clarissa knew the forest as well as she knew her own home. She and Josselyn had often followed its mossy paths in pursuit of rabbits and foxes, had carried picnics of figs and goat cheese and hard dark bread in simple baskets they had woven from the reeds that grew on the banks of its streams. She knew boulders and trees and waterfalls as landmarks that would guide her to her favorite hiding places and then direct her safely back home.

But she had never entered the forest after dark. The canopy of elms that marked the way in snuffed out the moon's light entirely, as she walked into the pitch black of deep night. She tried to distract herself from her fear by recounting in her mind the stories that Josselyn had told her. But too many of them involved ghastly beasts lurking or on the prowl in dark, menacing forests, and she decided to abandon that idea.

Then she remembered that Josselyn had sometimes told her stories from the Bible. The one Clarissa always begged for was the story of Moses. She loved the wondrous tale of a mother making a special basket for her baby son and setting him afloat in the river, saving him from the pharaoh's cruel death decree. Clarissa tried to will herself to be as courageous and resourceful as that young mother—and as the midwives she now knew from Beatrix had saved him at his birth.

She told herself the rest of the story as she walked. Moses grew up to be a great prophet who led his people out of slavery in Egypt. They were guided by God, who opened up the sea for them to walk on dry land, going before them as a pillar of cloud during the day and a pillar of fire at night. Clarissa scanned around her and peered deeply into the thick forest ahead of her, hoping—and believing for a moment—that she would catch a glimpse of that pillar of fire to show her the way forward. But all she saw in every direction was overwhelming darkness.

I'm only a girl, she thought, *no pillar of fire for me.* She had to rely on memory and the feel of the trees to keep her on the path. She moved slowly, stumbling over roots and rocks until she felt confident enough to raise her step and lengthen her stride. The haunting howl of a night creature sent chills racing up her spine. The earth felt spongy and not solid enough to support her, but she kept moving, too scared to stop—though she had to pause frequently to disentangle her velvet hem from the tentacles of vines and wayward branches.

She was emerging from a grove of pines into a small clearing, where the towering trees gave way to a thicket of low shrubs and the moon reappeared above her, when she heard a noise like thunder behind her. Closer and closer it came, until she recognized the pounding of hooves on the ground. She could not imagine why anyone would be riding through the forest in the middle of this late-October night, and she wondered if her weary mind was playing tricks on her.

But moments later she spun around and saw a very real horse bearing down on her. She leapt off the path as it galloped by, its rider shrouded in a black cloak. Clarissa saw the horse rear to a stop as the rider pulled up on its reins. She gasped when she realized that they were headed back toward her.

She clawed her way on her knees through the thicket of thorny shrubs, desperate to find a hiding place out of the revealing light of the full moon. The horse stopped several paces away from her, its rider holding his cloak across his face as he surveyed the area around her. Clarissa crouched low to the ground and held her breath.

After a few moments that felt like an eternity to her, they turned away. As they rode off, Clarissa caught sight of a distinctive patch of white hair on the right side of the horse's hindquarters, glowing in the moon's bright light. It reminded her of the Crusader cross hanging around her neck, and those she had seen on the shields and cloaks of knights.

She stayed hidden in the brush, her heart pounding, until long after the mysterious horse and rider had disappeared. Then she painstakingly extracted her dress and cloak from a tangle of thorns, wiped a few small spots of blood from scratches on her hands and face, and warily resumed her journey into the unknown.

§

The first faint hint of music caught Clarissa's attention, drawing her out of the numbing weariness that had overtaken her as she plodded along. She had no idea how long or far she had walked when she stopped to listen, disbelieving that anything so lovely could be drifting through the forest in the night. It drew her to another clearing, where what she spied took her breath away. She ducked behind a pine tree, rubbing her eyes to erase the impossible vision as a chill raced through her.

She peered around the rough trunk of the tree to steal another glimpse of the strange sight. At the center of a crowd and glowing in the light of a blazing bonfire stood a deer on its hind legs, laughing and then taking long drinks from a clay cup, its face human, its massive antlers seeming almost as tall as the branches of the trees behind it. Beside the deer, a sheep raised its cup against one held by a cow, and both grinned. These, too, stood on two legs. Clarissa quickly drew back behind the tree again and took a deep breath, her heart pounding as fiercely as it had when she had encountered the horse and its rider.

When she gazed around the trunk once more, she slowly scanned the huddle of people around the fire. They were a ragged band, she observed immediately. A young man in a gray coat covered with fraying patches played a soothing melody on a flute, while a slightly older man strummed a lute. Off to the side under a canopy of low branches, a few rough-looking boys took turns dunking their heads into a tub of water, one occasionally surfacing with an apple clenched between his teeth. Younger children slept with their heads resting in the laps of their mothers, perched on rough log benches.

Clarissa watched as a fiddle player stepped forward and immediately quickened the beat of the music. A toothless old man grinned and began thumping his knee in time to the lively tune with his right hand, stroking his gray whiskers with his left. Children blinked awake, rubbing their eyes and stretching their legs. The deer put down his cup and scooped up a young boy as the whole assembly stirred to life.

Women and men, some with young children in arms, sang and laughed as they circled around the fire. Older children chased one another, ducking in and out under the circle's clasped hands, the boys now prancing with scary masks on sticks, frightening the girls into contagious shrieks. Clarissa wasn't sure whether to be afraid or delighted.

The dancing went on for a while, until the fire shrank and the moon began to swell on its descent toward the horizon. Clarissa noticed the tops of the trees on the western edge of the clearing eerily silhouetted against its big, bright surface. When the music stopped, the group settled back onto the logs around the pile of glowing embers that had been the bonfire. An old man rose and gave thanks for a successful harvest. "We gathered here as the evening sun was leaving us," he said, "and now we are ready to greet the morning sun as we enter the dark half of the year."

Clarissa, suddenly overcome with weariness, yawned and leaned her forehead against the tree that hid her from the crowd. She closed her eyes, wondering if she could fall asleep standing up. That thought was interrupted by an energetic whooshing above her head. Startled, she looked up and saw an owl flapping its wings as it descended and then hovered near her face.

"Shoo!" she said loudly as she stepped away from the tree, frantically waving her arms.

Everyone turned in her direction. The screech owl, settling in after its nightly hunt, perched on a low branch of the tree, folded its wings, and joined the crowd in staring at her, its wide eyes unblinking. Clarissa felt immediately embarrassed about the fright the owl had given her. And self-conscious about her velvet gown, which in that moment she wished the night's roots and thorns had tattered into some approximation of the rags they wore, though she knew they had not.

"You're welcome at our Samhain celebration," said the old man warmly, a whistle escaping through the gap where front teeth should have been as he pronounced the ancient holiday's name.

"Samhain?" she asked.

"We come here at sundown on October thirty-first every year," he explained. "To give thanks for the earth's abundance and prepare ourselves for the dark time."

Clarissa thought of her parents, who in a few hours would be making their way to the cathedral to celebrate All Souls Day. Dressed in their finest clothes, they would solemnly light candles for Josselyn and her nameless daughter. They would be ushered by dirge-like hymns and enveloped in the heavy perfume of incense, surrounded by icons in gold frames arrayed before curtains of rich red and purple brocade.

"We burn the bones of the animals whose meat will sustain us through the long winter," the old man continued. "And some of us"—he nodded toward the deer, sheep, and cow, drinking again—"wear their hides to scare away the fairies in these woods who like to kidnap children." Clarissa noticed some of the youngest children nestle more closely to their mothers. The man turned and addressed the circle again. "On this night when the veil between the living and the dead is at its thinnest, we remember our loved ones who have crossed over to the next world."

As he spoke the last sentence, a young woman approached a pile of pine needles next to the fire ring. "Mama," she said softly through tears, her jaw quivering as she picked up a handful of the needles and dropped them on the embers. A circle of comforting older women closed in around the mourning girl as the needles flared briefly in a burst of light.

"Darwyn," murmured another woman as she approached the embers and dropped another handful of pine needles, staring at the burst of flame with sad eyes long after it had flared and disappeared. "Edwina" . . . "Oliver" . . . "Leif." It didn't matter to Clarissa that she didn't know the people behind the names.

"Sir Lancelot," a little boy choked out through his tears as he tossed his pine needles and then ran and buried his head in his mother's lap. "His hound dog," a woman standing next to Clarissa explained in a hushed tone.

When it seemed that the long procession of remembrances was winding down, Clarissa gathered her courage and stepped forward. She bent and scooped up pine needles in each hand. "Josselyn," she whispered as she dropped one handful. "Forestyne," she said as she released the other. The owl, keeping watch in the tree, let loose with a tremulous shriek that startled Clarissa and reverberated through her bones.

The name Forestyne had just jumped off her tongue, and she smiled as she said it. Gazing at the ephemeral but bright blazes of light that flared as fire consumed her pine needles, she told herself that Josselyn's daughter would have adored this forest just as her mother had. Oh, how Clarissa wished she had been given the chance to introduce her niece to its mysteries and delights.

At the edge of the fire, her grief overtook her again. Clarissa had never known life without Josselyn, even after her sister's marriage to Galorian. With her husband often encamped with the other knights in the forest, Josselyn had visited the manor frequently from their home an hour's ride away. She spent the nights of her visits stretched out on Clarissa's bed, where the sisters stayed up late whispering their secrets, until their eyes grew too heavy with sleep to continue.

The only time they had ever been apart for more than a few days was when Josselyn had gone away to spend a summer with their mother's sister and her family on England's southwest coast. Ten-year-old Clarissa had spent those interminable months pining for her older sister and secretly whining that her Aunt Adela hadn't let her come, too. Knowing that this time Josselyn wasn't coming back felt like more than she could bear.

Emptiness gnawed at her insides, born deep in the pit of her stomach. Clarissa couldn't have named it then, but her innocence died that night along with her sister and niece. She felt the emptiness spreading, draining her of hope. The trees around the clearing began to spin, and she swayed, clutching her stomach and keening her grief. A woman with her young daughter perched on her lap quickly set the girl down, leapt up, and stood next to Clarissa, holding her as she wailed.

After some time, calm returned to her. Clarissa buried her head in the woman's shoulder and then allowed this kind woman to lead her to an empty space on the logs. The woman sat back down in her spot and picked up her daughter again, but the little girl wriggled out of her mother's embrace. She walked with determination around the circle to Clarissa and clambered up into her lap.

Clarissa guessed her to be about three years old. She had flaxen hair and large doe eyes, and Clarissa couldn't help thinking that Josselyn's daughter would have grown to look just like this beautiful child. At that thought, two new rivers of tears streamed down her face. The little girl, dressed in a frayed and stained linen nightshirt that was too big for her, reached up and gently caressed Clarissa's cheek. Clarissa hugged her and managed a smile.

"Liliana," a voice said. The girl's mother had moved over next to them. "Her name is Liliana."

Clarissa looked into the eyes of the weary mother and said softly, "What a beautiful name."

"I'm Raisa," the woman said, squeezing in next to Clarissa on the log.

As the ritual of remembrance ended and all the tears around the circle were dried, the old man stood and spoke again. When he was done, he approached Clarissa and handed her a large turnip. Its core had been scooped out, and eyes, a mouth, and a very large nose had been carved into its side. "Just watch," the old man said, smiling. "You'll know what to do."

Clarissa noticed for the first time that every family had a large turnip or gourd. All had simple faces, farcical or frightening, carved into their sides. One by one, in the last moments of the receding night, each family approached the fire ring and scooped up a burning ember in its hollowed-out autumn vegetable.

"We carry an ember home to light our family's winter fire," Raisa whispered. "To remind us through the long dark time that we draw our light and warmth from each other, and from the spirits of our departed loved ones that hover close."

The flute player started up a haunting melody, and the others began to chant along around the ring. Clarissa thought she had never heard anything so wondrous. She thought again of her beloved Josselyn, who had a singing voice as clear and rich as a meadowlark's. Tears coursed down her cheeks once more as she stepped forward to capture an ember in her turnip—moved by the knowledge that through the long, cold days of the coming winter, this circle would cling to the memory of the communal bonfire that had warmed both hearths and hearts.

Clarissa joined the ragged parade of people carrying spooky, glowing, disembodied faces—lighting the way and scaring away any evil spirits that might be hovering—out of the clearing and into the forest in the direction of the town of Gladdington. Before entering the thick woods, she glimpsed a stab of brilliant red off to her right as the rising sun crested the eastern horizon. On her left, perched on the edge of the world opposite it, was a huge salmon-colored orb dusted with light purple shadows. The moon still seemed to be smiling at her.

As the light of dawn chased away the cold night, Clarissa wished for a hearth and wondered where her ember would find a home.

Four

The weary villagers slowly made their way back to their homes. Clarissa fell in next to Raisa, who held the hands of Liliana and her slightly older brother. A gaggle of other children followed along, the oldest looking to be about Clarissa's age. A man Clarissa assumed to be Liliana's father carried a boy with twisted limbs and a sweet smile.

"Where you headed?" Raisa asked her. Clarissa thought it odd that no one asked where she had been or to whom she belonged. She had no answer to Raisa's question. "You're welcome to stay with us for a while," Raisa said, not waiting for a reply. "We don't have much, but we'll share what there is." Liliana dropped her mother's hand and held her arms up to Clarissa, begging to be carried. Clarissa obliged, and Liliana laughed as Clarissa scooped her up in her arms.

The family's home on the edge of Gladdington was a one-room hovel, with dirt floors and a thatched roof. A rustic homemade table and a few crates were its only furnishings. Its frame was made of wattle—flimsy branches woven together. These were held in place with daub, a sticky plaster created from clay mixed with hair and dung from the family's one scrawny cow. Much to Clarissa's shock and chagrin, the cow shared the space, its body heat helping to warm the crude hut.

Liliana's mother cooked for her husband, Edmund, and their seven children in a sooty cauldron over an open fire in the center of the room. Clarissa had the thought that she was too hungry to sleep and too tired to eat. She ultimately decided that she was famished enough to down a bowl of Raisa's thin porridge before giving in to her exhaustion. Then she joined the other children on a pile of dirty straw in a dark corner, which was their shared bed. Had she been more alert she might have reconsidered, but she felt unable to stay awake another minute, and it was the only place to lay her head. Looking forward to a long rest, she fell asleep immediately.

She was surprised when she heard Edmund's voice shouting the names of his children. They grumbled quietly in response. "But, father, we were up all night," complained the oldest boy, rubbing his eyes.

"The sun's already high in the sky," barked Edmund. "We can't afford to lose the whole day. Move. Now!" The children lined up according to age, with the youngest at the front. "You too," said Edmund, scowling at Clarissa. "If you're going to be part of this family, you'll work." Clarissa gathered herself up and fell into line next to the girl who was the oldest of the children. "I'm Nerida," the girl whispered to her.

They marched outside. Even little Liliana marched, and the oldest boy carried on his back the one with twisted legs who couldn't walk. An assortment of battered wood boxes sat in a pile outside the door, and each child picked up one in a size that he or she could carry. Off they went, deep into the woods, marching behind their father. At the end of the line, Nerida and Clarissa were out of earshot of Edmund. "How often do you do this?" Clarissa wondered aloud.

"Every day," Nerida replied. "Except Sunday."

Clarissa expressed her dismay that they had to work after an all-night celebration. Nerida surprised her when she said, "But this is a good day. A short one." Usually, the girl explained, they were up at dawn and at work until dinnertime—gathering firewood to split and sell in the cold months, and hoeing, planting, weeding, and harvesting turnips and potatoes in the warm ones.

"When do you play?" Clarissa wanted to know.

"At Samhain," laughed Nerida. "And on Christmas Day." Clarissa noted the life that danced in the thin girl's eyes, despite her hard existence.

"They're not really our parents, you know," Nerida said offhandedly. She explained that children just kept showing up, some orphans, some dropped off by parents who were too poor to feed them, some sold to Raisa and Edmund.

"Sold?!" exclaimed Clarissa, incredulous.

"Some people are even poorer than us."

"How did you get here?"

Nerida didn't speak for a long time. "I ran away," she said finally. "My father . . ." Whatever it was her father had done was too painful for her to speak it. A few tears slid down her cheeks. Clarissa didn't ask her any more questions.

They went to work gathering sticks from the ground while Edmund and the oldest boy cut limbs and small trees with a simple saw. The one whose name Clarissa never heard—referred to only as "the crippled boy"—broke up sticks where he sat. Clarissa noticed that he had no shoes.

The five-year-old fought against his exhaustion until he was finally overcome and fell asleep under a poplar tree. Edmund cut a switch from the tree and whipped the sleeping boy on the legs. He sprang awake crying, and Edmund gave him another blow across the back as he ran off to pick up more sticks. Clarissa, filled with a mixture of sorrow and rage, looked toward Nerida, but the girl averted her gaze and kept filling her box with kindling twigs.

Clarissa was hardly suitably dressed for manual labor, but she was warmer than the children, who shivered in their rags. She stuck close to Nerida and Liliana, trying to turn their work into a game and telling stories she had heard from Josselyn to keep the little girl awake. By afternoon Clarissa's efforts were futile, and Liliana's eyes grew heavy with sleep. Mercifully, Edmund didn't disturb her as she napped on a bed of soft pine needles under Clarissa's wool cloak.

The day—shorter than usual to the others, but interminably long to Clarissa—dragged on. Hunger pangs and thirst gnawed at her. She kept a close watch on the sun, feeling her spirits lift a little when it began to dip toward the western horizon. But still Edmund made no move to release them from their labor. As twilight began to envelop them, Clarissa thought they should be heading back, but instead he ordered her and Nerida to go deeper into the forest. Clarissa saw the fear in Nerida's eyes and tried to go with her, but Edmund stopped her and sent her off in another direction. She wondered if this was punishment for their budding friendship.

As Clarissa stooped for a stick, she heard the shriek of a screech owl, waking up on the cusp of dusk for its nocturnal escapades. Or so she thought. But when she listened more closely, she realized that it was Nerida, sending her a signal that she was all right and still with her in the forest. Clarissa tried to imitate her and signal back to comfort her new friend, but her version of the call of a screech owl came out sounding more like the wail of a sick cat.

As full darkness descended, Edmund called them back. The children fell into line again, with Clarissa and Nerida once more at the back and out of his earshot. "You need to work on that," Nerida whispered, laughing at Clarissa's pathetic owl call.

Clarissa immediately thought of the day a few years before when she had tried to imitate Josselyn's singing, and her sister had said to her, "You sound like the frogs croaking by the lake." She shook away the memory, squeezed Nerida's hand, and said, "I'll practice." Then the weary parade headed back home in silence, carrying and dragging the day's haul of firewood.

Clarissa's back ached from the hours of stooping and lifting. Dinner was a bowl of the same thin porridge the family had eaten that morning. As soon as she finished hers, she tumbled into the pile of straw, wondering if she would ever feel rested again. She saw the cow, its tail swishing gently, wink at her—or perhaps it happened in her dreams.

§

Galorian attacked the pell over and over, thrusting and slashing the fixed wooden tower with all his strength—but none of his heart. When the last ounce of his energy was gone, he dropped his sword and fell on his knees to the ground, utterly spent. He put his face in his hands and tried to pray.

The last light of day filtered through the trees, dappling the forest floor with patches of gold as dusky shadows closed in. The mournful cry of a screech owl high in the branches above him caught Galorian's attention, prompting tears to pool in his eyes. He looked up. "Are you sharing my misery, then?" he asked of the owl. The creature's presence increased his sadness and released a cascade of long-buried memories.

Gazing at the pell, Galorian recalled his first encounter with the training device. He was only a small boy then. A slightly older boy had handed him a practice sword made of whalebone, almost as tall as Galorian and weighing twice as much as an actual weapon. "It'll build up your arms," the boy had explained, as young Galorian struggled to lift and aim it.

The owl shrieked again, and Galorian remembered the sad and unforgettable day when he had been taken from his home. *Has it really been two decades?* he thought. Recognized as an exceptionally strong and intrepid boy, he had been singled out at the tender age of seven. He wanted to cling to his mother on that rainy afternoon that changed his life forever.

But he went away quietly, looking back longingly at his parents. They stood side by side beaming their pride, while he memorized their faces and imprinted his last view of them in his mind to carry with him always. He cried for his mother every night for weeks, late at night on his hard palette, when he was sure no one could hear him. But over time his parents became a fainter and fainter memory, and he grew to feel at home in the huge castle that had become his new home.

Galorian gave himself over to his reminiscences as full darkness descended on the forest. He walked in his mind through the seven years he had spent as a page in the castle, serving a knight and being steeped in religion, manners, and the ways of chivalry—the first leg on the lengthy and arduous journey toward his own knighthood. He smiled as he recalled spending endless hours learning the strategy games of chess and backgammon, scaling walls and swimming lakes, hunting and sparring piggyback with the other pages to gain balance and strength. He remembered how he and his spirited young friends struggled to master the arts of holding shields, throwing spears, and wielding battle axes.

They took turns pulling one another on a wheeled wooden horse toward a target, practicing tilting a lance. Then they advanced to quintain training, charging on horseback at a shield-carrying dummy suspended from a swinging pole and weighted with a sandbag. Before he learned the feints necessary for staying astride a horse, the effigy, which was designed to resemble a menacing Muslim, knocked young Galorian out of his saddle more times than he could count. He laughed remembering.

But the sadness soon swept over him again. In his earliest days at the castle, Galorian grew close to a tender boy named Bradyn. They had the sort of friendship that allowed them both to brag about their futures as fearless knights and to share the little-boy sorrow of missing their parents. On a sunny afternoon, they borrowed two swift horses and rode to the forest, where Galorian challenged Bradyn to a race. Smiling and shouting "You're on!" Bradyn took off in a gallop, with Galorian following close behind.

Galorian wasn't sure what happened next—perhaps Bradyn's horse stumbled, or a low-hanging branch knocked him out of his saddle. All Galorian knew was that his own horse was charging full tilt and Bradyn was suddenly on the ground in front of him. He pulled on the reins with all his strength, but he could not stop in time. Bradyn cried out Galorian's name as his horse trampled his best friend.

Galorian leapt off, raced back, and knelt over Bradyn, who was breathing faintly and irregularly. Galorian picked him up and cradled him in his arms as he rode as quickly as he could back to the castle. Bradyn lived for three days. But he never awoke to hear his friend's fervent petitions for forgiveness and pleas for his life as Galorian knelt at his bedside day and night.

On the day that they buried his best friend, Galorian made a pledge to become an outstanding horseman in Bradyn's honor. That same day, he decided that he preferred the company of birds over humans. He buried his grief in what became his greatest love as a knight-in-training: falconry.

From the time that he could walk, Galorian had been intrigued by the large birds of prey that roosted on perches under mantel pieces in the dining rooms of fine inns while their owners ate dinner after a hunt. The boy Galorian ran after the baronesses who wore falcons as accessories, status symbols attached to their arms with jeweled chains. He followed the monks with birds perched on their shoulders into church, observing one Sunday when a hawk broke away and snatched the bread for the Mass off the altar.

The priest shooed the bird, its monk, and the boy out of the sanctuary, muttering oaths unbefitting a man of God.

During his days as a page, Galorian spent many hours in the castle mews. He cared for the peregrines, goshawks, and kestrels that sat patiently under hoods on their perches until he came each day to greet and feed them. One of his earliest tasks was to climb tall trees to remove bird-of-prey hatchlings from their nests and carry them safely to the castle for training. He watched in awe as Leland, the falconer, trained the birds for hunting, familiarizing them with his voice and whistle, rewarding them with morsels of food when they perched on his gloved fist. "They're not like us," Leland said to Galorian with a wink. "The females are bigger—and are the superior hunters."

Galorian learned to fashion the leather straps called jesses, which were tied to the birds' left legs, enabling them to fly for short distances until they learned to return on their own. He stitched pockets of bright red cloth, stuffed them with feathers and attached partridge wings. These the young page swung in the air as lures for the birds as they progressed through their lessons.

"For you!" announced Leland, his eyes sparkling with glee, early one morning when Galorian appeared in the mews. Perched on his gloved hand was the most beautiful bird the boy had ever seen. She was a merlin, with a shining silver-blue back and a buff breast, highlighted with flecks of orange and streaks of reddish-brown. And she was Galorian's to train.

Like most children of his time and place, Galorian had been raised on the magical tales of King Arthur and the Knights of the Round Table. And so he decided to name this enchanting creature Guinevere, after the elegant queen of the legend. Guinevere learned quickly and lived up to the reputation of merlins—fast and agile and an outstanding aerial acrobat who could pluck prey from the sky.

Galorian sewed a leather hood for her and embroidered it with gold and pearls, affixing on its top the bright feathers of a bird-of-paradise. He attached two small bells to his beloved bird's legs, enabling him to track her when she soared high out of sight. The bells bore the image of his lord's family crest, so that Guinevere could be identified and returned if she ever flew too far.

Galorian fretted occasionally that his beautiful and cherished bird might be stolen. But owning a bird of prey was considered a sacred duty, and the punishment for thieves was severe. At the age of eight, young Galorian had nightmares several nights in a row after witnessing a goshawk devour six ounces of flesh from the chest of an unfortunate man who was caught trying to steal it—the standard sentence for such a crime.

On one of his forays into the forest with Guinevere, Galorian discovered under a small pine a long-eared owl, dragging a broken wing. Two black ear-tufts stood up near the center of his head, above rust-orange eyes that scanned fearfully from side to side as Galorian approached. Beautiful black streaks ran the length of his tawny breast, and he stood on fully feathered toes.

"Hello," said Galorian softly, approaching with gentle steps. He carried the owl back to the castle and gave it a home in the mews. The owl stood on a wooden block with his right wing akimbo, too lacking in balance to inhabit a perch. He erupted with a series of exuberant hoots whenever Galorian and Guinevere returned from a hunting escapade, grateful for their gifts of shrews, voles, and mice.

"I tried to train an owl to hunt for me once," Leland told Galorian one day as they watched the newest resident in the mews down a fat mouse. "But they're slow as honey on a winter day. Their eye sockets take up most of their heads, leaving little room for brains." Galorian laughed. "And they're missing a crop in their throats to store food like the other birds. All that owl wanted to do after swallowing a reward was flap up to the nearest tree and take a long nap."

But Galorian loved the mysterious bird and tended him carefully. His owl reminded the young page of the one that perched on the shoulder of the wizard Merlin in the Arthurian tales. And so the boy Galorian lived happily in those days with an owl named Merlin and a merlin named Guinevere.

§

The screech owl high in the trees punctured the stillness with another plaintive cry, shaking Galorian out of his childhood reminiscences and jolting him back to the present. His memories of happiness turned into spasms of longing. "I've lost so much," he lamented into the night air, his voice cracking with despair. "My parents. My childhood home. Bradyn. The birds."

He swallowed hard before adding, "My beloved Josselyn and our daughter." The night before, he had left Aldrich in the dining room for several minutes and made his way to the birthing room. He gasped when he saw Josselyn cradling their child, both of them beautiful even in death. He reached down and picked up his daughter and then placed her back in Josselyn's arms. He kissed Josselyn on the forehead, his tears spilling onto her hair. And then he returned to the dining room to try to drink away his sorrow.

When he awoke that morning, still reeling from Josselyn's death, he didn't know whether to feel rejected or relieved when he discovered that her sister had run away. The only clear feelings he had were concern for Clarissa's safety and a measure of responsibility for the circumstances that had prompted her escape. He left the manor that afternoon, returning to the forest and the encampment of knights, hoping that the intense physical activity of their preparations would distract him from his grief and his guilt.

For ten long years he and his comrades had been getting ready for another Holy Crusade, keeping to a rigorous regimen that began each day with Mass and prayers at dawn. They devoted their days to sharpening their skills and increasing their strength. Galorian the boy who could barely lift a sword had grown into Galorian the knight who was renowned for his agile swordsmanship. He spent his mornings honing his exceptional equestrian abilities and his afternoons jousting with his fellow knights or attacking the pell. Evenings were devoted to the study of Latin and French, and to discussions with his comrades of warfare strategy and the use of siege weapons.

Galorian was ready and anxious to use his skills in battle on behalf of his faith—now more than ever. But the horizon was empty, with no new campaign to retake Jerusalem from the Muslims in sight. Dismayed and distraught, he could only wait.

In the stillness and chill of the night, he found it hard not to tally his losses over and over in his mind. *Has my life been wasted?* he wondered. *Have I been robbed of so much for nothing? Has it all been in vain?* The owl shrieked once more, flapped its wings, and took off into the dark expanse of sky. Galorian rose to his feet and called gently to his horse, the tears trickling down his cheeks.

§

Thankfully, it was Sunday when Clarissa awoke. No firewood to haul. Edmund was a confirmed pagan for whom Samhain was more than enough ritual for the year. But Raisa was a devout Roman Catholic, and she insisted that her children accompany her to the cathedral in Gladdington every Sunday morning. She bribed them with biscuits and honey.

Clarissa was grateful for her first solid food in more than a day. But she wanted no part of church. Although her faith, her prayers, and her love of Scripture had steadily deepened through her childhood, her love for the church had not. She was no longer dazzled by all the glitter and perfume. She knew that soon her parents would be sitting in their front pew, eyes riveted on the priest. Clarissa didn't care for Father Augustus—didn't like his fancy robes and his elite ways and his insistence on proclaiming the Mass in High Latin. She especially disliked the way he ignored the impoverished throng crammed into an alcove behind a screen in the back of the cathedral, separate and out of sight.

Nerida held Liliana on her lap, feeding her pieces of biscuit drizzled with dollops of honey. As the children ate hungrily, Clarissa realized for the first time that she had probably passed by them every Sunday. Perhaps they had been recipients of her gifts of sweets, which she subtly dropped out of her ample velvet sleeves each week as she left the cathedral with her family, hoping poor children would find and enjoy the treats.

The risk was small that she would encounter her parents in church. They would float in and out, oblivious to the poor souls huddled behind the screen at the back. And Galorian had likely already rejoined the other knights training in the forest. But Clarissa worried that she would stand out among the ragged crowd, dressed as she was. Questions would likely be asked. She announced that she would prefer not to go.

Raisa insisted that Clarissa join her and the children. Clarissa began to argue with her, but Nerida shot her a look that conveyed danger. Edmund stood up and moved to face Clarissa, towering over her. "The children of this house go to church," he declared with a menacing scowl. Clarissa knew then that, whatever the risks in church, there were more to be found in staying behind. She resolved then to get far away from Gladdington as quickly as she could.

Apparently the people behind the screen were used to seeing all manner of children show up with Raisa, and no one questioned or seemed to recognize Clarissa. She sat in a corner on the floor wrapped in her cloak, holding a swath of it across her face—there being no seats for poor people in the cathedral. A small break in the screen gave her a slice of a view. She strained to see her mother far away in her pew at the front, but she could not. She barely paid attention to Father Augustus, though when he listed the prayer concerns of the parish, one of his announcements stopped her cold.

"Prayers are requested for the family of Beatrix, beloved midwife, whose body was found on the forest path at dawn yesterday morning." The priest hesitated, and then added, "It appears to have been a murder." Clarissa gasped, and for a brief moment she stopped breathing. A murmur surged through the congregation as the shock registered. For years, Beatrix had caught the babies of both the wealthy and the destitute, providing equal care to all.

Clarissa shuddered when she realized that on the night of her own escape through the forest, the midwife had died there. She thought about the mysterious horse and rider in the clearing, wondering if she should tell

someone. But she knew she couldn't reveal what she had seen without revealing herself. Her cloak dropped open and the blood drained from her
face. Nerida whispered to her, "Are you all right?"

"Fine," said Clarissa, without looking at Nerida. But she was definitely
not fine. She was in a daze for the rest of the service, oblivious to the homily
and the prayers. When her parents filed past, Clarissa needed every ounce
of willpower to keep from stepping out, throwing herself at her mother, and
begging them to take her back. She missed her bed, and lamb stew, and the
warmth of fires in the hearth. She was beginning to feel that she couldn't
contain all her grief. She felt utterly alone in the world, and she had no idea
what she was going to do next. She fought back her tears, refusing to make a
scene. Nerida took her tenderly by the hand and led her out of the cathedral.

§

Edmund had observed his usual Sunday ritual, drinking cheap ale while his
family was at church and then sleeping off his drunken stupor through the
afternoon and night. When Clarissa was sure that everyone else was asleep,
she got up, then quietly woke Nerida and gestured for her to follow. They
crept out of the house. Clarissa grabbed her turnip with its long-cold ember
as they passed the pine tree under which she had carefully placed it, and the
two girls walked into the night until they were far enough away to whisper
without being heard.

"What do you think you're doing?" asked Nerida, a tremor of fright in
her voice.

"I don't belong here," Clarissa declared. "And neither do you."

Nerida slowly turned away from Clarissa. "I thought it would be better
here," she said as she unbuttoned the bodice of her plain dress and slipped
it off her shoulders. By the bright light of a moon just a sliver less than full,
Clarissa saw the scars that crisscrossed her new friend's back. She reached
out and gently touched them, as Nerida declared, "This is what happens
when you try to escape."

"I've already escaped," Clarissa said. "Come with me."

"The boys always run away when they're old enough," sighed Nerida,
readjusting her dress and turning back to face Clarissa. "They can fight, or
learn a trade. And they can protect themselves." She paused and took a deep
breath. "But bad things happen to girls."

"We'll take care of each other," said Clarissa, pleading. She had no idea
how they would do this, but she couldn't imagine Nerida remaining in this
horrible life, and she so desperately wanted not to be alone.

"I'm to be married. At noon on Christmas Day," Nerida declared then. "He's not so bad . . . a little slow." This made Clarissa laugh, and Nerida smiled, their faces illuminated in the moonlight. Nerida explained that she and her new husband would have to live with Raisa and Edmund for a while, but she hoped that someday they would be able to afford a place of their own.

"Do you love him?" Clarissa asked. Nerida looked at the ground and didn't respond. "Will he hurt you?" Clarissa asked then. When again there was no response, she said, "Nerida, you have the chance to choose freedom over fear."

Her friend looked up slowly, fixing her eyes on Clarissa's. "I'd rather live in fear," she said, "than die of hunger."

Though they had known each other for only two days, Clarissa thought she couldn't stand to lose someone else good in her life. But she knew she had to get on her way, and she didn't have the time or the words to convince Nerida to go with her. She had one question to ask before she could leave.

"Can you tell me about Liliana?"

Nerida smiled again. "She's magic," she said. "She showed up here dressed in lace and lying in a basket all decorated with bright ribbons when she was two days old."

Clarissa wanted more than anything to go back and rescue Liliana. She couldn't bear the thought of that winsome, beautiful child growing up under such cruelty and deprivation. But she knew she would risk everything if Liliana awoke and made noise. And Clarissa had no idea how she was going to take care of herself, let alone a three-year-old.

"I'll watch out for her," Nerida assured her. "And you're being watched over, too." She paused for a moment and then explained, "The owl is an omen of death to us. That's why the screech owl came to you the night you lost your sister and niece. Some people even believe that owls are the souls of people who have died." She smiled at Clarissa and said, "The owl is a messenger of good news, too. It shows up to bless newborn babies and accompanies people going through big changes. It won't forget you."

Clarissa wrapped her arms around her friend, and the two clung to each other for a few moments. "You must go," Nerida insisted. "Before they wake up and catch you."

Clarissa removed her cloak and handed it to Nerida. "For Liliana," she said. "To keep her warm." Then she carefully slipped her velvet dress over her head and handed it over, too. "For your wedding," she said, smiling.

Nerida, who had never owned anything so beautiful, could find no words in response.

"Are you just going to leave me standing here shivering under the moon?" Clarissa laughed. She helped Nerida remove her ragged dress made of coarse brown wool. Clarissa put it on and declared with a grin, "It suits me."

One last time she hugged her friend, now dressed in her favorite gown. She picked up her turnip and began walking away. Nerida raised her arms in the air, spun around twice, and whispered into the wind, "I'll never forget you," as Clarissa disappeared into the forest. A few moments later, a call that sounded like something between the screech of an owl and the wail of a cat echoed among the trees.

Five

Clarissa couldn't remember when she had last eaten or slept. The nights were cold and filled with far too many startling and unsettling noises for her to submit to her exhaustion. And the days brought too many people on the road who would be curious about a girl like her all alone. She had fallen into a pattern of hiding during the daylight hours and walking to keep warm and alert when it was dark. "The life of an owl," she said to her companion, warmly remembering Nerida's promise about the bird's protection.

"I should give you a name," Clarissa said to the screech owl, which had rejoined her soon after she had left Nerida and never strayed far from her. But she was too tired to think of one just then. The moon was on the wane, offering less and less light on the path every night. Six days had passed since she had jumped from the roof of her home. She had no idea how far she had traveled.

As the first pink hues of dawn chased away the last remnants of night on a morning that seemed like all the rest, Clarissa's eyes swept the landscape, searching for a place where she could lie down. She dragged herself under a small tree, far enough off the road to be out of sight, but not too far, as she felt her weary legs being less and less responsive to her demand that they carry her.

She sighed as she lay down on the hard ground, wishing she had her cloak to use for a pillow or to wrap around herself for extra warmth. She knew that she couldn't go on much longer. Winter was on its way. And she desperately needed to find something to eat. More than once she had wished that the silly turnip she carried had not been eviscerated of its flesh. Or that she had been brave enough to risk sneaking down and taking a stash of bread from the manor's kitchen the night she ran away.

All the crops were already harvested and in for the approaching freeze. Clarissa had found one rotting gourd in a field the day before and was so famished that she broke it open, brushed away the seeds, and dug into its pulpy center. That had been her only food in a few days. "Oh, Josselyn," she said to no one but herself and the spirit of her beloved sister, "if only you hadn't died in autumn."

She felt a sharp despair rising up in her. "Oh, Josselyn," she cried out, "if only you hadn't died at all!" She turned over and closed her eyes, feeling like all the world was against her. She gave in to a tantrum of the sort that she had occasionally exhibited as a very young and spoiled girl when she didn't get her way. Overwhelmed with a feeling that her life was unfair and unbearable, she kicked her feet and pounded her fists on the ground, until the last vestige of her waning energy was spent.

She was in that space between waking and slumber, where she often hovered despite her desperate hope to fall soundly asleep, when she was startled into full consciousness by a hideous face looming over hers. It was so close she could feel breath coming from the nostrils sniffing her. Clarissa sat up and shrieked, suddenly face to face with a baby dragon. The bulk of its body was about as long as Clarissa was tall, with a tail that doubled its length.

Clarissa scuttled backwards, still screaming, as the dragon shot out its long, red, forked tongue in her direction. It reared up on its hind legs and puffed out its throat, hissing at her. Clarissa ducked and covered her head with her hands to protect herself from the fire she knew it was about to breathe on her.

Nothing. It settled back down, still staring its beady eyes at her, flicking its very long tail from side to side. Clarissa took a deep breath. "You're not real," she declared confidently, thinking that perhaps the ugly beast was some kind of vision induced by her prolonged lack of sleep and food.

But it certainly looked real. It was colored a sort of brownish-yellow-gray, with bands of black around its body and tail. It had a pointy snout and long claws and was covered in scales. *You will grow into a frightful dragon,* thought Clarissa. *Especially once you master that fire-breathing trick.*

"Lizzie!" a voice called out behind her. "Are you bothering this nice, pretty girl?"

Clarissa turned and thought once again that perhaps she was hallucinating. Standing there was a man unlike any she had ever seen. He was tall and thin, dressed in green pantaloons and a tunic made of sewn-together patches of red and green and yellow silk. Cocked jauntily on his head was a hat with three points in the same colors, each topped with a gold bell. Even his upturned shoes matched—bells and all.

He had a flute peeking out of his deep left front pocket and a lute hanging from a strip of leather slung around his neck. He was holding another thin strip of leather in his right hand. To his left stood a donkey with enormous ears, hitched to a cart with large, solid wooden wheels, brightly painted to match the man's colorful outfit. The beast sported headgear that resembled a bishop's miter: tall, pointed, white, decorated with painted stones and pieces of coal, and streaming bright red and gold ribbons that reached almost to the ground.

With great flourish, the strange man removed his own hat. A tambourine fell out from under it. He made a swooping bow to Clarissa and announced with a smile, "Name's Jaxon." He murmured an apology as he slipped the leather strip around the neck of his dragon.

"Wh-what is that exactly?"

"Lizzie? Oh, she's a monitor lizard." He said this as if Clarissa had actually heard of such a thing. "Her real name," he told her with a wink, "is Her Majesty the Royal Highness and Regal Ruler of the Eminent Empire of England Queen Elizardbreath the First."

Clarissa laughed despite her effort not to. "You wait," said Jaxon confidently. "Someday we'll grow tired of kings and put a great queen on the throne, and she'll change everything."

Clarissa rolled her eyes and shook her head in disbelief. "But she won't be a lizard," she declared.

"I hope not," said Jaxon. "I'm just trying to get people used to the idea." He put his hand up to his chin and added, "Though I do know some lizards that would do a better job than some of the kings we've had."

Clarissa laughed again as Jaxon pointed at his scaly companion and launched into the story of Lizzie. "She's direct from the Holy Land," he explained. "I spend time with knights, you see. They tell me their stories about battles and conquests and love, and I turn them into songs and wander from coast to coast singing them.

"So one day this knight Rodney tells me he reached into his knapsack for his grub on his way back home from the Third Crusade and pulled out a bright orange reptile instead of his bread. A stowaway from the Holy Land desert. It was old Lizzie here. Well, young Lizzie, actually. Just a pup then. About the size of a hand and not yet faded to her mature color.

"Rodney kept her alive on beetles and grasshoppers. By the time he got back home to England, she was so big she had worn out her welcome. He thought she'd be a perfect sidekick for me. So now I catch the beetles and grasshoppers—and snails and fish and squirrels and mice and rabbits and birds—to keep her going."

Clarissa was pondering whether she believed the story when Jaxon added, "You're lucky. She's about to go to sleep for the winter. Hibernates from November 'til March and nobody gets to see her then. Gives me a break from having to catch bugs, which begin to disappear this time of year."

Lucky, thought Clarissa, feeling nothing of the sort. She couldn't help eyeing Jaxon's large knapsack. She figured he had some food in there, and she was almost—but not quite—desperate enough to ask for some.

As if he had read her mind, he asked, "You hungry?" He took the knapsack off his shoulder and pulled out a few brightly colored balls. "That won't do," he said, stuffing them back into the bag. Then he drew out a loaf of bread, followed by some currants and a chunk of hard cheese. It seemed like a banquet to Clarissa.

Taking a seat on a rock, Jaxon asked, "Who's your friend?"

"What?" asked Clarissa.

"Your friend there," said Jaxon, nodding at her funny-faced turnip sitting on the ground. "Nice nose," he declared. Before Clarissa could tell him the story of her Samhain turnip, he broke off a piece of bread and handed it to her, asking, "Where you headed?"

Clarissa hesitated a moment and then replied, "I have no idea." Then she hungrily stuffed the bread into her mouth.

They ate in silence for a while and then Jaxon asked, "Running away from home?" Clarissa affirmed his grasp of the obvious.

"What's so bad?" he wanted to know.

"They're forcing me to marry."

"Oh, that *is* bad," said Jaxon sympathetically. "A lot of that going around."

That made Clarissa smile. It had been days since she had smiled.

Jaxon suddenly jumped up and brought his foot down hard on the ground. "Beetle," he said, holding up the squashed specimen. Lizzie, who had curled up at his feet, swallowed it greedily in one gulp.

"Does she do tricks?" asked Clarissa, doubtful.

"Oh, you bet. She's very smart. Watch this." He popped up again and stood in front of the big lizard. "Stay right there!" he commanded. Lizzie didn't move. Didn't even pay attention, actually. "See?" he said. "She's brilliant!" Clarissa rolled her eyes. But she did smile again.

Jaxon sat back down next to her. "What was home like?" he asked, biting a piece of cheese off the end of a knife. Clarissa didn't know why she trusted this odd man, but she decided to spill her story to him. She began by talking about Josselyn, about how pretty she was and how beautifully she sang, about her fantastic tales and their adventurous forays into the forest. Slowly she made her way to describing Josselyn's death in childbirth and the news about the murder of the midwife Beatrix. Jaxon moved a little closer, recognizing the pain behind the words.

"Josselyn looked like my mother," said Clarissa, "crowned with the same beautiful golden hair." She sighed. "My dear mother." As she had done several times a day since she had left home, she wondered about her mother, what she was doing at that moment, whether she stayed awake at night mourning her older daughter and fretting about the whereabouts and safety of her younger one. Clarissa released the pang of guilt that stabbed at her. Then she said, "Unfortunately, I inherited my father's dark curls." That's all she said or thought about her father.

"They're beautiful," said Jaxon, eyeing her hair, and Clarissa blushed.

"My mother says they're the color of the raven," said Clarissa, feeling an intense stab of homesickness and longing for her mother's love and touch. She sighed and began describing for Jaxon the stunning views from her home's tower room, the peaceful pasture dotted with grazing sheep, and the orchard beyond the lake that was full of apples. She relayed every detail about the entrance to the manor: the stately double columns with their distinctive spiral pattern of crosses and shells, which she loved to trace with her fingers when she was a little girl; the flag emblazoned with her family crest—a proud green lion over a gold cross between two scallop shells, framed by oak leaves entwined with lilies. These had seemed overly showy to her before she fled, but now she would give anything to be able to run her hands up and down those pillars again beneath that familiar, fluttering flag.

"You're sure you don't want to go back?" asked Jaxon.

Despite her longings, Clarissa understood what fate awaited her if she returned. "I'm sure," she said. She drew hope from her belief that once Galorian left on a Crusade or married again, she would be free to go back home, where all would be forgiven.

Jaxon held out a handful of currants to her. Feeling full for the first time in days on bread and cheese, Clarissa took only a few. He tossed the others, one at a time, high into the air, catching them in his mouth and swallowing them with exaggerated gulps. "So, there's this nun place," he said when he had finished them off. "A convent. On the coast. They help out young women."

Clarissa perked up at this news. "How far?" she asked.

Jaxon thought a moment. "I'd say, for you, a two-day walk. You could be there day after tomorrow. Next day at the latest." He gave her some rough directions.

"Are you going that way?"

"Nah. Sorry. I wish we could take you there. But we're headed in the other direction." Clarissa felt an enormous sadness overcome her as he spoke the words. "I've got one more harvest festival to entertain before everybody hunkers down for the winter. Near Gladdington."

Clarissa's heart raced at the mention of the town close to her home.

Jaxon began gathering up the leftovers from their breakfast and stuffing them back into his knapsack—slipping what was left of the loaf of bread into her hands. Then he took a deep breath and picked up Lizzie, grunting and ducking as she tried to lick his face with her long forked tongue. He dropped the big lizard into the cart. She turned three circles, as a dog might, and then curled up again to sleep.

The donkey stood quietly, unmoving except for an occasional swish of his tail. Clarissa nodded in his direction and asked, "Is that His Majesty King Richard the First?"

"No," replied Jaxon, smiling at her. "That's Hubert Walter."

The name sent Clarissa into spasms of laughter. "Like the archbishop?" she asked. She had often heard her father talk in reverential tones about the head of the church.

"Yep," replied Jaxon. "I hear that the big church boss with the funny hat shares the name of my ass." He winked again at Clarissa. "When I got that donkey eleven years ago, I decided to name him The Most Reverend Primate Archbishop of Canterbury Baldwin of Forde," explained Jaxon. "But in no time, that eminent leader of the church up and died in Palestine, during the Third Crusade. So I changed my donkey's name to keep up.

"Next he was Reginald Lombardus, which seemed especially appropriate, because that archbishop was known to wear a hair shirt under his church vestments. But he lasted less than a month." Clarissa smiled at Jaxon as she stroked the beast's coarse, brownish-gray hair, taking note of the dark lines that came together and formed a cross on his back.

"The hardest time," continued Jaxon, "was the years eleven hundred and ninety-one to eleven hundred and ninety-three. The position of archbishop was vacant, and I had to call my donkey 'Hey You!' for seventeen months."

Clarissa laughed again. "I think he likes Hubert Walter," she said. Jaxon nodded warmly.

"Ask for Sister Mary Peter," he said as he swung a leg over Hubert Walter, who brayed loudly. "And be safe." The effect was comical as they plodded toward the road. Jaxon's long legs would have dragged on the ground had he not held them up at his sides at wild angles.

"Will you find out something for me?" Clarissa called after him.

"Anything," said Jaxon. She shouted her mission for him as he raised his hand in acceptance, never looking back.

§

Clarissa watched until the odd trio of donkey, lizard, and minstrel disappeared among the parade of travelers heading west. She felt lonely again then, but also more hopeful than she had since her escape. She had a destination, a place to wait until things settled down at home.

She was anxious to be on her way, but also weary and cautious. "A lot of help you were," she said to her owl, who had slept soundly on a tree branch through the entire encounter and still had its eyes tightly closed. She took note of its variegated brown, rust, and orange feathers, and the ear tufts that stood straight up on its small head, which was perched on its shoulders without a neck. "But you are strangely beautiful," she added.

Glad to have a satisfied stomach at last, Clarissa sighed. She closed her eyes as tightly as her owl's. And for the first time in several days, she fell soundly asleep, dreaming of nuns in long black robes and flowing headdresses floating in the sky among the clouds.

When she awoke, twilight was already creeping in. With a light step, Clarissa returned to the road and continued her journey east. But soon her steps grew heavy again. She wished for familiar landmarks by which to check her progress. That night seemed longer than all the others put together.

When the sun finally reappeared, she tried to sleep again, but her mind was racing with thoughts about the convent—whether she could find it from Jaxon's directions, who she would encounter there, how she would be received. She dragged herself through another night of walking. By dawn of the following day, she had not yet reached her destination, as she had hoped she might, and her spirit began to flag even more.

But as she settled under a tree to eat the last of Jaxon's bread, she saw a seagull circling overhead, a familiar sight from her family's brief summer visits to her Aunt Adela's home on the coast. She thought of all the times she and Josselyn had walked hand in hand among the dunes on the beach, eyes peeled for dolphins playing among the waves or riveted on the sand, searching for whorled shells with iridescent centers and the fan-shaped scallops that matched the symbols on their family crest.

Spotting the seagull made Clarissa's heart pound with anticipation. The soaring bird felt to her like a sign of good fortune close ahead. She took a deep breath before lying down and thought she noticed a tinge of salt in the air.

§

Even with a giant lizard in tow, a man on a donkey covers ground more quickly than a girl on foot. Jaxon got to the edge of Gladdington about the same time Clarissa reached the east coast. The air was cool, but the sun was bright, and for the citizens of Gladdington it was a perfect day for a festival. Pennants in brilliant colors snapped in a brisk breeze around the perimeter of the fairground.

Galorian was among the knights who hefted lances, while their squires burnished shields, in preparation for the day's jousting tournament. Spirited horses draped with silver armor pranced and neighed, anticipating their galloping charges. Parents scolded children who chased one another, giggling, among the hawkers of steaming pies and sellers of exotic birds.

Minstrels and jugglers roamed among the exuberant crowd, filling the air with color and music. Jaxon was a favorite among the entertainers. He had a little trick he did with Lizzie and a kerosene torch, maneuvering in such a way as to make it appear that his "dragon" was breathing fire. Adults oohed and aahed, while children, equally terrified and mesmerized, clapped and shouted "Do it again!"

Clarissa had told Jaxon that she had never been to any of the fairs that took place in the town just beyond the forest. And given Clarissa's description of her parents, he didn't expect them to show up among the bawdy and boisterous peasants who most appreciated his talent. But nonetheless, as he juggled bright balls in the air and sang his ballads, he constantly scanned the crowd for a blonde baroness in the company of a husband with dark, curly hair. He wasn't surprised that no couple matching their description appeared that day.

It was typical for traveling minstrels to seek out the hospitality of a well-to-do family. Jaxon received a few invitations, but he declined them all and headed into the forest on Hubert Walter, with Lizzie following behind in the cart, exhausted from her day of entertaining and ready to sleep it off for four months. Based on what Clarissa had told him, Jaxon followed the path that he assumed would eventually lead to the manor with the double columns and the family flag bearing the green lion. He was not disappointed.

It was about dusk when he knocked on the large oak door, between the pillars with the distinctive pattern of spiraling crosses and shells—just as Clarissa had described them. A servant appeared and, opening the door a crack, gave Jaxon a startled stare. "I'm looking for a place for the night," the minstrel explained.

Shocked by his dress, the young servant Catrain thought she had never seen anything so strange—until she caught a glimpse of the lizard. She let out a scream that caused the rest of the household to come running. The commotion upset Lizzie, who reared up on her hind legs, puffed out her throat, and hissed—which caused Hubert Walter to start braying relentlessly at top volume.

Thea gasped, covered her ears, and ducked. Aldrich laughed, which aggravated his wife. "They w-w-want a p-place to stay," stammered Catrain.

"Absolutely not!" cried Thea, straightening to her full height.

"Oh, why not?" said the baron. "It's been so depressing around here. We could use a few laughs."

"But he has a donkey," Thea said. "And that . . . that . . . *thing*!"

Everyone started talking at once—Thea, Aldrich, the servants. The word *dragon* was used more than once. Hubert Walter was still braying. Jaxon clapped his hands to settle them all down. "Perhaps we could just come in as far as the courtyard, where I could sing for our supper."

The buzz of conversation started up again immediately. Aldrich ordered the servants away from the door, to make way for the absurd trio. They moved reluctantly, as Jaxon led Hubert Walter, with Lizzie in tow, into the courtyard. "That's better," Jaxon declared as he smiled his brightest smile. Thea refused to look at him.

"If I could just sing you a song . . ." Jaxon pulled out his lute. "It's an original." He belted out a few notes to warm up his voice. And then he launched into his newest ballad, strumming as he sang:

> "I come to your fair city,
> With my face so pretty,
> My brain so witty.
> A man of class,
> Dragging my bony ass . . ."

Here he paused and said "Not this one," as he pointed to his rump, "but that one"—pointing at Hubert Walter, who was munching on one of the servants' caps. Young Catrain blushed. Aldrich chuckled. Thea rolled her eyes. It was obvious to Jaxon that the baroness's disgust toward the interloper in her home was growing with each stanza, but he pressed on:

> ". . . I sing a tale of a beautiful lass.
> With curls as black as the raven,
> Safe in her sacred haven,
> With a lover so divine,
> They sup on bread and wine."

The look on Thea's face immediately softened, and she locked her eyes on Jaxon's until he finished the song. Aldrich, clearly missing the message, clapped and shouted, "Well done!" He ordered the servants to bring dinner and mead for the minstrel, whom he slapped several times on the back, inviting him to spend the night.

"Unless the donkey and dragon are welcome in the bed, I'd just as soon stay outside with them," replied Jaxon.

Thea ordered the servants to gather blankets. As she handed them to Jaxon, mother and minstrel exchanged knowing glances, both aware that the cascade of questions bursting to be asked had to remain unspoken and unanswered. With tears in her eyes, Thea whispered a barely audible "Thank you."

Then Aldrich whisked his wife away. "Come, my dear," he said, grabbing her by the arm. "That wasn't so bad, was it?"

Jaxon fell exhausted into a pile of straw in the barn next to Hubert Walter and Lizzie. He smiled as he drifted off to sleep. He had conveyed a message to Clarissa's mother in the only way a man like him could get word to a baroness without arousing suspicion. He had let her know that her daughter was safe and in the loving arms of God, without revealing her location. He was very pleased with himself.

But he had yet to fulfill the mission that Clarissa had assigned him.

Six

"Smart girl," Thea whispered to herself, smiling, as she sank into the feather palette on her bed. It seemed to her that, since the night of Clarissa's escape, not an hour had gone by without Thea wondering and worrying about her. Especially in the silence and dark of night, alone in her room, she fretted about her daughter and quietly stormed heaven with prayers for Clarissa's safety.

At first, Thea had been angry. Having tragically lost her older daughter, she found it impossible to accept that her younger daughter was gone, too— and by her own choice. *How*, Thea thought bitterly, *could a daughter do this to her mother?* But over time all she felt was worry.

Now she tossed and turned, sleep eluding her as images of nuns crowded her mind. She wondered which of the scores of convents dotting medieval England had taken in Clarissa. She knew no way to find out. As much as she wanted to, there was no chance of sneaking out to the barn to ask the minstrel without being detected and creating a scandal.

Thea didn't know how to ride a horse or drive a wagon. Except for her weekly visits to the cathedral, and brief summer trips with her family to see her sister Adela on the coast, the manor alone had been her whole world since her marriage. Even if she had possessed more travel savvy, covering the entire country knocking on convent doors would have been absurd, if not impossible.

And, in the end, Thea knew that not knowing was best. How tragic it would be if she unintentionally led Aldrich and Galorian to her daughter. *She's safe*, Thea sighed. *That will have to be enough for now.*

She found herself envying the nuns in those convents. She pictured free, smiling women happily devoted to God and to one another. She marveled at Clarissa's wisdom to seek them out—and at her young daughter's courage. The thought had never occurred to Thea to escape the arrangement that her father and Aldrich had made for her future when she was a girl. She was only ten years old; how could she have imagined a world beyond the one that was chosen for her?

On her wedding day, she was dressed like a little doll in a white silk gown, with more pearls on the bodice than she was able to count. As she walked down its seemingly endless aisle, reaching up to hang on to her tall father's arm, she felt swallowed up by Gladdington's imposing cathedral. Her only duty that day, her mother had advised her, was to keep smiling. Always anxious to please, young Thea did her best, despite the tremors of fear that had set her knees knocking under her gown.

Her mother had not warned her of the duty that was expected of her that night. Confused and shocked by the pain, Thea cried herself to sleep every night for the first month of her marriage, longing for her mother and hiding her tears from Aldrich. How bittersweet that memory seemed now. Aldrich rarely came to her room or invited her to his anymore. Thea admitted to herself that she found some relief in that. But she was only thirty years old. *Is my life already over?* she wondered.

She rolled over on her side and felt an aching loneliness settle deep in her body. Tears slid down her cheek on to the pillow. Her daughters were gone. Her husband was distant, inhabiting his own world and pursuing his own desires. She tried not to care. But she could not help wondering where the servant Catrain, so simple and beautiful and young, was spending the night.

§

Clarissa stood at the door of a Benedictine convent. It was perched on a promontory just a stone's throw from breathtaking, chalky white cliffs, as far east as one could travel in England without falling into the sea. The hour was late, and except for the torch that burned beside the door, the imposing stone building was dark. Clarissa pondered for a moment whether she would receive a better reception in the morning, in the bright light of day. But she had walked so far, and was so very weary and anxious, that she knocked without giving it another thought.

She waited a few seconds and then knocked again, a bit more forcefully. The trap in the door slid open, and Clarissa saw a pair of eyes peering out at her. She had rehearsed what she was going to say many times, but now that the moment had arrived, her mind was blank. Apparently judging her safe for entrance, the sister behind the eyes unbolted the massive door, which slowly creaked open.

Clarissa had to suppress a giggle. Though she didn't yet know the name for the unusual headgear the nun wore, the wimple was so tight around the old woman's face that it revealed little more than the narrow trap in the door had. Clarissa, wrestling her amusement under control, did her best to plaster on her face a most holy expression and present herself as a solemn and earnest young woman seeking entrance. The effort was slightly compromised by the fact that she held in her hands a dried-up turnip with a ridiculous face carved in its side.

"The minstrel sent me," Clarissa finally managed to utter.

"The idiot with the ass and the lizard," the sister said under her breath. Clarissa had to stifle another giggle. This was not at all what she had expected to hear from a nun. The sister said nothing more.

"He said you could help me," Clarissa blurted into the silence.

"Did he now?" retorted the nun, bent over but eyeing Clarissa up and down with sideways glances.

"He said to ask for"—in her nervousness, Clarissa's brain was still failing her—"for Mary-with-a-man's-name-too."

"That would be half the convent," the sister muttered.

Clarissa heard a faint swishing behind the nun then, like a soft waterfall approaching. A sister that Clarissa guessed to be about the age of her mother—dressed like the other one in a long black robe and a wimple that covered her forehead, cheeks, and chin—gently pulled the older nun back inside. "Sister Mary Anthony," she said tenderly, "let's let this young woman come in out of the cold." She gestured for Clarissa to enter. "I'm Sister Mary Peter," she said with a warm smile, "the abbess here." Clarissa didn't know exactly what that was, but it sounded important, and she was immediately in awe of this kind woman.

"I'm Clarissa. The minstrel sent me," she repeated.

"Ah, Jaxon." The younger nun smiled again. "He keeps us entertained."

"Damn lizard," Sister Mary Anthony muttered.

"Will you excuse me a moment?" Sister Mary Peter took hold of the older nun's bony hand and led her, bent and shuffling, down a long corridor and out of sight. When Mary Peter floated back, she apologized to Clarissa. "She doesn't sleep well, and she often answers the door before I can get here." Clarissa nodded. "Let's find you a bed," said the nun. "We'll talk in the morning."

The thought of a bed brought tears to Clarissa's eyes. She had almost forgotten what a bed felt like. The one in the small room where Mary Peter left her was simple and hard, but it was a great improvement over the ground on which she had slept for a week. A crucifix on the wall kept watch over her and was a comfort. Stretched out beneath it, she considered the abbess's gentle compassion toward the old sister—and toward her, a stranger—and felt overwhelmed by Mary Peter's warm welcome. *As though the Virgin Mary—or Jesus himself—had showed up on the doorstep*, she thought, as exhaustion claimed her.

She wasn't asleep long. She awoke a few hours later, as if in heaven serenaded by a choir of angels. Their blended voices echoed through the long corridor from the chapel at its far end, where the nuns chanted psalms and murmured prayers. Clarissa got up and walked into the stone hallway. She gazed with longing down its length at the holy faces illuminated by candlelight and filled with peace. Spellbound, she watched until the singing stopped. Then she quietly slipped back into her bed and fell asleep smiling.

§

Jaxon woke before the sun appeared and headed back toward Gladdington on Hubert Walter, hauling Lizzie, anxious to find some answers for Clarissa. The merchants were throwing open the wooden shutters of their shops, ready to showcase their wares. Jaxon walked among the fletchers crafting their arrows, and the stringfellows at work on bow strings, past the dyers of wool and turners of wood, heading for the red-and-white pole standing prominently on a corner of the square.

A common fixture in most towns, a striped pole painted the colors of blood and bandages was a sign to the largely illiterate populace that this was the place to come to get an aching tooth pulled or a broken bone set—even the occasional infected limb amputated. Brimley, the town's barber-surgeon, cut hair, too, and Jaxon figured that this was the spot to get news and information. It didn't take long for him to find someone who had known Beatrix, the beloved midwife who had delivered babies for forty years.

Jaxon bought an apple from a cart and a sweet roll from the baker's shop and then followed the directions he had been given to the home of Beatrix's daughter, Ingrith. Amid clouds of flour, she was rolling out dough for her breakfast biscuits. She was a plump woman, with puffy cheeks set on a red face. When Jaxon mentioned the name of her mother, she burst into sobs, wiping her running nose on her sleeve. "She was planning to live with me!" Ingrith wailed. "Why didn't she stop sooner?"

Jaxon had no answer to this question. And he decided that she wasn't going to be of much help to him. "Did your mother have any other relatives?" he asked.

"Just a sister," she replied, sniffling.

Jaxon thanked her and set out for the forest, to follow Ingrith's long and complicated directions to the cottage of her aunt Zerah. When he arrived, he knocked and waited. A face peered warily around the door. Jaxon, explaining that Ingrith had sent him, introduced himself. "You have an unusual name," he said as he bowed to Zerah.

"It's biblical," she said, and a smile slowly crept over her face. "I'm a miracle. Thanks to my twin sister."

Jaxon was no Bible scholar, and he wasn't familiar with the unusual story found in its first book, Genesis. So Zerah told it to him. "A young widow named Tamar was about to give birth to twins. The first stuck out his hand, and the midwife tied a crimson cord around his wrist, so that she and the mother would know that he had come out first. But then he drew back his hand, and out came his brother.

"I put out my hand too and withdrew it," Zerah explained. "Beatrix came out first, and I was in distress in the womb. She grabbed my hand as she came out and wouldn't let go. I believe I would have died in there if she hadn't pulled me out. Is it any wonder she became a midwife?"

What a tale, thought Jaxon, feeling more than a little skeptical—but he always loved a good story.

"Zerah was the name of the second twin in the Bible story," she continued. "It means 'brightness' in Hebrew. Our mother liked that."

"Was the name of his brother Beatrix?"

Zerah laughed. "No. It was Perez. Fortunately, my sister was named for our grandmother."

"Did you wear a crimson cord?"

"Yes!" she said. "For over a year I wore a bracelet made of red ribbon, and Beatrix wore a yellow one. We looked so much alike that our mother never would have kept us straight otherwise."

The brightness matching her name, which radiated from Zerah's face, gradually began to fade. "A decade after our birth, the minutes that separated our arrival made all the difference in the world," she said softly, a faraway look in her eyes. "The elder daughter is always given away first. Our father made Beatrix marry his friend Udolf. He was an old man, hunched and bald and fat, with a half-shut eye that constantly oozed milky yellow tears.

"We were raised to obey, and Beatrix was too young to imagine disobeying our father. She knew she couldn't take care of herself on her own. So she endured her husband's beatings and beratings for over three years.

"But when she had a child, she changed. Udolf beat her badly for giving birth to a girl. One day Ingrith was crying. 'Keep her quiet!' he hollered. He grabbed the baby out of Beatrix's arms and dangled her in the air, then thrust her legs into a pot of scalding water. Her daughter's screams were more than Beatrix could bear. That night Udolf drank himself into a stupor, and she ran away. She carried Ingrith halfway across England, until she found a midwife in Gladdington who agreed to take her on as an assistant.

"Our father considered Beatrix dead. My sister didn't know the tradition that dictated that I had to be handed over to Udolf, to provide him with an heir. He told my father, 'They look the same. It makes no difference to me.' When Beatrix found out, she walked all the way back and risked her life to rescue me.

"We found this cottage hidden in the woods, far from any path we thought our father or Udolf would take if they ever bothered to try to find us. Beatrix, Ingrith, and I lived here together, getting by on the bit of food I was able to grow and the gifts Beatrix received from the few new mothers she assisted. But the day came when we knew that for us to survive, she had to make her home in Gladdington and work fully as a midwife. By then it seemed safe for her to be in town."

Zerah sighed heavily before continuing. "I love the isolation . . . and beauty . . . and quiet of this place, so I stayed. Beatrix came back often, bringing Ingrith for visits, sharing her food and money with me." She dabbed at the tears in her eyes and looked intently into Jaxon's. "My sister was so beautiful of spirit and so kind to everyone. Why would anyone want to kill her?"

Jaxon returned her anguished gaze. "I was hoping you could tell me."

§

The nuns were kind enough to let Clarissa sleep as long as she wanted that first night. It was past noon when she finally emerged from her cell, appearing groggy and yawning in the kitchen, where the midday sun was streaming in a high window. A young woman was kneading dough behind a large table and shaping it into loaves. Clarissa noted that she wore a habit similar to the Marys, but her head was covered in a simple white headdress rather than a wimple. *A pre-nun*, thought Clarissa, having not yet been introduced to the term *novice*.

"You're the new guest," the young woman said warmly, and Clarissa nodded. "Tomorrow morning you'll have this bread with beer. Our usual breakfast." Catching the surprise on Clarissa's face, she explained, "We make our own beer here. It's a lot safer to drink than the water." She reached into a cupboard for a large piece of that morning's breakfast loaf and, placing it into Clarissa's hands, directed her to the small orchard where Sister Mary Peter was overseeing the sorting of the last of the season's apples into baskets. Clarissa had finished the bread by the time she got there.

"Good morning, sleepy one," said the nun, holding out an apple.

Clarissa took it and thanked her with a smile. "It's been a week since I slept in a bed," she said. "It was delicious."

Mary Peter smiled back. "Would you like a tour?" They walked to the apiary at the edge of the orchard, where several hives of bees were beginning to settle from the buzz of frenetic labor into a pre-winter hum of lassitude. The tiny garden, whose rocky soil had produced a paltry crop of potatoes, carrots, and peas despite the sisters' summer of labor, was a patch of dark furrows with nothing to do but await spring.

The dormancy of the grounds was a sharp contrast to the activity in the buildings. Clarissa was in awe of the sisters who spun thread on large wheels, wove cloth on even larger looms, and added bright touches of embroidery to their work. But the place that took her breath away was the scriptorium. There, she was astonished to see sisters sitting stooped over simple desks, dipping large, stiff feathers into ink, illuminating the Holy Scriptures: copying them word by word and adding artistic flourishes. "I wish I could read them," she whispered, as she gently traced a few of those gorgeous words written on parchment with her right index finger.

"Then you've come to the right place," said Sister Mary Peter. Clarissa had been told more than once that teaching girls was a waste of time, but that didn't seem to be true here. She hoped she could stay long enough to learn a little—and maybe someday write elegant words in beautiful books. "You'd have to stay a while, though," said Mary Peter, as if reading her thoughts. "Hospitality is at the heart of our Benedictine way of life, and we provide for our guests for as long as they need to be here." She sighed as she said, "But most stay only a short time," causing Clarissa to wonder if this disappointed her.

Hoping she wasn't being impolite, Clarissa asked, "Why are there so many Marys here? And so many men's names?"

Mary Peter smiled at her. "When we take our final vows as nuns, we choose a new name to signify the new life we're entering. Many sisters choose the name of the mother of God, often paired with a favorite saint. I've always admired Saint Peter. He seemed so human, always wanting to do the right thing and often failing. But Jesus loved him deeply and built his church on Peter's faith." Clarissa smiled back at her, and Mary Peter said, "I'm happy to answer anything you want to ask."

Clarissa had been aware that England had many convents, but she knew next to nothing about them, so she had many questions. Mary Peter patiently answered them all. When Clarissa asked about her role, Mary Peter explained that people used many names for *convent*, including *priory*, *monastery*, and *abbey*. "*Abbess* means that I serve as a spiritual guide, or shepherdess, for the forty-five sisters who are part of the community in this abbey."

When the shadow fell across the three on the sundial in the garden, a nun swished past them to the chapel and rang the bell to summon the others to the time of prayer known as None. Mary Peter took a moment to explain to Clarissa the hours of prayer that were the backbone of the daily rhythm at the abbey. By the time Clarissa had dragged herself out of bed that day, the sisters had already observed Matins at two a.m., Lauds at first light, Prime at dawn, Terce at nine, and Sext at noon. Vespers and Compline were yet to come at six and eight that evening.

Clarissa was intrigued. "But how do you know what time it is at night?"

"By the rising of the constellations in the sky," Mary Peter explained.

"And when it's cloudy?"

Mary Peter laughed. "Then we just guess and figure that God is in as much a fog as we are."

In the chapel, Clarissa took a seat toward the back. She watched as the sisters filed in, genuflected by turn in front of the crucifix hanging behind the altar, and took their places in their prayer stalls. Their voices reminded her of Josselyn's, as melodious to her as the songs of the larks and thrushes in the meadow at home. Clarissa yearned for such a voice, to be able to sing clear and exquisite praises up to the rafters rather than self-consciously humming off-tune toward the floor as she did. The beauty of the mystical chants traveled right through her heart and settled into her bones, where they resonated with both the heaviness and the hope that she carried.

After the time of prayer, Mary Peter found her again and asked if she was feeling at home. Clarissa wanted to unburden herself to this kind nun, to spill her story and confess the secret that felt like such a heavy weight in her heart. But she understood now that Mary Peter was responsible for a whole community of women. She didn't want to be a bother—and she knew that she was one of the guests who wouldn't be staying long. She smiled and said, "I feel very much at home, thank you," and asked how she could be helpful.

"Just rest today," answered Mary Peter. "There will be plenty of time to help."

Clarissa was gratefully drowsing in her room when the bell rang at six for Vespers. She returned with the sisters to the chapel for the lighting of the candles and the welcoming of the night. When they filed out in silence, she was unsure whether to follow. She thought there was a meal. She *hoped* there was a meal. But she didn't know if guests ate with the community or somewhere else. She decided to follow.

No one spoke as the sisters took their places around six long, simple pine tables in a large room in the wing opposite the chapel. Clarissa hesitated, feeling lost and conspicuous. A sister with a gracious smile, who Clarissa guessed was about five years older than she, gestured at the empty seat across from her and whispered, "Just do what I do."

Clarissa stood with the others as Mary Peter led them in a unison grace in thanks for the meal. Then they all sat, each unfolding the linen napkin embroidered with a green fleur-de-lis at her place and putting it in her lap. Clarissa thought of her mother, who had a favorite silver necklace in the shape of a fleur-de-lis, and felt a sting of homesickness. The novices brought bowls of potato soup and pieces of bread, and Clarissa waited patiently along with the others while everyone was served.

The young sister across from her pushed back her chair and went to her knees. *The supper genuflection*, thought Clarissa. She did the same. When their faces met under the table, the sister mouthed "I dropped my napkin" as she waved it in the air, then put her hand over her mouth to stifle a laugh. When they sat back on their chairs, Clarissa's face was flushed with embarrassment, though she did her best to act as if nothing at all had happened.

At Compline at eight, in the shadows of the chapel, she wept her way through the psalm. Mary Peter had told her that monks and nuns had chanted these same words at this time every night for almost seven centuries, ever since the founder of their order, Benedict of Nursia, had created their liturgy:

> Answer me when I call,
> O God of my right!
> You gave me room when I was in distress.
> Be gracious to me, and hear my prayer.
> I will both lie down and sleep in peace;
> For you alone, O Lord, make me lie down in safety.

After Compline, the nuns entered into the Great Silence and went straight to bed. Clarissa had been awake for only a few hours. But when she settled onto her palette, she realized that she was weary again and ready to let go of the day, grateful that she would sleep in peace and safety as she had the night before. She looked up at the crucifix on the wall and said, "Goodnight, Jesus." Then she smiled, turned over, and whispered to herself, "I could like this life."

§

The next day Clarissa followed the schedule of the novices. She sorted apples with them in the morning. In the afternoon she appeared in the room where reading lessons took place. When she and the teacher saw each other, they exchanged grins. Her teacher was the sister who had dropped her napkin under the table the night before. She introduced herself as Scholastica, which Clarissa thought was a perfect name for a teacher. Scholastica explained that this was the name of Benedict's twin sister, the founder of the women's branch of Benedictine monasticism.

Clarissa relished every lesson and was grateful for Scholastica's attention and encouragement. She discovered under the sister's tutelage that she loved words: pronouncing them, spelling them, stringing them together in her mind. She anticipated with excitement the day when she would be skilled enough to put them down on paper. Mary Peter checked in on her from time to time and expressed admiration for her progress.

Except for having to get out of bed for Matins at two o'clock every morning, Clarissa fell easily into the rhythm of the convent. The busyness of the days, framed by the hours of prayer, kept her mind and heart occupied. But at night in her cell, she often cried herself to sleep. Hunger perpetually gnawed at her, and she yearned for food other than thin soup and hard bread—and for her soft clothes and the warm luxuries of her upbringing. Still, she awoke each morning grateful for a safe place to be, sheltered for a time among these kind and holy women until she could return home.

On the night of the new moon, she felt an ache and a stirring in her body that were new. She reached down and felt the trickle of warm blood. The terrible memory of Josselyn's bleeding came into sharp focus, and for a brief moment she feared that she was dying. But then she remembered her mother telling her about the bleeding that followed the moon, and the times when she and Josselyn had whispered together about it, and her panic subsided.

Never in the two weeks since she had been gone from her home did she long so strongly for her sister and her mother. She wanted to share this moment with them and receive their congratulations and comfort. Though she had not known it, beside the Samhain bonfire on the night of the full moon, the ache she had felt deep in the core of her was more than grief. Her body was moving into its time of fertility, releasing its first egg on its mysterious journey, just as her spirit was relinquishing its childhood innocence.

Pride and concern welled up in Clarissa in equal measure. She decided that after Matins she would speak to Scholastica and ask her how to take care of this new development. She looked forward to sharing the news of her blossoming womanhood with this wise sister.

"The curse," said Scholastica, shaking her head sadly when Clarissa told her in a corner of the chapel after the other sisters had filed out. Any words of comfort were erased in Clarissa's mind by Scholastica's lack of help and her pronouncement that "holy women don't bleed." She turned and walked away, leaving Clarissa feeling both stunned and confused.

"I can help," a voice whispered in the dark. Clarissa turned. "I'm Johanna," said a tall and smiling young woman who emerged from the shadows. "I was extinguishing the candles and tidying the chapel, and I couldn't help overhearing." Johanna wore the headdress of a novice, but Clarissa thought she looked older by several years than the other nuns-in-formation at the convent.

Picking up one of the small linen cloths on the altar, Johanna took Clarissa by the hand and led her outside. "It's true that most nuns don't bleed," she said. "But, far from being a sign of our exceptional holiness, it's because of our austere diet. Women's bodies shut down the usual functions when they lack proper nourishment to sustain a pregnancy." Johanna paused, and then she added with a warm laugh, "Not that any of us are trying."

Without speaking another word, she led Clarissa through the garden and across the cliff where the convent sat. They walked for a long time down a steep footpath strewn precariously with rocks, groping their way without a moon in the sky to shed light to aid them. When they came to a grove of tall trees, they skirted the edge until Johanna found the path that led to the bog at the center. She reached down and pulled up a clump of peat moss. "You put it inside the linen cloth," said Johanna, carefully wrapping the cloth she had lifted from the altar around the moss. "Use it for your monthly needs," she said, handing it to Clarissa.

As understanding dawned, Clarissa recoiled in horror. "But that cloth covered the bread of the Mass, the holy Body of Christ!" she protested.

"And do you think that your body is any less holy?" asked Johanna tenderly. Her words hung in the damp, salty air, unanswered. Clarissa was too stunned to respond. "We weave these cloths at the convent," Johanna continued, "and we have plenty." Pulling another clump from the bog, she explained, "Doctors call this blood moss because it's very absorbent. They use it on soldiers during the Crusades to stem the flow of blood from battle wounds." She paused a moment and then added, "I think it's the only good thing to come out of the Crusades."

The two women walked back toward the convent, making their way slowly up the path. When they got to the top of the cliff, still out of earshot of the sleeping sisters, Johanna said, "Let's sit for a minute." The night was cold, with a strong breeze coming off the ocean, and the two young women huddled close to each other.

For the first time that night, Clarissa shifted her gaze, which had been riveted on the precarious path, and looked up. From her balcony seat on the cliff, she took in the dark expanse above her, strewn with stars like sparkling gems. She gasped at their brilliance in the moonless sky. "They're all for you," declared Johanna. "A gift from God on this day that you've become a woman." She smiled, and Clarissa smiled back.

They sat in silence for a while, looking out over the sea and listening to the regular rhythm of the waves reaching the shore below them. Clarissa felt a deep trust in this new friend, and the moment seemed perfect for releasing the secret that still lay buried in her heart. But before uttering a word, she talked herself out of spilling it. Reveling in the enchantment and mystery of that night, she wanted nothing to spoil it.

Johanna interrupted her thoughts. "I love the church, and I love history," she said. "I read everything I can." She explained that, in the abbey library, she pored over the illuminated manuscripts of the Bible, the stories of the church's saints, and the works of the early Greek and Roman philosophers, at every chance she could grab away from prayer and work.

"The Roman hero Pliny the Elder believed that women's monthly blood turned wine sour, dulled steel, destroyed bees, and rusted bronze and iron," she declared. "He suggested that women should walk around cornfields naked, allowing their blood to kill off caterpillars, beetles, and worms." The two young women laughed at that image.

"Even the Bible says we're unclean and untouchable," continued Johanna, her tone somber once more. "Many of the sisters believe it." She paused and shook her head. "Even Sister Scholastica."

Then she turned and looked intently at Clarissa. "Please . . . don't you believe it," she pleaded. "When Jesus was on his way to heal an important synagogue official's dying daughter, a woman who had bled constantly for twelve long, lonely years reached out and touched his cloak. She was an outcast, a threat to the purity of her community. But instead of being offended and outraged, as expected of a holy man, Jesus listened to her story. He affirmed the power of her faith to bring healing and declared her body holy." She sighed. "We're all holy."

They sat in silence again as Clarissa let these words sink in. One by one the stars blinked out as the black of night gave way to the pink and aqua shades of dawn. Before long, a pinpoint of scarlet light appeared at the far edge of the ocean. Suddenly, Johanna erupted with delighted laughter. "The dolphins!" she shouted, pointing beyond the breakers. About a dozen of the sleek, gray creatures broke the surface in turn as they moved along the shore, the dawning sun glistening off their backs. Clarissa was mesmerized by their graceful, synchronized movement.

"Another gift," Johanna declared. She reached up and made the sign of the cross on Clarissa's forehead. "May you always shine like the stars and dance like the dolphins," she intoned. "And may you know yourself from this day forward as a woman blessed by God."

When Johanna put her arm around Clarissa, the newly anointed young woman leaned her head on the gentle and wise sister's shoulder. Grateful tears streamed down Clarissa's face. As the convent bell tolled out the hour of Lauds, she knew that she would always remember and treasure this night.

Seven

Scholastica found Clarissa after breakfast the next morning. "Please forgive me," she began. Clarissa noticed tears pooling in her teacher's eyes as she said, "I'm a widow." Clarissa was surprised. Scholastica explained, "It's not unusual. We come here in different ways. Some are promised by their parents when they are children and bring along dowries that help to keep us going. Others choose this life on their own as young women. And some of us decide to become nuns after we lose our husbands."

Clarissa noticed that the tears were beginning to slip down Scholastica's cheeks, and she reached out and put a comforting hand on the sister's arm. "I lost my husband and my two young daughters in a fire two years ago." Scholastica paused, unable to continue for a moment, and then spoke again softly. "It's difficult to be a widow . . . especially a young one. I was alone . . . stigmatized . . . without support. I needed a community. A place to grieve and be held up by the prayers of others.

"At first I was too sad to appreciate this life. It seemed like my only choice then, and I resented being here. But the sisters carried me through the worst, and over time I grew close to them and began to embrace their life." She smiled then. "Teaching the novices allows me to pour out the love and knowledge I would have shared with my daughters on other young women."

She had to stop again, and Clarissa gently squeezed her arm as Scholastica stared at the floor. When she gazed again into Clarissa's eyes, she brushed away her tears and said, "Last night you reminded me of my younger self . . . when the world felt full of promise . . . and I was full of joy, looking forward to marriage and children." She put her arms around Clarissa and drew her close. "I'm so sorry," she whispered. "I'm so very sorry for my hurtful words."

Clarissa, amazed that nuns weren't perfect and moved that anyone would care this much about what she felt, whispered back through her own tears, "It's all right."

§

The community in the abbey heard the approach before they saw it. The big wheels of the old cart creaked, Hubert Walter brayed, and Jaxon sang lustily as they arrived back from their foray in the west. Lizzie had been sound asleep for more than a week and would remain so for many more. "Ah, it's good to be home," announced the minstrel as he dished out smiles, a hug for Clarissa, and a wink in the direction of Sister Mary Anthony. The gnarled old nun wagged her finger at him, but Clarissa noticed that she was grinning at the ground when she turned back toward the kitchen and her labor of stacking dishes.

Stretching his arms into the air and yawning loudly, Jaxon headed straight for the shed at the edge of the garden that the sisters kept available for him and his strange menagerie. Clarissa, bursting to talk with him and learn what he had discovered, watched with dismay as he walked away.

The next morning Jaxon spied her in the orchard. He stood near her and helped to sort apples as he passed along the news. He began with the story of his loud arrival at the manor, reporting that Clarissa's parents were well, which was a great relief to her. Then he turned to the details of the mission she had given him.

"There isn't much to share," he began, as Clarissa's shoulders slumped with disappointment. He revealed the few facts he had gleaned from Beatrix's twin sister and a cluster of busybodies parked in Gladdington's barber shop and town square. "The midwife was found on the path in the forest. Strangely, no effort was made to hide her body." Clarissa stopped her work and looked at Jaxon as he continued. "She was stabbed through the heart, but not with a knife or a sword. The wound was made by a long instrument, as thick as my thumb but square, with a sharp point." He paused a moment and then said, "And there was a scarf around her neck that bore the crest of a leading Gladdington family, the Ashdowns."

Clarissa gasped. The Ashdowns lived in a neighboring manor and sat in a pew across the aisle from her own family's in the cathedral. She and Josselyn had known the daughters, the eldest of whom, Oswalda, had given birth under Beatrix's care to a stillborn son a few days before Josselyn and her daughter died. "Oh, Beatrix!" Clarissa cried, feeling the weight of so much tragedy and lamenting all the loss that was a regular part of a midwife's difficult work. *What a terrible time we women have*, she thought, for the first time in her life including herself in the company of women.

"They've arrested Lord Frederick Ashdown," Jaxon continued. "They have a motive—revenge for the stillborn birth of his heir. But it all seems a little fishy to me." Jaxon wondered aloud why a murderer would so obviously leave behind such damning evidence. "I think the real killer planted the scarf to draw suspicion away from himself." Clarissa gasped again. She thought of the poor Ashdowns, victims of this terrible wrongdoing. She couldn't imagine her friends' father committing such a crime.

"That's all I know," declared Jaxon. Clarissa was stunned into silence. "But I have some good news!" the minstrel announced cheerily. "Some knights at a jousting tournament in France decided it's time to make another go at taking back Jerusalem from the infidels. They convinced Pope Innocent the Third, and he just declared that there will be a Fourth Crusade. Your knight will be on his way back to the Holy Land before long, and you can go home!"

§

The messengers fanned out on swift horses, spreading the news throughout the empire to the far reaches of France and England. Word reached the enclave deep in the forest outside Gladdington. "Another Crusade!" shouted a huddle of knights as they raised their shields and clanged their swords in the air. *At last*, thought Galorian, going down on one knee and looking to the heavens in gratitude. For the first time in many months, he believed that his long journey to knighthood had not been wasted effort.

He had been elevated from his role as page at the castle to the position of squire when he turned fourteen in 1189, the same year that England, France, and Germany launched the Third Crusade to wrest the Holy Land back from the Muslim Saracens. The notorious Saracen commander, Saladin, had captured The True Cross in a battle near the Sea of Galilee, triggering the new military campaign. The Christian Crusaders could not tolerate Muslims holding the holy relic: wood fragments believed to be pieces of the cross on which Jesus Christ had been crucified.

Young Galorian had listened intently to the tales that filtered out from the Holy Land that year. He was both transfixed and horrified by the details that were related to him and the other knights-in-training. The Christians were losing the fight, decimated by starvation, disease, and unrelenting heat at the edge of the Muslim city of Acre on the Mediterranean coast. Clever Saladin had outwitted a Crusader blockade of the port by putting pigs on board his ships. The Christians, aware that Muslims were prohibited from eating pork, assumed that the vessels were some of their own and allowed them to pass through.

The Crusaders launched a counter-attack on the fortress in Acre. "We built gigantic wooden siege towers!" announced Cederic, a squire only slightly older than Galorian, who had been injured in battle and sent home to the castle. He gestured wildly with his hands as he spoke, and the younger squires and pages hung on every word.

"They're four stories high and hold five hundred men each. We covered them with hides and soaked them with vinegar and our own piss to keep them from burning!" Cederic crowed proudly. Then he said softly, "But it didn't work." The thought crossed Galorian's young mind that if the Christians couldn't subdue their enemies, the stink from the siege towers should have been enough to drive them away.

Cederic continued his colorful tale, explaining that thousands of peasant soldiers had scurried around, filling the moats surrounding the fort in Acre with rocks and brush to make a path as the towers lumbered forward to gain position by the walls. "Then the Muslims launched the horrible Greek fire," he declared soberly. He described the terrifying substance that spread quickly and burned even on water, which had rained down on them from the fort's parapets. It was nearly impossible to extinguish, except with sand, salt, or urine—the last of which the soldiers had apparently used up on the siege tower hides. "It was awful," said Cederic. "It burned up the towers and all the soldiers inside in a great blaze of flame."

For eight days the Christians and Muslims had clashed, as the oppressive heat baked the mounting mounds of bodies, covered in swarms of flies drawn to the stench of death. When winter came, thousands of Crusaders who had survived the battles succumbed to plague. "The live ones ate their dead horses!" declared Cederic, watching with an impish smile as the shock registered on the faces of the spellbound young boys. "And they filled up the moats with the corpses of their friends for the next siege." Horrified, Galorian grew restless to go to the rescue of the suffering soldiers.

The following June, his opportunity arrived. Standing on the deck of a ship, one of twenty-five in a fleet that sailed under the command of England's King Richard I, the sixteen-year-old knight-in-training took in the panoramic view of a multitude of brightly colored Muslim tents pitched along the Mediterranean Sea. He felt both fear and exhilaration. To the Crusaders at Acre, the approach of the English ships was the first sign of hope in a long stretch of despair.

The king took over command of the siege, and the city surrendered on July 12, 1191. A hundred thousand Christian soldiers had lost their lives in the campaign to take Acre. Among them was the knight whom Galorian had served as squire, tending his horse and keeping his armor and weapons at the ready. When his lord took a Muslim arrow in the chest, Galorian had picked up the knight's sword and shield, mounted his horse, and rode into a throng of charging Muslims.

It was an act of bravery that was not lost on King Richard, who at the same age was commanding his own army. The story of Galorian's courage and survival was a tale told round the Christian campfires that night. His fellow squires considered him a hero equal to the king, who emerged from that Crusade with the appellation Lionheart.

After seizing Acre, Richard and his army began the march to recapture Jerusalem. Galorian rode on his fallen lord's black steed, Thane. He was a coveted destrier—a warhorse with a highly arched neck, short and muscled back, and powerful hindquarters for turning and sprinting. Riding a strong and spirited horse whose name meant Warrior, carrying his fallen knight's sword and shield, Galorian found his spirit swelling with the pride and passion of a holy mission ordained by God.

After several skirmishes between the armies of Richard and Saladin, the two military leaders entered into negotiations. These included an unsuccessful attempt to marry off Richard's sister to Saladin's brother. Ending the Third Crusade, their September 1192 truce kept Jerusalem under Muslim control but allowed Christian pilgrims free and safe access to its holy sites.

Disappointed that they had fallen short of their goal, a despondent Galorian turned back with the other Crusaders as they began the long journey home. Only a battlefield promise by the king kept him from lapsing into complete despair. But before he reached England, Galorian learned that fulfillment of that promise would be delayed; his king had been shipwrecked and captured. When Richard was finally freed—with a ransom equivalent to more than twice the annual government revenues of England—the king came home and honored his pledge.

§

Galorian slowly made his way to the cathedral in Gladdington. Having just turned seventeen, he was humbled knowing that his king's trust in him had expedited this moment. He felt the great weight of the honor being placed upon his shoulders.

On his last night as a squire, Galorian ceremoniously shed the clothes of that role and immersed himself in a bath of purification, praying that the taut strength of his young body would serve him well. He then donned a simple robe and walked alone down the long aisle of the empty cathedral's cavernous sanctuary, bathed in the light of candles and buoyed by the hovering presence of the Holy Spirit.

When he reached the altar, upon which lay the new sword and shield that would be his for life, young Galorian fell to his knees. He kept vigil there all night, bent in fervent prayer, beseeching God to make him a worthy and valiant knight. His head was bowed for most of ten hours, but from time to time he looked up and allowed his gaze to fall on the icon behind the altar, a portrayal of the crucifixion of Jesus Christ. His eyes moist with pious tears, Galorian prayed to be as humble, courageous, and willing to offer up his life as his Lord had been.

In the morning, he carefully put on a white vesture symbolizing purity, a red robe representing nobility, and the black stockings and boots that were a sign of his readiness to die for the cause for which he would fight. Knights, nobles, and onlookers packed into the cathedral for the Mass, where Father Augustus enumerated the sacred duties of knighthood. Then the priest stepped behind the altar and blessed Galorian's sword and shield.

Galorian swore to "defend to his uttermost the weak, the orphan, the widow, and the oppressed." Under threat of eternal damnation should he fail to uphold the Code of Chivalry, he vowed to obey authority, speak truth always, protect the defenseless, fight for the welfare of all, act gallantly toward women, avoid traitors, attend Mass daily, observe fasts and abstinences, and never refuse a challenge from an equal or turn his back on an enemy.

King Richard himself picked up his royal sword and, placing the end of its blade flat on kneeling Galorian's shoulder, commanded, "Arise, Sir Knight." As he stood, Galorian felt a chill travel from the crown of his head down his spine. His sponsor stepped forward and attached spurs on his heels and girded his sword at his waist. The new knight picked up his shield, which caught and reflected a glint of blinding sunlight that was spilling in through one of the cathedral's massive windows.

The shield was emblazoned with a coat-of-arms that was Galorian's alone. Centered at its top, colored the azure blue of truth and loyalty, was a large falcon in profile with raised wings: the symbol of one who did not rest until he achieved his objectives. In its talons the falcon gripped a shield. In the shield's upper left quadrant was a gold pattée cross —square with flared ends—on a background representing the white-with-black-spots of ermine fur, the symbol of dignity. In the shield's opposite corner, imposed on the same ermine background, was a purple crescent, carried by knights who had been specially honored by the king and signifying hope for even greater glory. The other two quadrants were solid gold, the color of generosity, and deep purple, the shade of justice. The shield was encircled with a green wreath of laurel, representing peace, triumph, and loyalty in love.

Galorian's young new squire, Silas, appeared at the back of the cathedral and led the knight's black steed down the long aisle that Galorian had walked the night before. Thane wore silver headgear with raised falcon wings, mirroring the symbol on Galorian's shield, and armor that covered him to his knees. In one smooth movement Galorian mounted the spirited stallion, which reared and pawed the air. Thane then pranced proudly back up the aisle holding his head high, seeming to understand the import of the occasion, the brisk claps of his hooves against the slate floor reverberating throughout the massive sanctuary.

A blare of trumpets escorted Sir Galorian with great fanfare from the cathedral. A feast was spread for fellow knights, nobles, and royalty. Plates were heaped with venison and swan; goblets overflowed with the best wine. Dancing lasted late into the night, flowing into a tournament the next day at which England's newest and youngest knight showcased his equestrian skills and impressed all challengers with his dexterity with sword and jousting lance.

That day, so full of pride and promise, had grown very distant as the months dragged on without apparent purpose. But now, every moment of it came back to Galorian with sharp clarity. The answer to a decade of prayers was at hand. The Fourth Crusade was about to be launched.

§

Clarissa felt a wave of relief at Jaxon's announcement about another Crusade. Galorian's skill was widely known, and she felt certain that he would be among the knights leading the new campaign. As she watched Jaxon walk back toward the abbey, she was sure that her minstrel friend was right. Before long, Galorian would be gone and she would be able to return home safely.

But, as she tossed an apple in a basket, she realized that she felt something in addition to relief. She couldn't quite name it. *Doubt . . . misgiving . . . regret?* She was suddenly overcome with an uneasiness that surprised her. She took note of a strange warmth she felt toward the soon-to-be-departing knight.

She picked from a basket the least blemished apple she could find, sat down on the ground under a tree, and took a bite of the ripe red fruit. The splendor of Galorian's dubbing ceremony into knighthood came into focus in her mind. It was her earliest memory, witnessed when she was four years old from her family's front-row pew in the cathedral. Her mother told her later that Clarissa referred to that event as "the day the horse came to church." And for days afterward, she had run through the manor, imitating the way the black steed had reared up right before her eyes.

Seven-year-old Josselyn had been more focused on the knight. Though Clarissa didn't remember it, years later Josselyn would claim that on the night of Galorian's ceremony, while the two sisters were stretched out on Clarissa's bed recounting the day, Josselyn had asked her, "Did you see how the blue bird at the top of his shield was the same color as his eyes?"

What Clarissa did recall about that night was that it was the first time her sister entertained her with a simple story. It was, not surprisingly, a tale about a brave, handsome, blue-eyed knight. "I'm going to marry him," Josselyn announced at breakfast the next morning, claiming to have dreamt of her wedding to Galorian and causing her mother to smile. Clarissa chose to believe that her own dreams that night had been filled with her escapades riding a swift black horse and slaying dragons in a dark, scary forest.

Now a decade removed from that moment, the poignancy of the memory settled into her heart. For the first time since leaving home, she wondered if she had done the right thing by running away. *What young woman wouldn't want to be given in marriage to a knight as magnificent as Galorian? Is there a better man in the land? Wouldn't Josselyn be happy for me to be with the husband who treated her so honorably?*

Clarissa, choking back tears, leaned her head against the trunk of the apple tree. She began to feel overwhelmed by a deep ache of longing. Several minutes passed before she realized that the emptiness she felt was not about Galorian. The person she longed for was Josselyn. She missed her sister. Oh, how terribly she missed her beloved sister.

She dried her eyes and felt clarity emerge again. There was so much she wanted to see, so much to learn and experience. She was far from ready for marriage, and certainly not prepared to birth and care for children. And to be the wife of her brother-in-law would certainly feel like a betrayal of Josselyn's love for him.

And yet . . . she couldn't deny that she felt a stabbing pang of sadness when she thought about Galorian leaving for a distant and dangerous land.

Eight

Clarissa and Johanna snuck off wordlessly to the cliff after Compline most nights. They endured the cold blasts that roared off the sea, wrapped together in Johanna's wool blanket and warmed by their conversation. As the nights unfolded, Clarissa revealed pieces of the story of her escape.

She spoke of her life in the manor and her leap from the roof, the Samhain celebration, meeting Liliana and Nerida, and her rude awakening on the road by Lizzie. She scrunched up her face like Sister Mary Anthony's and mimicked the wizened nun's rough welcome to the convent. With perfect intonation, Clarissa delivered her favorite line from that night: Mary Anthony's description of Jaxon as "the idiot with the ass and the lizard." She and Johanna stifled their laughter to keep from waking the sleeping sisters.

Several nights passed before Clarissa found the courage to speak of what happened in the birthing room the night Josselyn died. She wept through the telling, as Johanna held tightly to her hands. After spilling the details of her anguished goodbye to her beloved sister, Clarissa said, "When I picked up the baby . . ." She wanted desperately to tell Johanna exactly what had happened next, but she could not. All she said was "she was gone." Her secret was still safe.

In early December, she helped Johanna adorn the chapel altar with greens from the pine trees and sprigs of holly that bore clusters of startlingly red berries. A hope blazed in Clarissa's heart that she would be home by Christmas. She became more fervent in her prayers and often knelt alone in the chapel when the sisters were gone, lighting candles in front of the statue of the Virgin Mary in hopes that her petition would be answered.

The priest from the nearby town of Dover came every Sunday afternoon to say Mass for the sisters. Opposite in demeanor from the flashy and pompous Father Augustus in Gladdington, Father Dudley was a small man, bent with age, so soft of voice that Clarissa had to strain to understand his words. Observing vastly more life and faith in the sisters than in this man of the cloth, she found it increasingly difficult to sit still for the priest's solemn Sunday incantations. She and Johanna referred to him as Father Deadly, suppressing giggles whenever his name was mentioned.

On the first Sunday afternoon of December, Clarissa was sitting in the chapel in her usual place, toward the back near the left wall, when to her utter shock Father Augustus himself swept into the chancel to say Mass. Clarissa was still wearing Nerida's wool dress, as well as a hooded cloak that the sisters had lent her for warmth when the first winds of winter had begun to stir. She pulled the hood around her face and wished—for the only time since her arrival at the abbey—that she wore a wimple, to hide even more of her features.

"Father Dudley is away," announced Sister Mary Peter. "And Father Augustus has come from Gladdington to offer the Mass in his place." Clarissa glanced furtively at the sisters sitting in their holy stalls at the front of the chapel, holding their prayer books. *Did none of them think it odd that a priest would make such a long journey to bring them the Mass?* Their stoic faces betrayed no surprise. With her heart pounding and panic rising in her throat, Clarissa pondered what to do. *Can I slip out without drawing attention to myself? Unlikely. Can I get through the Mass without Father Augustus recognizing me? Equally improbable.*

She slumped down in the pew and kept her face buried in her prayer book as she murmured her way through the service. *How tragic it would be,* she thought, *to be discovered just as I'm beginning to glimpse my day of freedom dawning, almost close enough for me to grasp it.* When the time came for the congregants to file up to receive Mass, she took advantage of the commotion to slip quietly out the side door.

Only she and the priest's black horse were outside the abbey on that brisk afternoon. The latter was tethered to an oak tree in the courtyard by the door from which Clarissa had emerged. As she passed by the horse, her owl—which had made itself at home in the tall tree during Clarissa's stay at the convent—stabbed the cold air with a shriek of danger that pierced her heart.

That's when Clarissa noticed an unusual white marking on the horse's right flank. It resembled a knight's cross, square with flared ends. She gasped in alarm. Then she ran as quickly as she could to her cell, where she curled up on her palette, burying her head under her blanket.

§

Two weeks before, on a Monday morning, Thea had made a visit to the cathedral. Bickford, the livery servant, drove the wagon into Gladdington. Thea did her best to look composed as they bumped over the rutted roads through the forest. She sat under a canopy of blue linen, draped over the top of the wagon to keep a drizzling rain off of her.

When they arrived, Bickford stayed with the horse and wagon while Thea entered a dark hallway on the cathedral's ground floor. Her shoes struck a staccato path over the stone floor as she made her way to the large room where other penitents waited to make their confessions to Father Augustus. When her turn came, Thea walked to the private chamber in the corner. She bowed on the kneeler, on the other side of a partition from the priest, who bent to listen. A square of wood lattice separated their faces. An ornate gold crucifix hung on the wall behind Father Augustus, who waited for Thea to begin.

"Bless me, Father, for I have sinned . . ." she whispered. After the required preliminaries, she spilled the truth that she had kept sealed in her heart for almost a month: "My daughter ran away to escape a marriage arrangement. A minstrel told me that she is in a convent, but I have not told my husband or tried to find her."

Father Augustus leaned in closer. "Do you know where she is?"

"No," answered Thea, shaking her head, her eyes fixed on the floor.

"How do you know this minstrel speaks truth?" asked the priest.

Thea described gentle and good-natured Jaxon, detailing his unique appearance and his unforgettable visit to the manor, affirming her trust in his message. Father Augustus quickly waved the sign of the cross toward her and offered words of absolution. When Thea stood up, he reached up and pulled a red velvet curtain across the lattice, signaling an end to confessions for the day.

Feeling grateful release from the burden of her secret, Thea made her way back down the long hallway. She was stepping into the wagon on Bickford's arm when Father Augustus stood abruptly and called for Rowan, the young priest-in-training who assisted him with his vestments and preparation of the altar on Sundays. "I'm sending you on an urgent mission," the priest declared. "There's a girl in trouble, and you need to find her."

§

During the night that followed Clarissa's abrupt exit from the Mass, she dreamed that she was riding the black horse with the cross on its flank. Holding tight to its reins as her cloak flew behind her, Clarissa raced through the dark forest near Gladdington on its back. At the far edge of the forest, it reared up, as Galorian's steed had done at his dubbing, pawing the air against unseen enemies as Clarissa clung to its neck.

The horse began to haunt her dreams. Sometimes it spoke to her. "You must find the truth," it told her one night, and she awoke in a cold sweat, shaking with fear.

"Are you all right?" Johanna asked her the next morning after early prayers.

Clarissa hesitated. "I'm fine," she said. In the days that followed, she considered confiding in Johanna or Jaxon about what she had seen. But she always talked herself out of it, convinced that this was a mission for her alone. Her prayers became even more regular and fervent.

A week before Christmas, Clarissa went to speak with Jaxon. "It's time for me to go home," she announced to him outside his shed. She couldn't imagine spending Christmas apart from her mother, deprived of feasting and gifts. "Galorian is surely on his way to the Holy Land by now," she declared. She wasn't sure that she actually believed it, but by stating it aloud she tried to persuade Jaxon and convince herself at the same time.

Her minstrel gave her a weak smile. "I'm happy for you," was all he said. Then he walked into his shed and came out with a worn leather bag, which he had embellished with a few patches of bright silk. "To carry your things," he explained, and Clarissa thanked him.

When she shared the news of her departure with Johanna, tears ran down her friend's cheeks. "I wish you would stay," pleaded Johanna. "You're safe here—and you could have a bright future with books." She smiled through her tears. "But I know you belong at home."

The day Clarissa left, she hoped to slip away and avoid emotional goodbyes. But Johanna was by the front door, waiting. She took Clarissa's hand and pressed a perfectly round, milky-white stone into her palm. "It's from the beach below the cliff," she said.

Clarissa smiled and nodded. "Where we watched the dolphins and had our best talks."

Their eyes met and once again Johanna's brimmed with tears. "Carry it with you," she said. "So that . . . so maybe you won't forget."

"How could I ever forget you?" said Clarissa. She reached in and pulled something out of the bag Jaxon had given her. "It isn't much of a gift," she said. "Certainly not one that will last, like your stone." Her turnip still held its burnt ember, its face now caved in. "But it once held warmth and light," Clarissa said as she handed it to Johanna, "the very gifts you shared so generously with me." She hugged her beloved friend goodbye. And then before her own tears could engulf her, she ran to find Jaxon.

He helped Clarissa up onto Hubert Walter. "I'll send a servant on horseback from home," she reminded him, "to lead your donkey back to his minstrel." She gave Jaxon a smile, and she could see that he was trying to return it.

Clarissa asked him for directions to Zerah's cottage and listened carefully to his detailed description of landmarks and turns. "Tell her I sent you," said Jaxon. "She'll let you stay as long as you need to." Clarissa smiled at him again. "You're sure you don't want me to come?" he asked. But they both knew that Hubert Walter couldn't carry them both. And Clarissa understood that what she had to do, she had to do alone.

"I'll be fine," Clarissa answered. He nodded. Their goodbye was wordless. Clarissa felt a great heaviness in her heart, not knowing if or when she would see this good man again.

The sisters surrounded her, murmuring wishes for traveling mercies and promises of prayers. Mary Peter gave her a basket filled with bread and apples for her journey, and Scholastica rushed forward and embraced her, whispering "Go with God" into her ear. Clarissa thanked them all. And then she turned Hubert Walter onto the path that led down the cliff toward home.

§

Clarissa was extremely grateful on her journey for the steadfast donkey, whose ears she rubbed three times a day when the two of them stopped to share from their bounty of apples. She kept the bread for herself. The nights were bitterly cold, and she was relieved that she had to spend only two of them on the road out under the stars. It was a slow journey of prod and plod, but the familiar path and the goal of home buoyed her spirit.

She tried to think through a strategy, unsure of exactly what she would do when she arrived. What seemed clear was that as soon as she was back with her parents in the manor, getting away again would be virtually impossible. They would watch every move she made. So she decided to head first to the cathedral in Gladdington, to face Father Augustus. She had no idea what she would actually say to him.

Three days later Clarissa walked down the long hallway in the bottom of the cathedral that led to the place where confessions were made. She waited in the large room, as one by one the penitents rose and made their way to the priest's chamber in the corner. When her turn came, Clarissa took her place on the kneeler. Her knees shook as she lowered herself, her face just inches away from Father Augustus's on the other side of the lattice screen.

She wanted to mention the unusual marking on his horse's right flank. She wanted to tell him that she had seen that horse in the woods the night Beatrix was murdered. But when she looked up to speak, she caught sight of the crucifix on the wall behind the priest, and the words froze in her mouth.

Her eyes were fixed on the figure of Jesus on the cross. She could feel the pulse of her heart pounding in her head, and she had to stifle a scream. The crucifix was bleeding. Tiny drops of blood were sliding from the pierced wound in Jesus's side, down the gold crucifix to its pointed end.

"Mary, Mother of God," she whispered, her eyes wide. She stood up abruptly and bolted from the room. She burst out of the door of the cathedral and into the cold air, clutching Josselyn's cross at her neck and gasping for breath.

§

It was a very long and winding way to Zerah's cottage in the woods, far from the heart of Gladdington. Clarissa was comforted to have her screech owl flying above her. "Thank you, Owl," she said to her loyal companion, embarrassed that in all this time she had not been able to conjure an interesting name for the bird.

Clarissa thought it odd that she hadn't known that the midwife Beatrix had a twin sister. But Zerah seemed to want it that way, living a reclusive life on the edge of things, never putting in an appearance at the cathedral or other places where she was likely to be seen. Her cottage was small, constructed of hardened mud and topped with a thatched roof. Clarissa knocked on the door, and it opened a crack. "I'm Clarissa," she said to the eyes that peered out at her. A shiver bolted through her and set her teeth chattering as she spoke her name.

Before she could say more by way of introducing and explaining herself, Zerah threw open the door and welcomed her in. "Come sit by the hearth," she said. Clarissa leaned gratefully on Zerah's arm as she ushered her toward a fire that filled the room with light and heat. She sighed as she sat by the blaze and let it envelop her with its warmth. She tried not to register the shock she felt being in the presence of this woman who was not Beatrix but looked exactly like her. She caught her breath and searched for the right words to say. She began by talking about the night she lost Josselyn and her daughter. "Your sister showed great concern for me," she said.

"Yes, the minstrel told me your story," said Zerah. "A very long time ago Beatrix escaped from a marriage to a brutal, hideous man named Udolf. When she found out that our father had handed me over to him after she ran away, she bravely snuck back one night and rescued me. She stood outside a window several paces away and called to Udolf to distract him.

"While he raged at her for leaving him and threatened to kill her, I ran out the door. I grabbed Beatrix's hand and we took off running. We could hear Udolf huffing behind us, but he was too old and fat to catch us." She added hastily, "Beatrix knew that your sister's husband is not such a horrible man. But she believed that no young girl should be forced into marriage."

"I'm so sorry that you lost Beatrix," said Clarissa.

"Yes. I miss her. But we had a long life together. You lost your sister so young."

That prompted Clarissa to pick up her story again. She mentioned spying the horse with the unusual cross on its flank on the forest path the night Josselyn died, and seeing it again at the abbey. She took a deep breath and then declared, "I think the priest had something to do with the murder of your sister." She paused and drew another breath. "In fact, I think I've seen what he used to kill her."

Zerah's mouth dropped open. She looked as if she were about to speak, but no words came out. Clarissa waited, wondering what Zerah wanted to say but could not.

"Clarissa," Zerah said softly, reaching out and stroking her dark curls. The old woman's weathered face was etched with concern and what looked to Clarissa like fear.

"What is it?" Zerah's hesitation to answer told Clarissa that she didn't know how or where to begin to say what was troubling her. "What is it?" Clarissa repeated more insistently, as worry began to overtake her.

Zerah sighed and pulled back her hand from Clarissa's hair. "I just want you to know that I'll do anything I can to help you." The hour was late, and Zerah pointed to a blanket by the hearth, wished Clarissa a restful night, and abruptly left her.

Clarissa, crestfallen, had hoped for some answers. She had no idea why the priest was mixed up in Beatrix's murder. Despite Zerah's words, she felt all alone and on her own to figure out what had happened. *How can I possibly find the truth?* she wondered. *And if I do, how will I get anyone to believe me?* She knew that the word of a thirteen-year-old girl would hardly be heeded by the men who could do something about it—especially since her insight came through a spiritual vision. *How can I ever explain the mystery of the bleeding crucifix?* Having on her side a reclusive old woman, and a minstrel with a fire-breathing fake dragon and a donkey named after the archbishop, could hardly help her case. Father Augustus had the weight of the church behind him—and all the power.

She curled up under the blanket, feeling determined to find out what she could. But she knew that committing herself to finding answers meant that she might not see her mother again for a very long time. Surely if she went home, her parents would make her give up the search. Home was so close—and yet unreachable, it seemed, as long as she persisted in discovering and exposing the truth. She fell asleep under the enormous weight of that sorrow.

She awoke with a start in the middle of the night. Another dream had unsettled her. She threw a log on the fire and sat staring at the blaze, her arms hugging her folded legs and her chin resting on her knees. Then she laughed out loud. "It just might work!" she said to herself. She pulled the blanket more tightly around her shoulders and fell back to sleep, smiling.

Nine

Clarissa spilled her dream and her plan to Zerah as they chewed on pieces of hard, dark bread just after dawn. "You must tell your mother," Zerah told her.

"But she'll try to stop us," Clarissa argued.

"Your father could help us. A man of his status would give some protection if things go bad."

"He'll never do it," Clarissa insisted.

"You won't lose anything by asking."

Clarissa was afraid that she would lose everything—her clarity, her courage, her resolve—if her parents tried to stop her. But Zerah eventually won out. And that afternoon, as Clarissa was knocking on the big door under the family flag, between the pillars with the spiraling crosses and shells, she was thankful that Zerah had convinced her to come home. Her heart beat rapidly with the anticipation of seeing her mother. She thought she might jump out of her skin as she waited impatiently for someone to unlock the door and let her in.

Catrain answered her knock and squealed with astonishment. Clarissa urged her to quietly find her mother and tell her to come to the door. Thea came at once and threw her arms around her daughter's neck. "You've come home!" she exclaimed, her eyes welling with joyful tears. Then she stepped back and looked Clarissa up and down, expressing concern about how thin she had become in her almost two months away. "And what's that you're wearing?" she asked. But before her daughter could answer, Thea took her by the hand and said, "Come in and get something to eat."

Clarissa pulled in the other direction, taking her mother instead toward the barn. She still believed that she wasn't safe at the manor, and she wasn't ready yet to be discovered by her father. She told her mother about

Father Augustus and the horse and the crucifix, about her dreams and her plan. Thea took it all in, trying not to convey her shock.

"We must tell your father," Thea said. "He'll help." An expression of doubt overtook Clarissa's face. "Things have changed since you've been gone," her mother assured her, adding, "He's not a bad man." Thea shared with Clarissa the effect that the false arrest and imprisonment of his friend Lord Frederick Ashdown had had on Aldrich. Clarissa found herself wishing that he had been as moved by the death of Josselyn and her daughter, but she quickly dismissed that thought and listened closely to her mother.

"Your father is sure that Lord Frederick was not capable of murdering the midwife. And if he had," she said, "he surely would not have been stupid enough to leave her body on the forest path with a scarf bearing his family emblem wrapped around her neck." Clarissa nodded.

"When Lord Frederick was arrested," Thea continued, "your father expected the cathedral priest to extend compassion and consolation to him and his family. But Father Augustus was quick to offer condemnation instead." Thea shook her head sadly. "He seemed overly eager to accept the pronouncement of Lord Frederick's guilt."

Thea explained that Father Augustus had sent his representatives both to Lord Frederick's jail cell and to his wife at their home. The churchmen had insisted that, in exchange for a large donation to the cathedral, the priest could ensure that Frederick would not languish in the way-station for lost souls known as purgatory. And for an even more generous gift, the man of God could guarantee that he would not spend eternity in hell for his crime. "Your father was furious when he found out. I think he will be very eager to hear your information about Father Augustus."

Clarissa wasn't sure that her father would believe her, but she wanted so desperately to be back home, sleeping in her own bed, eating her favorite foods, and talking with her mother, that she was willing to take the risk of telling him. Their reunion was formal and awkward, as their relationship had always been. They did not speak of Galorian, or of Clarissa's escape. Thea beamed encouragement across the room to her daughter as Clarissa spilled what she knew.

Aldrich paced, taking in the astonishing information without looking at her. Clarissa felt her pulse quicken as she began to tell her father of the plan that had been revealed to her in a dream. He wasn't critical to its execution, but Zerah had convinced her that having a witness of such high social standing would increase the prospects of justice ultimately being carried out.

"I will do it," Aldrich declared, surprising Clarissa with the immediacy of his response. "For the sake of Lord Frederick and his family . . . that he might be set free. And for the peace of the midwife's sister." Clarissa was filled with gratitude and relief. But she wished that her father had added, "And on behalf of my very brave daughter."

§

"Sit down, child," Thea said gently to Clarissa. "It will be fine." But Clarissa could not stop pacing. She walked again to the south wall of the dining room, trying to hear the sound of the wagon. *Oh, how I wish this room had windows,* she said to herself. "Please sit and eat something," begged her mother, trying to tempt her with milk and sweet bread loaded with raisins.

But Clarissa could not eat. Not until she knew that everything had gone according to the plan. "Why is it taking so long?" she asked, knowing that there was no answer to her question.

At last, her fear-filled ruminations were interrupted by the arrival of the wagon at the manor. Clarissa stopped pacing and focused on the door. When her father and Zerah walked into the dining room, she couldn't read the expression on their faces. "Did something go wrong?" she asked.

They did not answer. Aldrich walked wordlessly to his daughter and embraced her. Such affection was rare between them, and Clarissa was as confused by the gesture as she was about his silence and Zerah's downcast eyes. Her father stepped away and then began quietly. "The room was overflowing with people who had come to make their confessions on this day before Christmas. When it was Zerah's turn, she approached the priest's chamber and knelt."

Zerah picked up the story. "I kept my shawl wrapped around my face and looked at the floor. When Father Augustus bent close to hear my confession, I whispered, 'I have a message for you from God himself.' Then I lifted my head and unwrapped my shawl so that our eyes met. The shock was clear on his face. He blurted out loudly without thinking, 'B-b-but you're dead! I killed you myself.'"

"The whole room heard him," said Aldrich. "He stood up abruptly and pulled the red curtain across the lattice, his face just a few shades paler than its color. I stepped out from behind Zerah, where I was hiding, and walked around to his side of the confessional. I took him by the arm and began to lead him out. But before we left, I grabbed the crucifix off the wall."

Clarissa, who realized she had been holding her breath, let out an audible sigh of relief. "So he confessed to killing Beatrix. In front of a roomful of witnesses."

"That's good news," Thea chimed in.

"Yes," said Aldrich. "But there's more." He looked at Clarissa. "I think you should sit down for this," he said, and she obeyed. Clarissa listened as her father related the story of Beatrix's murder and the events that led up to it.

I cannot live with this, thought Clarissa. *The horror of it is too much to bear.* She wanted to run into her mother's arms, and at the same time she felt an overwhelming urge to flee out the door. But she was blinded by tears and felt nailed to the floor, like she had on the night that Josselyn died.

Thea made no attempt to stifle her own wails. She rocked and keened, a sound ancient and primal, which Clarissa found at once both comforting and terrifying. Zerah moved over and took Thea in her arms, while Aldrich put his head in his hands and groaned, loudly and repeatedly.

§

On Christmas Eve, Clarissa and her family always went to the cathedral. It was her favorite night of the year. She loved feeling embraced by joyful music and bathed in warm candlelight under fragrant pine boughs at midnight. But no one in her family was going to the cathedral this year.

Thea had taken to her bed soon after hearing the report. Clarissa had something she desperately needed to say to her mother, but her father had told her that Thea needed to be alone and was not to be disturbed. Aldrich too had gone to bed early, as did Zerah, who had accepted Thea's offer to spend the holidays at the manor. The house felt cold and empty as Clarissa sat staring at the fire in the hearth in the dining room.

She walked over to a shelf and pulled down one of her father's prized goblets. She found the cache of mead that she knew he thought he had hidden in a secret place. She poured the goblet full and raised it in the air. "To you, Josselyn. Oh, how I wish you were here to share Christmas." Clarissa took a sip. It was strong and sweet. She took a few more sips. "It's just not the same without you," she said, feeling the weight of her loss on this most special night of the year, as tears streamed down her cheeks.

She awoke early on Christmas Day, groggy, wedged into the dining room chair where she had fallen asleep, with an empty goblet in her lap. In years past, she and Josselyn would have bounded out of bed just after dawn to see what treasures the magical day held in store for them. But this year what prodded her to move was the growing anxiety she felt about her need to speak with her mother.

By mid-morning Thea still had not emerged from her bed. Clarissa was clear about what she had to do, and she knew that this was the only day she could do it. She grew desperate as she watched her window of opportunity for action closing. As the morning began to slip away, she told herself, *I must do it now. Before it's too late.*

She went to the barn and climbed onto Hubert Walter, hoping she would find what she was looking for and praying that her parents would forgive her for any hard feelings they might have about what she was about to do. She rode as fast as the donkey could move and was extremely relieved when she approached the clearing in the woods a few minutes before noon and heard the familiar strains of fiddle and flute.

How sad, she thought, *that Nerida's family is too poor to afford a wedding in the cathedral. And how fortunate for me that I knew just where to find it.* As on the night that Clarissa had escaped, a huge bonfire blazed in the center of the circle. The heat from it and the mid-day sun—as well as the energetic dancing she knew was to come—made the winter day tolerable, she supposed, for an outdoor celebration.

At the sound of the music, Clarissa slid off Hubert Walter and tied his rein to a pine sapling. She walked until she caught a glimpse of Nerida, who was standing between Raisa and Edmund, in the woods beyond the circle and out of sight of the expectant crowd, not far from where Clarissa had hidden on the night of Samhain. Nerida was dressed in Clarissa's green velvet gown, looking beautiful with sprigs of holly woven into her braided hair. Clarissa, filled with joyful gratitude to see her friend after their two-month separation, ducked behind a broad oak tree.

She knew she didn't have much time. But she hadn't yet figured out exactly what she was going to do at this precise moment. Raisa was holding the hand of Liliana, who was wearing a new wool dress and carrying a basket decorated with bright ribbons, filled with evergreen boughs, pine cones, and holly berries.

As Nerida leaned in to whisper something to Raisa, Clarissa emitted a strange and, she hoped, unmistakable sound. She had practiced, as she had promised Nerida she would. She was counting on the fact that no screech owl would be calling in the middle of the day and that none sounded quite like her, so that Nerida would know immediately what she was hearing.

Clarissa watched from behind the tree as Nerida glanced in her direction and then spoke again briefly to Raisa. The musicians changed their tune to a distinctive lilting number. Nerida turned and began walking toward Clarissa. Edmund shot Nerida a scowl but followed Raisa as she led Liliana to the edge of the circle.

"I'm not sure whether to be overjoyed or worried to see you," Nerida said to Clarissa as they hugged.

"What did you tell Raisa?"

"That I needed a moment alone to say a quick prayer that I'll be a good, obedient wife." Clarissa rolled her eyes, and both girls laughed. Then Nerida added quickly, "I have to go. I'm supposed to be walking in with Edmund right this moment."

"I've come for you and Liliana," Clarissa declared. "You don't have to go through with this. You can come and live with me." There wasn't time to explain everything.

The music kept repeating itself, and even from a distance, they could see that Edmund was growing impatient and angry. "I can't disappoint them now," said Nerida.

"But—"

"Clarissa, I know you mean well, but I just can't. I'm not you."

Clarissa spoke as fast as she could, filling in a few essential details, pleading with Nerida, but to no avail. "Then send Liliana over here to me," she said. "I accept that you can't choose freedom for yourself, but I'm choosing it for her."

The look on Nerida's face told Clarissa everything she needed to know. She understood that Liliana was the one thing in Nerida's life that gave her joy, and she recognized at that moment that the loss of her would be more than Nerida could bear. "This is my wedding day," Nerida retorted, "and I won't have anything to do with sending Liliana away. If you want her, you'll have to figure out how to get her."

With that, Nerida turned and ran toward the circle. She arranged a smile on her face as she entered it, her arm linked with Edmund's. Liliana skipped in front of them, handing out pine cones and sprigs of holly to the appreciative crowd.

Clarissa felt a desperate panic overtake her. She stood behind the oak tree and watched Edmund give away Nerida, a piece of property being transferred from father to husband. Wilfred, the groom, shuffled his feet throughout the brief service, looking awkward and uncomfortable in borrowed trousers that were too short and a wool tunic that was too tight. Clarissa never saw him make eye contact with Nerida, who pledged to obey him, while he made the more vague promise to honor her. With the pronouncement that they were "man and wife," Clarissa knew that her friend's sad, subservient role in life was sealed.

A gaggle of men closed in on the groom and slapped him on the back, while the musicians launched into a tune for dancing. Soon everyone was up on their feet. The women spread sweet pastries on a makeshift log table, and Edmund hauled out the ale.

Clarissa noticed that the day seemed quickly to be no longer about Nerida, and she was thankful that the bride was able to slip away without drawing attention to herself. Nerida found Clarissa behind the tree. "Take her," Nerida said, weeping tears that were part grief and part joy. "When I get a chance, I'll send her over here to you. Take her to a good life." She gave Clarissa another hug and rushed back to the party.

Clarissa waited, her heart pounding. Everyone in the circle was caught up in the dancing and drinking. Children chased one another around its edge. Clarissa watched as Nerida caught up to Liliana. She imagined the words Nerida was saying to the girl: "Do you remember our nice friend Clarissa who told stories and played games with you? She's back there waiting to say hello to you."

Liliana picked up her basket and ran toward the tree. Clarissa stepped out and, as she swept up the laughing little girl in her arms, asked her, "Do you want to take a ride on my donkey? His name is Hubert Walter." Liliana smiled as Clarissa lifted her onto the donkey's back and then settled in behind her.

It was mid-afternoon when they arrived at the manor. Clarissa asked Catrain to entertain Liliana while she went to find her parents, who were sitting by the fire in the dining room. When Clarissa appeared, Thea rushed toward her with her arms outstretched. "You're safe!" she exclaimed.

Aldrich stood up and scolded, "Where did you disappear to on Christmas Day without telling us?"

Clarissa swallowed her dismay. "I've brought you a Christmas present," she began. But before she could prepare her parents or explain, Liliana ran into the room, twirling around in her new dress. She had tucked a holly sprig into her golden hair. Thea gasped when she saw the basket decorated with ribbons that the girl was carrying.

"Mother, Father, this is Liliana," said Clarissa. "She's your granddaughter."

Ten

———————————

"Why didn't you tell me?" Clarissa was trying to keep her voice calm. "Why didn't *she* tell me?" It was three days after Christmas, and finally Thea was ready to talk. Liliana was at Clarissa's feet, playing with a small pile of simple blocks that Aldrich had made years before for his daughters, from the wood of an apple tree that had fallen in the orchard.

"I knew something was wrong that Christmas," Thea began. Her eyes were focused on a point far in the distance. "Any good mother could have seen that something was wrong." She took a deep breath while Clarissa waited, anxious for her mother to fill in the gaps that yawned between her knowledge and the truth.

Thea brought her gaze to rest on Clarissa. "She was your age then. I could see that she was becoming infatuated with Elbert. Do you remember the young livery servant who used to take care of the stable and horses?"

Clarissa nodded. "I used to tease her about him, to make her blush. I was surprised when he disappeared so suddenly."

"Your father was very displeased. He reminded Josselyn of who she was. And then he dismissed Elbert from his post and sent him away.

"Early in Christmas week, Josselyn asked me if she could take a horse into Gladdington, to make her confession to Father Augustus about the error of her misplaced love for Elbert. She wanted to go before the Christmas crowds started streaming to the cathedral. I had been telling her for a long time that I would let her ride alone when she turned thirteen. And she seemed so sincere in her need to see the priest. I told her to speak to Bickford"—the whiskery and toothless old man Aldrich had hired to replace Elbert—"and have him saddle up a gentle horse for her."

Thea stopped and sighed, her eyes focused in the distance again. "When she came back, she was clearly upset. She went right to her room and shut the door. I knocked and spoke her name, but she said 'Please, just go away.' When I returned later with a tray of food for her supper, she asked me again to leave her alone. I could tell that she was crying."

Thea paused again and swallowed hard. "I don't know if I can ever forgive myself for not overriding Josselyn's wishes and insisting that she tell me what was wrong. But I just thought that Father Augustus had been hard on her, reminding her of her station in life and demanding that she give up her childish foolishness. And that she was upset over Elbert."

Thea sighed again. "Maybe she didn't want to spoil our Christmas. Maybe she thought we wouldn't believe her." She looked at Clarissa. "I'm sure she wanted to protect you from the painful truth. You were only ten." Clarissa remembered then how hard Josselyn had fought her mother that year about having to go to the cathedral on Christmas Eve—and Thea's insistence that the family always went together.

"As the weeks went by," continued Thea, "Josselyn grew increasingly sullen and distant. The voluminous gowns we wear make it difficult to detect . . . but still, I should have known. A good mother would have sensed it.

"When Josselyn finally told me in May that she was expecting a child, I immediately assumed that she had not gone to see Father Augustus that day in December, but instead had arranged a tryst with Elbert. I contacted your Aunt Adela and made plans for Josselyn to spend the summer with her, hoping to avoid tarnishing our family with shame."

"I remember that spring," Clarissa said. "I remember her impatience with me and the unhappiness in the house. I was disappointed about not getting to spend the summer with Josselyn on the coast, but I wanted her to go. I wanted her to come back happy again."

"I prayed for her every day," said Thea. "I wanted to visit her, but your father thought she needed to 'take responsibility' and 'learn a lesson.' He refused to allow me to make the trip." Tears slid down Thea's cheeks. "When the time for the birth came close, I took some of my household money and paid Beatrix to go to your Aunt Adela's home and catch the baby. I sent the midwife off with prayers, an infant's gown made of white lace, and a basket decorated with bright ribbons."

§

A knock on the door of the dining room interrupted them, and Zerah slipped in. "May I?" she asked, as she took a seat at the table. She looked from mother to daughter as she began to spill the words she needed to say. "Beatrix told me what happened and made me swear not to tell another soul. She was worried about Josselyn's safety. And yours.

"I never connected what happened to Josselyn with the murder of my sister until the night you came to see me, Clarissa. My heart was racing as you talked, and it was like pieces of a puzzle falling together in my head. I wondered whether Beatrix's death freed me from the secret she made me promise to keep. I wanted to tell you everything I knew." Zerah sighed. "But I decided you should hear it from someone closer to you. I told your father the day we went to see the priest, so that he could tell you both."

"She was so alone," lamented Clarissa. "I wish I had been there with her when Liliana was born."

"I know my sister took good care of yours," said Zerah. And then she revealed the story that Beatrix had told her, as best as she could remember it.

"After a hard labor, Beatrix asked Josselyn if she wanted to see the baby. Josselyn had turned it over and over in her mind for weeks. She was afraid she would always regret it if she didn't see her child. But she was afraid that if she did, she wouldn't be able to let the baby go. Or worse, she might despise it for reminding her of her pain and shame.

"She decided in the moment that she wanted to see her. Beatrix laid the baby in her arms. Josselyn held her daughter and kissed the top of her head. She whispered to her, 'You're beautiful.' My sister let them fold into each other for a few moments. Then she leaned over them both, made the sign of the cross over the baby, and blessed her: 'May you always know that you are holy and loved, my child.' When she said those words, Josselyn began to cry.

"Beatrix pried the baby out of her arms and set her in the basket you sent along, Thea. 'She'll be all right,' Beatrix told Josselyn. 'You'll both be all right.' But Josselyn wouldn't calm down. Beatrix sat on the edge of the bed and took her hand, rubbing it to try to soothe her. Josselyn sobbed for a long time." Zerah looked at Clarissa. "Then your sister looked into the eyes of mine and asked, 'Does being the daughter of a priest make a child holy?'"

§

Zerah paused to collect herself before continuing. "Finally the truth spilled out with her tears. Josselyn told Beatrix about going to the cathedral before Christmas, about making her confession about Elbert and then commenting on the beautiful gold crucifix on the priest's wall. Father Augustus asked her if she wanted a closer look. He led her in by the hand, pulling the red curtain across the lattice."

Clarissa could feel anger rising in her throat. "It all happened very quickly," said Zerah. "Josselyn didn't know how to stop it. She wanted to scream, but the priest told her to be very quiet and held his hand tightly over her mouth. He told her that this was God's way of making sure she had only pure thoughts and pure relations. It would make her a more holy woman, he said.

"When it was over, Josselyn stumbled toward the door, afraid that her legs would collapse beneath her. Father Augustus grabbed her arm and turned her to face him. 'If you speak about this to anyone,' he threatened her, 'God will punish you and your family with horrors you can't even imagine.'

"Josselyn's shame was like a millstone she thought she had to drag around alone." Zerah looked at Thea and said, "She didn't want to upset you." And then, turning to Clarissa, "Or to scare you." Zerah paused once more, longer this time, as if considering whether to speak what she said next. "And Josselyn said she could not face the wrath of her father, who she thought would blame her for polluting a man of God." Thea nodded and cast her eyes down at the floor.

"When Josselyn finished telling my sister what had happened," Zerah continued, "the sobs shook her whole body and left her gasping for breath. Beatrix held her close and whispered, 'Hush, child, it's not your fault. Hush now, it's going to be all right.'

"When she stopped crying, Josselyn leaned back against the pillow. Beatrix smiled at her, and Josselyn returned the smile. I think she felt free of that millstone for the first time in nine long months. Beatrix stroked her face and said again, 'This is not your fault.' She added, 'And it's not God's fault, either. God does not will such suffering for his children. When people hurt, he's right there crying with us.'

"Josselyn nodded, trying to believe my sister's words. Then she pleaded, 'You mustn't tell my parents.' Beatrix used all the power she had to try to persuade Josselyn to tell you the truth, but it did no good. Josselyn told her, 'I decided months ago that I would rather keep this secret and bear it myself than inflict pain, or harm, on my family. God gives me strength.'"

Zerah fixed her eyes again on Thea, who looked up to meet her gaze. "Beatrix was moved by the strength and faith of your daughter," she said. "When they finished talking, Beatrix picked up the basket by the bed and told Josselyn, 'There are families that are happy to have more children. Your daughter will be well taken care of.'

"Josselyn didn't know how desperately my sister hoped that she was speaking truth. All Beatrix knew for certain was that she would hand over this precious baby in her beautiful lace gown and festive basket to a woman who was in touch with couples looking for children. She kissed Josselyn on the top of her head and whispered, 'All children are holy.' Then she walked out the door with Josselyn's daughter."

§

"Oh, poor Josselyn!" wailed Clarissa.

"And poor Beatrix," added Thea, looking with compassion on the mid-wife's twin sister. She hesitated a moment and then asked, "Do you know the rest of the story?"

Zerah said with a sigh, "Father Augustus isn't talking. The details are hidden in his cold heart and gone to the grave with Beatrix. But I know some of the events that led up to her murder, and I've imagined many times what must have happened that night in the forest." Both Thea and Clarissa leaned in to hear what Zerah knew.

"Except for telling me," said Zerah, "Beatrix held Josselyn's secret for three years, wanting to honor your daughter's wishes and protect her and all of you. But when Lord Frederick's eldest daughter, Oswalda, gave birth to a stillborn son, a fire awakened in my sister. Father Augustus scolded her when he came to sprinkle water over the dead child on the bed between her and Oswalda. He shouted at her, 'You should have summoned me earlier! I'll baptize him, but it's too late to do any good. His blighted soul will spend eternity in the fires of hell!' Oswalda wailed when she heard those words.

"Beatrix stared up into the cold eyes of the priest as he got ready to bless the water and hissed at him, 'I've seen how you abuse the power of the church. I know what you did to Lord Aldrich's daughter.' She took a deep breath and then said to him, 'And someday your punishing God is going to catch up with you.'

"Father Augustus looked down at her scornfully. Ignoring her warn-ing, he waved his gold crucifix over the bowl of water, murmuring words that Beatrix couldn't understand while she tried to comfort Oswalda."

"Your sister was so brave," said Clarissa.

"Yes," said Zerah, smiling at Clarissa, "we both had very brave sisters." She turned to Thea and asked if there was any wine or mead in the house.

"I'll get it," said Clarissa, relieved for a break in the story and the hor-rible conclusion that she knew was coming. She got up quickly, walked to her father's allegedly secret stash of mead, and poured Zerah a cup. As she handed it over, she thought that perhaps she should feel guilty in the pres-ence of her mother about knowing the location of his special store. But Thea just gave her a smile.

Zerah thanked Clarissa and took a sip of mead. "That's all I know," she continued. "But here's what I imagine happened. On the way out of Lord Frederick's manor, Father Augustus spied a scarf bearing the Ashdown family crest, maybe hanging on a peg by the door, and slipped it into a pocket in his robe. A few nights later, he came here to mutter words of blessing over another bowl of water and another dead child. I think that on his way back to Gladdington in the middle of the night, he must have overtaken Beatrix walking home on the forest path.

"I picture him dismounting from his horse and blocking her way. I imagine her facing him as he waved his gold crucifix at her like a weapon. I hear her saying, 'Do what you're going to do.'" Zerah shuddered and stopped to take another swallow of mead. And then she ended her story. "I believe that my brave twin sister died that night whispering a prayer of thanks for a good life, knowing she would be welcomed into the loving arms of a merciful God."

§

Zerah, Thea, and Clarissa sat in silence, each lost in her own imaginings about exactly what had happened on that dark forest path. Liliana began to fuss at Clarissa's feet. Clarissa looked at her niece and then at her mother. "Does Galorian know?" she asked.

"No," said Thea. "He was so in love with Josselyn and anxious to marry her that we didn't want anything to spoil it. Your father insisted on double the expected dowry—a gesture, he hoped, that would buy Galorian's silence if he ever found out that he had married damaged goods."

Clarissa cringed at the phrase her mother used to describe her sister. Then she reached down and gently lifted Liliana into her lap. The little girl turned her hands into tight fists and began crying for Nerida.

Clarissa never questioned that she had done the right thing by rescuing Liliana from a childhood of labor and poverty punctuated with cruelty. Edmund cared about the children only as workers, and Raisa was worn out by too many mouths to feed and bodies to clothe. Clarissa doubted that they would put much effort into trying to find out what had happened to Liliana. But she had not considered that her niece would miss the only family she knew. Especially Nerida, who had cared for her like a mother.

Clarissa felt helpless, and Liliana's inconsolable tears cut through her like a knife. Thea held out her arms and said, "Here, let me try." Singing gently, she held and calmed her granddaughter as she walked around the edges of the room. Aldrich came in, his face somber. Clarissa couldn't imagine that there could be any more bad news, but she could see that her father was struggling to know how to begin what he had come to tell.

"There was a fire," he said, looking directly at Zerah. "Some men from the village appeared at your place with their hunting bows and took aim at your thatched roof with flaming arrows." Thea and Clarissa gasped in unison. "I'm so sorry," said Aldrich. "There's nothing left."

Clarissa, frightened, could tell that there was more. "This morning around dawn, Catrain discovered one of our ewes on the front stoop," continued her father, looking at Thea, who had set Liliana down so that she could focus on her husband's disturbing report. "The sheep's throat had been slit, and someone had spattered the blood on the door. Three rough-looking men stepped out from the shadows and told Catrain—" Here he stopped, swallowed hard, and looked sympathetically at Clarissa. "They told her that it was a warning, and that 'the same thing will happen to the conniving daughter of this house who trapped the priest and spread lies about him.'"

Clarissa's mouth dropped open, and she began to tremble. Her mother ran to her side and held her close, as Aldrich sat down next to them and Zerah moaned quietly over her loss.

Eleven

They left just after midnight that very same night. Zerah rode one of the manor's gentle young geldings, and Clarissa followed on Hubert Walter. She was wrapped in a thick wool tunic, a Christmas gift from her parents to replace the cloak she had given to Liliana.

Thick clouds scudded across the bright face of a full moon, blown by a fierce wind that pierced Clarissa through to her heart. *Such a cruel irony*, she thought, *to be leaving home again so soon under the same watchful full moon.* Snow began to fall as she and Zerah made their way across the pasture, slowing the pace of the animals and blanketing the world in an eerie quiet.

Throughout that day, Clarissa and her parents had floated many plans, trying to determine the best response to the threats. Several involved having Aldrich or one of the servants accompany Clarissa and Zerah for protection. But, in the end, it seemed best for the two women to slip out as quietly and unobtrusively as possible, without having to spare a servant from the manor or deploy Aldrich, whose absence was likely to be noticed by men who would be paying attention.

Clarissa was preoccupied that day with worry for her father. She understood that the manor wasn't a fortress. She didn't know quite how to ask, but for her own peace of mind, before she left she blurted out the question that was eating at her: "Father, will they try to hurt you?"

Aldrich had answered without hesitation. "No," he said, reaching for her hand. "They tried to scare me by threatening to hurt you—and I believe they would if you stay. But they need my mutton and honey and apples—and my taxes for their Holy Crusades. They may not like me anymore, but it doesn't serve their interests to harm me." Clarissa tried to trust his confidence.

Her father's answer gave her a thin thread of assurance to hang onto as she left. The other sliver of hope that sustained her was knowing that, by the time she and Zerah reached the abbey, Bickford would already have made his way to Edmund and Raisa's home and spoken to Wilfred about going back with him to the manor, to replace the fragile and failing livery man.

"I'm knocking on doors, looking for a young man who's willing to work," Bickford would lie, knowing that he would approach no other doors. He would disclose to Wilfred the pay for taking care of the horses. And then he would offer Wilfred and his new wife a room in an elegant manor on the other side of the forest beyond Gladdington.

Bickford would bring them in the wagon. And when they arrived, Thea would inform Nerida of another job opening at the manor. "Would you be interested in being my granddaughter's nursery maid?" she would ask. "Maybe you'd like to meet her before deciding." The thought of it made Clarissa smile all over, filling her with warmth to keep the bitterly cold night at bay, if only for a moment.

The chestnut gelding pranced and stomped in the snow, snorting white clouds of warm breath into the dark and frigid air. Hubert Walter did his best to keep up, prodded on by Clarissa's vocal encouragements and the gentle digs she made with her heels in his ribs. A stab of familiar sound pierced the quiet, and Clarissa felt a brief surge of relief in knowing that her screech owl was watching over them. But it didn't erase her loneliness.

Their three-day journey back to the convent was a blur to her. Clarissa was numbed by the cold, and by the lightning-quick change in her circumstances. She had just begun to live into the joy of being home when everything was snatched away from her again. And this time she had no hope of returning any time soon—if ever. But she could not allow herself to believe that she might never see her parents again. Better not to think about it. Better just to be thankful that she and Zerah had escaped unharmed.

The closer they got to the coast, the busier the flow of people—far more than Clarissa had ever seen before. Small companies of knights on proud horses, their tunics emblazoned with the Crusaders' cross, stormed past them. Throngs of foot soldiers marched in ragged clumps through the woods. Wagons creaked under the weight of swords and lances and maces piled high for battle.

Clarissa and Zerah arrived at the abbey in the middle of a frigid afternoon, chilled through to their aching bones, yearning for a bowl of hot soup and a long sleep in a warm bed. Word spread quickly among the sisters that Clarissa was back, and several left their work and ran to greet her. Jaxon came at once from his shed. Without speaking a word, he gently lifted Clarissa off of Hubert Walter and carried her inside, her head nestled against his comforting shoulder. Johanna brought a bowl of porridge to Clarissa's cell. Though she was bursting with questions, she sat in silence while Clarissa sipped the warm broth. When she finished, Clarissa fell into a deep sleep, clutching the hand of her dearest friend.

§

Since living at home wasn't possible, the abbey was Clarissa's second choice. But she feared that the men who had left the death threat on the manor doorstep would show up there. *They may already be on their way*, she thought in a panic, imagining her enemies joining the massive movement of humanity and horses that had overtaken the road, heading east.

The morning after her arrival, Clarissa wasted no time calling together her friends to help her hatch a plan. She spilled the story to Johanna, Jaxon, Scholastica, and Mary Peter, seeking their advice and guidance. They recognized that all the activity on the road could work to their advantage. When the plan was agreed upon, Clarissa invited Zerah, who was exhausted by their trip, to hear it. She listened carefully, and then she sighed, "I'm just too old. I'll never keep up."

Clarissa opened her mouth, thinking to persuade Zerah, but Johanna spoke before Clarissa could utter a word. "I'll go!" her friend said, her eyes dancing with the promise of adventure. "I'll go with you."

"But Zerah—"

Before Clarissa could say more, Zerah interrupted. "I'm used to praying and being alone," she said. "Whatever time I have left, I want to spend in the peace and quiet of this place."

"We'll keep her safe," chimed in Mary Peter. Then, with an urgency that reminded Clarissa of the midwife's tone on the night that Josselyn died, she said, "You must get on your way quickly." She smiled and added warmly, "Your whole life is waiting for you."

Clarissa turned to Johanna. "I'm not sure I can do this," she said, her voice trembling.

"Aren't you the girl who ran away from home?" said Johanna. "You've already proven that you're brave." She reached out and took her friend's hand.

"Are you sure you want to leave here?"

"You'll need my help," said Johanna. Then she added with a grin, "My whole life is waiting for me, too."

"But the sisters—"

This time it was Mary Peter who interrupted her. She smiled at Johanna and said, "We've always known that Johanna would leave us someday to see the world."

Jaxon slipped back to his shed. Clarissa suspected that he was hoping to escape the sorrow of another farewell, but she followed him. In keeping with the comfortable way that had grown between them, they spoke few words—only enough for Clarissa to be assured that Jaxon would return the gelding to her father on his next trip to Gladdington.

She had retrieved her shriveled turnip from Johanna. She handed it to Jaxon—"to keep away the bad and sad spirits," she explained. He took it and managed a smile. Smiling back, she said, "It would never survive the trip."

"I'll take care of it for you," said Jaxon. Then he disappeared for a few minutes and returned with the gifts that would make their plan work. They embraced briefly, and then Jaxon said, "Now go." Clarissa thanked him again, rubbed Hubert Walter's ears one last time, and blew a kiss to the still-sleeping Lizzie. Then she returned to Mary Peter and sat still while the abbess took a pair of scissors to her hair, creating a sea of dark curls at Clarissa's feet.

§

Late that night, Clarissa and Johanna joined the large stream of humanity making its way to the suddenly bustling port of Dover. Clarissa wore leather breeches and a white linen shirt, anchored with a red sash at the waist and topped with an odd little three-cornered hat. Her stockings were beige, and her shoes were so big that she had to stuff them with dead leaves to make them stay on her feet. Johanna laughed when she saw her friend's get-up, to which Clarissa replied, "You should see yourself." Johanna was practically a mirror image.

When the sisters, who had never seen Jaxon dressed in anything but his garish minstrel outfits, laid eyes on these clothes he had pulled out of an old trunk in his shed, they gaped in amazement. "I was normal once," he explained, hurt by their surprise.

The apparel enabled Clarissa and Johanna to blend into the crowd on the shore, milling around in the shadow of white cliffs that glimmered in the moonlight like huge pearls, awaiting transport across the channel to France. Disguised as men, they avoided the questions and dangers that surely would have accosted them as two young women on their own. They wandered unobtrusively among the throngs of anxious foot soldiers on the beach, surveying the situation and trying to determine their best move.

The masts of ships bobbing offshore appeared above clouds of fog that draped the outer edges of the harbor. In front of these, the gangway was being lowered on a cog—a flat-bottomed, steep-sided ship with a large triangular sail furled and lashed in place. It thudded heavily on the sand. A man attempted to lead a frightened and resistant horse up its planks and into the cog's hold, while two others pushed from behind. Canvas slings awaited the loaded horses, to stabilize them for the short but choppy ride to Calais.

Farther down the shore, Clarissa and Johanna discovered a dock loaded with barrels and crates, filled with provisions for the march across France to Venice, Italy. There the Crusaders would embark on ships again for the journey across the Mediterranean Sea to the Holy Land. Clarissa and Johanna hovered by the dock, watching as men hoisted crates to their heads and waded through the shallow water to a galley waiting to receive the cargo. None of them paid attention to the large barrels that sat close to the two young women.

Clarissa and Johanna got the same idea at precisely the same moment. They had understood that their disguises were adequate for meandering among a late-night crowd on a fog-shrouded beach. But they would never have passed for men in the close quarters on a ship.

They smiled at each other. Without saying a word, Johanna pried open the lid of a barrel and jumped in. Pulling the lid tight over her head, she sank into a small mountain of flour.

The first barrel that Clarissa opened was full to the brim with oats, leaving no room for her. The second as well. She panicked, fearing that she would be left behind and wondering what would happen to her if she were discovered. With her heart pounding, she quickly opened a third barrel and, spying some space, jumped in.

The stench was overpowering. She curled up in the top of a barrel of salted fish. She wondered how she would tolerate being in that position with that company for the crossing, but she was too frightened to move. She secured the lid and held her breath.

Before long, she heard voices. And then she felt the barrel tipping over. She stifled an urge to cry out in alarm. The barrel rolled round and round on its way to the shore. She worried that she would faint from the motion and the smell of the fish—or, worse, lose that night's supper. She focused her thoughts on Johanna and prayed that her friend was safe.

Her head still spinning dizzily, Clarissa felt a great relief flood through her when she was stood upright again. Soon she heard the clamor of a few dozen men taking their places at the oars. When their voices subsided, Clarissa dared to raise the lid a crack and take a peek at the scene around her. She wondered which of the virtually identical barrels on the deck held Johanna.

The fog began to lift as the ship raised its anchor and started its crossing. Clarissa heard the flapping of sails unfurling in the brisk wind and felt the galley surge forward as it captured the breeze. A familiar shriek came with the wind. Clarissa peered above her to catch a glimpse of her owl, reappearing to her delight. *A good omen for my journey*, she thought. The bird's outstretched wings were silhouetted against the ghostly sails, reflecting a bright, waning moon that had just peeked out from behind the fog. They flapped vigorously to keep up with the galley.

Clarissa smiled. "I really must give you a name, Owl," she whispered once more to her winged friend. But before she could ponder the possibilities, her ears caught another reassuring sound. A family of dolphins, drowsing under the sea in their nightly somnambulant state, surfaced slowly by turn to draw breath, in rhythm with the synchronized dip of the oars. The sleek and smiling creatures moved just below Clarissa, keeping pace with the ship, almost within her reach. Her smile transformed into a grin.

The galley sailed into the year 1203 as it churned toward Calais. Clarissa thought of times past, when greeting a new year meant feasting and games with her family and the servants in the dining room of the manor. The evening always ended with a sweet cake at midnight, the flavor chosen by Clarissa, who had the good fortune of celebrating her birthday on the first day of the year.

This year she turned fourteen in a barrel, accompanied by dolphins and a screech owl, far from home and covered in stinking fish. *What a birthday*, she thought, laughing to herself. She closed the lid, pinched her nose against the stench, and curled up again in her barrel, wondering what adventures awaited her in her new country.

§

When she felt the thud of the boat against the shore, Clarissa slowly lifted the lid of the barrel. Torches, stuck into sand, burned along the beach. Daylight was still at least an hour away, and the men from the ship were caught up in the task of unloading the provisions. She decided she could emerge safely.

Taking a moment to stretch and steady her cramped legs, she spied Johanna and calmly walked over to her, resisting the urge to run and throw her arms around her friend and draw attention to them. "You won't *believe* what I had to put up with," whispered Johanna, shaking flour out of her hair and coughing a small cloud of white powder. She took a deep breath, paused, and then asked, "What's that horrible smell?"

"Dead fish!" answered Clarissa, wrinkling her nose in disgust. Johanna tried unsuccessfully to suppress a cascade of laughter. "It's not funny," Clarissa declared. But then she too joined in the amusement of her predicament.

"Hey!" One of the oarsmen, with a crate of cheese balanced on his head, heard the female laughter coming from what appeared to be men and, his suspicion raised, called out in their direction. "They're stealing food!" he shouted, to grab the attention of one of his comrades standing closer to them. The second oarsman dropped what he was carrying and headed at top speed toward them. Clarissa exchanged a quick glance with Johanna. And then she ran as fast as her legs, stuck in ill-fitting shoes and still adjusting to life outside a barrel, would carry her.

"Faster!" shouted Johanna, who was on Clarissa's heels, dodging barrels and leaping over crates with her.

As Johanna passed her, Clarissa caught a glimpse of their pursuer closing in on them. "That way!" she shouted, pointing past Johanna while she ran in the opposite direction. Her plan worked. When they split up, the oarsman became confused about which one to follow. Clarissa glanced back. She saw him careening into a large barrel of honey, which tipped over and spilled a stream of its sticky contents, along which the poor man slid until he slammed into a barrel of flour, which coated him from head to foot. He cursed and Clarissa laughed, as she circled around and caught up with Johanna.

Panting, they leaned against a rock wall with their hands on their knees, trying to catch their breath. "We have to get out of here before the sun comes up," said Johanna, gasping for air. Clarissa nodded. They started walking away from the shore, blending into the crowds leaving Calais. They began reciting to each other the directions that Sister Mary Peter had given them. The walk to the Benedictine convent in Liège would take a few days, she had told them.

Clarissa reached into the pocket of her shirt and pulled out two salted fish. "For our breakfast," she announced, grinning, as she tossed one of the slippery herrings to Johanna. They ate hungrily. Then, after one last look across the channel toward home, they set their sights to the east, walking toward the sun as it breached the horizon and spattered pink streaks across the lightening sky.

They were on a coastal road that took them past a sweeping beach, whose white sand reflected the sky's changing hues. A few seagulls noisily greeted the day, standing at attention like one-legged sentries, lifting one foot and then the other off the cold strand. Clarissa found it comforting that the French beach resembled the windswept coasts of home.

The Crusaders were heading south, away from them, and traffic on the road was sparse. But Clarissa and Johanna hadn't walked far when a family in a wagon pulled up beside them. Upon seeing them, the woman sitting next to her husband on the front bench exhibited astonishment that couldn't be disguised by a language difference. Her outburst was punctuated with pointing and animated gestures. That's when it occurred to Clarissa that two young women dressed in men's clothing—one covered in flour and the other reeking of dead fish—was not a typical sight on the road.

Clarissa didn't understand her words, but once the woman calmed down, she gestured for them to climb up on the wagon and join the four children in the back. Relieved of the need to understand or make conversation, Clarissa sank into the straw beneath her and began to doze as the wagon bumped along the coast and then headed inland. The last thing she remembered before falling asleep was the child next to her pinching his nose as he pointed at her and exclaimed, "Ewwww!" Clear in any language.

Twelve

"Why don't they just take all our money and send us all to the poorhouse?" Aldrich was standing by the large oak table in the dining room, loudly bemoaning their predicament to Thea. They had stopped worrying that someone was going to poison their sheep or do them harm; the baron had apparently been right that their presence and their goods were needed and safe.

Controversy in Gladdington about Father Augustus had shifted from loud commotion and denial to quiet acceptance of the priest's lifelong change of address to the jail. He had been saved from public hanging only by virtue of his vocational calling from God.

Days had passed without any word from Clarissa. Though Thea had learned to trust her daughter's resourcefulness, she couldn't help wondering and worrying again about her whereabouts and safety. In her absence, Thea was grateful to have Liliana, Nerida, and Wilfred at the manor, though she often felt sad that Nerida was saddled with such a dull husband. Liliana was an endless fountain of joy, and her presence lifted Thea's spirits.

Aldrich had returned to being often volatile and angry after Clarissa's abrupt departure, and Thea was tired of hearing his tirades about the Fourth Crusade. Of course enormous resources were required to move tens of thousands of soldiers across two continents. And the cost of the weapons, armor, transport, and food for these campaigns was a huge burden on every family in England. *But,* she thought, *if men don't want to pay for it, they should stop fighting wars.*

Clarissa's bold escape had given Thea courage, and she spoke to her husband more directly than she ever had before, no longer feeling compelled to keep her thoughts to herself. "Be grateful," she said sharply, "that we're not among the hordes that really are ending up in the poorhouse—or worse, in jail. We have Galorian to thank for that." Every family without young men—or with ones who refused to sign up for the Crusade—was obligated to pay a "Saladin tithe," named for the dreaded Muslim leader and equivalent to ten percent of the value of their money and possessions. Galorian was still considered their son-in-law, and his role as a knight spared them this burden. Many families were barely making enough to survive before the tax, and those who couldn't afford it watched helplessly as fathers and brothers were dragged off and thrown into prison.

"And thank your God that you're not a Jew," Thea continued. It was widely known that Jews, who had the legal status of draft animals in medieval England, were taxed at a rate of twenty-five percent, and King Richard regularly seized their property to finance his military campaigns. The cathedral was abuzz every Sunday with stories of arrests and land thefts from poorer neighbors and Jews, the stuff of truth mixed with gossip—though no one, it seemed, was outraged or offended enough to do anything about it.

Aldrich's list of complaints went on. He blasted the king for selling political offices and titles, royal castles and land, and for forcing towns to buy the right to govern their own affairs—all to raise more money for the Crusade. "I heard a man in town quote King Richard saying, 'I would sell the city of London if I could find a buyer.'" Thea rolled her eyes and returned to the needlework in her lap.

Undeterred, Aldrich carried on, lamenting that the peasants who had once been available to work his garden and orchard were now off dying as soldiers in the Holy Land; that the profits he once made were being siphoned off by the king and the pope to fight the wars; and that the whole country was on the verge of collapse for lack of funds for the proper maintenance of England. "And yet," said Thea, her eyes still on her work, "you never question the righteousness of the Crusades." She sighed. "You complain in private—and then you pay up, like all the other men who can afford to do so. And so the dying continues."

§

For weeks the knights, foot soldiers, and weapons had streamed from the far corners of Europe to Venice, where a fleet of two hundred ships set sail from the Italian city's lagoon. Banners whipped from every masthead, some emblazoned with the Lion of Venice, others bearing the coats-of-arms of the noblest houses of France. Four silver trumpets blared from the lead vessel, which carried the doge, or duke, of Venice. More than eighty years old and nearly blind but full of vigor, Doge Dandolo sat in state on the deck under a silk canopy painted imperial vermilion to match the color of his galley.

Other ships answered with the call of hundreds of trumpets, joined by the beat of drums and the rattle of tabors. Excitement pulsed through the air as the Fourth Crusade was officially launched.

Galorian stood on the deck of the galley behind the doge's. Feeling the wind on his face, his heart racing in rhythm with the beat of the drums, he was flooded with the same exhilaration that had visited him on his first trip to the Holy Land more than a decade before. But, this time, not with the fear.

He wore a suit of armor that was custom-made to fit his body exactly, transforming him into a living fortress. His doublet, a quilted coat made of linen, was stuffed with grass for extra padding. Over it he wore a knee-length shirt of chainmail to further protect his chest, arms, and groin. Even his socks were made of small steel rings linked and welded together into chainmail—as was his coif, the hood protecting his head. From the iron plates riveted on his boots to the spiked gauntlets covering his hands and the visored helmet that would sit on his head during battle, Galorian was as protected as he could be from the attacks of his enemies.

Confident and prepared, he was anxious for the next battle to retake Jerusalem. Like his Crusader brothers, he believed that God was on their side and would bless their valiant effort. Standing next to him on the deck was Silas, his young squire. Galorian recognized the mixed expression of excitement and apprehension on the boy's face—the same that had been on his own as a squire approaching the Third Crusade.

A twinge of sorrow crept into Galorian's spirit as the massive fleet headed out into the Mediterranean Sea. He recalled for a moment his dubbing into knighthood and the man who had performed it. "I wish King Richard could be here to see this grand launch," he said to Silas. "It was he who changed the strategy of the Crusades."

"How?" asked his squire.

"In the first two Crusades, soldiers moved in massive sweeps by land across Europe and Asia. But King Richard knew that water travel was faster and cheaper and brought us by ship in the Third." He placed his hand on the squire's shoulder and said, "I was about your age then, standing on a boat just like this."

"What was the king like?" asked Silas. Galorian proudly related stories about the bravery and military prowess of the king who had earned the name Lionheart.

"Did he die in battle?" the boy wanted to know.

Galorian sighed. "When Pope Innocent the Third announced this Crusade, King Richard was locked in a conflict with the king of France. The pope sent his assistant, a cardinal, to try to bring peace between them, and

King Richard was so furious that he threatened to cut off his . . . well, you know . . ."

"Head?"

"Private parts." Galorian actually blushed as he said it. Silas's eyes grew wide. "That cardinal high-tailed it back to Rome as fast as he could," Galorian said, grinning, and Silas managed to grin back as Galorian continued the story.

"King Richard vented his anger by attacking a French castle. He came out of his tent one evening and was amused to see a French defender on top of the castle wall using a frying pan for a shield. He called up to applaud the man's resourcefulness and, while he was distracted, a crossbowman shot an arrow into his left shoulder. The surgeon who removed it mangled his arm, and the wound quickly became infected.

"The king demanded to see the archer, who turned out to be a mere boy. The boy naturally expected to be put to death. But King Richard forgave him, handed him a hundred shillings, and declared over him, 'Live on and by my bounty behold the light of day.'" Galorian sighed again. "That's the kind of man he was."

"I like that the boy got to live," Silas responded.

"Unfortunately," said Galorian, "others were not as gracious as our king. Once King Richard died from the infection, a captain ordered that the boy be flayed alive, his skin removed piece by piece, and then hanged." Silas gulped loudly. "King Richard's big heart was embalmed with frankincense—one of the gifts given to our Lord at his birth—and buried in Normandy. His entrails rest where he died, and the rest of his body is buried at the feet of his father in an abbey in Anjou." Silas tried to picture the scattered organs of the king, wondering if they looked any different from an ordinary man's.

With the loss of King Richard, the hero of the Third Crusade, England stepped back into a mostly supporting role in the Fourth. But for Galorian and the other English knights, participation in the Fourth Crusade was an act of honoring their fallen king. "We're going to recapture Jerusalem," Galorian explained to Silas, "for the great man whose determination to do so was unwavering."

The Venetians had agreed to supply the massive Crusader fleet with 10,000 oarsmen and a year's provisions for 33,500 men and 4,500 horses, in exchange for 85,000 marks of silver and half of all the plunder from the Crusade. But when the planned date for the launch arrived, the Crusader legion numbered less than a third of expectations—too few to pay the agreed-upon charter fee. Just when it seemed that the Fourth Crusade was about to collapse, the Venetians made a counter-offer. They would supply their fleet if the Crusaders would help them conquer Zara on the Adriatic Sea. It was a Christian city, but one that was a naval and commercial rival of Venice.

The mostly French leaders of the Crusade, who recognized Galorian's bravery as a young man in the Third Crusade and respected his strategic savvy, had already agreed to his proposal to make the city of Cairo, Egypt, their first target. They planned to secure that center of Muslim power as a stronghold for launching the campaign to recapture Jerusalem. Galorian urged them to stick with the plan and argued vigorously against the assault on the Hungarian city of Zara.

Pope Innocent III threatened to excommunicate from the church any Crusaders who took part in the diverted attack. But the leaders of the Crusade felt backed into a corner by the Venetians. They agreed to the change in plan, counting on their pope to quickly forgive them so that the Crusade he had announced and launched would go forward.

Standing on the deck now, Galorian felt frustration crowding out the exhilaration he had felt moments before. "Just a little detour," he explained to his squire, patting the boy's shoulder. "And then we'll take Cairo." The ships sailed toward Zara.

Days later, horses and soldiers stormed into the city. Galorian took note of the banners marked with crosses that Zara's citizens had hung from their windows and the city's walls—to remind the Crusaders that they too were Roman Catholics. He watched an old woman grab the flag from her window and run into the street, waving it vigorously. The woman stood her ground as a French knight on horseback rounded a corner and headed toward her. Her language was unintelligible to the invader, but her agitated and desperate plea for reason and mercy could not be missed.

Galorian was sure that the knight would pass her by in pursuit of more formidable and significant conquests. He watched in horror as the knight charged at the old woman at full gallop. She collapsed to the ground, her screams echoing along the street. Clutching the banner to her chest, she died instantly from the sword thrust, which pierced the cross emblazoned there before entering her heart. The knight laughed, withdrawing his weapon as a dark stain of blood spread over the cross. Then he galloped off to find his next victim.

Sickened by the sight, Galorian turned Thane back to the edge of the city. He dismounted, pressed down by the weight of the shocking and shameful brutality he had just witnessed. Kneeling by a fortification wall, he prayed for God's forgiveness for the error of their assault. And for a return to clarity of purpose for the Holy Crusade.

§

After a long journey of walking, interspersed with much-appreciated wagon rides, Clarissa and Johanna appeared on the doorstep of the Benedictine convent in Liège four days after they left England. The young nun who opened the gate ushered them to a small room, saying, "Mother Agnes Luc will be with you soon." As soon as the abbess appeared, a memory came to Clarissa—of late-summer days when she and Josselyn would sneak off to the far edges of the orchard to climb forbidden trees, bouncing on their limbs to release a cascade of fruit. They gathered up apples in their skirts and carried them to a secluded clearing to let the sun dry them for winter snacking. The old nun's face reminded Clarissa of the apples they left too long: shriveled and sallow and hard. But though that face seemed frozen in a perpetually sour expression, and the abbess had an unfortunate wheeze when she spoke, she welcomed them and received their greetings from Sister Mary Peter.

The convent held twice as many sisters as the abbey in Dover. It too was an imposing stone building with a candlelit chapel, filled with nuns bustling about their work or sitting quietly in prayer. Consistent with the order's Rule of Saint Benedict, hospitality also hummed at the heart of this one's life, and Clarissa and Johanna were embraced warmly by the sisters. Falling easily back into the rhythm of daily prayer, they felt immediately at home.

Agnes Luc put Mathilde, a novice, to work at once teaching French to the two young Englishwomen. Clarissa was a particularly quick study, loving the beauty of the language and devoting herself to learning it. She was happy for the distraction, doing her best to put thoughts of home and fears about safety for herself and her family behind her. The best plan, she believed, was to keep busy, focus on the future, and not think too much about what she had lost. She wanted to convince herself that she could be happy in this new land, and she threw herself completely into the life of the abbey, even deciding after a week to declare herself a postulant, the first step toward becoming a novice and then a vowed nun.

Though she and Johanna grew to love the sisters, Agnes Luc remained a mystery. She was so different in spirit from Mary Peter—from all the nuns they had met, in fact—and from what they expected of an abbess. Mary Peter chose to be called Sister, a sign of her equality with the others in the community. But Agnes Luc insisted on Mother when she was being addressed—and Mother Superior when she was being described. When Johanna asked Mathilde one day how Agnes Luc had come to her role in the community, the novice hesitated. Then she said simply, "The bishop favors her."

"But I can't imagine she's who the sisters want," Clarissa declared.

Mathilde looked around furtively. "Things are hot around here," she said, barely audibly. "It doesn't matter what the sisters want." Then she hurried out of the room, leaving Clarissa and Johanna to exchange troubled glances and wonder just exactly what she meant. It didn't take long for them to discover a clue.

They relished exploring the dusty archives in the convent basement, searching for local history. "Listen to this," Clarissa said late one afternoon as she blew a thin layer of dust from a document penned on fragile parchment. "Liège produced a martyr." She was thrilled to discover a saint that Johanna didn't already know.

Clarissa read aloud the fascinating story of Father Lambert le Bègue. Then she repeated the highlights in English, to make sure that her friend didn't miss any of the details. "He was the priest at the Chapel of Saint Christophe, not far from here," Clarissa explained. "He worked among tanners, weavers, and carpenters. He found them to be holier and more sincere than his priest colleagues." She smiled at that. "He translated some of the Holy Scriptures from Latin into simple, vernacular French, so that all could read them. And he told the laborers about something called 'the priesthood of all believers,' convincing them that they could pray directly to God without needing a priest to do it for them."

Johanna commented, "I imagine that didn't go over too well with the other priests."

"Exactly," responded Clarissa. "They accused him of heresy, failure to preach to the elite, and opening Scripture to the unworthy! But what really got him into trouble with the big church leaders was accusing his colleagues of corruption for charging lots of money to perform baptisms and burials." In her imagination, each of those priests looked exactly like Father Augustus.

"The church came down hard on him," Clarissa continued. "Father le Bègue was arrested and thrown into prison in the year eleven hundred and seventy-seven. He died soon after he escaped, as a result of what he suffered there." She took a deep breath. "Seems like Liège is a dangerous place to speak truth."

§

"We must return to the plan and set a course for Cairo." Back on board one of the galleys that had carried them across the Mediterranean, Galorian was struggling to keep his voice calm and even as he pleaded in French with his comrades leading the Fourth Crusade. He was disturbed at the proposal of another detour.

"We subdued Zara quickly and easily," argued a French knight. "We can do the same to Constantinople. Doge Dandolo is insisting."

Constantinople—named for Constantine the Great, the first Christian emperor of the Roman Empire—was the center of Eastern Orthodox Christianity, which had for centuries been at odds with the Roman Catholic Church of Western Europe. The great city was the capital of the Byzantine Empire, which was embroiled in a scandal involving greed, political intrigue, and family rivalry—with one royal brother blinding another in order to steal the position of emperor. "If we overthrow the usurper to the throne and install the rightful emperor," continued the French knight, "the doge will release us from our debt to him, draft the Byzantine navy into service to carry us to Cairo, and bring the Eastern Orthodox Church under the authority of the pope."

"That's absurd!" exploded Galorian, no longer able to contain his frustration and anger. "For centuries Constantinople has been a Christian bulwark between us and marauding Muslim Arabs and Turks. Why would we turn against her now?"

"Her citizens are traitors to the Christian faith," replied the French knight curtly. "They prefer diplomacy and trade over war. And they choose to tolerate—and even assimilate—our enemies, the Muslims." He shook his head. "Christians and Muslims living side by side inside city walls—unthinkable!"

Galorian continued to make a case for returning to their original plan. But he was outvoted by the other leaders, who saw only the prospect of quick power and prosperity. They had readily accepted bribes from the doge, who was anxious to seize the opportunity to increase Venice's commerce and control in the East. And so it was that the Soldiers of the Cross, pledged to fight Muslims, set themselves against Christians in one of the world's most ancient and splendorous cities.

The Crusaders overwintered in Zara, parceling out meager rations and shivering through brutal cold as they waited for favorable weather to revisit the continent. "God, and the sun, are smiling on us," announced the French knight with whom Galorian had argued, when warmth finally returned to the land. "On to Constantinople!"

Anxious to get on with their mission, the Crusaders shook off the languor of winter, prepared themselves for battle, and set out for the great city.

Early on a June morning in 1203, Galorian stood on the deck of his galley and caught a bright glint of sunlight in the distance. As the ships closed in on their target, he saw the source of the reflected light: the gold spire atop the massive dome of a grand cathedral rising out of the center of Constantinople. "God help us," whispered Galorian into the wind as he went down on one knee. His fellow Crusaders were mouthing similar prayers, but with a different intent.

The fleet escorted the restored Byzantine emperor to the edge of the city, so vast that the ten largest cities of Western Europe could have fit within its walls. When the emperor's galley appeared, the response of the crowds was not the cheers the visitors had anticipated, but a hail of arrows. As Galorian had feared, the citizens of Constantinople let it be known that they felt more resentment than gratitude for the intervention of foreigners in their political affairs.

Constantinople was fortified with high walls, a deep moat, and a strong chain across its harbor. The Venetians snapped the chain and attacked, while the French rowed ships carrying siege weapons up to the city's imposing castle tower. Giant slings called trebuchets released heavy boulders, as many as two thousand in a day pounding its walls.

"Over here!" A filthy and hunched man standing by a massive catapult known as a mangonel was trying to get the attention of Silas, who had wandered onto the deck of the galley. Galorian saw that the man clutched an object in his left hand. Though it was indistinguishable from a distance, Galorian felt a chill of suspicion bolt through his body and immediately moved closer.

"Load it on the catapult!" yelled the man, thrusting the object at Silas. Too late, Galorian saw the terror on his squire's face as the bloody stump of a human leg was forced into the boy's arms.

Galorian immediately inserted himself between the man and Silas. "Let him be!" he shouted, knocking the grisly, dismembered limb to the deck. Tears spilled down his young squire's cheeks as he turned, trembling, and fled.

"He'll learn," said the man to Galorian with a sneer. "War will make him a man." Then he laughed, exposing a mouth absent of front teeth, as he loaded the severed leg and a bucket of horse manure into the mangonel. At his feet was a pile of enemy body parts, disease-ridden Crusader corpses, dead animals, sharp poles and darts—all designed to impose maximum distress and discomfort on the people on the receiving end inside the castle. Beside him were casks of tar, ready to be set on fire and hurled, burning, against the fortified walls.

"Let him be!" repeated Galorian in the tone of a threat, glaring into the man's rheumy eyes. Then he turned and went in search of his frightened squire. He found him curled up in the straw among the horses in the ship's hold.

§

For eight months, Clarissa and Johanna lived the life of prospective nuns in France. They gained proficiency in reading and writing French, acquired the skills of weaving cloth and brewing beer, and cared daily for the people suffering with leprosy that congregated outside the convent gate. Clarissa at last achieved her goal of working in a scriptorium, copying Scripture onto smooth pages of parchment with a stiff hawk's quill. Her love for words grew, especially sacred ones. As she worked, she enjoyed picturing the colorful images and artistic flourishes that Brother Cyrille, the Cistercian monk who now served the Chapel of Saint Christophe, would add when she was finished. Crosses and flowers, saints and dragons would lurk among and weave their way around the letters she so meticulously etched on the pages.

She was coming to the end of the Gospel of Matthew one morning when she encountered the verses that took her breath away. Her hand quaked as she copied them. She read them over three times. And then she ran to find Johanna.

"Listen to what Jesus said!" Clarissa insisted as they began to walk around the grounds of the abbey, as if her friend had never before heard the words. She read from a sheet of thin parchment, the ink on it barely dry: "'I was hungry and you gave me food, I was thirsty and you gave me something to drink, I was a stranger and you welcomed me, I was naked and you gave me clothing, I was sick and you took care of me, I was in prison and you visited me.'"

Clarissa looked into Johanna's eyes. "The people who heard this asked how it could possibly be. How could they do these things for Jesus? And Jesus told them, 'Whatsoever you do unto one of the least of these my brothers, you do unto me.'" Clarissa sighed. "I never heard *that* preached at the cathedral in Gladdington."

That same night, a large and exotic bird appeared to Clarissa in a dream. It was an azure-blue falcon, with a massive wingspan and gold bells attached to its feet. When it shook the bells, Clarissa awakened with a start. And then she heard the faint but persistent shrieks of her owl outside the thick walls of the convent.

She got up and slipped into the corridor. Removing a torch from the wall, she followed the sound and found her owl perched on the front gate. Below the bird, slumped against the iron gate, was a figure moaning in pain. Clarissa recognized her as a girl, about her own age, whose feet she had recently washed, tenderly wiping the disfiguring sores that had relegated the poor soul to the status of social outcast.

"Please help me," the girl pleaded when she saw Clarissa. Opening the gate after dark was against the rules of the convent. But echoing in Clarissa's heart were the words of Jesus that had so moved and troubled her, in which he called poor and suffering ones members of his family, his own brothers. *And surely*, she thought, *he must have meant sisters, too.*

As Clarissa agonized about what to do, the girl's face was suddenly illuminated, a bright halo framing it with golden light. Clarissa looked again and saw the face of Jesus. The gaze from his suffering eyes pierced her through to her heart. She heard Jesus say "Whatsoever you do . . ." She gasped and fell to her knees. Her owl let out a primal, spine-tingling cry and, flapping its wings vigorously, flew high into the branches of a nearby tree.

The vision faded quickly. Face to face with the girl, with only the gate between them, Clarissa knew what she had to do. She slid open the gate and knelt by the girl's side. Her breathing was slow and heavy, each rattling inhale sounding as though it would be her last. A small huddle of people, all wearing the ragged white robes and bells around their necks that distinguished them as lepers, stood a short distance away, some crying.

"Why has God abandoned me?" the dying girl asked, her eyes riveted on Clarissa's.

Clarissa groped for words. "I don't know" was all that she could choke out. The girl took her final labored breath in Clarissa's arms. Clarissa looked to the sky, tears streaming down her face, and whispered, "Welcome your dear sister home, Jesus."

The others moved in to carry the body away. But before she released it, Clarissa lifted the bell hanging on a leather strap from around the girl's neck. She placed it around her own, next to Josselyn's cross. Clarissa knew in that moment, with more clarity than she had ever possessed before, that something was terribly wrong with a world that condemned some people to die outside the gate with nothing, while others had warm beds and more than enough food and clothing and money. "It isn't right," she said through hot tears to the small crowd huddled around. "And I'm going to wear this bell until it's right."

Her owl flew back and, landing on the gate, emitted a screech of punctuation. Clarissa whispered "Thank you" to the bird that always appeared when she needed reassurance. Then she slipped back inside the gate. She watched as the ragged clump of humanity, with the bells around their necks jangling mournfully, slowly carried their dead friend away into the mist-shrouded night.

Thirteen

For most of a year, the Crusaders and the Byzantine defenders clashed. By the spring of 1204, feeling more than ready to end their relentless campaign, the invaders planned a massive final assault on Constantinople. Knights on horseback stormed off boats onto the shore, backed up with the arrows of legions of crossbowmen. Siege weapons lumbered forward and hurled their dastardly and deadly ammunition. Foot soldiers under cover of what they called turtles—large rounded hulls turned upside down on wheels—attempted to break through the city's brick walls. But to no avail. After several hours, the Crusaders were forced back once more.

"Look!" exclaimed Silas, laughing, as he pointed to a spot on the top of a castle wall. There, a few defenders were adding disgrace to defeat by dropping their breeches and displaying their bare backsides to the retreating soldiers. Galorian clapped one hand over the young squire's eyes and pushed him with the other into the ship's hold.

Silas collapsed in the straw by the horses. He continued to laugh uncontrollably, his mouth wide open, a wild and unfocused look in his eyes. Galorian got up close to his face and repeated the boy's name a few times, until Silas quieted down and stared back into the knight's gentle eyes. Then with a heavy sigh Silas turned away, curled up at Thane's feet, and began to sob. Galorian held him and repeated over and over, as if trying to convince himself, "It'll be all right."

A new attack was planned for the morning of Monday, April 12. The day before, every soldier took Sunday Mass and received God's blessing from the priest for the next day's assault. Also that day, all the prostitutes accompanying the Crusader army were hustled onto a ship and sent away, to minimize the soldiers' distractions and allow total concentration on the task at hand. Galorian was very glad to see the women go, as he had been arguing for some time that they should. All of them left except one, a loud woman with fiery eyes and a disheveled mop of cascading hair that reached to her waist. She had hidden in the straw by the horses and bribed Silas with a kiss in exchange for his silence when, to his shock, he discovered her there.

Pope Innocent III had sent a cautionary letter to the leaders of the assault, forbidding the Crusaders from committing atrocities against other Christians. But the leaders failed to share it with the foot soldiers. Bright and early on Monday morning, the fleet attacked, aided by a strong and favorable north wind. Horses and soldiers swarmed out of the transport ships and into Constantinople.

Galorian rode Thane toward the huge dome he had spied from the ship's deck. Underneath it, he found his comrades engaged in reckless mayhem in the heart of what for seven centuries had been the world's largest and greatest cathedral. Galorian had learned from his research that ten thousand workers had labored for six years to build the stunning Hagia Sophia, and now he was witnessing a company of Crusaders hell-bent on destroying it in a day.

Galorian pleaded for reason and respect, but his voice went unheard over the commotion of destruction. He watched as the invaders desecrated a thousand years' worth of priceless treasures, destroying Greek, Roman, and Orthodox antiquities. They burned sacred manuscripts, slashed paintings, and smashed holy icons and sculptures. They stripped the walls of gorgeous mosaics depicting Jesus and the Virgin Mary, Christian saints and angels. Yelling "To the ships!" they carried the precious art out through the cathedral's massive marble doors toward the harbor, to be hauled back to Venice.

Galorian heard shouts of "The head of John the Baptist!" and "The hair of the Virgin Mary!" as soldiers ran through the rotunda waving the body parts of saints they had raided from ornate reliquaries. The invaders carved up a piece of The True Cross, as thick as a man's leg and decorated with gold and precious jewels. One wrapped himself in a shroud he claimed was the burial cloth of Jesus and wore the Crown of Thorns that had reportedly sat on the Savior's head.

Laughing derisively, a French knight burst into the holy sanctuary with the prostitute from the ship slung over his shoulder. He dumped her on the sacred Eastern Orthodox patriarchal throne and ordered her to sing bawdy songs, while he served his friends church wine in holy chalices. When the knight raised a chalice in an obscene toast, Galorian had seen and heard more than he could endure. Intending to knock the cup out of the knight's grasp, Galorian charged at him, shouting "Stop!"

But before he reached him, Galorian felt the grip of a powerful hand spin him around. Blinded by his fury, he had not seen the knight who had come up behind him. The knight lunged at him, making a sharp thrust into

Galorian's left shoulder. Stunned and speechless, Galorian stared blankly as the knight pulled back his sword. Then he watched helplessly as the crazed warrior jumped onto the sacred cathedral altar, where he began hacking into pieces the silver plates he found there.

Galorian stumbled out of the cathedral and slowly mounted Thane. Clutching the reins with one hand and using the other to keep pressure on his wound, he plodded toward the coast. Silas had stayed hidden in the hold of the galley. He called out "My lord!" when he caught sight of the stain of blood on Galorian's shoulder. Galorian dismounted and, with Silas's help, removed his armor and shirt.

Stretching out on the straw, Galorian said calmly, "I'm fine." The chain mail had allowed only the sword's tip through. And the attacking knight, Galorian understood, had been intent on sending him a message, not in-flicting a mortal blow. Still, he recalled the circumstances of his king's death and whispered a prayer.

Silas left and returned with water, lifting some to Galorian's lips and us-ing the rest to carefully clean away the blood. Then he doused the spot with vinegar, as he had observed others do to stab wounds. Galorian flinched briefly but then smiled at the boy and thanked him for his care. "I'm fine," he repeated. Though he felt less fine than he had ever in his life felt before.

§

"You cannot wear a bell around your neck in the convent." The Mother Superior in Liège was in a no-nonsense mood. Clarissa bowed her head politely as Agnes Luc continued. "It's too distracting during prayers, and it interrupts the silence we keep for God."

Clarissa considered the abbess's response an unfair overreaction. The bell was muffled against her wool habit, and it barely made a noise at all unless she shook it intentionally, which she did not do in the convent—certainly not during prayers. She pondered her reply carefully. "But doesn't God love the lepers?"

"Of course God loves the lepers," answered Agnes Luc curtly.

"I was in the scriptorium a few days ago, copying the Gospel of Mat-thew," said Clarissa, hoping to explain adequately. "It says that whenever we welcome a stranger, or feed someone who is hungry, or visit a person who is sick or in prison, we do that very thing to our Lord Jesus Christ."

"Yes," said the abbess impatiently.

"That means that Jesus himself is hungry and in prison. And it means that Jesus is a leper." Clarissa paused for emphasis. "Would we force Jesus to wear a bell to announce to everyone that he is sick and unclean—to scare people away?"

A noisy fit of wheezing, which Clarissa noticed always got worse when Agnes Luc was under stress, overtook the abbess. "I don't make the rules," she said between gasps.

"And maybe we can't change them," Clarissa retorted. "But I promised to wear this bell to let the lepers know that, like Jesus, we are with them. To remind myself that Jesus shows up at our gate every day." She paused and added softly, "To remind us all."

Agnes Luc dismissed her with "You may go now." Clarissa turned and walked out, clutching the bell around her neck, her serious demeanor gradually melting into a smile.

§

Moved to do more than copy words of Scripture, Clarissa wanted to understand them. To *live* them. She and Johanna petitioned Mother Agnes Luc to allow them to participate in weekly lessons at the Chapel of Saint Christophe. Thirty years had passed since Father Lambert le Bègue had been arrested for heresy, and the abbess responded, "With that trouble-making priest long gone, I don't see the harm."

As soon as they were out of earshot, Johanna whispered, "Obviously she doesn't know Brother Cyrille—a man cut from the same cloth as Father Lambert."

Clarissa smiled as she said, "Two men of the cloth cut from the same bolt of humble, strong, discomforting wool."

They walked to the chapel every Wednesday afternoon, grateful for the gift of this brief freedom. They wore the simple black robes and white headdresses of Benedictine novices, still inhabiting the time of preparation that was required before taking the perpetual vows of nuns. They both knew that, once those vows were made, even this limited freedom outside the abbey walls would disappear.

On their walk home one evening around dusk, as the stone front of the gray convent came into view beyond the trees, Clarissa stopped and faced Johanna. "I can't stay here," she announced. She looked for the shock she expected to see on Johanna's face, but she saw only her friend's usual peaceful demeanor. "Are you surprised?" Clarissa asked.

"Only that it took you this long to reach that conclusion."

"I know that good, holy women with deep faith and abundant compassion live within the cloister walls," said Clarissa. "But those walls are starting to feel like a prison to me. I need to be out among the people." A smile spread over her face. "Did you see how they really love the Scriptures?" Brother Cyrille had carried on Father Lambert's legacy of translating the sacred texts into the vernacular language of ordinary people, and the understanding and exchanges among the villagers who showed up each week were animated and inspiring to Clarissa.

"'Blessed are you who are poor, for yours is the kingdom of God,'" she recited, quoting the day's lesson from Jesus's familiar hillside sermon in the Gospel of Luke. "'Blessed are you who are hungry now, for you will be filled. Blessed are you who weep now, for you will laugh.'" She smiled and looked toward the sky. "Don't you see?" she said, bringing her gaze back to Johanna, unable to contain her excitement. "They understand in a way that we never will that Jesus came for *them*!"

Clarissa's smile began to fade as she noticed the tears gathering in Johanna's eyes. "What is it?" she asked, reaching for her friend's arm.

"*I* understand," whispered Johanna. She took a moment to gather her words. "My family left me with the nuns in Dover when I was ten years old. They dumped me on the stoop of the convent with a crust of bread, knocked on the door, and left." Johanna swallowed hard. "The image of my parents and my three older brothers fleeing in our wagon is the last picture I have of them. That was over ten years ago." She took a deep breath. "They couldn't afford to feed me. That's what they told me. And it's true we were often hungry." She paused again. "They decided they could feed the boys. The boys were worth something."

Clarissa felt great sorrow and shame overtake her. In the year that she had known Johanna, she had been so focused on her own troubles that she had never once asked her friend about her story. "I didn't know," she choked out remorsefully. "I'm so sorry, Johanna."

"As soon as the nuns taught me to read, I spent as much time as I could with my face buried in Scripture and the books of the abbey library," Johanna continued. "I thought that if I could fill up my head with knowledge . . . if I could cram it full of details, there would be no space left for memories of my family. I was so angry, and so resentful, and so sad, for so very long. Why do you think it took me a decade to decide to sign on as a novice?"

"Why did you?" asked Clarissa. "What changed?"

Johanna smiled. "I finally recognized Jesus. The *real* Jesus. Not the distant, fancy one in the cathedrals, high on a shiny gold cross, wrapped in a royal robe and topped with a jeweled crown like a king, who never existed. But the one who was born in a stable to poor parents on the run. The one whose first cradle was an animal feeding trough. Who lived as a child in exile, hidden from the wrath of cruel rulers who wanted to kill him.

"I couldn't ignore this child who grew into a man who never owned a thing and never had a home, who healed lepers, and taught ordinary people, and had a special love for outcasts. Whose acts of compassion and thirst for justice riled up the leaders, who killed him like a common criminal." She paused and sighed. "Hardly what you'd expect for the Son of God."

She opened her eyes wide then. "But that was the point. Don't you see, Clarissa? God didn't become human to convince us of his power. He came down to earth vulnerable and poor, to let us know that he shares our pain. *Maybe*, I thought, *Jesus can understand my suffering, too.*"

Clarissa's mind and heart were racing as she tried to take in the words. Then Johanna began softly reciting: "'The Spirit of the Lord is upon me, because he has anointed me to preach good news to the poor. He has sent me to proclaim release to the captives and recovery of sight to the blind, to let the oppressed go free.'" As she finished, she slid to the ground and leaned wearily against the rough trunk of a tall pine. "Those are words from Jesus's first sermon," she explained, "the one where he announced his mission in his hometown of Nazareth by reading from the scroll of the prophet Isaiah." She sighed heavily. "If we're followers of Jesus, then his mission is our mission. And we too have been anointed."

Clarissa pondered this for a moment. "I believe you," she said, not entirely confident that what she was saying was true. She joined her friend against the tree. Clutching Johanna's hand, she declared, "I trust you." Those were words she could utter without a shadow of doubt.

As they sat in silence, Clarissa's heart began to beat even more rapidly, as if it were about to leap out of her ribcage and soar into the sky. She was overwhelmed by a feeling she couldn't explain or contain. With more conviction than she had ever before mustered in her life, she declared to her dearest friend, "Your Jesus is the one I want to follow." Then Clarissa swallowed hard, feeling her spirit crash as if the wings of her heart had been abruptly clipped. She looked at Johanna. "But how do we do it?"

Neither spoke for several minutes. Then Clarissa asked, "What fate is there for us? Living as nuns enclosed in the dark shadows of that convent?" She shook her head, imagining that possibility. "Or married to men determined to subdue us—by words, or neglect, or beatings." She took a deep breath. "Or are we doomed to die in childbirth?"

Before Johanna could respond, Clarissa declared, "I want to be free." Silence fell between them again. Clarissa was beginning to understand the costly truth of those words. She had already paid a price for freedom. And she felt sure there was more yet to pay. "But where can we go?" she lamented, aware that she had just enumerated the entire spectrum of choices available to them as young women.

"We're limited only by our imaginations," declared Johanna, turning to gaze into her friend's eyes and taking her other hand in hers. Then she added, "And our fear." This seemed to Clarissa to be an answer equal to "I have no idea." Johanna spoke again. "*Men* can live on their own. Men can work and earn money. Men can marry without fear."

All true, thought Clarissa. Then she looked to the sky again and asked, "But what about *us*?"

§

Two days after he was wounded, on the third and final day of the brutal sack of Constantinople, Galorian rode back into the center of the city. He had difficulty taking in the savage and surreal sights that attacked his senses. The French knights were continuing their drunken rampage of destruction, while the Venetians wantonly plundered and pillaged, loading their ships with precious treasures. Fires blazed unchecked, burning wide swaths of devastation. Countless numbers of Constantinople's half a million defenseless citizens had been brutally massacred, their lifeless bodies strewn around the streets.

In the city square, Thane reared in reaction, slipping on a river of blood from the massive slaughter. Galorian leapt to the ground as his beloved horse fell hard on his side. The knight gently coaxed Thane back on his feet and led him toward an alley, away from the mayhem in the square. From a far corner of the alley, Galorian heard screams. He followed them and came upon a knight, his sword bloody at his side. A young man and woman lay a few paces away, fallen together in death. Beyond them lay two lifeless young boys.

The knight straddled a young girl on the ground, tearing at her clothes with one hand as he tried to silence her with the other. "Mama!" she cried over and over between screams.

"Stop!" ordered Galorian, drawing his sword. The drunken knight laughed and ignored him, throwing off his armor and fumbling with his own clothes while he kept the girl pinned to the ground. "Stop!" Galorian repeated. Still the knight persisted. "Now!" shouted Galorian, feeling a rage he had never before known rising up in his chest. The knight reached clumsily for his sword. Galorian raised his own and thrust it swiftly into the man's heart. "I said 'Stop,'" he muttered as he stumbled backward.

Galorian took a moment to catch his breath. And then, as the full import of what he had just done overtook him, he crumpled to the ground, tears coursing down his face. The corpse was lying with limbs askew and eyes wide open, looking straight at him in a ghastly death stare. Galorian noted with sorrow how young the dead knight was. "We're supposed to be on the same side," he choked.

Then, slowly and deliberately, he pulled his sword out of the knight's chest and let it clatter to the ground. For a few moments, Galorian's body shuddered with sobs. Then he staggered to his feet and, leaving the sword behind, began to walk slowly out of the alley.

The girl's crying broke the daze that gripped him. He looked back over his shoulder at her, lying next to the dead knight. *She's just a child,* he thought. *An orphan now.* Thane stood over her protectively. Her eyes pleaded.

Galorian thought then, as he had so many times since he had lost them, of his beloved Josselyn and their daughter. Overcome with his own sorrow, he hesitated for a moment. And then he turned around and walked back. Kneeling by the girl, he removed his riding cloak and wrapped it around her. Her dark eyes, still filled with terror, were fixed on his. "Don't be afraid," he said in a language he knew she didn't understand. "I won't hurt you."

He reached over to the dead knight and grasped at the large gold pendant hanging around his neck. Galorian yanked hard on the square cross whose bars flared into fleurs-de-lis, breaking the chain and placing the cross inside his glove. He glanced at his sword and left it where it lay.

He picked up the girl, still trembling with fright, and set her gently on Thane. Then he put a foot in the saddle stirrup and lifted himself up behind her. As they trotted out of the alley, he cradled her close to him. He noticed the thick band of gold around her left wrist, which she fingered nervously as they rode.

They approached the edge of the city square. Constantinople's wounded and dazed citizens wandered the blood-soaked streets among billows of black smoke, accompanied by choruses of anguished moans. In one corner, a knight barked orders at huddles of Crusader foot soldiers, who were struggling to drag four huge, solid bronze horses toward the ships. In another, soldiers were gathered around a fire, melting down a holy statue. A whole company wrestled with a massive statue of the Greek goddess Hera, whose head was so large that four yokes of oxen they had found and drafted into service could barely carry it off.

"Hold on," said Galorian when they had passed through the bloody square, and the girl let out a slight whimper as he dug his heels into Thane's side. They sprinted to the edge of the city as fast as the horse could run. When the sails of the galleys in the harbor came into view, Galorian sighed with relief. Then, fully aware that she couldn't comprehend what he was saying, he whispered to the girl, "I have no idea what I'm going to do with you."

§

Johanna and Clarissa walked together around the abbey every evening, try-ing to hatch a plan for their future. They talked and prayed and consulted Scripture but came up against what felt like only dead ends. Clarissa began to despair and started spending more and more time in the convent's base-ment archives, out of sight.

Late one night, when all the sisters were sound asleep, hunched with a candle over the ancient hagiographic manuscripts that contained the stories of the saints of the church, she stumbled upon inspiration. Catherine of Alexandria, she discovered, was the daughter of a pagan king who had ruled the Egyptian city in the early fourth century. She had a quick mind and had devoted herself to the study of art, science, and philosophy. At fourteen—Clarissa's age—Catherine had encountered and converted to Christianity.

Clarissa devoured the details of the young saint's life and then hurried out of the basement to wake Johanna. "You won't believe who I discovered!" she said, shaking her friend to rouse her. Johanna shot Clarissa a sleepy and skeptical look and then rolled over toward the wall. Clarissa put a hand on her friend's shoulder and turned her back to face her. "Catherine of Alexandria."

Rubbing her eyes, Johanna said, "Yes, I've heard about her." Clarissa's face fell, and Johanna added, "But I don't know much about her."

"She told her parents she would only marry someone who was smart-er, richer, and more beautiful than she was. And then she saw a vision of the Virgin Mary giving her in mystical marriage to Jesus." Clarissa was breathless with excitement as she continued to reveal what she had learned about the astonishing Saint Catherine. "She visited the Roman Emperor Maxentius and told him to stop persecuting Christians who refused to bow down and worship idols. He answered her by getting fifty of the best pagan philosophers to debate her. She won the debate and converted them all to Christianity!

"So then mad-as-a-dog Maxentius had them all burned to death. He threw Catherine in prison and had her tortured to try to get her to recant her faith, but she wouldn't do it. In fact, she converted the two hundred visi-tors who came to see her—and all her guards and the emperor's wife! Max was so mad he killed his wife and all the guards, too."

The story tumbled out of Clarissa as fast as she could spill it. "So then he tried something even worse than torture on Catherine—he proposed to her. But she decided she would rather be a martyr than be married to that dog, so she explained to him that she was already married to Jesus."

Johanna was fully awake now. "So Maxentius condemned her to a horrible death on the spiked breaking wheel, imagining her limbs being slowly stretched and her bones painfully broken. But Catherine remained calm throughout the ordeal and prayed, and the wheel miraculously broke instead of her body. So the emperor had to settle for having her beheaded. She died praying for mercy, asking Jesus to extend his wounded arms toward her and receive her into heaven."

Johanna's eyes were wide with wonder. "Now that I know the whole story," she said, "I can honestly say that in all my years of study, I have never encountered anyone as amazing as Saint Catherine of Alexandria."

"But that's *not* the whole story," said Clarissa. "Angels carried Catherine's body to Mount Sinai in Egypt. And in the sixth century, a monastery was built there and named after her. People still pray to her, asking to be as pure and strong and brave as she was. Asking Saint Catherine for the strength to love God and serve him as faithfully as she did."

Clarissa took a deep breath. "If only we could."

Fourteen

Galorian, responsible now for two traumatized youngsters—one of whom did not speak any of the three languages he knew—pondered his options. Nothing remained to tie him to England. Having been removed from his parents at a young age to begin his knighthood training, he had no familial bonds. His wife and child were dead. He had lost his fervor for the Crusades and his affection for the culture that spawned them.

But Silas, he knew, needed to get back home as soon as possible. The siege against Constantinople had ended the Fourth Crusade, and the soldiers began immediately streaming back to Europe with their plunder. Wandering amid the post-war chaos on the shore, Galorian spied the galley that had brought them and turned Silas over into the care of the kindest English knight he knew for the return journey.

Silas, crying, clung to Galorian for several minutes before relenting to go. Galorian sent him off with the words "Be brave" and a prayer for safe travel. It was the best he knew to do for the boy who never should have been a squire in war.

The girl was another matter. Galorian didn't want to imagine the horrors that would visit a young girl among soldiers drunk on wine and victory. He had gone back into the city alone, hoping to locate a convent or orphanage to take her. But the devastation of Constantinople was complete. Her home no longer existed.

Galorian did not possess the language to explain his predicament to anyone in the city. So he decided to return once more, this time with the girl, with the intent of finding and handing her over to a loving family that had survived the horror and was remaking a life among the rubble. But when he placed her on Thane and pointed his horse toward Constantinople, she cried and shook so violently that he abandoned that plan.

"Aminah," she said, placing her hand over her heart, when he set her back down on the ground. Then she reached for Galorian's hand and pressed his palm against his chest.

"Galorian," he said, smiling. She smiled back. "I guess we're stuck with each other," he sighed.

He had a map of Egypt. He had studied the passage to Cairo. For a long time he had hoped to lay eyes on that great city. And so he decided to find a way to get there.

In normal times, mercantile ships traversed the Mediterranean Sea regularly between Constantinople and Alexandria, the Egyptian seaport just north of Cairo. Gold, grains, and textiles were exchanged between those prosperous cities. After the Crusader conquest, Constantinople had nothing left to trade. But at the edge of the activity on the shore, Galorian overheard the name "Alexandria" whispered and spied a huddle of young men quietly wrestling a gold statue into the hold of a boat. It had apparently been overlooked by the Crusaders who had systematically seized or destroyed everything of value—or maybe it was stolen from some while they slept off their revelry in a stupor of drink and exhaustion.

Galorian took a quick inventory of his appearance. Except for his boots, he had shed his armor. His shirt was stained with blood at the shoulder. He had abandoned his sword, and his shield was with Thane, who was tied to a tree out of sight. No one, he thought, would mistake him for a fearsome knight. He said a quick prayer and, with one hand open and the other clutching Aminah's right hand, approached the young men, smiling.

They stopped their work and gazed at the pair with mistrust. Galorian, still smiling, said "Alexandria." He reached into a shirt pocket and took out the large, solid gold cross and chain that he had removed from the neck of the knight, hoping that these enterprising young men would view it as fair passage. For several moments, nobody spoke or moved.

Then one of the group stepped forward, grinned, and grabbed the cross. Holding it over his head in a gesture of triumph, he said something to which the others gave loud assent. *Do they understand the value of the gold?* Galorian wondered. *Are they intrigued by the enemy's cross? Or are they simply glad to have some European plunder?* He would never know the answers—or why the young men chose to accept it. But he was relieved that they did.

Untying Thane, Galorian whispered a prayer of thanks for this small miracle. He led his horse and Aminah into the hold, which the three of them shared with a naked, life-sized statue of the Greek god Hercules. Galorian modestly wrapped him in his riding cloak, which made Aminah giggle. Then she curled up in the space under the bow to sleep.

Galorian walked up onto the deck. Through the language of panto-
mime, the young man clutching the cross conveyed to him their plan to cash
in the statue for rice and other food in Egypt. He launched the boat out onto
a sea swarming with Crusader vessels making their way back to Western
Europe. The Crusaders apparently had little fight left in them. None paid
attention to the boat with the gold statue hidden in the hold that was headed
south toward Africa.

§

As soon as the spring sun began to warm the earth, Johanna and Clarissa
petitioned Mother Agnes Luc with a request far wilder than making weekly
forays to the Chapel of Saint Christophe. To their utter shock, the abbess
gave quick assent to the pilgrimage. "There will be many pilgrims on the
road," Agnes Luc asserted. "They—and God—will watch over you and keep
you safe." Clarissa and Johanna wondered aloud later if her response was
more an indication of her desire to be rid of them for a while than a holy
blessing.

Clarissa had come to equate protective safety with Saint Catherine,
which is the name she finally bestowed that season upon the screech owl
that had been her one constant companion since her first escape from
home. "She can't just be Owl forever," she explained to Johanna. "She's bold,
she's loyal, a true saint of an owl. And like Catherine after her beheading,
she has no neck."

Johanna rolled her eyes and groaned. "Saint Catherine it is."

Soon after receiving her name, Saint Catherine the Owl began keeping her distance, spending more time in the trees in the heavily forested
tracts around the abbey. The mystery of her disappearances was solved one
evening at dusk when Clarissa caught sight of another owl, slightly larger
than Catherine but otherwise an exact replica. He was engaged in an odd
dance—hopping, bobbing, bowing, snapping his bill, swiveling his small
head and even winking one large eye at a time at Catherine.

The elaborate courtship ritual apparently had the intended effect. The
owls touched their curved beaks and began preening, running their beaks
up and down through each other's orange-brown feathers. Clarissa laughed
at the spectacle. The two love birds, apparently embarrassed in whatever
way birds get embarrassed, flapped their wings and headed for a large hollow in an oak tree. It was high enough to be safe from predators but, thankfully for Clarissa, close enough that she could observe them until she left on
her journey, the first travel adventure that Catherine sat out since they met.

Agnes Luc had been right about the safety Clarissa and Johanna would find on their journey. The Fourth Crusade had reignited interest in Jerusalem, and throngs of European pilgrims were making their way to the Holy City, heading in the same direction. Clarissa and Johanna were never alone on the road that cut southeast toward the Mediterranean Sea.

But the first travelers to offer them a ride were not Christian pilgrims, but a family of Jews from Calais. Malakai, the father, wore a knee-length robe and the pointed yellow cap that French law forced Jewish men to wear to make obvious their faith. He graciously invited them to take a seat behind his wife, Natania, and their two young sons, Levi and Yosef, in their comfortable wagon. Johanna immediately took his hand and stepped in.

Clarissa followed gingerly. "Are you sure this is a good idea?" she whispered in English as she settled next to Johanna among boxes and clothes, hoping not to be overheard or understood.

"Why not?"

"I've heard that Jews kidnap and kill Christian children and use their blood in their religious rituals."

"That's nonsense," Johanna retorted. "Just a tale invented by their enemies to scare us and justify persecuting them." Clarissa had heard the stories of Jews having their property seized, being arrested and expelled from France, even being massacred and burned at the stake—just for being Jews. "It's no wonder they're leaving," said Johanna, shaking her head sadly. "If we're lucky, they're going all the way to Jerusalem and can take us most of the way to the monastery."

As it turned out, the family wasn't leaving France at all, just making a visit for several days with relatives near the Italian border. But Clarissa and Johanna were grateful that they were carried across the country by the family of Jewish bakers, who generously shared their bread along the way and left two rye loaves with them for the rest of their journey. They thanked Malakai and his family profusely for their kindness.

As they got out of the wagon, Clarissa and Johanna took in a view that they never could have conjured in their imaginations. Rising before them were the breathtaking Alps, so tall that snow rested on the highest of the purple peaks. "Oh my!" gasped Clarissa when she caught her first glimpse of the seemingly endless mountain range. "How are we going to get around that?"

"I don't think around is possible," laughed Johanna. "I think we're going to have to go over."

As they stood frozen in amazement, surveying a vast carpet of bright green moss dotted with tiny white flowers that led to the peaks, a loud entourage of wagons overtook them. A man emerged from one and, spying them, introduced himself in French as Pietro, an Italian cloth merchant. Waving his hands toward the wagons loaded with colorful linen, muslin, and wool, he immediately told Clarissa and Johanna how much success he always had trading his fine silk for cloth in France—and how he loved their country's lavish textile fairs and all things French.

"I've just spent two months in Champagne, the heart of commercial exchange between northern and southern Europe," he said excitedly. "What people, what opportunity, what a time!" The garrulous merchant spoke in such glowing terms about French food and fashion, and the beauty of French literature and language, that Clarissa and Johanna didn't have the heart to tell him that they were English. "My son was born twenty-three years ago when I was here for the first time in France on business," declared Pietro. "My dear wife named him Giovanni, but I call him Francesco—'the Frenchman'!"

Pietro inquired about the destination of the young women. "Perfect!" he exclaimed. He was on his way back to Italy with the cloth he had acquired in France. "I'm headed to Rome," he said, "where my ship is waiting to take me around Italy and on to Egypt to sell my cloth there. To the glory of God, I will see that you get there safely."

Pietro helped Clarissa and Johanna up onto one of the wagons, where they gave thanks for their good fortune as they settled into a cushiony pile of wool dyed a deep shade of purple that matched the mountains. The entourage lurched forward, passing through the sea of moss and flowers and onto the rugged path that led up to the pass through the Alps. The wagons groaned and swayed as they moved over the rough terrain, slowly gaining height.

Johanna took in every breathtaking view, but Clarissa peeked out only occasionally from under the wool cloth into which she had burrowed. Soon she was groaning along with the wagon wheels, as dizzying images of tipping over and spilling down the steep and treacherous slopes raced through her mind. As the sun slid behind the peaks, she began to wonder where they would spend the night and was grateful when a simple house came into view—despite its being perched precipitously on the side of a mountain. Staffed by gracious monks, it was the first of several Alpine hostels they found along the pass that catered to Christian pilgrims on their way to Rome and the Holy Land.

When the band of travelers finally crossed the border and then entered a low, wide valley, Clarissa smiled for the first time in several days. Returning the smile, believing completely in her words, Johanna announced confidently, "The worst is over." She had no idea how wrong she was.

§

"I have only to make a stop at home to pick up more silk," Pietro said as the entourage moved forward into the heart of Italy. "We'll spend tonight there." As they crossed the broad Umbrian Plain, the setting sun cast a scarlet sheen over a picturesque town built up a mountain in a series of terraces. The pink and white limestone houses glowed in the resplendent light, as a towering castle on the mountaintop above them kept watch over villagers streaming home at the end of their day's work. Clarissa took a deep, exhilarating breath, imprinting the enchanting scene on her memory.

Pietro helped Clarissa and Johanna down from the wagon and into his textile store, which was affixed to the side of his considerable mansion, the largest and finest of the homes they had spied in the town. They immediately heard loud snores in a corner, where they saw a left foot and right arm sticking out from under a small pile of blue velvet fabric. Pietro hurried over, threw the cloth off the young man who was sleeping there, and shook him awake. "Francesco," he said angrily, "we have guests."

His son looked at him with one eye closed and then rolled over. His clothing was askew, his silk shirt damp with spilled beer, which had filled the air with a sour odor the moment Pietro removed the cloth that covered him.

"Get up!" yelled Pietro, turning his son and shaking him again, harder this time. Clarissa had the sense that the merchant's reaction would have been even more violent had she and Johanna not been there. Francesco stared at his father, grinning, but did not move. Then he closed his eyes again, succumbing to a bout of hiccups.

Pietro turned away. "Worthless," he muttered under his breath. He shot a look at Clarissa and Johanna, sadness replacing anger and disgust in his eyes. "He went off to war three years ago. I thought the army would cure him of his love of frivolous parties and strong drink and the unmanly silliness of the troubadours. But he came back worse than when he left." The merchant shook his head. "He was a prisoner of war for over a year, and when he was finally set free and came home, he seemed to think that his life should be one endless party."

Pietro turned away and strode out of the room. Clarissa looked with pity and some consternation on the dissolute young man lying akimbo on the pile of cloth, a stream of drool making its way down his chin. He was a decade older than she, yet apparently lost as to the path and point of his life. She knelt beside him and took his hand in hers. She touched his forehead, which burned with fever. "I'm going to pray for you," she said, "that you might turn your life over to God so that he can make something of it."

Francesco opened his eyes, blinked, and stared at her. "You do that," he said, grinning again, a hiccup convulsing him.

Clarissa dropped his hand and got up quickly. As they left the shop, following a servant who had come to lead them to their room for the night, she grabbed Johanna's arm. "Such a waste," Clarissa whispered. "I'm afraid he's not going to amount to much."

§

The young servant led them out of the shop and into the heart of the mansion. They walked up a wide staircase made of Italian marble, with a shimmering pattern of gold inlaid in the bannisters. The servant escorted them into a cavernous room and left a tray heaped with bread, cheese, and fruit. "Master has gone to bed," she explained in apology for the less-than-lavish supper. "There will be a large breakfast for you in the morning."

The room had two large beds, each topped with a bright red canopy and surrounded with gauzy sheets of shimmering silk that flowed to the floor. The palettes were soft and thick. The down-stuffed coverlets swaddled Clarissa and Johanna in cozy warmth.

"This is the best bed I've ever slept in," sighed Johanna.

Clarissa immediately thought of the people with leprosy outside the convent gate, the girl who had died in her arms, and the ragged children who begged on the streets of Liège. She wanted to feel anger—or guilt—about the extravagant comfort of this place that reminded her so much of home. "Me too" was all she said as she sank more deeply under the thick coverlet, anticipating a night of luxurious slumber.

Early in the morning, the servant returned and led them back down the marble stairs. She ushered them to chairs resembling royal thrones at each end of an ornately carved table, which was so long that Clarissa could barely see Johanna once they were seated. Each had a boiled goose egg in a gold cup next to a steaming plate heaped with rabbit stew over biscuits. Clarissa let her eyes feast on her breakfast for a moment and then lifted the egg out of its cup. She set it on the table and gave it a shove toward Johanna. The egg rolled and rolled and rolled, plunging them into a fit of giggles.

The door opened and Pietro swept into the room. Johanna hastily grabbed Clarissa's egg and buried it in her stew while they wrestled their laughter under control. "And did you sleep well?" asked Pietro, bowing to each of them. Johanna and Clarissa nodded solemnly. The busy merchant left as quickly as he had come, to oversee the hitching of the horses to the wagons. As soon as the door closed behind him, they burst into laughter again.

After breakfast they were on their way to Rome. Seeing the ancient city with its holy and stately buildings was an unexpected bonus. Pietro took them on a brief detour to view the elegant Lateran Palace. "The pope lives there," he explained. "I thought you would like to see his home." Standing next to the palace was the splendid Basilica of Saint John Lateran, gleaming in white marble. "It's the Mother Church," explained Pietro, "the oldest in Europe." Clarissa and Johanna smiled broadly to let him know that they were grateful and suitably impressed.

At the port, they watched as servants loaded the wagonloads of cloth on board a large galley. Pietro invited them as his special guests to sit with him in the most comfortable corner of the deck, where they had a splendid view and ate and drank whenever it pleased them. Clarissa reveled in their trip across the Mediterranean in the lap of luxury, enjoying the gentle spring breezes and the warmth of the sun on her face, the rocking of the waves and the wonder of new sights. "I wish we could do this forever," she proclaimed to Johanna, popping a plump olive into her mouth as they rounded the southernmost tip of Italy.

Johanna laughed and then pointed toward the eastern horizon. A convention of angry, gray clouds was gathering there. "You might soon change your mind," she said.

For four hours they were pelted by rain and tossed by relentless waves. Clarissa clung to the railing at the edge of the deck and to Johanna, feeling that she was spilling everything she had eaten in three days into the stormy sea. "You're right," she said when she could finally speak again. "Nuns are not made to be sailors."

§

Galorian rejoined Aminah in the hold of the boat. She whimpered softly as she slept, breathing heavily. Occasionally she cried out as if in the clutch of a nightmare. Galorian replayed in his mind the horror of the knight's assault on her and imagined the brutal murder of her family, trying to fathom the heaviness of the grief she carried. He thought of his parents for the first time in many months, recognizing that he too had been made an orphan of sorts at a young age. He remembered how devastated he had felt and how many nights he had fallen asleep longing for his mother.

She can't be more than ten or eleven years old, he thought as he watched Aminah sleep. A great sorrow overcame him, knowing that one so young and innocent had lost and suffered so much. When she cried out again, he felt a compelling urge to hold and try to soothe her. But he was afraid of startling her and adding to her terror. And so he just watched her from the other end of the hold, unable himself to surrender to sleep.

When they stepped at last onto African soil, Galorian bowed to the young men in the boat, a gesture of thanks for safe passage. As he and Aminah made their way on Thane toward the heart of Alexandria, she began to tremble, fingering her bracelet again nervously and burying her head in his chest. Galorian put a protective arm around her as Thane carried them through the jammed, narrow streets of the port city. They arrived at a large bazaar, crammed with people shouting and moving among rough tables spread with goods, which stretched as far as Galorian could see. Pointing and gesturing, he managed to buy fruit and bread for the duration of their journey.

They slept on sandy ground at the edge of the city, with Thane between them. Galorian could hear Aminah's quiet weeping as she fell asleep. He wanted again to try to soothe her, but he feared that the gestures of comfort he had offered on the back of a horse in daylight would be misinterpreted on the ground in the dark of night. And so he kept his distance and prayed for her peace of heart.

They headed out at dawn the next morning. Aminah flashed Galorian a smile as they left Alexandria, and he wondered if the city had been a painful reminder to her of Constantinople—or if she was letting him know she was glad to be with him still. He was both anxious to reach Cairo and dreading the moment when Aminah would understand that he was giving her away.

Thane moved slowly until he caught his rhythm in the desert sand, and then they kept a steady pace. They rode in silence as the blinding brightness of the sun expanded to fill the sky and the heavy air around them. Galorian noted that his inability to communicate with Aminah felt as stifling as the heat.

Just then she turned her head toward him, patted Thane three times, and pronounced a word in Arabic. She said it again, with more insistence, and Galorian understood that he was to repeat it. Aminah laughed at his attempt. Then he said "horse," and she spoke it back to him. Aminah pointed at a rock and gave him the Arabic word for it, and he gave her the English, both pronouncing awkwardly the other's language. *It's a start*, thought Galorian, smiling at his young companion's creativity.

They passed the rest of the morning that way, as Aminah pointed at sand, sun, cloud, tree, hill, bird—until she ran out of objects in the rather depleted desert. Then she touched her eyes and nose, mouth and feet, and uttered words for each. She turned again toward Galorian and patted his arm three times, giggling as she pronounced a word. Galorian, not sure what amusing term she had chosen to describe him, said "knight" back to her.

They stopped in the worst heat of the day to share water and bread while Thane rested, and then they started up again. Aminah turned toward Galorian once more, with a crushingly sorrowful look that caused a grave concern to rise up in him. Then she said a word. Immediately her expression changed, as she fake-laughed and beamed Galorian a broad smile, uttering another word. Then she cowered and shook and pronounced a third.

Galorian mimicked her expressions, following them with proclamations of "sad," "happy," and "scared." They took turns trying to outdo each other looking "worried," "angry," and "confused." With her mouth open wide and eyes popping, Aminah's dramatically conjured portrayal of what Galorian could only assume was "startled" sent him into a spasm of laughter. That day as they exchanged vocabulary lessons, they laughed easily and often together.

In late afternoon, Aminah pointed far into the distance. Galorian looked and saw a cluster of massive, ancient pyramids rising out of the sand. They shimmered in the fading light. Aminah chattered on with obvious delight about the rare spectacle.

Galorian was the first to spy the immense statue with the body of a lion and the head of a man. "What creature walks on four legs in the morning, two legs at noon, and three in the evening?" he asked Aminah, who smiled at him without comprehension. Galorian remembered from his lessons in Greek mythology that this was the riddle that the Sphinx, which strangled and devoured anyone who gave the wrong answer, had posed to Oedipus. The monster destroyed itself when the great Greek hero answered correctly: "Man. He crawls when a child, walks on two legs when grown, and uses a walking stick when old."

The towering Sphinx beckoned to the pair of weary travelers. When they reached it, Galorian helped Aminah down from Thane, and they settled into the shadow of the massive statue, getting their first respite of the day from the sweltering heat. They shared a sweet pomegranate and some bread, watching as the sun collapsed from a yellow blaze that filled the sky into a red disk that hovered on the horizon. Aminah was asleep, snoring lightly, before the sky turned dark. That night the Sphinx kept watch over them with a sly and knowing smile.

Fifteen

Clarissa, more than ready to return to life on solid ground, was grateful beyond words when the coast of Africa finally came into view. She and Johanna thanked Pietro for his kindness and generosity. The merchant sent them ashore with an oarsman in a small craft and a pledge to meet them again there in eighteen days, to provide their return passage to Europe. Then he busied himself attending to his cloth.

The land where they disembarked overwhelmed Clarissa's senses. People of every hue of human skin were crammed into the open bazaar in the heart of the port of Alexandria. Lamb carcasses, quartered and hanging, hovered above baskets of rice and bright fruit in varieties Clarissa had never before laid eyes on. Vendors dressed in long white robes called out in a cacophonous chorus of Arabic, Coptic, and Greek, trying to lure customers to buy their fragrant spices and colorfully woven rugs.

"Look!" cried Clarissa at least a dozen times in their first hour there, pointing out wonders in all directions to Johanna. She had a hard time believing that she was in Egypt and the city that was home to her inspiration, Saint Catherine. She and Johanna might have chosen to linger, but they had a lot of ground to cover and understood that they had to keep moving if they were to meet up again with Pietro at the appointed time. *But how to find their way in this teeming city where many languages were spoken but no one seemed to know theirs?*

They wandered until they spied a tall man under a towering palm tree in the heart of Alexandria's marketplace. He stood at the center of a noisy and demanding throng of people, who were shouting out words in a stew of languages. The man gestured and barked out orders in response.

Clarissa and Johanna observed for a few minutes at the edge of the crowd, and then Johanna shouted, "Saint Catherine's Monastery!" Her voice was lost in the uproar. Clarissa caught on: the man was playing the role of multilingual ride coordinator, orchestrating the apparent chaos into order and connecting people with common destinations. She joined Johanna and they shouted together, moving ever closer to the center as the crowd gradually dispersed in small matched clumps. They pushed and shouted until they were almost hoarse, and at last they were close enough to be heard.

When they had yelled "Saint Catherine's Monastery!" for what felt like the hundredth time, two men about the age of Johanna waved their hands in the air. The tall man nodded at them and gestured to Clarissa and Johanna, and then put out his hand. It took a moment for Johanna to understand. She fumbled around in a pocket until she located a coin among the few that Agnes Luc had given them. She slipped it into the man's palm, giving Clarissa a glance that said she hoped it was acceptable currency and a sufficient sum. He barely glanced at it, and then moved on to the next customers.

The two young men smiled at Clarissa and Johanna, bowing repeatedly, and then hurried toward the edge of the bazaar. Johanna started after them, but Clarissa grabbed her by the elbow. "They're Muslims," she whispered.

"What did you expect?" said Johanna. She started walking again toward the men. Clarissa followed, a step behind.

"I expected Christian pilgrims—like us!" she said. "They don't even speak French—and certainly not English."

"It will be an adventure," Johanna declared. Never had she spoken truer words.

The distance between them and their guides was rapidly closing. "But what if they're not really going where we want to go?" Clarissa fretted aloud. "And how do we know they won't try to kill us while we're sleeping?"

"We don't," said Johanna. "But God will protect us." She picked up her pace and glanced back at Clarissa. "Aren't you the girl who ran away from home?" she called over her shoulder. "Try to have some courage."

Clarissa felt her face redden. She was furious that Johanna refused to take seriously the risks of two young Christian women heading off into the Egyptian desert with strange Muslim men they had just met—with whom they couldn't even communicate. But, seeing no other choice, she kept following her friend.

The two men began gesturing and speaking rapidly in Arabic as soon as they spied an older man, who rushed forward to greet them. He bowed and flashed a long, mostly toothless smile at Clarissa and Johanna. Then he touched the headdress that wrapped his forehead and flowed down to cover his neck, and gestured with palms up toward Johanna and Clarissa's. He touched the sleeve of his robe and then gestured at theirs. Then he laughed.

Clarissa felt herself relax a bit and managed to laugh, too. Except for the differences in material and color, all five of them were dressed essentially the same. *Maybe this won't be so bad*, she told herself.

"Asim," said the older man, thumping twice on his chest with his right palm. He nodded toward the taller of the young men and said "Kafele," and then identified the other as "Madu." Johanna and Clarissa introduced themselves. Then they all smiled at one another again for a long while, realizing with some awkwardness that they had reached the end of their conversational capacity.

"Oh," said Johanna, reaching into her pocket for another coin, hoping once again that it would be acceptable. She handed it to Asim, who turned it over and over, causing Clarissa to wonder if he had ever laid eyes on a French coin before. Asim smiled again, put it in a pocket in his robe, and gestured for them to follow him.

§

Johanna forged ahead, following closely behind their three guides, while Clarissa moved cautiously a few paces behind her. After several steps, Johanna turned around to look at Clarissa, wrinkling her nose and placing her hand over it. Clarissa was confused about the gesture, until a repulsive, overpowering odor assaulted her. She widened her eyes in terror when she located its source.

Three shaggy, lumpy, towering brown creatures, with big calloused knees and oversized feet and nostrils, stood tied to a wooden rail at the edge of the desert. Johanna stopped to look them over and give Clarissa time to catch up. Then they walked tentatively together, hand in hand, toward the odd beasts. One bellowed a rude greeting, the second hurled a bundle of spit in their direction, and the third let loose an avalanche of odoriferous dung.

If they had not heard every Christmas of their lives the story of the Three Wise Men from the East following a star to Bethlehem to honor the Baby Jesus, Clarissa and Johanna would not have known about camels. Nor would they have been able in their wildest imaginations to conjure such creatures. The ones in the Christmas story were noble and picturesque— gentle silhouettes following a bright star against a backdrop of shimmering dark-blue sky. Not at all like these ghastly beasts.

Clarissa's mouth dropped wide and stayed open so long that Johanna said, "You're going to catch sandflies."

"I'm not getting on one of those," Clarissa declared defiantly.

Johanna stood without moving for a few moments and gulped loudly. And then she began to laugh. Uncontrollably. She laughed so hard that tears came to her eyes. "Didn't I tell you it would be an adventure?" she said. Clarissa glared at her. "Would you rather walk to Saint Catherine's?" Johanna asked when she finally got control of herself. Clarissa shot her another icy stare and then started walking forward once more. A determined stride masked her fear and disgust.

The three men had each untied and positioned himself by a camel. Kafele ordered his to its knees and beckoned to Clarissa. Taking her hand, he helped her clamber up into the large saddle adorned with bright green and red tassels that sat atop the animal's monstrous hump. The camel swung its long neck around and put its face up to Clarissa's, lifting its large lips to reveal huge yellow teeth, startling her to the point that she almost tumbled from her precarious perch.

An array of aromas immediately overwhelmed her: a pungency that reminded her of the pine forests of England, sweetness like the lavender of the manor's garden, and a sharp spiciness that bore no hint of recognition to anything she had ever smelled before. Beside her were large baskets crammed with bottles and boxes and jars, each one filled with an herb or spice or oil. Together they created a feast of fragrance.

But none was strong enough to mask the overpowering stench of camel.

On Kafele's command, the dingy beast below Clarissa bellowed obnoxiously as it raised its backside in a cloud of dust, its crusty knees still on the ground, almost pitching her forward over its head and into the sand. Once she regained her balance—though not yet her composure—she looked over and saw that Johanna was struggling at the same angle to stay on Madu's camel.

As the behemoth beneath Clarissa swayed and stood up fully, and she rose slowly and dizzily into the air, the import of being on the final leg of a holy pilgrimage caught up with her.

Still, she could not keep from giggling. Kafele looked up at her, thumped his camel on the chest, and said, "Quibilah." Clarissa repeated it as best she could, assuming it to be the beast's name. She and Kafele exchanged smiles as he took the reins and led her into the desert.

Madu followed, leading Johanna on a slightly larger camel that was also laden with spices and oils, as well as a basket of food and a large bladder filled with water. Asim had mounted his camel, the largest of the three, with more grace than Johanna and Clarissa combined had mustered. Lashed beneath the baskets at its sides were a rolled camelhair tent, wooden poles, and three rugs.

Her three guides, Clarissa surmised, were spice merchants heading east to sell their wares. She wondered if Kafele and Madu were brothers—and if Asim was their father. Or perhaps a grandfather? She figured she would never know.

The day was already slipping away, and the small caravan moved slowly over the sand. Clarissa immediately bemoaned the black wool habit that swathed her in discomfort and seemed to absorb every ray of the beating sun. She couldn't help coveting the white, airy robes of her traveling companions. When the sun set a few hours later, releasing the suffocating heat, she whispered a prayer of thanks. And she gratefully received the gift of a vast dome of sky splashed with shades of pink and orange, fading to a deep aqua and finally black. When the last tinge of color disappeared, the sky filled up with more stars than Clarissa had ever before seen.

That evening the odd little group sat on the ground and shared a simple supper. The bread was coarse and dry, but Clarissa found the yogurt surprisingly delicious—until Johanna commented, "It must have been made from camel's milk." Clarissa immediately dropped her bowl into the sand. At the end of the meal, Asim stood in front of Clarissa and Johanna with his palms toward them and his ten fingers extended. Uncomprehending, they nonetheless nodded and smiled.

The men pitched the tent for them and slept under the stars a short distance away. Clarissa and Johanna dug nest-like pits in the sand under the canopy with their hands, trying to create comfortable space for their stiff backs and sore muscles. The temperature had plummeted and Clarissa, shivering, now longed for some of the day's heat. She and Johanna crawled into their places, too exhausted to say a word, trying to draw the last hint of warmth from the sand.

Clarissa, curled up tightly, felt enshrouded in a desert silence that was deeper even than the silence of the convent. She tried to let it seep into her soul, to invite her into prayer, to bring her peace. But she could not get her cold, exhausted, aching body comfortable. Worse, she was unable to tame and settle her mind. She realized that her fear that their new companions might kill her in her sleep was unfounded: she would *never* fall asleep in this desert.

She chastised herself for coveting the men's lightweight clothes. She scolded herself for being fearful and deficient in faith. Already feeling bad enough about her failings, she hated to add cursing to her sins, but the situation seemed to call for something stronger than she was used to uttering. She had heard Kafele and Madu blurt out an Arabic word whenever something went wrong—a rein tangled or precious water spilled. She didn't know what the word meant or how to spell it—only how it sounded. She muttered the unfamiliar oath into the night, then followed it with "Even the tent smells like a camel!" She felt immediately better.

Johanna laughed and beamed a smile to Clarissa in the dark. "Go to sleep, my dear friend," she said. "And dream of camels." Clarissa wished it would be that easy. But long after she heard Johanna quietly snoring, she was still tossing and turning in the desert sand.

§

Galorian and Aminah arose early the next morning, ready to push on. Galorian was grateful that his young companion was an uncomplaining traveler. She smiled more and more often at him, and a comfortable ease settled between them. He hoped that she felt completely safe in his care.

A few hours after they set out, they reached the great Nile River. Galorian allowed Thane to drink his fill, while he and Aminah, who was wide-eyed with wonder, dangled their feet in the cool water under a towering palm tree. After sharing another meal on the bank, they moved on and got their first glimpse of the gem that was Cairo.

As in Alexandria, the sprawling bazaar in the heart of the city was the center of activity. It hummed with the frenzy of quick and loud transactions as fish and fruit, fabrics and fragrances were exchanged. Galorian listened carefully to the medley of languages that ricocheted around the market, but he heard none that he comprehended. He knew that Aminah understood the Arabic that predominated, but he had neither the words nor the heart to explain to her his plan. He could hardly expect her to negotiate her own removal from him.

She began to shake again, as if sensing their impending parting, or perhaps because being in a city reminded her of home and all her losses and made her fearful. Hand in hand, they wandered among the tables of the bazaar until the sun began to crawl toward the western horizon. As both night and despair began to close in on him, Galorian muttered to himself, "This is going to take a miracle." Deciding to give up for the day, he led Aminah back toward the busy street where they had entered the market.

He heard the voice of a man speaking French. Galorian rushed to him.

Earlier in the day they had passed the merchant, posted in a prominent spot, but Galorian had not heard him speak. After greetings and introductions, the man named Pascal, who stood behind a table stacked with delicate lace, explained that he was born and raised in France but had lived in Cairo for more than thirty years. His father had traveled throughout southern Europe and northern Africa, carrying Pascal and his brother to distant locales to sell his fine French lace. As a boy, Pascal was fascinated and enamored with Egypt, and as a young man he moved the trade to Cairo when he inherited his father's business.

Galorian shared highlights of his own story, explaining with near desperation his need to find someone to care for Aminah. "You're in luck," said Pascal. "My brother also lives in Egypt, and he runs just the place that can help. It's a crossroads for good, God-fearing people from many places. I'm sure he can find someone to take the girl."

Though the journey was longer than he had hoped, Galorian received the directions from Pascal with relief. He embraced the kind Frenchman, expressing his gratitude. As Galorian turned, leading Aminah by the hand, Pascal shouted after him, "Don't worry, it will work out. My brother is a holy man. He believes in miracles!"

§

Quibilah had a lot to say. He seemed to keep up a running conversation with himself. Clarissa heard odd burbling noises constantly rumbling around in the vicinity of what she assumed to be the beast's stomach, which from time to time burst out in raucous belches from deep in his throat. After a sleepless night, she passed the time the next morning trying to come up with words to describe this constant camel self-serenade, hoping to keep herself awake and avoid tumbling off his back into the sand.

At lunch, she and Johanna compared their thoughts. "Not exactly a bellow," Johanna commented about the camel clamor to which she also was subjected.

"More persistent than that," observed Clarissa.

"And loud," added Johanna. "Like a rumble of rolling thunder that doesn't quit."

"Like the incessant wail of a mad goose with a stomachache strangling in a deep pool of gurgling water calling out over and over for help."

"Exactly."

A few hours later, as they settled in for supper that evening, Clarissa grinned at Johanna and said, "I've got it. It's a gurgleburblegrumblerumble."

Grinning back, Johanna asked, "How long did it take you to come up with that?"

"All day."

Johanna laughed. "Well, at least you had something to do."

On that second night of their journey from Alexandria, Clarissa received her bowl of yogurt with a smile, determined not to offend her hosts.

She pantomimed to indicate that she would enjoy it later in the tent—though she had no intention of eating it. She ate a piece of bread, chewing painstakingly and for a long time to make it moist enough to swallow.

When the meal was finished, Asim stood in front of her and Johanna and held up nine fingers. Clarissa nodded this time with understanding, growing alarmed when she realized that the old man was indicating how many more days they had to travel to reach the monastery. "We'll never make it back in time to meet up with Pietro again," she lamented to Johanna before saying goodnight, forgetting the bowl of yogurt by her head that she had intended to dispose of in the dark.

Though exhausted from lack of sleep and the grueling trek—and determined to have a more restful night—Clarissa hovered for hours on the edge of wakefulness. Despite more tossing and turning, digging and burrowing, she still could not find a comfortable position in the sand. She envied Johanna's ability to fall asleep so easily.

Sometime in the hour before dawn, Clarissa turned over and stared into a face that was lapping up her yogurt with a long tongue. It looked scary and yet familiar. "Lizzie!" she shouted, her loud exclamation jolting Johanna awake. It took a moment for Clarissa to remember that Lizzie was on another continent entirely. She jumped up and tried to shoo away the monitor lizard. "Go!" she yelled, waving her arms wildly, bent at the waist in the short tent.

Johanna sprang up and joined her, hollering at the scaly beast that was about the size of a large dog. It ran in circles with Clarissa scrambling behind, still flapping her arms madly, and Johanna on her knees chasing them both, trying to drive out the repugnant reptile. Clarissa spied the half-eaten bowl of yogurt on the ground and hurled it at the lizard. "And don't come back!" she yelled as it fled out of the tent and into the last vestige of night.

Just then the tent collapsed on her and Johanna, burying them in a blanket of dusty camel hair. They were coughing and trying to get free when the men rushed over to check on the commotion. Clarissa noticed when they lifted the tent off of her that the corner was smeared with yogurt, and the still-not-empty bowl was in plain sight. She didn't know whether to feel worse about waking everyone or revealing to her hosts that she had ungraciously failed to eat the supper they had given her. There was no way to explain.

Johanna began cleaning up the disarray, but Clarissa sank into the sand and didn't move. Hot tears of frustration stung her eyes. She was exhausted, and nothing felt holy about this pilgrimage. The intrusion by Lizzie's cousin reminded her of how much she missed Jaxon, and soon she was caught up in painful longings for home, overwhelmed with memories of her mother and Josselyn, Nerida and Liliana.

Months had passed since Clarissa had succumbed to her rawest emotions. For several minutes, sharp pangs of sorrow and anger tormented her as she recounted her losses, feeling stabbed by the unfairness of it all. Quibilah bellowed at the rising sun, and Clarissa stuck her tongue out at him, for no other reason than she thought that doing so would make her feel better. Then she looked at Johanna accusingly and whined, "You told me when we conquered the Alps that the worst was over."

Johanna, smiling sympathetically, had one word for her in response: "Gurgleburblegrumblerumble."

Clarissa glared at her. "Are you saying that I sound like a complaining camel?"

"Exactly."

Before Clarissa could react, Asim began to chant in a melodious drone. Five times during the previous day, he had sung in this way. Each time he had pulled out the three rugs lashed to his camel, handing one each to Kafele and Madu. The men had then walked several steps away from Clarissa and Johanna, scooped up sand and rubbed it on themselves, stood and then knelt with their foreheads on their rugs, murmuring their prayers.

Clarissa was immensely grateful for this regular respite from the back of her cantankerous camel. But each time it happened, she and Johanna stood by awkwardly, unsure what to feel about the unchristian ritual and what to do with themselves while it was going on. That morning Johanna noted the obvious: their guides' times of prayer at dawn, midday, midafternoon, sunset, and evening coincided exactly with Lauds, Sext, None, Vespers, and Compline. She and Clarissa had opened their prayer books together each morning on this sojourn, but they had made no attempt to keep the hours of the liturgy that they observed at the abbey throughout the day.

Clarissa found Asim's chants immediately calming. Though she had a hard time admitting to herself that three male Muslim strangers were opening space and inspiring her to regular Christian prayer, she realized on that morning of the reptilian rampage that this was what would get her through the challenges of the journey. Minutes after the lizard scrambled away, at Asim's first call to prayer that day, the men knelt on their rugs while Clarissa and Johanna observed Lauds a short distance away. Facing the rising sun, they filled the awakening desert with the mixed murmurs of faith.

At breakfast, Asim grinned at Clarissa and handed her an empty bowl and an extra piece of bread. Then Kafele helped her back onto Quibilah. Before he could pick up the reins, Johanna gestured for him to help her up as well. His puzzled look turned into a smile as she settled into the saddle behind Clarissa, who was taken completely by surprise.

Kafele grabbed Quibilah's reins, climbed up on Madu's camel, and gave Madu a hand up. The two men moved to the front, leading Quibilah, with Asim on his camel behind them.

"I'm sorry about comparing you to a camel," Johanna whispered to Clarissa. "I was trying to get you to laugh and forget your troubles."

"I know."

"Lean back," said Johanna gently. "Let me be a wall for your sore back and aching spirit."

Clarissa sighed in gratitude for her dearest friend and leaned into her sheltering love. The camels took off in a trot. That night, after supper, Asim held up four fingers. Clarissa felt flooded with hope.

Sixteen

The trek across the desert felt like equal parts ordeal and adventure. On their third day, Kafele turned around to get Clarissa and Johanna's attention and gestured toward a point in the distance. Seeming to rise magically out of the sand and gleaming like brown gems in the late afternoon sun was a cluster of towering pyramids. Before long, the odd caravan passed by the lion-like Sphinx, which stared at them with a mysterious and unsettling smile. Overtaken by awe, Clarissa, who had talked non-stop in Alexandria, was rendered speechless by these wonders.

When they reached the Nile River, she gave a cheer, grateful for the abundance of water and the lush greenery around it. Their guides led the camels to drink at the bank. Clarissa—who never in her wildest thoughts as a child could have imagined laying eyes on this great river that saved the infant Moses in her favorite Bible story—paused to take in the wonder of it and the exotic beauty of the scene spread out before her. She wanted to tell Johanna what this moment meant to her, but she couldn't locate the words.

Pulled by the river's magic, Clarissa slipped off her shoes and waded in, careful not to be swept away by the powerful current. She dipped her hands in the water and gently pressed it to her face, which had felt for two days like it was on fire. Johanna soon stepped beside her. Clarissa splashed her gently. Johanna splashed back. Before long they were drenching each other, laughing wildly, releasing the tension of the long trek.

The ride into Cairo was short, but the sun's heat was so intense and the air so arid that their heavy habits were dry by the time they arrived on that bright Sunday morning. Asim, Kafele, and Madu headed straight for the bazaar at the heart of the city and immediately went to work setting up their wares on a conspicuous corner bordered by two busy streets. Clarissa and Johanna stood close by, taking in the sights.

"I hear French!" declared Clarissa after a few moments, amazed at their good fortune. She led Johanna toward a stall nearby, keeping her eyes on their three guides. The lace merchant named Pascal was just beginning to introduce himself when they heard chanting and turned to see a long procession coming down the street. A man in front carried a massive wooden cross festooned with colorful flowers. Following him were several other men wearing long black robes, gold crosses around their necks, and hats that reminded Clarissa of pillows. Behind them was a throng of men, women, and children, the youngest of whom were tossing flowers to onlookers.

"Coptic Orthodox Easter," said the French merchant.

"You're not a believer?" asked Johanna.

"I gave up church a long time ago, in France. Too elitist for my taste," he said. "And too serious." Clarissa recalled the sleepy and solemn Easter mornings she had spent in Gladdington's cathedral under the hawkish eye of Father Augustus. A shudder went through her as she remembered the man she had tried for so long to forget.

The huge crowd kept coming. "They'll march by the cave over there, where they believe Mary, Joseph, and the Baby Jesus lived while they were in exile in Egypt, fleeing from Herod's death decree," Pascal explained. Clarissa looked in the direction of the cave and felt an overwhelming desire to see it. "Then they'll go on to the Hanging Church—so called because the sanctuary is suspended over the gatehouse of an old Roman fort. Some call it the Staircase Church, because you can only get into it by walking up twenty-nine stairs." He described some of the church's most prominent features in detail.

"Go," said Johanna, smiling, to Clarissa, "before you jump out of your skin."

"Are you sure?"

"I'll stay here," said Johanna, "and make sure our friends don't leave without us."

Clarissa fell in with the throng, feeling swept up in the tide of resurrection joy. At the cave, she peered in and saw a burning oil lamp, the ground around it strewn with flowers. A chill of excitement raced through her as she stood at that place where Jesus himself had once lived.

She rejoined the procession, walking in silence through a colorfully decorated gate, across a courtyard flanked by bright mosaics, up the twenty-nine steps toward three carved wooden doors, and into the unusual church. The timber ceiling was steeply arched, and as Pascal had said it was intended to do, it made her think of Noah's ark. But what captured her attention was the high white marble pulpit. It stood on thirteen graceful pillars, representing Jesus and his twelve disciples. Carved on its stairs were a cross and a large shell. They were the same figures that circled the pillars of her family's manor in England. The symbols of home. She couldn't hold back the tears seeping from her eyes.

When people were packed into every possible space in the church, one of the patriarchs in a black robe stood and shouted a phrase from the front. The crowd thundered a response. Clarissa could not comprehend the words, but she recognized the cadence. She had heard that proclamation and response in the Gladdington cathedral every Easter morning of her life: "Christ is risen!" . . . "He is risen indeed!"

Clarissa raced out of the church and back to Johanna, saying breathlessly, "You have to go. My turn to stay." She pointed Johanna toward the sacred cave and the magnificent church. As Johanna turned, Clarissa spoke her name. Johanna looked back, and Clarissa grinned and shouted, "Christ is risen!"

Johanna grinned back at her. "He is risen indeed!"

§

Thane sank at times into sand up to his knees as he carried Galorian and Aminah across the Sinai wilderness. Galorian took spells leading his horse by the reins to lighten his load. A scorching sun beat upon them, creating an unquenchable thirst in beast and humans. They stopped at mid-day to wait out the worst of the heat in a thin shadow cast by a stray boulder. And then they rode again.

On the last full day of their journey from Cairo, the orange light that danced in the air suddenly turned gray, as if a curtain had been pulled across the sky. From atop Thane, Galorian stared to the west, trying to comprehend the shift. Soon the source of the mystery visited them with a fury.

The sandstorm plunged them into a blinding darkness. Galorian leapt from Thane and quickly lifted Aminah off and to the ground. He pulled on Thane's reins until the horse knelt. Then he sheltered Aminah under his body as the sand whipped him from all directions, swirling like a tornado of tiny pellets. Aminah cried, and Galorian crouched over her more closely to protect her from the sudden and painful assault.

In a few minutes the storm was over, moving east and trailing a blanket of sand in its wake. Aminah opened her eyes and smiled at Galorian, and he smiled back, grateful that they were unharmed. Then he cast his glance toward Thane.

The poor horse lay prone several paces away, his head on the ground, his hindquarters covered in a mountain of sand. He raised his head and struggled to stand, pawing at the ground with his front legs, but his back legs were paralyzed by the weight of the sand. After several tries, he set his head back down on the ground with what sounded to Galorian like a loud, defeated sigh. Galorian scrambled to his horse's side, and Aminah followed. With their hands they dug and scooped away sand until Thane was free. The great steed stood, shook his head and neighed loudly, and then collapsed back on the sand.

Galorian stretched out on his side, his head propped on his beloved horse's ribs, gently stroking the exhausted beast's neck. Aminah watched them for a while. Then she wordlessly curled up against Galorian, in the hollow created by his chest and his knees. And that's how the three of them slept until the sun reappeared in a yellow blaze the following morning.

§

By the time Johanna returned from the church, Asim, Kafele, and Madu had sold most of their spices and oils, saving only the jars in one basket on Asim's camel. The little group headed back to the desert to rest up for an early start the next morning.

Clarissa's resurrection joy faded quickly. The following day was the hardest of the journey for her. No astounding wonders rose before them. No cities or rivers punctuated the arduous, monotonous, and seemingly endless trek across the Sinai wilderness. Her face still burned as if on fire, and she could not slake her thirst during the searing heat of the day. She dreaded another night shivering and worrying about lizards and spiders, scorpions and jackals and hyenas—all the grotesque creatures she had been told inhabited the deserts of Africa. It felt like things couldn't get any worse.

The caravan stopped for sunset prayer. Clarissa was trying to sink into the peace of Vespers, to find comfort in images that were dramatically different from the stark landscape around her, as she and Johanna recited Johanna's favorite psalm: "The Lord is my shepherd, I shall not want. He makes me lie down in green pastures. He leads me beside still waters. He restores my soul . . ."

Their recitation was accompanied by the chants of their Muslim companions several steps away. The light was an unusual orange, the breeze carrying an odd sensation of portent.

Suddenly Kafele popped up and shouted at them in words they didn't understand. His arms animated with urgency, he yelled again. Clarissa and Johanna stared blankly. He gestured behind them at the western horizon and they turned. Clarissa couldn't identify exactly what she was seeing, but she knew that the gray wave that had blotted out the sun and was rushing toward them couldn't be good.

Kafele, Madu, and Asim ran toward the camels. Clarissa and Johanna followed, imitating the actions of the men. They burrowed into the sand as close as they could to Quibilah, who was kneeling on the ground. A great hurricane of sand passed over them, pelting them with stinging force. Clarissa closed her eyes as tightly as she could and clung to Johanna. Quibilah shifted slightly and bellowed with discomfort, but he stayed put.

Johanna quietly launched into completing the recitation of the psalm that had been interrupted by the sandstorm: ". . . Yea, though I walk through the valley of the shadow of death, I fear no evil; for you are with me . . ."

In a few minutes it was over. Thanks to the wall that Quibilah had created, Clarissa and Johanna were unharmed. Their companions, talking rapidly all at once, ran over to check on them. They all smiled and nodded several times to indicate that everyone was fine.

They stayed right where they were for the night. No one said much at supper. Clarissa, shaken by the storm, sick of dry bread, exhausted and aching and ornery, wondered just how much more of this holy pilgrimage she could take.

She endured the next day mostly in silence, trying to be thankful that no sandstorm or monitor lizard broke up the grueling monotony. That night, after supper, Asim stood up. He beamed a toothless smile directly at Clarissa and held up one finger. She melted into tears of relief.

§

Never was Galorian so grateful to see anything as he was to glimpse the tall, granite walls of Saint Catherine's Monastery, rising like a castle fortress amid the waves of desert heat. He rode Thane slowly around the perimeter and was perplexed to discover that the only entrance was a small door high off the ground. He saw no obvious way of reaching it.

"Hello!" he shouted up to the closed door. Nothing. He shouted again, this time in Latin. Then he tried French. "Anybody there?" He looked around and spied a rope. He pulled on it, hoping it was attached to a bell inside. After a few minutes, a monk opened the door, stuck out his head, and called to him in French, inquiring as to who he was and the nature of his visit.

Galorian decided to state his case simply. "I'm Galorian, a Christian knight," he called back, "and I'm seeking someone to care for a young girl I rescued in Constantinople." The monk pulled back inside and closed the door. For a few agonizing moments, Galorian was unsure what to do, wondering if their long and arduous trek had been in vain. But then the door reopened. By a series of ropes and pulleys, a large, sturdy basket descended along the wall and landed at his feet.

"Get in!" the monk shouted. "One at a time." Galorian placed Aminah carefully in the basket, reassuring her with words she didn't understand when he caught the fear in her eyes. "Afraid," she said to him, gripping her gold bracelet for courage as the basket made its ascent. The monk helped her out at the top, and Galorian saw her look down at once to make sure he was following.

Galorian secured Thane to the wall, promising to come back down with water and food as he gently stroked the neck of his faithful, bone-weary horse. Then he climbed into the lowered basket for his turn to be raised up to the door. "What an entrance," he commented as he stepped out of the basket at the top, stomping clouds of dust off his boots.

"Yes," said the monk, introducing himself as Father Alain, the abbot of the monastery. "We are isolated and have many enemies. This protects us—and allows us to lower food to the hungry nomads who find their way to us." He pointed to the machicolation, a parapet with large openings in its floor, which projected over the monastery's entrance. "When we have to, we use that to pour boiling olive oil on our attackers," he explained. "We have a lot to protect."

"We come as friends," said Galorian quickly. "Your brother sent us." He described his encounter with Pascal at the Cairo market, reporting that his brother had been kind and helpful and sent along warm greetings to Alain. Galorian was unsure how much to say about Aminah and decided only to mention that her parents had been killed in the siege of Constantinople. He also wondered what to say about himself and settled on stating simply that what he had witnessed there had created a great uneasiness and some doubt about his calling as a knight.

"Nasty business in Constantinople," said Alain, shaking his head and gazing at the floor. "Unforgiveable." Then he looked again at Galorian. "You're welcome here," he said warmly. "It's a good place to rest and pray and listen for the whispers of God for a while. And many holy and compassionate people come through. I will find someone suitable to care for the girl."

Then Alain turned to Aminah and spoke to her in Arabic. She smiled and responded. The abbot looked back at Galorian and said, "She wants to thank you. She thinks you are a very good man." Aminah then repeated the word that she had used to describe Galorian when they were learning words together on their journey. Alain laughed. "And handsome, too."

Galorian blushed. Recognizing that they had been through so much together and that this was their first opportunity to communicate easily, he thought that he should have many things to say to Aminah. But he felt oddly at a loss for words. He wasn't yet ready to tell her why they had come to the monastery. "Please tell her that I think she is very brave," he said. "And pretty, too." And then it was Aminah's turn to blush.

Father Alain called to a young monk to bring some bread and figs for the travelers. "You can stay among the brothers, participate in prayers and meals, and walk freely wherever you wish," Alain said to Galorian. Then he explained that monastery protocol forbade any association between men and women, beyond Father Alain's welcome and attention, and that he would escort Aminah to a room in a small wing reserved for female pilgrims who visited.

Galorian smiled reassuringly at Aminah as she left with Alain. The monk soon returned. "She fell asleep at once," he reported." Shall I take you to your room?"

Galorian followed Alain to a small cell with an inviting bed. But, despite the arduous journey, he was more curious than tired. He left his shield in the corner and took off exploring the many halls in the vast complex. He soon discovered what Father Alain had meant when he claimed that the monks had a lot to protect. The monastery held a vast collection of ancient holy manuscripts and icons, some of the latter more than five centuries old. Images of the Madonna and Child, and of Christ's nativity and crucifixion and resurrection, adorned the walls. Special niches were reserved for the icon of Saint Catherine, the monastery's namesake, and the oldest known Christ Pantocrator, an image of the haloed Savior with his hand raised in blessing.

Galorian wandered into a cavernous room covered in gorgeous mosaics depicting scenes from the Bible. He paused to admire each one, along with the ornate chalices and reliquaries on pedestals in front of them. Remembering how many similar sacred objects had been destroyed by his fellow Crusaders in Constantinople, he felt a great sorrow sweep over him.

He heard footsteps. "Would you like to see our Crusader art in process?" asked an approaching monk, who introduced himself as Brother Matthias, the oldest of the monastery's iconographers. He stroked his very long gray beard as he said to Galorian with a grin, "I have to tuck it into the rope cincture around my waist when I work."

He led Galorian into a large alcove. Two monks with brushes in hand were seated and hunched over small tables. They kept at their work, not pausing to acknowledge the visitor.

"The ancient Egyptians made portraits of their dead by applying hot beeswax colored with pigment to panels of wood," explained Matthias in a whisper. "These were attached to the covered faces of their mummies, to identify who was where. After the First Crusade, we European monks adopted this encaustic process, one of the world's oldest painting techniques, in the making of our icons. Saint Catherine's Monastery is a center for the development of this rare and beautiful hybrid art form, the stunning result of a blending of Christian images and Muslim genius."

It took a moment for Galorian to take this in. "I'm glad to know," he said in a hushed voice to the old artisan, "that one good thing has come from the meeting of cultures that has otherwise led to such bloodshed and devastation."

§

The final day of their journey seemed endless to Clarissa. When the high, fortress-like walls of Saint Catherine's Monastery finally came into view around sunset, Asim shouted and prodded his camel into a fast trot. The other camels followed, bouncing along at a rapid pace, causing Johanna to grip Clarissa tightly, and Clarissa to utter the Arabic oath again.

When they reached the monastery, Asim was already on the ground, still shouting, walking with his arms outstretched toward a monk with a broom in his hand. The two men kissed each other on both cheeks, like long-lost brothers. Asim looked up at Clarissa and Johanna and talked rapidly, too excited to remember that he was explaining in a language they didn't understand.

When Asim paused, Johanna spoke to the monk in French, hoping he would understand her. "We've been inspired by Saint Catherine," she said, "and we're very glad to be here."

He smiled warmly and responded, also in French. "I was born near Paris—though I haven't seen France in nearly four decades. You are welcome here." Clarissa sighed with relief at the realization that someone at the monastery spoke their language.

The monk turned to Asim, Kafele, and Madu, addressing them in Arabic. All three spoke at once, shouting questions. The monk smiled again at Clarissa and Johanna. "There are many things they would like to know," he said. "Let's go inside. I've swept away enough rocks for today."

Clarissa believed that, after their desert escapades, nothing could surprise her anymore. But nothing had prepared her for the basket ascent to the monastery's high entrance. The monk insisted that she and Johanna go first.

"I might as well get it over with," Clarissa said under her breath. She closed her eyes as tightly as she could and gave her best try at being fascinated rather than terrified. Johanna, of course, bubbled with excitement about the unusual entrance when she arrived at the top.

It took some time to get everyone up the wall and inside. When they were all together again, the monk ushered them into a small room and invited them to sit. "I'm Father Alain," he said to Clarissa and Johanna. "I'm the abbot of the monastery. After thirty-some years here, they've finally given me a turn as spiritual leader." He laughed. Clarissa liked Father Alain immediately. He spoke with a humble, gentle spirit, and his eyes sparkled with warmth and welcome. "There's much to discover and discuss," he said.

Asim, Kafele, and Madu handed Alain an array of jars and vials and boxes. "Ah," the abbot said gratefully, "the best cumin and cardamom in Africa!" One at a time, he opened the jars and took a sniff, as fragrances of saffron and cinnamon, anise and mint, and spices Clarissa couldn't identify permeated the room. "The cook will be very pleased," Alain proclaimed.

He opened a box that contained a white resin, releasing the pungent aroma that had reminded Clarissa of the pine forests of home. "Frankincense," he said to her and Johanna. "We burn it during prayer and use it for burials."

He reached for another box and laughed heartily when he saw what it contained. "I knew you wouldn't forget," he said to his three friends. From among dozens inside, Alain pulled out what appeared to Clarissa to be a brown pebble the size of a wren's egg and held it up. She had no idea what she was seeing. "It's a mixture of cinnamon and myrrh, boiled with honey, rolled into pellets and then hardened," the abbot explained. "You see, we tend to get lots of grit and sand in our bread here, from the stones that grind our flour and . . . well . . . because we live in a desert."

Clarissa silently concurred with his dour assessment of the local bread. "These tend to wear down our teeth," continued Alain, "and make our mouths smell . . . well, let's just say, less than pleasant." He examined the pellet in his hand. "Sucking on one of these every day helps. And, I've also been told that myrrh is a cure for baldness." The abbot touched his smooth head and, laughing again, added, "Though I have yet to see evidence of that."

A young monk appeared at the door and handed Father Alain a tray heaped with olives, figs, pomegranates, and cheese. Clarissa worried that the others could see her salivating. "Please," said the abbot, gesturing for her and Johanna to help themselves first.

Asim was fidgeting in his seat, clearly growing impatient. He voiced another eruption of questions. Father Alain spoke to him briefly in Arabic. Then he turned to Clarissa and Johanna and switched again to French.

"They want to know where you are from, what your life back home is like, how you pray, why you have come to Saint Catherine's." He laughed once more. "And they'd like to know how it was for you riding the camel."

"We have some questions too," said Johanna. She thought for a moment and then, joining the monk in warm laughter, said, "I guess they're the same ones . . . except for the camel." Father Alain, moving with ease between Arabic and French, translated as they spoke to one another. In the course of their conversation, Clarissa and Johanna learned many things about him and their traveling companions.

The abbot was the son of a lace merchant, who had carried him and his brother Pascal along on his trade forays to exotic lands. "Pascal?" asked Johanna, assuming that it was more than coincidence that they had met a French lace merchant in Cairo by that name.

Alain, delighted, confirmed that they had indeed met his brother. "Just yesterday, I received a good report about him from a knight who also encountered him at the Cairo market," he said. And then he continued with his story.

"I saw many wonderful places when I was a boy, but I fell in love with Egypt. And with God. And so I have been here for most of my life." Alain felt honored to be the abbot of the monastery, but he was just as happy sweeping away rocks, a task he believed every monk was obligated to take a turn doing. Though it was a challenge to meet every one of the hundreds of pilgrims who visited each year, he considered it his personal duty to welcome each guest to Saint Catherine's.

The kind abbot had known Kafele and Madu since they were young boys. Their parents were mercilessly killed during the Third Crusade by a marauding band of English knights, who swept through the Sinai Peninsula on their way to the Holy Land. Asim, the boys' grandfather, had raised them. For generations their nomadic Bedouin ancestors had kept the monastery stocked in spices and oils for the monks' religious rituals and for food preparation and preservation. Asim inherited and grew the trade to include the markets of Cairo and Alexandria, and eventually the entire northeast corner of Africa. His two grandsons had hopes of expanding it even farther. "It may not be obvious," said Alain, "but they are very successful spice merchants."

Alain then repeated the men's questions to Johanna and Clarissa. Johanna spoke up, offering profound thanks to Asim, Kafele, and Madu. "We are novices at the Benedictine Abbey in Liège, France," she began. She explained their life at the convent, their times of prayer and their ministry with people who suffered from leprosy. She described in detail the landscape of France. "We don't have camels," she said, and the room erupted in laughter.

Clarissa noted that, as with the merchant Pietro, Johanna chose not to reveal that they were English. It dawned on Clarissa that, for Johanna, her life began in earnest when she arrived at the convent in Dover. It did not seem to Clarissa like a good time to talk about her days as a spoiled child in an English manor—or the circumstances that had led to her escape from it. The group of new friends talked together for a long time. Finally, Father Alain said, "I can't imagine that there could be, but are there any more questions?"

"I have one," piped up Clarissa. "What does Quibilah mean?" She waited for the abbot to translate. Kafele smiled at her and spoke a word.

Alain looked back at her and said, "It's an Egyptian name that means 'peaceful.'"

Clarissa, delighted, smiled back. "I have one more." But she hesitated and then said, "No, never mind." She would probably never know the meaning of the Arabic oath she had employed in her worst moments on their journey.

Kafele spoke next. Alain translated. "He is saying 'We will come to France. We will visit you. Next year.'" The abbot smiled. Asim nodded and grinned. Madu stepped forward and handed Clarissa and Johanna several bottles and boxes of spices, which they received gratefully. Clarissa felt a pang of sadness knowing that, despite her new friends' intentions in the moment, she would never again see these three good and generous men who had faithfully guided them through trial and travail across the Egyptian desert.

Seventeen

"We must climb the mountain," Clarissa whispered to Johanna on their second morning at Saint Catherine's. The only women present for Lauds, they were sitting behind a screen in the chapel, out of sight of the monks. The monastery's rules were strict for women pilgrims, who were limited to their wing of cells and this chapel and were forbidden from any contact with the monks, except Father Alain. Clarissa was feeling revived after a day spent mostly sleeping, in a simple but comfortable bed with, thankfully, no sand in sight. Her day-long nap had been interrupted only by times of prayer and simple meals of bread, cheese, and fruit that were slid under the doors of the women's cells morning and evening.

Though the holy place where they sat was commonly known as Saint Catherine's Monastery, the official name was The Sacred Monastery of the God-Trodden Mount Sinai. It rested in the shadow of the great biblical mountain upon which the prophet Moses received the Ten Commandments from God. "Has this heat made you lose your sense?" was Johanna's whispered response to her friend's declaration about climbing it. But by breakfast Clarissa had convinced her.

They rested another day, gathering their strength, and set out in the cool of night with a loaf of bread and a sheep bladder filled with water. The climb was steep, and they moved slowly under an eyelash of a moon and a blanket of bright stars. About halfway up, the crude switchback path gave way to a mountainside of boulders. They scrambled on hands and knees, making slow progress, their long habits an encumbrance. For a brief moment, Clarissa wished for a camel.

Just before dawn, they reached the top and, panting, settled triumphantly into a cleft on the eastern side of the mountain. A strong wind buffeted them as they huddled close together, their arms wrapped around each other. Clarissa thought of the night they had spent on the cliff when she first arrived at the convent in Dover, watching the stars fade as the sun rose and the dolphins began to dance. She felt flooded with gratitude and anticipation.

But one corner of her heart still ached with homesickness and grief. On the top of that holy mountain, she felt Josselyn's spirit close to her. *Oh, what would you think of me now, dear sister?* she wondered. *Would you be proud . . . or alarmed?* Fingering the cross that still hung around her neck, next to the leper's bell, Clarissa whispered into the wind, *Say another prayer for me, Josselyn.*

Soon a brilliant point of scarlet light appeared on the eastern horizon. And before long the whole Sinai wilderness was flooded with sunlight. Clarissa drank in her first panoramic view of that stark, barren land, the heat already radiating in waves from the desert floor just minutes after dawn. The thought came to her on that sacred mountaintop that this would be a perfect moment to be granted some spectacularly deep insight about life, some stunning revelation of wisdom and truth.

But any hope of that was interrupted by a blunt proclamation by Johanna: "If I had lived here, it would have been a forty-year-long gurgle-burblegrumblerumble." She and Clarissa had begun employing the term in every situation that made them want to bellow and holler like camels—which was often on this holy pilgrimage.

"What do you mean?" asked Clarissa, turning to face her.

"I would have whined, just like our ancestors in the faith did when they were here." Johanna began to describe the oppressive slavery the Hebrew people suffered under in the pharaoh's Egypt.

"I know the story," interrupted Clarissa. "Josselyn used to tell it to me." She shared with Johanna then what their stop on the bank of the Nile River had meant to her, and how she had loved as a little girl the story of the floating basket and the baby who grew up to lead his people to freedom, chasing a blazing pillar of fire.

"And between slavery in Egypt and freedom in the Promised Land," said Johanna, "they spent forty long years in this wilderness . . . because God thought they had a few things to learn." She swept her arm over the vast expanse of hot sand and rocks below them. "They muttered and groaned and complained. Some wanted to go back to the security of slavery, awful as it was, rather than face the uncertainty of freedom in this barren place."

"How did they survive?" Clarissa wanted to know. She was already beginning to wonder if she could make it through a week and couldn't imagine spending forty years in this searing, desolate spot.

"Every day God rained down bread from heaven. They called it manna, which means 'What is it?' They gathered it up and ate it."

"The same food every day for *forty years*?" said Clarissa. "I would have grumbled, too."

"But God took care of them. And as long as everybody took only what they needed, it worked. If they got greedy and took too much, or hoarded it, the manna rotted and sprouted worms. But if they shared, they always had enough. Every day."

Clarissa pondered that for a moment and then, beginning to grasp the astounding truth, said, "So, in the emptiness of this place, with nothing else to rely on, they depended on God. And they didn't have to fight or steal or use each other, because everybody got a fair share." She sighed. "And nobody went hungry."

"They were the people of God," said Johanna, "a community committed to living by faith, dedicated to the common good." Clarissa's mind was racing. "Before they left this wilderness," Johanna continued, "God told the people to put a piece of manna into a jar and carry it with them to the Promised Land, to remind them of how they were supposed to live. But of course they soon forgot, and greed took over. Before long the powerful ones were overworking and exploiting their neighbors and forcing some to be slaves. The rich expanded their huge mansions and massive vineyards, while the poor suffered in tiny hovels and starved. Wars broke out over food and land.

"God sent the prophets to try to set things right. They cried God's tears, railing against the rich, demanding food for the hungry and justice for the widows and orphans and exiles. But the people didn't listen, and they just kept getting meaner and greedier. So God said, 'I guess I'll just have to go down there myself and show them what compassion and justice look like.'" Johanna sighed. "And they crucified him."

She shook her head sadly. "It seems some people will do *anything* to protect their greed. The lessons of this wilderness were lost long ago, and I'm not sure they will ever be recovered."

Her mind still racing and her heart beating wildly, Clarissa whispered, "I wonder where that jar of manna is now."

§

Galorian, haunted by his thoughts and unable to sleep, wandered the monastery at night. He sat often in one of its dozen dark chapels, praying for wisdom and a clear path. Three nights after his arrival, he took a detour from his usual route and stumbled upon a most unusual and startling holy site at the heart of the great building. He ran his hands along the symbols etched on the room's walls, a motif of crescents and stars. No crucifix dominated the front. Instead, Galorian saw a pulpit unlike any he had ever seen. Steep stairs led up the ornately carved wooden tower. Beside it was an equally elaborate prayer stool.

In the morning, Galorian asked Father Alain about it. "Ah, you've discovered our mosque," said the abbot.

"A mosque within a Christian monastery?"

"Six hundred years ago, Mohammed frequented this site, befriending the monks, whom he considered his brothers in faith," explained Alain. "The monks requested the protection of the prophet. In the year six hundred and twenty-six, Mohammed issued an immunity covenant, commanding his fellow Muslims to share their crops with the monastery brothers, to guarantee their safe travel throughout the area, and to refrain from taxing or making war on them.

"Saint Catherine's would not have survived without it. In gratitude, the brothers converted one of the monastery's chapels into a mosque in the year eleven hundred and six, soon after the First Crusade. The Muslim pulpit, or minbar, is the only one of its kind in the world."

"And is the mosque used now by Muslims?"

"Unfortunately, it is not properly oriented toward Mecca for prayers," explained Alain. "But on special occasions, it gets used by local Bedouins, who bring us supplies and help to maintain the grounds here, like their ancestors before them did through all the centuries of the monastery's existence."

That night, when all the monks were asleep, Galorian returned to the exotic holy room. He lit a few candles and then sat and gazed at the great Muslim minbar. His eyes grew moist as he remembered his night in the cathedral before his dubbing into knighthood. As he had prayed then for strength to be a valiant knight, he prayed now to follow God's will, wherever it might lead him.

For a brief moment, the candles flared and burned more brightly, shooting off sparks of light. Then Galorian heard a voice speak to him: "You have heard that it was said, 'You shall love your neighbor and hate your enemy.' But I say to you, Love your enemies and pray for those who persecute you." Galorian recognized the words as ones spoken by Jesus during his most famous sermon, addressed to a hillside of followers trying to understand the nature of the kingdom of God.

But how do I love my enemies? he wondered. He had read those words from the Gospel of Matthew many times before, but he thought that night that he had never really heard them. Images flashed through his mind: the streets of Constantinople running with blood, the rampage of destruction in the cathedral, Silas's fear, Aminah's terror, the dead knight in the alley. He bowed his head and prayed to God to be given the clarity and conviction to respond to the unsettling command of love.

§

The next morning Father Alain told Galorian about the brotherhood of knights vowed to protect sacred shrines and pilgrims on the route to Jerusalem, hoping that this might be the answer to the young man's search for his future. "The Knights Templar are granted the coveted Saint Catherine's cross," the abbot said. He described the cross set within a wheel, a symbol of the one that the Roman Emperor Maxentius had used to try to break the monastery's brave namesake. "It would be an honor to join them."

"Thank you, Father," responded Galorian, his words breaking with emotion, "but I won't be enlisting in their endeavor. As clearly as I have just heard your voice, our Lord spoke to me last night." He related to the abbot the struggle he had endured in the dark quiet of the mosque.

"Of all the words of our Savior," Galorian declared, "these are the most difficult: 'Love your enemies.'" He paused for a moment and then asked, "Was he misguided? Was he naïve?" He paused again, pondering his own questions, while Alain waited in silence.

"Surely Jesus Christ was not naïve about the power of the Roman Empire to torture and kill him on a cross," Galorian continued. "And yet he refused to fight back against his enemies—and forgave them even as he took his last breath." He shook his head in consternation. "How, then, can we stab and skewer and slay people he commanded us to love? Is it possible to love your enemy and thrust a sword through his heart?"

Galorian paused once more and stared into the sympathetic eyes of the old monk. "If you can embrace a mosque within your walls, then surely I can embrace Muslims within my heart."

Father Alain smiled. "Real truth," the wise abbot said, "is always big enough to recognize that there is more than one truth."

Galorian fell to his knees then. "Father, will you hear my confession?" Right there, he spilled the story of killing the knight who was attempting to rape Aminah. "There must be a better way than all this killing and destruction," Galorian lamented. "There must be some way other than war." He gazed up at the holy man who hovered above him. "I want to throw my life on the side of brotherhood and peace, as our Lord did."

Father Alain bent down, offering absolution with the words "Galorian, beloved child of God, you are forgiven," sealing them with the sign of the cross on Galorian's forehead. Pools of tears gathered in Galorian's bright blue eyes. "Arise now," said Alain gently. Those words pierced Galorian's soul. The last time he had heard them was when his king had declared him a knight.

He rose slowly and turned to leave. Then, turning back, he said, "There's one more thing." Alain followed him as he walked into a small open courtyard. Galorian had remembered seeing there an array of tools used in the monastery's olive grove and gardens. He picked up a heavy spade. "When I became a knight," he said, "I was told that if I should ever disgrace my calling, the spurs would be hacked off my boots and my shield would be hung upside down as a sign of dishonor. I am choosing to dishonor my calling as a knight in order to honor my calling by God."

Galorian handed the spade to the monk, who hesitated for a moment. But then Alain lifted the tool and made repeated blows against Galorian's spurs until they separated from his boots. Alain then dipped his right thumb into a large urn filled with olive oil and placed drops on the forehead of the former knight three times, offering a blessing for strength, wisdom, and peace.

When he got back to his room, Galorian picked up his shield from where it leaned in the corner and turned it upside down. He smiled. He had never felt so free. That evening he exchanged his knightly garb for the simple, hooded, brown cassock of a monk. He walked barefoot to the mosque inside the monastery to spend the night offering prayers of gratitude and petitions for a clear path and a peaceful spirit.

§

The night after she and Johanna climbed Mount Sinai, loud sobbing in a room down the hall startled Clarissa awake. It had been so quiet during their stay on the women's wing that they had assumed that they were the only ones there. Clarissa groaned silently, her muscles aching from the climb, her body craving sleep. She knew that, unlike her, Johanna would sleep through almost anything, and she needed to go.

She walked to the door of the room, knocked softly, and then peered inside. She was surprised to see a young girl curled up on the bed, trembling and gripping a thick gold bracelet that wrapped her left wrist. Clarissa walked in, sat down next to her, and began stroking her long, dark hair.

The girl, with tears flooding down her cheeks from eyes that matched the color of her hair, sat up and threw her arms around Clarissa. Startled, Clarissa didn't know what to do except hold her, repeating over and over,

"Shhh, it's going to be all right." After a few minutes, she began reciting psalms of comfort and continued until the girl fell back to sleep.

In the morning Clarissa told Johanna about her discovery and asked Father Alain about the girl. He told her what he knew about the orphan named Aminah. "She was brought here by a kind knight," explained Alain, "who is looking for someone to care for her." Clarissa left the conversation feeling pity for the girl, who was scared and seemed all alone in a desolate part of the world. For the rest of that day, Aminah inhabited Clarissa's heart and prayers.

That night, when the rest of the monastery was sleeping and there was little chance of encountering a monk, Clarissa snuck down to the library. As in the abbey in Liège, she was anxious at Saint Catherine's to learn as much about saints and church history as she could. Descending the steps to the vast treasure trove of archives was like entering another world, and as always before, the knowledge she discovered flooded her with amazement and resolve.

"There were desert fathers and mothers!" she whispered excitedly upstairs a few hours later, gently shaking a sleeping Johanna, who made no effort to resist the interruption.

"Yes," said Johanna, sitting up drowsily, "they were my favorite discovery in the abbey library in Dover." She tried to rub the tiredness out of her eyes as she declared, "Quite an odd bunch."

"One named Syncletica sold everything she had, gave all her money to the poor, and lived as a hermit among the tombs," said Clarissa.

"And Theodora of Alexandria lived with monks in this Egyptian desert disguised as a man, a secret she kept until she died," added Johanna.

"I can beat that. Daniel the Stylite stood alone on a pillar near Constantinople for thirty-three years. Even though his feet were covered in ulcers and his scanty clothes were blown away by the wind, he kept on celebrating the Mass and healing the sick and handing out spiritual advice on top of that pillar."

"Do you understand why?" asked Johanna, who was now fully awake and glad to be talking about one of her favorite subjects. "The Christians before the desert mothers and fathers, the ones who lived in the first three centuries after Jesus, followed his commands to love God and their enemies, and were thrown to the lions for refusing to bow down to the emperors or fight in the army. But in the fourth century, when the emperor Constantine the Great declared Christianity the official religion of the Roman Empire, the followers of Jesus faced a challenge far worse for the faith than martyrdom.

"Most gave in to the seductions of greed and power and violence. Fortunes were amassed and devastating wars were launched in the name of God. So a faithful remnant escaped to the desert—*this* desert—in order to keep the true witness alive. They came here to remember what their ancestors had learned in this same wilderness after they were freed from slavery: how to live simply and peacefully and justly for the good of all.

"Most of them started out as hermits, but they soon learned that the power of their faith and witness grew when they lived together in communities, sharing what little they had and taking care of each other. And so they eventually got around to building monasteries. Like this one—one of the oldest in the world. All the religious orders, including us Benedictines, can be traced right back to this desert." She smiled warmly at Clarissa. "All it takes is a few faithful souls to keep the witness alive."

§

Taking short naps throughout the day, Clarissa abandoned her efforts to sleep at night, deciding it was less important to her than exploration, which she could do only under the cover of darkness if she wanted to remain undiscovered. She anticipated and savored her nightly journeys, tiptoeing into the corners of the vast holy compound to see what she could learn about the monastery's early inhabitants, and what unimagined wonders awaited her.

One night she wandered down into the deepest, darkest bowels of the monastery in search of the remains of Saint Catherine. Feeling her way along a rough wall, her heart pounding, she turned a corner and gasped as she bumped into someone. "Excuse me!" she blurted into the dark. As her eyes gradually focused, she had to stifle a scream of horror. Standing in front of her was a skeleton, dressed in black church vestments, a rosary in its hand, a crucifix around its neck, and a cap emblazoned with a white cross perched on its skull. The plate at its feet identified him as the monk Stephanos, a sixth-century hermit who lived on Mount Sinai near the cave of Elijah the Prophet.

Clarissa had stumbled upon the charnel house, a crypt below the monastery's Chapel of Saint Trifonio. Behind the frightful monk, lit by candles, was an eerie mountain of skulls, centuries' worth from the men who had lived and prayed within the monastery walls. She left quickly, feeling the hollow stares of the saints following her.

In another chapel she found the sprawling roots and limbs of the bush that Father Alain had told her about, appearing to sprout from atop a large stone altar. "Saint Catherine's was built on one of the most sacred sites in all of history," the abbot had explained. "The monastery contains the bush that burned with fire but was not consumed when God spoke through it to give Moses his call to be his people's liberator."

"But that was so long ago!" Clarissa had responded.

"Yes," said Alain, "but this very rare type of rose bush, found only here in the Sinai wilderness, sends out roots and regenerates itself and can live for thousands of years."

Clarissa removed her shoes, as Moses had done on this very spot of holy ground centuries before. She reached up and touched the gnarled roots of the miraculous bush. *Is the fingerprint of Moses deep in there?* she wondered. *The fingerprint of God?*

She recalled the conversation she and Johanna had shared on their walk down Mount Sinai a few days before. "I want to tell you my favorite part of the story about Moses," Johanna had said. She began to relate the tale of the midwives Shiphrah and Puah. Clarissa interrupted and explained that Beatrix had told her about the two brave women who refused to bow to royal threats and saved all the newborn Hebrew boys the pharaoh had commanded them to kill.

Johanna nodded and continued. "The pharaoh's next move was to order that all the boy babies be thrown into the Nile to drown. You know the story of Moses's mother, Jochebed, who turned that river of death into a river of life by setting her son afloat in a basket among the bulrushes. The basket was discovered by the pharaoh's daughter, who took pity on the baby and decided to save him. And the baby's own sister, Miriam, stepped out from her hiding place on the river bank and offered to find a Hebrew nurse for the baby. So her brother Moses ended up being raised by their very own mother."

Johanna sighed. "Everybody knows about Moses. But almost nobody knows that he lived to be a prophet because of five courageous, creative, and clever women." Clarissa considered this as she and Johanna reached the end of their descent from the mountain. "And to think," Johanna had said as the monastery shimmered into view, "the pharaoh didn't even consider girls important enough to bother having them killed."

§

Clarissa pondered the wonder of that story again now as she stood quietly in the shadows of the Chapel of the Burning Bush. She pictured God appearing to Moses on this very site, tapping him to take up the mantle and lead the Hebrew people out of slavery. "But I don't speak well," Moses had demurred. "I stutter."

Clarissa felt God urging her, too, onto a path that was unknown and frightening. She knew, as apparently Moses had, that a great deal would be required of her. *But I'm only a girl*, she thought. In her imagination she heard the voice of Johanna repeating, "But aren't you the girl who ran away from home?"

Clarissa smiled then, trying to dispel her fear, remembering those five women who had saved the life of the prophet and changed the course of history. She recited their names, lighting a candle for each from the flame of the altar's lamp: Shiphrah, Puah, Jochebed, Miriam, and the pharaoh's anonymous daughter. And then she heard the voice of God speak to her as surely as he had spoken to those women and to Moses: "Find your sisters and set them free."

My sisters? Clarissa could think only of beloved Josselyn and the enormous loss of her. *Who are they? And how can I set them free when I don't know what freedom is?* She felt doubt gnawing at her, but she stayed by the sprawling bush, kneeling now, her heart open, her eyes glistening with tears. She gazed at the large oil lamp on the altar, whose dancing flame always burned. *Like the pillar of fire that blazed all night and showed the way*, she thought.

She began to pray. *Please, God, help me. Make plain what you want me to do. Show me the way. And give me the courage of Moses, and the women who saved him, and blessed Saint Catherine.* When she finished her prayer, Clarissa got up. She walked out of the chapel with Johanna's words echoing in her heart: "And we too have been anointed."

Though she didn't yet know the way, Clarissa felt a renewed determination to trust that God would open a clear path for her and guide her on it. She smiled, her steps light as she made her way back toward her room. But her newfound confidence was immediately shaken when she took a wrong turn in the maze of corridors and became disoriented. She tried not to panic as she groped her way along, hoping for a familiar landmark.

A chapel she had not seen before appeared in front of her. Its wooden door was different from the others. Curious, she opened it and peered in. She noted the strange symbols along the walls, lines of crescents and stars instead of the usual accent of crosses. She slipped inside and took a step toward the unusual pulpit at the front.

But then she saw, in the flickering candlelight, the hooded cassock of a monk bent in prayer. She gasped in surprise, unused to encountering others on her late-night forays throughout the monastery. When he heard her, the monk looked up and began to turn his head toward her. Clarissa felt a chill run down her spine. Then she quickly ducked out of the chapel before their eyes could make forbidden contact.

Eighteen

Clarissa looked in on Aminah whenever she left or came back to her room during her nightly ventures. The young girl was often awake and in tears in the middle of the night. Clarissa held and soothed and rocked her back to sleep. When Clarissa ran out of psalms to recite, she sang some of Jaxon's bawdy ballads, overcoming her embarrassment about the raspy, off-tune quality of her voice and taking comfort in the fact that the girl had no idea what words she was singing.

On the morning of Clarissa and Johanna's last full day at the monastery, Father Alain summoned them. They expected a simple farewell and were stunned when he shared what he had to tell them.

"You're sure?" said Johanna.

"Yes," said Father Alain. "Aminah sat in that chair where you're sitting now, with her eyes fixed on the floor, and said to me, 'I'd like to go live with the nuns.' I've been checking on her every morning since she arrived, and I know that you've been watching out for her, comforting her when she gets frightened."

"But we don't speak the same language," said Johanna.

"And she's a Muslim," added Clarissa.

"Yes," said the abbot. "I had imagined a nice Muslim, Arabic-speaking family for Aminah, but I have not been successful at locating one willing to take her. I reminded her that you are Christians who live far away in France and don't speak Arabic. And I asked her, 'How will you communicate with them?' She said in a whisper, 'We communicate.' I told her that I would speak with you about caring for her."

Clarissa and Johanna had no need to discuss it. The quiet girl who seemed so vulnerable and alone had captured their hearts and become a regular part of their conversations and prayers. Clarissa was aware that, although Aminah was only a few years younger than she, the girl had stirred maternal feelings in her. With one silent glance exchanged between them, Clarissa and Johanna gave their mutual assent.

"We would be honored to have her," Johanna declared. "There will be challenges to overcome, but we can give her a good home at our convent in Liège. If you believe it's a good plan, we would be happy to carry her with us when we leave tomorrow." Father Alain gave his joyful blessing to the arrangement.

"Before we go," said Clarissa, "may I ask you something?" She was too curious not to ask, and she knew that their imminent departure meant that any reprimand she might receive for disobeying monastery rules would soon be left behind. "I came across a chapel." She described its unusual symbols and pulpit. She didn't mention the monk she had glimpsed there.

"So you found our mosque," said Alain, in a tone that, to Clarissa's relief, registered delight more than reproach. He told them the story of Saint Catherine's centuries-old relationship with Muslims and the miracle of a mosque at the heart of a Christian monastery. "We try to embrace all truth here," said the abbot, as Clarissa tried to fathom the import of his words.

§

Father Alain went in search of Galorian. The abbot shared with him the good news that two nuns from France were willing to care for Aminah. Though Galorian was aware that his request countered centuries of protocol at the monastery, his first response was, "May I meet them?"

"I've met them," replied Alain. "They are devout and kind. You can trust that Aminah is comfortable in their company and happy to be among women. They will take her to their convent in Liège and take good care of her there." Galorian was relieved to hear the monk's words. But he also felt a stab of sorrow at having to release into the care of the nuns the winsome young girl who had been his constant companion across sea and desert.

The next morning, Alain brought Aminah to Galorian for a farewell. She gazed into Galorian's eyes with a broad smile. "Happy," she said in English, placing her hand over her heart, as she had done when she first met him and told him her name. Galorian smiled back at her and, mirroring the gesture, said softly, "Happy."

The smile slowly faded from Aminah's face, and tears began to slide down her cheeks. "Sad," she said. Galorian tried to keep his own tears at bay as he said, "Yes. Sad." Aminah ran to him and threw her arms around his waist, and they held on to each other for a long time.

Galorian walked with her to the monastery entrance, where the basket
waited to carry her down the wall. As Alain lowered the ropes, Galorian
peered far below at the two women dressed in black habits and white headdresses, waiting in the horse-drawn wagon that Alain had arranged for
them. When the basket reached the ground, they got up and helped Aminah
out. She walked to the corner of the monastery where Thane, eating and
resting after Galorian's morning ride, was tethered. Galorian felt a wave of
poignant sadness wash over him as he watched the young girl stroke his
beloved horse's neck for the last time.

Aminah turned away from Thane and walked slowly back to the
wagon. The two nuns helped her up, and she settled in between them. As
the driver guided the wagon away, Aminah waved up at Galorian. Though
he was too far away to see her face clearly, he was sure that she was smiling.

The two nuns waved at him as well, and he waved back. Their gesture
prompted a memory of Josselyn, the way she always stood outside their
home and waved until he was out of sight whenever he had to rejoin his
comrades in the forest or leave on knightly escapades. A chill of sorrow
sliced through him.

When Galorian could no longer see the wagon, he turned back into
the monastery, grateful that Aminah would be well cared for in France, but
weighed down with the grief of another loss.

§

"She can't stay here," Mother Agnes Luc pronounced sharply. Clarissa, Johanna, and Aminah were standing in front of the abbess's small desk in the
convent in Liège, just back from their sojourn at Saint Catherine's. Their
return had been uneventful compared to the journey there. Crossing the
Egyptian desert in a wagon was slow but far more comfortable than on the
back of a camel.

During the trip, Aminah had sat quietly with her eyes closed when
they stopped for prayers. She slowly revealed the English words she knew—
pointing at various objects along the way and naming them. "The knight
must have taught her," said Clarissa to Johanna. Aminah entertained them
with her amusing portrayals of an array of emotions, and smiles passed
readily among them. On their first night in the desert, Clarissa had declared,
"I think she feels safe with us," as Aminah slept soundly in her arms on the
back of the wagon under a bright half-moon.

The merchant Pietro, exactly where he had promised to be, was delighted to see Clarissa and Johanna again and anxious to hear everything

that had happened to them. If he was bothered by their new companion, he didn't let on. "There's plenty of room in the boat," he said, and Aminah received his gregarious welcome with a characteristically shy smile.

Thankfully, the Mediterranean was calm for their crossing. With Clarissa's encouragement, Aminah overcame her reticence about partaking of the lavish food on board, and when they arrived at Pietro's mansion in Italy she settled comfortably into a canopy bed. After an overnight there, the merchant was anxious to return to France with the cloth he had acquired in Egypt. He carried Clarissa, Johanna, and Aminah through the Alps and bid them farewell a short walk from Liège.

But now it seemed their luck had changed. Though Clarissa took some comfort in the fact that Aminah couldn't understand Agnes Luc's words, her glare and disdainful tone were unmistakable. "But isn't hospitality our holy calling?" asked Clarissa, stunned by the abbess's response.

"Yes, but the Muslims are the enemies of Christ."

"And didn't our Lord command us to love our enemies?"

The abbess sighed. "Our Lord was not acquainted with the terror of Muslims."

Clarissa protested, "But his enemies tortured and nailed him to a cross in an excruciating death. Surely that's terror, if ever there was—"

The Mother Superior cleared her throat loudly to interrupt. "The girl cannot stay," she repeated, before a fit of gasps and coughs silenced her.

Clarissa sighed and decided to try a different approach. "But how can she come to know our blessed Savior and turn from her heathen ways unless we take her in and show her the truth?" The old nun was unmoved. Silence reigned between them for a moment.

"Then we'll go with her," Clarissa declared, shooting an uncertain look in the direction of Johanna. "We promised to care for her, and we can't just put her out on her own in a country where she knows no one and cannot speak the language."

Mother Agnes Luc shook her head and stared at the floor for a few moments, closing her eyes and folding her hands as if in prayer while her breathing calmed down. Then she looked up at them and said, "There's a house. On the coast. Not far from Calais. The church owns it and has made it available to us. We thought we would use it for times of rest, but nuns don't rest much." Clarissa had to stifle a smile as the abbess continued. "You two and the girl can stay there until you find another home for her." Her tone grew even sterner. "You are not to leave the house, do you hear me? We'll send food every other week."

As dusk began closing in, Clarissa slipped out of the abbey and headed toward the forest, intent on a long walk to clear her troubled spirit of its misgivings. She knew that she had pushed too far this time, that she and Mother Agnes Luc would never see eye to eye and the convent would never again be her home. As she walked, she heard an unmistakable, comforting screech and gazed up at the oak tree where she had last seen Saint Catherine. There sat her loyal owl, welcoming Clarissa back from her long journey.

Catherine was not alone. Her suitor, now mate, peered down at Clarissa and added his own tremulous chorus of joyous screeches. Small, downy wings flapped around them, as a nest of curious, big-eyed owlets tried to get their footing and push their way to the front edge for the best view. Clarissa laughed out loud and then exclaimed, "What a beautiful family you have, Saint Catherine!" She felt immediately better.

She began reciting one of her favorite passages of Scripture, from Jesus's long mountaintop sermon in the Gospel of Matthew: "Look at the birds of the air; they neither sow nor reap nor gather into barns, and yet your heavenly Father feeds them. Are you not of more value than they?" As a young girl, Clarissa had heard and loved those words, as well as the ones that followed about the lilies of the field: "they neither toil nor spin," but God clothes them in beauty and glory. "Will he not much more clothe you?" asked Jesus.

When Clarissa had come across and copied the same words in the abbey's scriptorium, she committed them to memory. She believed their promise: "all these things"—food, shelter, clothing—will be given to those who "strive first for the kingdom of God and his righteousness."

When she was a pampered child in a comfortable manor, she had every reason to trust God's provision. She had everything she needed or could possibly want. But now a thick cloud of doubt began to envelop her. She felt her delight over Catherine's new family evaporate, as envy seeped into her spirit. *Could I possibly be jealous of a bird?* she wondered. She was. She gazed up at the happy family in their cozy home, nestled in the hollow of a tree as if held in the palm of God. And she felt suddenly abandoned.

The words of Jesus that had once comforted her now seemed like a mockery, and she vented her growing anger at God. *What about the hunger and neglect Johanna and Nerida endured? Where were you when my own sister suffered unspeakable violation? What about the pitiful, dying lepers in their rags outside the gate? Have you forgotten them? Are they beyond the promise of your provision? Are they somehow less valuable than the birds and the flowers?*

With an intense and anguished fear gripping her soul, Clarissa fell to her knees and began to weep. *How can I trust that you will take care of me? How can I believe that your words aren't just empty promises? Are they true only for people with enough money to make them true?* She curled up on the ground, feeling all alone as the night closed in around her and a chill breeze began to stir the leaves on the trees.

And then she felt a warm embrace. Johanna had found her. Clarissa cried unashamedly as her dear friend held and rocked her at the base of the oak tree. Through her sobs, she spilled the gripping fear and doubt. "It's so unfair," she said. "How can we expect people who have nothing to trust God?"

"But don't you see?" said Johanna, wiping her friend's tears. "They're the ones who trust him the most. They're the ones who know they need him."

"But how can we trust his promises when so many good people are hungry and poor? Jesus's words seem like a lie." As soon as she had leveled the charge, she regretted it. But she couldn't change how she felt.

"Do you remember what Jesus said exactly?" asked Johanna, as she repeated the verse that so troubled Clarissa: "Strive first for the kingdom of God and his righteousness, and all these things will be given to you as well." Clarissa sniffled a few times and then focused on the face of her wise friend. "It's not a promise to individuals," said Johanna. "It's a promise to a community . . . to the people of God. There's more than enough of everything we need to go around." Clarissa thought carefully about the words as Johanna continued.

"*Righteousness* means 'right relationship.' It means living justly, as God intended us to live, knowing that we are all created in his image. Do you remember the lesson of the Sinai wilderness?" Clarissa nodded sheepishly. *How quickly I've forgotten,* she thought. *Just like the people who spent forty years there learning.*

"People—not God—break the promise, making others suffer because of their envy and violence and greed," continued Johanna. "But if we live according to the kingdom, treating each other as God's equally beloved children, then no one is hungry or poor. Then God's audacious promise holds."

Clarissa was sitting up straight by the time Johanna finished speaking, a glint of brightness having returned to her eyes. "Do you think we can do it?" she asked. "Do you think we can create a place where people want to follow Jesus so much that they're willing to share and take care of each other and live in peace as equals?"

Johanna answered without hesitation. "I'd sure like to try."

§

Unsure of what the future would bring them, Clarissa and Johanna spent the day before they left the abbey spreading farewells. They thanked each of the sisters for welcoming them and accepted gifts of food. They took bread to the people hovering outside the gate, receiving their gratitude and offering blessings.

That night, Clarissa stopped by the oak tree to say goodbye to Catherine and her brood. With a little push from their parents, the four owl chicks were learning to flutter to the ground and hop back up to their nest. But they hadn't yet mastered flying, and Clarissa understood that Catherine's place was with them. "I'll miss you," she said, surprised at how deeply sad she felt that their long and unusual companionship had to come to an end. Catherine, for the first time since they had met, swooped down and alighted on Clarissa's arm. She offered a plaintive farewell that was something between a trill and a purr, and then she flew back to her youngsters in the nest.

Clarissa didn't sleep at all that night, her heart racing and her soul churning with a mix of excitement and dread. In the morning she and Johanna started out, returning the way they had come when they first set foot in France, with Aminah between them. They walked for stretches and accepted rides when they were offered.

Clarissa's spirit was expectant as they headed northwest toward the sea. She couldn't tell what Aminah was feeling, and she didn't have the language to ask. She wondered how much the girl understood and whether she felt fear or disappointment that the convent would not be her home. Then it dawned on Clarissa that Aminah had shown her how to ask. She turned down the sides of her mouth as she said, "Sad?" Aminah shook her head. Clarissa cowered and asked, "Scared?" and Aminah shook her head again. Then Aminah grinned at Clarissa and said, "Happy." Clarissa was relieved that Aminah seemed glad simply to be in the company of her and Johanna—and seemingly unaware of just how uncertain her future was.

They arrived late in the afternoon a few days later at the coast. They passed through a small village and wound their way up a steep path to an old stone house at the edge of an overgrown pasture. Clarissa raised a storm of dust as she pried open the thick door of the house, vacant but for a small army of mice that scurried into the corners at the sound of their footsteps. She threw open the shutters, breathed in the salt air, and sighed, "We're home."

They peeked in all the corners of the house, which had a large central room with a hearth, and a table and chairs, surrounded by four smaller rooms. "Perfect!" proclaimed Johanna. And then they went right to work sweeping away the dust and sand and cobwebs, aiming to make the place comfortable before night set in. They found straw in the barn in the adjoining pasture and made several trips back and forth, carrying piles of it for makeshift palettes. They shared a loaf of bread and then, tired from their travel and labor, headed toward sleep around sundown. But Johanna interrupted that plan, saying, "Let's go see!"

They followed her up a stony path that ran between the house and the barn along the pasture, ending at a bluff that jutted out over the sea. It was so high above everything around it that it afforded a panoramic view in all directions. They swept their eyes over the property's small apple orchard, large pond, and swatch of pine forest. England was right across the channel, and Clarissa thought that if she looked hard enough, maybe she would see the abbey perched on Dover's chalky cliffs. Johanna interrupted that thought, exclaiming, "We can see both sunrises and sunsets here!"

"You sound like someone who's planning to stay a while," said Clarissa, grinning, and Johanna grinned back. Then they heard an unmistakable sound in the sea below them.

"Dolphins!" they shouted at the same time, pointing out for Aminah the beautiful creatures squeaking with delight as they leapt the breakers crashing toward the shore. "The amazing thing," said Johanna to Clarissa, "is that they may be the very same ones we saw from the cliff across the channel the night we became friends."

As the dolphins and the sun disappeared, they walked back to their new home under a crescent moon that hung in the night sky like a smile. Clarissa knew that they would put no effort into finding another home for Aminah. She slept long and peacefully that night—for the first time in many months.

§

Clarissa and Johanna agreed that Aminah's Christian formation and language lessons were their first priority. "But which language do we teach her?" asked Clarissa.

Both she and Johanna acknowledged their desire to make English the official tongue of the house—to return to the words that were most familiar and reminded them of home. And Aminah had already incorporated a number of English words into her vocabulary. But Johanna stated the obvious: "If we're going to get to know the people around us, we must speak their language."

And so each morning, after shooing out the mice, reciting morning prayers, and sharing breakfast, they broke open the books they had borrowed from the shelves of the abbey library in Liège and taught Aminah

French, while they worked on polishing their own. Like Clarissa, Aminah loved words and picked up new phrases quickly. The hours spent with books were happy ones for them all.

After two weeks, just as provisions in the house were getting dangerously low, two novices from the abbey appeared in the doorway with food as promised. "I'm going to go back with them," whispered Clarissa to Johanna that night. "It's time to talk with Mother Agnes Luc again."

Clarissa understood that their petition was likely to be rejected, but she also knew that they had to pursue their dream. She rehearsed the conversation in her mind several times on the way back to Liège. On her first morning there, she went to see the abbess about the house. "It would just be empty, except for the mice, if we weren't there," she pointed out. "We'll use it until we can buy it."

Mother Agnes Luc let out a dismissive and condescending laugh, forcing Clarissa to see the absurdity of her proposal. *What was I thinking?* she wondered. *Women can't buy property. And we'll be lucky if we can figure out how to feed ourselves.* She sighed in embarrassment, unable to shake the word *preposterous* out of her head.

"And just how do you propose to earn money?" asked the abbess, a frown plastered on her face. Clarissa was stunned that she had ever thought that the difficult old woman would consider letting them have the house just because no one else was using it.

"By selling bread and beer," she replied. It was the first thing that came to her, and it flew out of her mouth without thought. She hoped that the abbess wouldn't remind her of how often her bread refused to rise and her beer tasted like foamy vinegar.

Agnes Luc inhaled a huge wheeze and exhaled another scoffing laugh. "You cannot possibly think that you can take care of yourselves." Clarissa assured her that they could. She pleaded and begged until the abbess relented. As with their request to journey to Saint Catherine's, Clarissa believed that she was finally willing to say yes to get her and Johanna out of her sight and away from the abbey.

"We'll pay when we can," Clarissa said, whispering "Thank you" as she bowed before Agnes Luc. The bell still hanging around her neck jangled as it struck the floor, and Clarissa had to stifle a smile. The Mother Superior glared at her. As Clarissa turned and walked toward the door, Agnes Luc shouted after her, "I'm not in the least responsible anymore for what happens to you!"

Clarissa opened the door and stepped out into the hall. Mathilde, who worked in the abbey garden now, appeared from around the corner and hastily handed her a large basket. It contained five heads of cabbage, half a dozen cucumbers, and what appeared to be the abbey's entire crop of carrots. "There are some seeds from last fall's gourds beneath them," whispered the young woman, smiling. "If you plant them now, you'll have some food for the cold months."

Clarissa embraced and thanked her, grateful as she was taking her leave to be reminded of the generosity that resided within the abbey walls. Despite her difficulties with Mother Agnes Luc, Clarissa realized with immense thankfulness that during her time in the abbeys in Dover and Liège, she had encountered many women who had taken to heart Benedict's encouragement to live "with hearts overflowing with the inexpressible delight of love."

Still in Clarissa's embrace, Mathilde leaned in more closely and spoke softly into her ear. "It's a secret vote," she said. "The bishop sits in the confessional, and the sisters pass by one by one and tell him through the lattice screen their choice. An abbess is elected for life." She released Clarissa, then turned and disappeared down the long hallway.

Clarissa opened the convent's iron gate and walked out slowly, turning over in her mind Mathilde's words. Only the bishop knew who among the community had actually been elected abbess by her sisters. Clarissa realized then how anxious she was to be away from this place that, despite the strength of the women inside, was ultimately under the often-invisible but always-ironclad control of churchmen. She knew she was as happy to be away from Agnes Luc as she was sure the Mother Superior was to be permanently rid of her and Johanna. She took one look back. Then she stepped with confidence onto the forest path leading to the road that ended at the coast.

She grinned when she heard a familiar shriek. Catherine, her mate, and their brood were flapping above her, the little ones seemingly happy to be on a journey, trying out their newly feathered wings. Clarissa sighed. "Now I'll have to give you *all* names," she said, laughing.

She was anxious to see her friends waiting by the sea and to tell them about her conversation at the convent. Once inside the shelter of the forest, she picked up her pace. "Into the wilderness then," she declared, her eyes gleaming with hope as she threw off the head covering that marked her as a future nun.

When she arrived at the house by the sea, Clarissa blurted out the good news. "We have a home!" she announced to Johanna and Aminah from the doorway. They smiled broadly and clapped in response. Then Clarissa fell into a seat at the table and sighed, "Now what are we going to do?"

Nineteen

Galorian lingered far longer than he had anticipated at Saint Catherine's Monastery. "God has given you a humble and gentle spirit," Father Alain said to him a week into his stay. "You are welcome to stay as long as you like."

The former knight framed his days with rides on Thane after Lauds at dawn and before Vespers at sunset, taking advantage of the cooler parts of the day. He added wonderings about Aminah to his daily thoughts about Josselyn. He spent an hour each morning studying passages of Scripture that he had learned since childhood, many of which he had memorized. But the words spoke to him differently now. *How had I been so mistaken for so long?* Galorian wondered, recalling his years of preparing for war in the name of the Prince of Peace.

He was particularly moved by an image that had been preached by the prophets Isaiah and Micah: "They shall beat their swords into plowshares, and their spears into pruning hooks; nation shall not lift up sword against nation, neither shall they learn war any more." Galorian found great joy in the monastery gardens and olive orchard where the prophets' image became real for him, as his hands that had wielded sword and shield now plowed yielding earth and pruned fruitful trees.

After a few weeks of instruction and observation with Brother Bernard, the rotund monk who had tended the monastery grounds for more than four decades, Galorian became the keeper of the bees. He enjoyed the task of cutting the wax from the tops of the honeycombs and gathering the sweet treasure from the hives. He was content to abandon the lessons of war in order to learn the agriculture of abundance.

A long, triangular garden jutted into the desert, an oasis surrounded by barren wilderness and rugged granite peaks. "How did ever you get a garden here?" Galorian wondered aloud.

Bernard laughed. "Many monks hauled a great deal of soil from far away over many generations," he explained. Wooden barrels caught what little rainfall fell, and troughs directed melting snow off the mountains into large clay pots for storage. The result was a splendid and totally unexpected garden.

Of particular fascination to Galorian was the plot dedicated to the dye plants the iconographers needed for their spectrum of colorful pigments. Galorian had not forgotten that their technique of encaustic painting was born of peaceful Christian and Muslim cooperation, and he desired to make a contribution to their art. As he had spent much of his childhood obsessed with birds, he now brought the same curiosity and attention to learning about dyes.

In the center of the garden was a cluster of weld, commonly known as the dyer's weed, with tall stalks of bright yellow flowers. Dotted among these were saffron crocuses in a shimmering yellow-gold shade, and safflowers resembling the thistles of England but bright orange in color—one of the world's oldest crops, according to Bernard. Surrounding them was a circle of low, sprawling woad plants, producing the indigo needed for the deepest blue pigments.

Trails of madder, an evergreen with red roots, climbed the garden walls. Scarlet resin was harbored in the tap roots of the pungent giant fennel, also known as stinking gum or Devil's dung. Dominating one corner of the garden was a tree filled with pomegranates, loaded with hundreds of brilliant red seeds. Next to it stood a gnarled shrub of henna, its leaves a source of reddish-brown dye—a discovery, said Bernard, which ancient Egyptians had applied in their cosmetics.

Not everything the iconographers needed could be found in plants. Clusters of scale insects called kermes clung to a scrub oak in another corner. The parasitic bugs were easy to harvest, as they attached to one branch and never moved, feeding on the tree's sap. The dried bodies of the females were bright crimson in color.

More exotic even than the insects to Galorian was the bucket of sea snails that Bernard had gathered on a journey to the Mediterranean. The slimy creatures lived inside spiny shells and possessed glands that secreted mucous of a rich purple shade. They were most likely to emit the dye when poked—a task known as "milking the snails." It was not Galorian's favorite chore.

He was constantly spreading flowers, roots, leaves, the rinds of fruit, and the bodies of bugs beneath the hot desert sun to dry. These he and Bernard crushed into colorful powders with mortar and pestle. They melted the beeswax that Galorian cut from the honeycombs and mixed each pigment carefully. Galorian was largely an observer in the last step of the process, not yet a master of the delicate art of proportion.

After three months of work in the garden, Galorian made a request of Brother Matthias, who agreed to take him on as an apprentice iconographer. The former knight embraced the art of making icons as a holy calling, observing and studying and praying for several weeks before dipping a brush into the pigments. Creating eternal objects of sacred beauty, Galorian believed, was the new path that God was opening for him.

His teacher was kind. After viewing Galorian's first attempt, which looked like nothing more than colorful lumps of wax on a piece of wood, Matthias said gently, "It takes time. None of us could do this when we first tried." But Galorian's second effort was no better. Nor his third. His icon of the Blessed Virgin possessed small eyes and such oversized cheeks that she looked a bit like a fish taking in sea water.

Galorian saved Matthias from having to tell him the sad truth. "I've decided to return to the garden," he announced late one afternoon when he showed up at the usual time for a lesson. "I miss the physical work."

Matthias responded generously, "It is as holy a calling to tend the dye plants as to paint the icons." Galorian grinned at him, and they both laughed. Then Galorian went in search of Thane for their nightly ride. They trotted into the desert as the sky transformed into a palette of brilliant hues: crimson and orange, with clouds in rich shades of purple and aqua streaked across the broad expanse. Galorian laughed again. As he urged Thane into a canter, he uttered into the wind, "Only one Artist is a true master."

§

Clarissa was ecstatic that Saint Catherine and her family had accompanied her all the way from the abbey to the coast, not least because they kept the mouse population under control. Summer was well under way, with too little left of the growing season for Clarissa and her housemates to cultivate a serious garden. But they spent an afternoon together on their knees, opening the warm, pliant earth between the house and the pasture with their hands, planting the seeds from the abbey's gourds. Before long, delicate green vines began to take over their humble patch of earth.

While they waited for the fall harvest, they had their fill of carrots and cucumbers and cabbage soup. They kept to the rhythm of the convent, punctuating their days with shared meals and prayer. During the latter, Aminah sat quietly, listening to the psalms and recitations, always retiring to her room for several minutes when they were over.

Early one morning after Lauds, Clarissa caught a glimpse of the young girl on her knees, her black cloak spread beneath her and her forehead bowed to the floor. Clarissa paused and listened. She didn't comprehend the words, but she could not mistake their fervency. Egyptian men offering praise to Allah in the Sinai wilderness was something she had come to accept in exchange for their guidance and protection, but a girl doing the same in her Christian home on the coast of France felt like quite a different matter.

Clarissa cleared her throat. Startled, Aminah sat up at once. "I'm praying," she said tentatively. "I watched the path of the sun to decide which way. Mecca is over there." She nodded in the direction in which she faced.

Clarissa realized then that their shared prayers had not been enough, that she had mistakenly assumed the impact they were having on Aminah, and that it was time to begin the girl's Christian formation in earnest. "Aminah," she said, "I want to introduce you to the One True God."

"Who is that God?" asked Aminah.

"The Father of our Lord Jesus Christ," explained Clarissa, "who died to save you from your sins and"—she said it gently—"your wrong beliefs."

"Sins? I'm only eleven," said Aminah. "And I already have a God."

Clarissa measured her words carefully. "But, Aminah, surely you know that your religion is violent. Muslims have spread terror far and wide, murdering thousands of our faithful Christian Crusaders in the name of your god Allah."

As soon as Clarissa had pronounced the holy name, Aminah was ready with her response. "But surely you know that Christianity is a violent religion," she said, mimicking Clarissa's tone. She continued haltingly, a child thrust into an adult conversation, grasping for the words to explain a complicated truth in a language not her own. "Your Crusaders invaded our land . . . destroyed our homes and stole our property . . . killed us . . . all in the name of your One True God."

Tears spilled down Aminah's cheeks. "Is your terror more—" She paused, clearly groping for a word that she could not find. "Does it hurt less?" she said finally. "Let me tell you what your Christian Crusaders did to me." She choked out phrases she couldn't complete. "My parents and brothers . . . if not for the knight who saved me . . ."

Sobs were wracking her body. Clarissa walked over, knelt, and took Aminah in her arms, rocking her as she had on the night they had met. Clarissa had heard from Father Alain the bare-bones version of her story, but Aminah had not until that moment tried to speak to Clarissa about the trauma she carried in her body and soul. Sharing it was so difficult that Clarissa imagined Aminah would never speak of it again.

Aminah held out her left arm to give Clarissa a close view of the gold bracelet on her wrist. "My mother gave me this on my eleventh birthday," she said. "Do you see this?" She rubbed her finger along the elegant raised flourishes shaped into a heart at the center of the band. "They're Arabic letters. They spell *Salaam*. It means *peace*. Islam is a peaceful religion. Just like you say your Christianity is a peaceful religion." She sighed. "Muslims and Christians, the same: not all who claim to follow do so in truth."

Clarissa was stunned by the wisdom coming from one so young. That night she barely slept. She prayed for understanding, struggling through that long night to surrender whatever had to be released for her to see the truth.

Before Lauds the next morning, while Aminah was still asleep, she announced to Johanna, "I think the church has it wrong. Why should we all be killing each other, Christians and Muslims and Jews? Surely there's a better way to deal with our differences." Johanna smiled slightly as Clarissa spoke.

"And don't we all want the same thing," continued Clarissa, "no matter what name we give the God we all pray to? Peace . . . enough food . . . freedom to decide about our lives." Johanna's smile grew. "I'm going to ask Aminah for Arabic lessons," Clarissa declared. "And an introduction to Islam. I want to understand it."

The smile overtook Johanna's face as she said, "We'll learn together."

§

The bread and cabbage and cucumbers were long gone. An unexpected early frost had killed the tender blossoms on the gourd vines; there would be no harvest. As Clarissa sat in the kitchen gnawing on her fourteenth gnarly carrot in a week, she tried also to swallow the gnawing fear that overtook her whenever she tried to imagine how two young former almost-nuns and their eleven-year-old Muslim companion would survive in a world that offered them no work, no protection, and no security. All they had was each other, and Clarissa tried desperately to believe that it was enough.

She knew that, with time, they would venture into the village of Balnéaire, which they could see below them from atop their bluff. But they weren't quite sure yet how to go about it. *How can we be a helpful presence,* she wondered, *in this land that is still so alien to us?* As aspiring nuns, she and Johanna had been granted the safety of the cloister and the immediate trust of the people outside it who believed in the church and needed their care. As women on their own harboring an "enemy," they were likely to be viewed as outlandish—even dangerous—strangers. They were vulnerable to

the stares and whims of people who didn't understand. And so they decided
to stay put on their bluff for a little while.

Clarissa was deep in thought when a noisy interruption announced
itself. The braying and the creaking of wheels were unmistakable. Knowing,
yet disbelieving, she raced to the door. There she beheld Jaxon atop Hubert
Walter, slowly approaching on the path. Jaxon, she noted, was dressed more
sedately than she had ever seen him, in dark pants and a fraying brown
jacket.

Shouting his name, Clarissa ran out and flung her arms around the
minstrel's neck. So many months had passed. In all that time, she had not
sent word back home, still fearful of being discovered by those who intended her harm, and not sure how to do it even if she had wanted to. And now
she was overjoyed that Jaxon had found her.

He returned her warm embrace. But when she drew back, Clarissa
could see that his face was troubled. He seemed not to know where to begin
to explain his presence. After a long silence, he said, "I've come to take you
home."

Clarissa felt her joy melting into distress. "But—"

"Just for a little while," Jaxon said. "It's your mother." Shifting uncomfortably, he changed the subject to a report on his journey. "I had a hard
time finding you. I knew the nuns in Dover sent you to Liège. Mother Agnes
Luc—now *there's* a cranky nun—she directed me back here. It was a long—"

Clarissa couldn't bear the suspense. "What about my mother?" she
interrupted.

An even more pained expression overtook Jaxon's face. "Your mother
is dying," he blurted out. "Taken ill with fever." Clarissa's eyes grew moist as
Jaxon continued. "Last week I went to the harvest festival in Gladdington,
like I always do. I stopped by the manor, hoping your mother might have
news of you that she could share somehow."

Clarissa moved over beside Hubert Walter and ran her hands along
the donkey's ears, leaning in close and whispering his name, trying to focus
on anything but another irreplaceable loss. *How can I possibly bear the death
of my mother?* she wondered.

"He's Reginald now," said Jaxon, nodding toward his donkey. "New
archbishop. As of July." He flashed Clarissa a smile, but it was not returned.

"Did you leave Lizzie at home?" she asked.

More silence dropped between them. "Ah, there's a sad tale," said Jaxon
finally. "She went to sleep last winter and never woke up." He looked down
at the ground and scuffed at the earth with his right foot a few times. Then
he brought his gaze back. "We need to go. It's been over a week since I left."

We need to go now." He swallowed and looked intently at Clarissa, their sad eyes meeting. "Before it's too late."

Clarissa led Jaxon inside and introduced him to Aminah. He bowed, took her hand and kissed it, and she smiled shyly at him. When Johanna appeared, she hugged Jaxon and shook her head in disbelief, repeating his name over and over. Clarissa shared her need to return to England at once. She noticed the concern on Johanna's face and the fear on Aminah's. "Yes, you must go," insisted Johanna. She moved over and put an arm around Aminah. "We'll be fine," she said, "waiting here for you to come home."

Jaxon went to the barn to get some straw for the cart. Aminah packed a few carrots and apples in a basket and handed it to Clarissa. Clarissa hugged her gratefully and said, "I'll be back soon."

Aminah smiled and said, "I'll pray for you and your mother. Be safe."

Within an hour of when they had arrived, Jaxon was directing the donkey now known as Reginald back down the path, pulling Clarissa, curled up in a tight ball in the straw in the cart, stunned and filled with sorrow.

Twenty

$\bigwedge$ shaft of sunlight slipped in through a narrow opening in the brocade curtains and spread itself across Thea's face. Her breathing was heavy, her pale lips moving in a murmuring cascade of words that Clarissa could not understand.

Leaning over the bed, Clarissa planted a kiss on Thea's forehead, the tears dropping from her eyes into her mother's. Thea's forehead was hot, as if on fire. Clarissa reached for the cloth and basin by the bed, wiping Thea's brow and reciting psalms to her, feeling the power of doing for her mother what she had failed to do for her sister.

She stayed there for hours, refusing food and Catrain's offer to spell her for a while. The shaft of sunlight shifted gradually away from her mother's face and across the room, finally disappearing altogether as night crept in and filled the space. Clarissa lifted a candle from its bronze holder and stepped out to light it from the torch in the hall. When she returned, her mother was gone.

She did not throw herself upon her mother's body and sob as she had imagined she would. Instead, she closed Thea's eyes and gently kissed her hands, arranging them as if clasped in prayer. Clarissa calmly recited the prayer that had hovered on her lips as Josselyn died: ". . . Holy Mary, Mother of God, pray for us sinners, now and at the hour of our death. Amen." And then she went to find her father.

Aldrich entered the room and gazed at his wife. He knelt by the bed, put his right hand over hers for a moment, and then rose and walked out. As soon as he was gone, Clarissa reached up and gently removed the silver necklace from around her mother's neck. She had always loved that shiny necklace. She remembered fingering it as a young child in her mother's lap, tracing the fleur-de-lis symbol that was engraved on it and tapping the bright blue lapis gem in its center. She carefully hung it around her own neck, tucking it under her robe next to her heart, beside Josselyn's cross and the young girl's bell.

She planned to return to France before anyone outside the manor knew she had slipped home. She understood that she was probably being unnecessarily cautious, but she still felt afraid there. And she didn't relish facing the curious crowd at her mother's funeral, or tending to the brooding aloofness of her father. Whatever warmth had been kindled between them by his concern over Beatrix's murder seemed to have evaporated in the intervening months of Clarissa's absence.

There was just one thing Clarissa wanted to do before she left: spend a day with Liliana and Nerida. She climbed into bed very late that night, thinking of her mother and anticipating the next day. Tossing and turning, unable to fall asleep, she heard a gentle knock and saw the door open a crack. A figure glided into the room.

"Don't be scared, it's just me," whispered Nerida, and Clarissa smiled in the dark. Nerida slid into the bed next to her. They spent that night with their hands clasped together, mourning the loss of Thea and sharing the truth of their lives. Clarissa couldn't help thinking of all the times she and Josselyn had stretched out together just like this, pouring their thoughts and hopes into the dark heart of a long night.

At breakfast the next morning, Clarissa got her first glimpse in a year and a half of Liliana. "You've gotten big!" she declared, as she gathered up her niece in her arms, overcome once again with the beautiful child's striking resemblance to Josselyn. Liliana giggled and held tight around Clarissa's neck.

The day turned unseasonably warm, and Clarissa enticed Nerida and Liliana into the forest with a picnic lunch. They shared it under a large willow tree at the edge of a stream, a favorite spot for Clarissa and Josselyn when they were young girls. Clarissa and Nerida picked up the threads of the previous night's conversation, while Liliana waded and played in the dancing sunlight.

"Now that your mother is gone, Liliana and I have no reason to stay here," said Nerida. "We want to go with you."

Clarissa had not been surprised to hear the night before of Nerida's unhappy marriage, but still she was startled. She thought about the hardships and uncertainties of life on the northern coast of France, especially for a child. She did her best to consider Liliana's well-being and not reveal her excitement about Nerida's desire. "But there's more security for you and Liliana here," she responded.

"And when have *you* ever chosen the secure path?" Nerida smiled. Then they laughed, collapsing together in a joyful embrace. Spying them,

Liliana raced out of the stream in a splash of water and threw her wet arms around them both, giggling.

Wilfred did not put up a fight. Aldrich had begun treating the young man as his heir apparent, and they were both preoccupied with the business of the manor. Nerida had failed to provide her husband with an heir—or even a daughter. He felt no tie to Liliana, and no warmth toward either her or Nerida.

Clarissa consulted with Jaxon. Adding two people to their trip, with one being a child, complicated it. She knew Reginald couldn't carry and haul all four of them across England. "Nerida and I can walk," Clarissa said, "with a break in the cart when we need it. At a donkey's pace, it won't be hard to keep up. And when we get to Dover, Nerida, Liliana, and I can rest up at the abbey for a few days before we go on to France."

"And let you have all the fun?" exclaimed Jaxon. "In France, I won't be just a minstrel, I'll be a *troubadour*!"

"You mean you'll come with us? And stay?"

"Forever," said Jaxon. "You're the next best thing to Lizzie. With her gone, where else would I want to be?" He winked at Clarissa. "We'll take turns riding and walking."

On the morning they left, Jaxon appeared in what he apparently believed was the appropriate attire for a troubadour in France: striped red-blue-and-yellow silk pantaloons and a bright green shirt with voluminous sleeves, covered in a pattern of large black diamonds. Perched on his head was a pointed purple hat, taller than Reginald's miter and emblazoned with a gold moon and stars. It reminded Clarissa of something the wizard Merlin from the King Arthur tales would have worn. Liliana giggled when she saw him and begged to sit in his lap atop Reginald.

Wilfred was notably absent. Nerida thanked Aldrich for his kindness. Clarissa hugged her father and wished him well, knowing that this was likely the last time she would see him. She wished that she could conjure some sadness, but she could not. Liliana blew him a kiss.

As they turned toward the path, Aldrich said, "Just a moment." From the direction of the barn came Wilfred, riding Magnus, the baron's favorite stallion. He was driving three young sheep—two beige and one black—which scampered on spindly legs and bleated an unholy racket. "You'll need the horse to get around," explained Aldrich. "And the ram and ewes will be the start of a flock that will keep you warm in wool during the cold winters to come."

Clarissa embraced her father again and, moved by his generous gesture, said, "I love you."

"I love you, too, Clarissa." It was the first time the words had ever passed between them. "Now go," said the baron, slipping a heavy bag of coins into his daughter's hands—far more than enough, she surmised, to pay for their passage across the channel to France and get them through the winter.

Wilfred helped Nerida slide into the saddle behind Clarissa and then arranged the sheep in the cart. The stallion pranced in anticipation. Jaxon raised his right hand in the air and dug his heels gently into Reginald's side. As the company of friends headed toward the coast, the grief Clarissa felt over losing her mother began moving to the edges of her heart. Flooding in and pushing out the sorrow was her joy at being on her way to live in France with all the people she loved most in the world.

§

On the ride to Calais, Clarissa pondered which was worse: crossing the channel in a barrel of dead fish, or in the hold of a boat with a spirited horse, three bleating sheep, a donkey in a bishop's hat, a giggling girl, and a juggler in silk pantaloons. The odd company reached the French coast before she arrived at a conclusion.

"I'm a *troubadour!*" Jaxon announced as the boat touched the shore. He hurried off, got down on his knees, and kissed the ground. Liliana, who had sat wide-eyed throughout the crossing, scampered off like a drunken sailor on legs not yet accustomed to land, anxious to see the delights of her new home. They made their way through the market shops of Calais, stocking up on winter staples: barley, lentils, flour, honey, spices, butter and cheese, turnips and gourds from gardens that were closer to the sea, warmer and more protected than theirs. Clarissa gave thanks that there wasn't a carrot anywhere in sight.

They headed along the coast, passing through the village of Balnéaire and winding their way up the path as the sun began to set. Clarissa prodded Magnus into a trot. Nerida leaned into her back and whispered, "Thank you for bringing us."

When the house near the bluff came into view, Clarissa commanded, "Go, Magnus!" He took off in a gallop, and Nerida clung even more tightly around Clarissa's waist. Clarissa took in deep gulps of the familiar salty air and then shouted to her friend, "Welcome home!"

At the crest of the bluff, she pulled up on the reins. From atop Magnus, she and Nerida watched the sun drop and the sky turn brilliant crimson as the evening breezes began to stir. Feeling the sting of the wind on her cheeks, Clarissa was anxious to be enveloped in the warmth of home and to share it with Nerida. But she guided Magnus to circle back, down past the house, and they followed behind Reginald as he trudged up the path with Jaxon and Liliana and the still-bleating sheep.

When they arrived at the house, Clarissa could see that Johanna and Aminah were very glad to see her—and astonished at the menagerie of humans and beasts accompanying her. Hugs were shared all around. Jaxon bowed and kissed Aminah's hand again in greeting, and the young girl blushed and giggled—at either the gesture or Jaxon's outlandish outfit. Johanna immediately placed a pot of water to boil over the fire, throwing in a handful of barley, a splash of honey, and some licorice root, her favorite drink for celebrations. Liliana made herself right at home, moving from lap to lap as the women caught one another up on events since their parting, sipping cups of the hot barley water in the light of a fire blazing in the hearth.

"What do you call this place?" asked Nerida. When her question was greeted with silence and shrugs, she said, "We need a good name." The others agreed, and they launched into a conversation to find one. They considered naming their new home in honor of a saint of the church, but their favorite had already been bestowed on a screech owl. They pondered the points of natural beauty around them, but couldn't settle on a name involving Coast or Bluff. They talked about their mission, trying out being the House of Faith, or Peace, or Hope.

"How about the House of We-Have-No-Idea-What-We're-Doing?" offered Clarissa, and they all laughed.

Johanna began thinking aloud, scanning through images that had meaning for them. Her eyes brightened when she reminded them of the lesson of the Sinai wilderness. "Manna was the sign of God's steadfast provision, and the people's trust, and the importance of living generously and justly. It was a daily reminder that everything they needed would come to them, and there would always be enough to share."

"Manna House," said Clarissa, smiling. "I like it." The others murmured their agreement. And so it was.

In the days that followed, they all understood that the pressing task before them was to survive the winter. Though at first glance having a troubadour among them didn't seem like much added protection or security, they were grateful for Jaxon's presence. He went to work gathering up wood to keep their hearth filled.

He left around dawn each morning with Reginald from the barn where they slept in the straw next to Magnus and the sheep. Clarissa considered it unkind that Jaxon had to share accommodation with the animals, but everyone knew that a single man living in a house with a group of women was a scandal that would have made connecting with their neighbors even more difficult than it already seemed. "It's twice as big as my shed at the convent in Dover!" exclaimed Jaxon, as if he were living in a spacious manor rather than a drafty barn.

Jaxon spent his mornings filling his cart with wood from the forest beyond the bluff, about half of which he carried back to the house and the rest he exchanged in Balnéaire for fish and more staples. More important than what he brought home from the village were the relationships he built there. He routinely stopped upon his arrival to eat his lunch in the small town square. By the time he was finished, he was juggling turnips or gourds in the air with a crowd of giggling children around him, pushing one another for a turn to touch his silky sleeves or pet Reginald's enormous ears.

From the day he arrived, Jaxon added color and charm to an otherwise drab winter landscape. He infused warmth and whimsy into an isolated coastal outpost, which was buffeted for months by frigid gales that blew off the sea. Jaxon did what Clarissa and her sisters had not figured out how to do: he got the odd little community on the bluff noticed and accepted by the people of the village.

It didn't take long for the children to begin following Jaxon home. They showed up ragged, hungry, and cold. When a snowstorm blew through in early December, their number grew. They clamored for rides in the juggler's "sleigh," which Jaxon had fashioned by nailing two large runners hewn from an arched bough of a yew tree to the wheels of his cart. The children piled in for rides up to the bluff, and Reginald plodded patiently under the strain of the extra weight.

Between Aldrich's coins and Jaxon's barters, there was always enough food acquired to share. The house hummed at a high pitch with the joyful noise and activity of children, who knew they would always find something to eat and someone to love them there. Clarissa and Nerida delighted in preparing the food, and Liliana was their most dedicated server.

Soon parents—curious, or hungry, or both—began tagging along with their children. The first to venture up the bluff was Genevieve, a widow with six young ones ranging in age from two months to seven years. The weary young mother, with a distinctive red birthmark on her forehead, peered in tentatively.

Clarissa gestured her inside, finding her a seat amid the chaos, near the fire. Over the din, Genevieve explained that her husband, a coppersmith, had been taking his wares to the market in Calais the week before when his horse slipped on ice and the wagon overturned on him. "I don't know how I'm going to feed all these children now," she said.

"They're always welcome here," said Clarissa. "And you are, too."

Day after day villagers crammed around the table in Manna House, in the room that no longer seemed so big. Cooking went on at the hearth all day long, commencing as soon as morning prayers were ended. Clarissa and her companions tumbled onto their palettes each night, too tired to speak. "We need to set some limits," Johanna declared one morning at breakfast, her voice hoarse from exhaustion.

Setting limits felt like failure to Clarissa. She wondered aloud if Jesus ever said no to any of the people who cried to him for bread or healing, all the ones who crowded around to touch his hem or tell the truth of their lives. Johanna reminded her of the stories of Jesus slipping off in boats, or escaping to the desert, trying to elude the clamoring crowds and find some time alone to pray. "We need to keep our rhythms of prayer and solitude," she declared. "We still need to put God first."

"But the needs of God's children are so great," said Clarissa, "and we have so much to share." But she knew in her heart that Johanna spoke truth.

"I can help," piped up Jaxon, who overheard their exchange. Jaxon, it turned out, was the possessor of many skills beyond juggling. A few days later, as soon as the last remnant of the blizzard's snow had melted from the ground, he began felling limbs and binding them together for the frame of a building between the house and the barn.

The young women of Manna House hauled buckets of soil from the edges of the garden and sand from the beach below them, which they mixed with water and straw. Thanks to the animals, they never lacked for dung, the other critical ingredient in the daub they smeared on the wattle frame. To their delight, they discovered that both young ewes were pregnant, due to increase their small flock—and its useful output—by spring.

The little community worked in the early afternoons, when Jaxon returned from town and the faint winter sun cast just enough warmth to keep the muddy daub from freezing. The young women shivered as they toiled under Jaxon's direction to raise a center for their ministry of hospitality, hoping to have it completed by Christmas.

The endless trips down the steep and narrow path to the beach for sand were particularly exhausting. Clarissa, her arms and back aching, wished desperately that the path were wide and passable enough for Reginald and the cart to do the hauling. On the fifth day, noting how much work they had yet to do to complete the project, she began to despair of ever finishing it. "This is impossible," she declared.

Johanna laughed and said, "I don't think so." She pointed down the hill. Coming up the path from Balnéaire was a parade of townspeople, led by Genevieve and a gaggle of grinning children. From the smallest child to the oldest grandmother, each villager carried a cup, or pot, or bucket.

Without saying a word, they fell in next to the young women, hauling sand and soil to the building site. Before long, Jaxon began to hum, and the whole crowd joined in singing, transforming their hard labor into shared joy.

When the walls were up, several of the women and children joined Jaxon in gathering up sheaves of dried grass and heather, which he layered and wove for the thatch of the roof. Determined to finish the center on time, Jaxon labored tirelessly, his devotion to the work as pure as his young women friends' was to prayer. And often, Clarissa noticed, after a long day of construction, a light burned in the barn well into the night, causing her to wonder what Jaxon was up to and when he ever slept.

§

Two days before Christmas, Clarissa grabbed a handful of her father's dwindling coins, led Magnus out of the barn, and rode to Calais. She was on a search for ingredients that weren't available in a village as small as Balnéaire.

The next day the young women of Manna House awoke even earlier than usual and devoted themselves to a long day of creating holiday treats. On her third try, Nerida mastered the art of making pastry shells that wouldn't break a tooth, gaining a new understanding as to why such edible containers were commonly called coffins. Aminah took on the task of filling them with currants and thick crème made with almond milk and eggs, proudly showing off the sweet and beautiful custard tarts when they were done.

Clarissa rolled out pastry in thin sheets and helped Liliana use a saucer to cut it into circles. These Johanna fried in hot oil over the fire to create crunchy crispels. Liliana, insisting that she needed no further supervision, drizzled honey over them, getting as much on her hands and in her hair as on the delicate pastries. In the afternoon, they all collaborated in the making of fig pudding, caraway-seed cookies, and rosewater cakes spiced with nutmeg.

When they were done, flour covered the floor, honey dripped down the walls, and piles of nutmeg and cinnamon and seeds were scattered across the table. They were exhausted. They sighed, laughed, exchanged sticky hugs, and went to their rooms to take a short nap before the party began.

They dedicated their new center on Christmas Eve. A throng of villagers stood in the large, open, circular room that someday would hold several tables and benches. A fire roared in the heart of the hall. Scattered candles and pine boughs added additional warmth and a sweet pungency to the festivities.

Saint Catherine and her brood had slipped in unnoticed, until they flapped their wings and screeched a welcome from the highest point of the building's frame. Jaxon circulated among the crowd juggling and singing ballads, an owlet perched precariously on his shoulder. He winked at each of the many children, who immediately stopped whatever they were doing and joined the parade that snaked along behind him through the festive hall.

When Jaxon stopped singing, Nerida moved next to the fire. All eyes were focused on her as she offered warm thanks to the gathered crowd. "You made this possible," she said in halting French, having been coached by Johanna. She smiled broadly, her arms spread wide in welcome. "It belongs to all of us."

Johanna stepped forward to share the vision of the young women of Manna House for their new center. They planned to serve a mid-day meal open to all every day, conduct Scripture study on Sunday evenings, and convene a school for girls five afternoons a week. A few of the boys groaned at the mention of a school for girls, but several of the girls gasped with delight. The rudimentary school in Balnéaire did not welcome them, and they understood that they were being presented with a rare opportunity.

"We talked for a long time about what to name this space," said Johanna. Clarissa was taken aback. They had all talked at length about the name for their house, but she had not been part of any conversations about a name for their new center. Johanna gave a nod and Jaxon stepped forward. He had in his hand a large piece of wood.

He held it up above his head so that all could see what was engraved in its bark: "Welcome to the Josselyn Center." Johanna explained the name. And then she beamed a smile at Clarissa and invited her forward to offer the prayer of dedication. For one of the very few times in her life, Clarissa was utterly speechless. She forgot the words she was going to pray. Instead, she asked simply that all who passed through the doors of the Josselyn Center would be blessed. Her voice choked as she spoke the name.

The villagers clapped. Jaxon pulled out his flute and launched into a lilting tune, as the crowd began to mill around again. A few young folks moved around the fire, formed a circle, and began to dance. Clarissa hugged Johanna and whispered, "She would have loved it. This place is filled with joy . . . and beauty . . . and faith. Just like Josselyn."

After a few songs, Jaxon stopped and clapped his hands together vigorously. "There's one more thing!" he announced in English, as Johanna translated for him. Jaxon, who in most settings relied on the universal languages of music and laughter, had been too busy working to conquer even a rudimentary grasp of French.

He pulled six small copper balls out of his bag and, to the children's amazement, began juggling them all at once. He tossed them so high that Catherine's owlets left their perch under the roof in search of protection. When he had the crowd's full attention, Jaxon caught the balls one by one and held them up, a signal to the young man waiting by the wide double doors at one end of the hall.

The young man opened the doors, and a group of boys burst into the room. They were laughing and rolling a massive, round slab of thick wood, twice their height. Younger boys followed, carrying two frames and a piece of wood that, except for its slightly smaller size, was identical to the first. "I got the idea from King Arthur and his knights!" exclaimed Jaxon, his eyes sparkling in the firelight. "A round table—where all are equal and everybody can reach and share the bounty the earth gives us."

The boys struggled to set the huge slab of wood on the large frame, and a few men stepped forward to help. Placing the smaller frame on top of it, Jaxon dropped the six balls within its edges. Then he helped the younger boys nest the other circle of wood inside it. He gave a conspicuous nod, and girls streamed from four directions, carrying trays heaped with the day's production of sweet treats and steaming mugs of hot, spiced cider. These they set on the tabletop, as an aromatic infusion of cinnamon and nutmeg wafted through the room.

Jaxon proudly showed the crowd how the round top turned on the copper balls, so that a hungry person could stay put and bring the food around. It seemed like a magic trick to the villagers, who stepped up and took turns spinning cookies and custards and cakes to one another, pointing and laughing. "When we have benches, it'll seat twenty!" declared Jaxon, beaming with pride. "Plus all the children on laps!"

Clarissa was astonished that her friend had pulled off making the table after putting in long hours every day on the center's construction. And that he had kept it a surprise. She moved over next to Jaxon. Grinning, she said to him, "I need to stop in the barn more often."

Jaxon, returning the grin, said "Merry Christmas, my friend."

"Yes. It is," replied Clarissa. "The merriest." Then she gave her favorite troubadour a warm Christmas hug.

Twenty-one

The young women of Manna House did more than survive the winter. The Josselyn Center resounded throughout that bleak season with the joyful noises of meals being shared and lessons being learned. Jaxon and a few of the village men crafted benches and three more round tables, which for a couple of hours in the middle of every day held steaming bowls of soup and thick slices of bread.

On Saturdays the residents of Balnéaire filed up the path for a special meal, summoned by the pungent smell of herring and cod cooking over the fire. The families that could afford to offer contributions expanded the feast with cheese from their cows and their favorite sweet desserts.

On weekday afternoons a steady stream of girls, as young as four and as old as fifteen, made their way to the center. They showed up with a loaf of bread or a basket of eggs, declaring "I want to read." Their eagerness was an inspiration to Clarissa.

One six-year-old appeared with a small pig under her arm. Clarissa smiled weakly to disguise the frown that revealed her true feelings about the gift. She failed to get a good grip when the girl tried to hand over the piglet. The poor, frightened creature tore through the classroom in a frenzy, squealing, while the youngest students chased after it, with Liliana in the lead. Clarissa noted to herself that day how much she would have appreciated coins, but she was grateful for every odd payment for an education that came to her and her sisters.

On the second day of school, a fisherman barged into the center during Johanna's reading lesson. He grabbed his two daughters from their seats on a third-row bench and roughly dragged them, weeping, out of the classroom. "There's cooking and cleaning to be done," he said gruffly, "and babies to take care of!"

Clarissa followed them outside, intending to stop him and bring them back. But the girls' shaking heads and pleading eyes signaled that any attempted intervention would only make their punishment more severe. Clarissa walked back inside carrying a heavy sadness in her heart for those bright and eager young girls, realizing that it was nothing short of a miracle that more fathers hadn't shown up to drag their daughters home.

A few days later a grandmother, hunched over, dressed in rags and missing most of her teeth, brought a young girl to school. "Would it be all right if I just waited for her here?" she asked as she sat on the floor in a corner, introducing herself as Sapientia. Clarissa immediately grabbed a chair for her. *What harm can it do*, she thought, *to have this poor old woman with us?*

The next day Genevieve, holding her two-month-old, decided to wait for her daughters in the same corner. She shot Clarissa a look that asked if it was all right for her to be there, and Clarissa nodded back. Genevieve began to nurse her son as she recited her letters. Before long a small throng of women longing to read hovered at the back of the room, taking lessons with their daughters and granddaughters.

Soon a few envious boys, some of whom were among the groaners in response to the announcement of the girls' school at the Christmas party, began ducking out of the overly rote and rigid village school and hanging around the door each afternoon. The oldest, a rough-looking chap named Clovis, who always appeared with a navy blue Greek fisherman's cap cocked over one eye, eventually vocalized their hope for an invitation to come inside. Clarissa and Johanna, trying to keep afloat a school that was already beyond capacity for girls who had no other educational opportunities, knew that this was where they had to draw the line on their generosity. They gently shooed the boys away.

The girls received instruction in reading and writing. Clarissa and Johanna also attended to their spiritual formation with Christian Scripture and prayer. And every Friday afternoon, on the weekly Muslim holy day, Aminah gave them an Arabic vocabulary lesson and a teaching from Islam. Clarissa was unwavering in her commitment to having Aminah enlighten their students to the truths of another faith, hoping that they would grow into young women more tolerant than she herself had recently been.

On the Friday of Aminah's first lesson, Johanna introduced her to them as a teacher as well as a student and explained the values of understanding and acceptance. Aminah walked among them, offering each one a close look at the exquisitely delicate Arabic letters engraved on the gold band that was a gift from her mother. "*Salaam*," she said, tapping on the bracelet wrapping her left wrist. She asked them to repeat it together, and then she told them, "It means *peace*."

Clarissa and Johanna had proposed to Aminah that she teach ten new words or phrases each week. And so that first day she also taught them the Arabic words for *gold* and *bracelet*, and the more practical *yes* and *no*, *hello* and *goodbye*, *please* and *thank you*. And she introduced them to *Allah*, the Muslim name for God.

That was too much for one of the mothers, whom Clarissa had noticed shifting impatiently in the corner as Aminah shared the lesson. She sprang up at the mention of Allah, pointed at Aminah, and angrily shouted, "Infidel!" Then she strode to the front of the room, seized her daughter by the arm, and stormed out.

Another mother followed the first, grabbing her daughter by the hand, yelling as she yanked her out the door in a fury, "Why do you think we have the Crusades?" Clarissa overheard one of the women say loudly to the other when they met outside, "Do you think we could build a wall around France to keep the likes of her away?"

The students sat, unmoving, in stunned silence. Clarissa's concern focused immediately on Aminah. She was surprised and pleased to see that Aminah seemed only mildly shaken by the outbursts, standing her ground and keeping the few tears in her eyes under control. Aminah confessed to her later, "I expected worse."

Once again Clarissa considered it miraculous that more upset parents hadn't wrenched their daughters out of the school. Apparently most of the older women had decided that they were willing to accept the unusual curriculum each Friday afternoon in exchange for learning to read and write. Clarissa hoped that some even appreciated it. Aminah's shy and endearing demeanor helped considerably.

During those winter weeks, Aminah taught many vocabulary words and covered several aspects of the Five Pillars of Islam: profession of faith, ritual daily prayer and charity to the needy, fasting during the holy month of Ramadan and making a pilgrimage to Mecca once during one's lifetime. Though younger than several of her students, Aminah knew her faith well, kept their attention, and was a patient teacher. And she made clear that she cared as deeply about them as she did about the lessons she was sharing.

Clarissa and Johanna were delighted to spend their Sunday evenings opening Christian Scripture with the villagers, as they had done in the chapel in Liège, and Nerida and Aminah were regular participants. After pondering several possibilities, they decided to begin the dawning year of 1205 by exploring together the Acts of the Apostles. "It feels like we're giving birth to something," explained Johanna, "and Acts tells the story of the birth of the church."

She read the Pentecost story to the gathered group on the first Sunday evening in January: "When the day of Pentecost had come, they were all together in one place. And suddenly from heaven there came a sound like the rush of a violent wind, and it filled the entire house where they were sitting. Divided tongues, as of fire, appeared among them, and a tongue rested on each of them. All of them were filled with the Holy Spirit and began to speak in other languages, as the Spirit game them ability."

Blasted that winter by unrelenting gales off the sea, huddling as close as they could to their hearths for warmth, the people of Balnéaire understood the power of the Holy Spirit that came to the earliest believers as tongues of fire in a rush of violent wind. Johanna read on and then said, "When people from all over the known world were together in Jerusalem and erupted in languages that everyone could understand, onlookers accused them of being drunk." Some of the villagers laughed. "But," Johanna continued, "the Apostle Peter stood up and let them know what was true, reminding them that God had promised to pour out his Holy Spirit on his people, uniting them, inviting men and women, young and old, to share visions and dream dreams."

She paused a moment and then asked the Sunday night group, "What are your visions and dreams for your life?" The villagers were reluctant to answer at first, but then one by one they responded. Their dreams were simple: safety, enough food, more warmth, happy and healthy children.

When they had each taken a turn, Johanna declared, "The church loves to read the Pentecost Scripture every year, but we usually stop before the end of the story and miss its true power. What happened after the Holy Spirit came?" Answering her own question, she began to read again from the manuscript in her hand: "All who believed were together and had all things in common; and they would sell their possessions and goods and distribute the proceeds to all, as any had need."

"Nobody showed up with a plan," explained Johanna. "It's just what happened when the followers of Jesus were filled with the Holy Spirit. They began to live like a family, sharing everything they had, making sure that no one among them was hungry or hurting."

Sapientia, who had sat quietly in a corner, stood up, shuffled over to Johanna, and lifted the manuscript out of her hands. The old woman moved her left index finger slowly over the page as she read, trying out her new skill aloud for the first time. She pronounced the words painstakingly, in a halting but clear voice, as she finished the story: "Day by day, as they spent much time together, they broke bread at homes and ate their food with glad and generous hearts, praising God and having the good will of all the people."

Sapientia looked up and smiled her toothless smile at the gathered group. "That's us," she said. And then she slowly carried her bent-over body back to her seat.

§

In early March, when the slightest hint of spring visited the bluff, Clarissa decided it was time to shake off winter and begin exploring the corners of the coast that she had not yet discovered. Walking alone was her favorite form of prayer. Each day she wandered a little farther, until one sunny morning she came upon a treasure hidden in a cliff wall: a large cave.

The tide was out, and Clarissa walked on moist sand into the far reaches of the dark expanse. "Hello," she called out, just to make sure she was alone. "Hello . . . hello . . . hello," answered the walls of the cave, each echo a little softer and more distant. Clarissa sat on a large wet rock in the center and reveled gratefully in her discovery, wondering if she would share it when she got back to the house or keep it as her special secret.

The tide reversed while she sat there praying, and the window of time for leaving without having to wade in the frigid water—or, worse, swim through it—began to close. Clarissa walked out of the cave and, eyeing the jutting cliff above her, decided to scramble up to it. While she settled in and drank in the view all around her from the top, faces of the girls in the school visited her, rolling through her mind one at a time.

She knew that most of the oldest ones would be married within the year—and mothers by the next. A few would die in childbirth. The rest would be bound to the relentless demands of children and husbands—kind ones, if they were lucky, but more likely the sort who would beat them. *How I wish I could hand them confidence along with education,* she thought. She yearned to instill in them a sense of their preciousness, an understanding of the sacredness of their bodies as well as their spirits. She remembered again her night on a cliff like the one on which she now sat, when she and Johanna celebrated her budding womanhood and Clarissa felt that everything changed for her.

As she walked back toward home, she knew that she was too excited to keep her discovery of the cave from her sisters. She wondered how they would respond to the wild idea she was about to propose to them.

§

Galorian gave thanks for every day at Saint Catherine's. But when spring arrived, and he began closing in on a year there, he felt as restless as the desert streams that had come to life. Early in his visit, he had donned the garb of a monk, but in all his months at the monastery he had made no commitment to Father Alain and his brothers. He asked for a meeting with the abbot.

"I think the time has come," said Galorian. "I'm grateful for every act of generosity and kindness that has been extended to me here. And for every bit of knowledge I've gained. I needed to be here to rest and recover and pray." Father Alain listened intently. "But it's time," continued Galorian. "It's time for me to leave the shelter and isolation here and find my own place in the world."

The abbot nodded. "Where will you go?"

"I don't know," answered Galorian. "That's why I wanted to see you. To ask you to pray with me that I will find a path and a place. I want to serve the church, but I'm not sure how."

"I knew this day was coming," said Alain. "And I've already thought and prayed some about your future. I have an opportunity for you to ponder. I've just received word from a brother in Rome that holy men are needed at the Lateran Palace to dedicate themselves to organizing the relics and records of the church. You are a man of God with a clear devotion to the church and fluency in Latin. I could put in a good word for you. Are you interested?"

The invitation seemed to Galorian like the opportunity of a lifetime. "Yes," he said, smiling, as joy flooded his soul. "Yes, I am."

Soon Galorian was making the rounds, thanking Matthias and Bernard and all the brothers who had welcomed him. Matthias sent him off with a small icon of John the Baptist that was among the first the artisan had created. Bernard gave him a jar filled with small packets, each bearing seeds or bulbs labeled woad or fennel, madder or crocus or safflower. "Plant them in a sunny plot," said the monk, "and you'll grow a garden of dyes."

Then Bernard handed Galorian a wooden box with small holes in the top. "Not sea snails, I hope?" said Galorian, smiling as he lifted the lid, and Bernard laughed. What Galorian saw was not much less surprising than a box of snails would have been. About a dozen of the languid kermes scale insects were inside, attached to a sap-drenched twig of scrub oak.

"They'll come back to life when it gets warmer," said Bernard, "and by next spring you'll have enough bugs to dye all the robes at the Lateran Palace!"

A week later Galorian left on Thane, carrying the gifts and a letter from Father Alain. He didn't relish the long re-crossing of the desert, and he felt especially alone, his thoughts turning often to Aminah and their shared journey. But he was filled with anticipation about a bright future in the church. His hope carried him all the way back to Alexandria, where he found passage on a boat to Rome.

His first glimpse of the spires and domes of the great city awed him. He couldn't help thinking of Constantinople, imagining what outrage and sorrow would visit the citizens of Christendom if this seat of Western Christianity were ever destroyed as his comrades had destroyed the heart of Eastern Christianity. As he led Thane out of the boat and made his first footstep on the ground of Rome, Galorian knelt, bowed his head, and silently pledged his determination to do what he could to preserve the history of the church. "May it live on forever," he whispered as he breathed in the holy air.

§

For several days, Clarissa and Johanna announced that there would be a special program for their students age eleven and older. Clarissa was delighted that Johanna had supported her idea. After school on a Wednesday afternoon in mid-March, when the mothers and grandmothers had taken the younger girls home, the two of them led twenty-three young women on a walk to the cave.

Inside, Johanna placed a large candle on the rock in the center. As the students gathered around her, she started at the very beginning, reading the first sentence of the Holy Scripture: "In the beginning when God created the heavens and the earth . . ." The waves of the ocean at the edge of the cave added a rhythmic backdrop to the dramatic story of creation. ". . . the earth was a formless void and darkness covered the face of the deep, while a wind from God swept over the face of the waters."

Johanna proclaimed the first words uttered by God, forcefully enough for them to echo throughout the cave: "Let there be light!" She read to the young women about the world emerging out of chaos through the breath of God; about the sun and the moon and a multitude of stars emblazoned on the dome of the sky; about flowering plants and creeping animals and swarms of amazing creatures in sea and air. She reminded her listeners, riveted on every word, that God pronounced each element of creation good.

She ended the reading: "Then God said, 'Let us make human beings in our image, according to our likeness.' In the image of God, male and female, God created them. And God saw that it was very good." Johanna looked around the circle of eager young women. "Do you believe that you were created in the image of God?" she asked. "Do you know that you are here because God chose to breathe divine breath into you, and that you are more precious to God than the sun and the stars? Do you accept that you are part of the creation that God declared *very good*?"

The young women stood wide-eyed, the tears of some reflecting the light of the candle, as Johanna continued the lesson. "Everywhere you turn, people will tell you that as a woman you are physically weak and morally inferior—doomed to live a life of submission." Johanna took a long pause. "Don't believe it," she pleaded. "*Please don't believe it.*"

She held up the manuscript from which she had just read. "We have the truth right here: you were made in the likeness of God." She lowered the pages and took the time to look each of the twenty-three young women in the eyes. Then she said, "I hope that whatever happens to you in your life, you will always remember this moment and this truth."

Clarissa handed a candle to each of them and invited them to come forward one at a time, to light theirs from the large candle in the center representing God's light. Several of them wept openly as they stepped forward, their hands trembling. When all held a lighted candle, Clarissa declared, "Like communities of women since the beginning of time, living close to each other and to the earth and its rhythms, we enter our times of fertility on the full moon and bleed together when it's new. We will come to this cave every month on the new moon to remember that we are God's precious daughters and that our bodies are a sacred part of God's good creation. We will come here to celebrate that each and every one of us reflects the beautiful light of God."

Clarissa led the young women out of the cave. The sky had darkened, and a myriad of brilliant stars sparkled overhead. In the quiet of the encroaching night, she heard the movement of dolphins. They came close to the parade of young women, leaping and squeaking in greeting. Awestruck, the women continued their candlelight procession in silence back to the Josselyn Center.

§

The pounding on the door was loud, frantic. Clarissa awoke in the middle of that late-March night with a start, threw her tunic around her shoulders, then swooped out of her room and opened the door wide. She took one look at the gaunt child who stood trembling on the stoop under the light of a full moon and thought, *She could not have mustered the strength to knock with*

such urgency. Then Clarissa noticed the horse-drawn wagon on the road
that led to town, moving swiftly out of sight into the night.

As Clarissa opened her mouth to speak, the girl's knees buckled, and
she tumbled toward the ground. Clarissa caught her before she landed and
carried her inside, cradling the precious child. There were bruises up and
down her arms, and one under her left eye. Her threadbare clothes had been
torn. Once they were inside the house, the girl wrapped her arms around
Clarissa's neck, buried her head in her shoulder, and wept.

Clarissa guessed her to be a little younger than Aminah, who had just
turned twelve. Clarissa held her close and tried to soothe her. The girl was
mute, traumatized into silence by whatever terror had visited her. Clarissa
carried her to her room and laid her on the bed. She gently removed the
girl's clothes, washed the tears from her cheeks and the blood from the inside of her thighs. She found a clean linen nightshirt for her. "You're safe
here," she said.

Clarissa knelt by the bed and, stroking her hair, hummed lullabies and
recited psalms to the child until almost dawn. Exhausted, the girl closed
her eyes and moved to the edge of sleep several times, only to awaken with
gasps and screams, as fragments of nightmares visited her. "Hush now,
child," Clarissa whispered tenderly again and again. "It's all right. You're in
God's hands."

The next morning the young women of Manna House agreed immediately that they should provide a home for the poor girl. Clarissa surrendered
her bed to her and made up a palette on the floor for herself. She and the
others had to coax food into the frightened child. A few swallows at each
meal. For days she did not smile or speak, living nameless among them.

"We have dolphins," Clarissa announced to her one morning. "Would
you like to see them?" The girl nodded, allowing Clarissa to take her by the
hand and lead her down the steep path and along the beach in the direction
of the cave, where Clarissa frequently encountered the playful sea creatures
during her walks.

The first smile came when the girl saw a young dolphin break the ocean
surface and spring toward the sky. She clapped as two others followed, leaping out of the water in a synchronized dance. The three creatures circled
near the shore, the young one bobbing its head, beaming smiles and squeaks
in the girl's direction.

"My name is Lisette!" she called out, excitedly. "What's yours?" Then
she charged toward the dolphins with her arms outstretched.

"No!" shouted Clarissa, dreading the cold shock that would hit Lisette
when her feet met the water. But she kept running until she reached the
sea. And then she leapt in. Far from emitting the startled cries that Clarissa

expected to hear, Lisette giggled as she jumped the waves, heading straight for the dolphins.

They circled around her, moving their slick backs under her outstretched hands, and three more appeared. One stopped and gently nuzzled her face. Lisette reached out and grabbed the fin on its back. Clarissa stood on the shore, mesmerized by the sight as the dolphin swam through the waves in smooth arcing movements, staying close to the surface and carrying Lisette, who laughed with delight.

The girl's lips were tinged blue, and she was shivering from head to toe when she emerged from the water, smiling. Clarissa threw her tunic around her and carried her to a spot in the bright, warming spring sun. The child laughed again, and Clarissa felt a wave of gratitude and relief wash over her. Lisette was going to be all right.

§

The new moon in April fell two weeks later on the night before Easter. Clarissa and Johanna led the students to the cave again. They warmly invited Aminah to join them, but as with their first gathering, she declined. The composition of the group had changed slightly. A few of the older women, catching the excitement of their daughters and granddaughters, asked if they could join the ritual. A few others forbade their daughters from participating again, scolding Clarissa and Johanna and reminding them that "ladies don't speak of such things."

Johanna stood in the dark by the rock at the center of the cave, while Clarissa positioned herself by the entrance. "Tonight we'll keep the Easter vigil," Johanna announced. "And during this year, until next Easter, we'll come to this cave every month to hear the stories of our sisters in the faith that I've been blessed to discover. We'll learn together about many women who reflected the light and likeness of God—and who inspire us to do the same."

This was Clarissa's cue to step outside the cave and pick up the torch she had left stuck in the sand there. "The Light of Christ!" she proclaimed as she re-entered the cave, holding the torch high.

"Thanks be to God!" responded the circle in unison. Balnéaire was too small to have its own village church, but through their childhood years the families of the young women had carried them to the cathedral in Calais for the celebration of Easter—even if they attended at no other time during the year. They knew exactly what to say and do—and what to expect. Clarissa repeated the proclamation twice more, and they answered. Then she lit a

candle held by one of the young women, who lit the candle next to hers.
Light spread and filled every corner of the dark expanse, which enclosed
them like a womb of hope and blessing.

They spent that entire night together, moving more deeply inside the
cave and then up onto rocks as the tide came in and filled the space with
sea water. Clarissa reminded the young women that their Savior spent three
days in a tomb very much like the cave where they now waited. Throughout
the night they prayed and listened to passages of Scripture that spanned the
faith story from creation to crucifixion. They sang hymns, which reverberated off the walls in rich harmonies, until the tide went back out and the sky
outside began to lighten.

"Christ is risen!" proclaimed Clarissa at dawn.

"He is risen indeed!" came the shouted response. Then the young
women blended their voices in a chorus of "Alleluia," singing it over and
over.

They gathered in a circle again. Johanna moved to the center, her arms
raised high, holding a shallow bowl and a clay jar. Whispers rippled through
the group. "Surely it's not bread and wine," Clarissa heard one of the mothers say. "Only a priest can serve the Mass," said another.

"This Easter," Johanna announced, "we will share a communion of
milk and honey. They remind us that God, who nourishes us, has given us
the gift to nourish others. And they help us to remember that we live and
move in the sweetness of our Risen Lord." She handed the milk to Clarissa,
who dipped a finger into the bowl and took a taste, then passed it to the
woman next to her. They did the same with the jar of honey.

Clarissa tried to read the expressions on the faces as the milk and
honey were passed around the circle. The young women appeared mesmerized and moved by the ritual. But Clarissa couldn't tell if the mothers and
grandmothers felt the same, wondering if any were offended and whether
they would tell their husbands what had happened in the cave when they
got home.

Clarissa's concerns evaporated back at the Josselyn Center as the
students, many with tears in their eyes, hugged her and Johanna. They offered their thanks and spoke nonstop about the night they had all shared.
Then they spread out across Balnéaire, heading toward home and shouting
"Christ is risen!" as the sleepy village awoke to Easter morning.

The women of Manna House rested for a few hours and then feasted
for the rest of the day in their home. Clarissa felt deeply at peace as the quiet
day with her sisters unfolded. Nothing, she thought, could rob her of her
joy that Easter.

But that night as she settled, happily exhausted, into her palette on the floor, Lisette whispered to her from her bed. "Sister Clarissa," said the girl. She didn't say more for a few moments. "I didn't bleed," she finally blurted out. "I didn't bleed with the others."

Clarissa sat up. She responded gently. "You've suffered a terrible trauma, Lisette. It may take your body some time to recover." She tried to sound reassuring and to convince herself as she spoke. "It's been a long day," she sighed as she lay back down wearily. "Try to sleep now."

Twenty-two

By late spring the coins from Clarissa's father had run out. Jaxon's fire-wood business came to a standstill, as the people of Balnéaire needed wood only a few hours a day to cook rather than all day and night for warmth. Clarissa and her sisters had been on the coast for almost a year, and she tried to release the guilt she felt about not staying in communication with the nuns in Liège. She was too embarrassed to let them know that the women of Manna House had no money to pay even a modest amount toward the property on which they were living, and that they had constructed a building without even alerting Mother Agnes Luc, let alone securing permission.

They were saved that season by the villagers, who kept whatever misgivings they may have had about the odd little community on the bluff and their troubadour to themselves. The generous people of Balnéaire helped them plant a large garden, sharing seeds and bulbs garnered from the previous year's harvest. They scattered rye, oats, and barley in one corner. Beets and beans, turnips and gourds and onions, cabbages and carrots and cucumbers were planted in long beds.

A father of five daughters at the school brought a wood box containing a queen honeybee and set it at the edge of the garden, and soon a noisy swarm of worker bees followed and took up residence. A man who attended the community's Sunday night Scripture study gave them a bolt of linen, which his wife had made from the flax in his field. "You'll need some light clothing for the warm months," he said, bowing as he presented the gift.

Clarissa was grateful not to have to suffer through another summer in her black wool habit. "It's perfect!" she exclaimed, returning the bow and showering him with thanks. The linen was gray-brown—the dull shade always worn by her neighbors, who couldn't afford the brightly dyed cloth of the rich. Clarissa thought, but didn't say, that the color would be a constant reminder to her and her sisters to be humble, sharing a life of simplicity with those who were too poor to live any other way. Nerida and Johanna went to work at once sewing simple robes.

Clarissa joyfully assisted at the birth of the lambs that spring. Each of the ewes delivered three, tripling their small flock to nine. All the newborns were healthy and playful, a source of delight for everyone—especially Liliana, who appointed herself their caretaker under Nerida's supervision.

Though they had only three mature sheep, the community invited their friends for the shearing soon after Easter. Men from the village, arriving with their families, brought their expertise, clippers, and bags for the wool. The yield was small, as they expected—but enough, Clarissa hoped, for the plan she and Johanna had hatched. They handed the wool over to a neighbor for the long process of cleaning and carding, then spinning into thick thread and weaving.

The day turned into a marvelous celebration of the arrival of spring. Clarissa loved everything about it—the sun warming her face, the laughter of her neighbors and friends, the lambs gamboling in the pasture and the children splashing in the pond, the feasting and dancing to Jaxon's music that lasted late into the night. As they watched the last remnant of villagers finally start down the path toward town, Clarissa turned to Johanna and said, "We should do this every year," and Johanna agreed.

Jaxon took the advent of warm weather as an invitation to begin building himself a shed close to the house—"one like my accommodations at the Dover abbey," he said. Clarissa was glad that Jaxon would soon be moving out of the barn into his own space. He also set about constructing a comfortable home for the bees. He spent many hours crafting wood boxes and stacking them on top of one another into a pillar at the edge of the garden, creating a beehive that was the envy of all their neighbors.

Aminah announced that the Muslim holy month would begin that year on April twenty-third, and that she would be observing the traditional Ramadan fast. "I'll keep it with you," piped up Johanna.

Clarissa, feeling that Johanna's eagerness left her no choice, chimed in, "Me too"—having little idea of what she was volunteering for. She knew that Jesus had fasted from food for forty days in the desert before launching his ministry, and that his followers often connected fasting and prayer. Sister Mary Peter had told her once that giving up food for short periods of time helped the nuns shift their focus from physical well-being to spiritual growth, from the things of this world to the ways of God. But Clarissa, who loved food, felt that their diet was already meager enough, and she never felt called to this particularly humbling spiritual discipline.

When Aminah explained that they would not be eating or drinking between sunrise and sunset for a month, Clarissa almost gasped out loud.

On the day that she realized that Ramadan fell at a different time each year, she muttered to herself, "Why couldn't it have come in December, when the sun rises late and sets early?" Instead, they were observing the Muslim fast on the cusp of summer and the year's longest days.

Clarissa stuffed herself each morning before sunrise. She wished that, like Aminah and Johanna, she could embrace fasting as a way to deepen her prayer life and her faith. But instead she dragged herself through the days, tracking the sun's path across the sky and dreaming of the meal that awaited her as soon as it disappeared. The one delight of Ramadan for her was that Aminah, who was deeply moved by her Christian sisters' act of spiritual solidarity, insisted on preparing all their evening meals.

Aminah possessed by far the best cooking skills among them. Clarissa and Johanna had turned over the Egyptian spices from Asim, Kafele, and Madu to her when they had arrived at the house on the coast. By fall the spices had run out. When Clarissa was stocking up for their holiday baking, she was overjoyed to find a vendor of Eastern spices at the large market in Calais. She had bought a few jars and presented these to Aminah on Christmas Day, proclaiming proudly, "A taste of home for you."

As May twenty-first approached, Aminah spent many hours planning the meal for Eid al Fitr that would mark the end of their month of fasting. She had just enough cardamom, cumin, and saffron left from Clarissa's Christmas gift to pull together a marvelous celebratory feast. The centerpiece was lamb cooked in the spices and drenched with mint sauce. Alongside it were the first of the garden's early peas and a special sweet bread baked with honey, cardamom, and raisins.

Clarissa hesitated to eat the main dish, until Aminah announced, "It's not one of ours. I traded with a neighbor for one of his lambs." Clarissa knew that Aminah owned little of value, and she looked immediately at the young woman's left wrist. Her gorgeous bracelet, the gift from her mother, was gone. Clarissa was both moved and saddened that Aminah had made such a great sacrifice for them, parting with the exquisite gold band that had been a source of deep comfort to her. But she had never seen Aminah as joyful as she was on that day when she prepared the feast for them all.

Clarissa savored every bite of the extraordinary meal, anticipating with excitement what would come after it. When they finished eating, she nodded at Johanna and asked Aminah to close her eyes for a moment. When she opened them again, in her lap lay a gorgeous prayer rug, beige with a striking pattern of black diamonds, created from the wool of their first shearing. Aminah's smile was radiant. "Thank you," she whispered to her generous and cherished sisters, clutching the rug close to her as tears pooled in her eyes.

That spring of 1205, Jaxon's shed grew and grew. Clarissa thought it a bit extravagant for a troubadour, but she kept her feelings to herself. Jaxon's generosity and hard work had sustained them through the winter, and she was too thankful to question his expansive construction. On the day that he put the finishing touches on the building, Jaxon invited her to come and look at it. "I changed my mind about a shed," he said. "Your house is getting crowded. This is for all the other girls who will show up like Lisette. Word's getting out that there's kindness and refuge here, and there's no telling how many will come."

"But what about you?" asked Clarissa, as grateful understanding dawned.

"I'm happy in the barn," replied Jaxon, punctuating his words with his characteristic wink.

Nerida and Liliana moved into one room of the new house, with Lisette in another. The young community referred to it simply as Q Cottage. They understood that Quibilah Cottage would be a challenge to remember and pronounce, especially for their neighbors. When questioned, the young women smiled and answered that the "Q" stood for "Quiet."

Jaxon's prediction came true soon enough. "How did you know?" Clarissa asked him a few weeks later when the new house was almost full of young women who had shown up on the doorstep seeking safety and shelter.

"I've seen it all over England," he told her, "and here in France. A man who can't stand a girl saying no to him forces himself on her, so she's ruined and can't marry anyone else. Or he kidnaps her and makes her marry him." Clarissa had never heard Jaxon speak in such an angry tone—or about so serious a subject. He shook his head sadly. "Where else are they going to go to escape?"

Clarissa was moved by the parade of girls that appeared on the stoop, the would-be child brides whose mothers deposited them there and the young ones who mustered the courage on their own to run away, as she had done. The day students in the school were all from Balnéaire, but the girls who moved in came from Calais and places even farther distant. They were ushered there on a secret network run by kind and courageous women, who spread the word and made sure the girls arrived safely at the community on the bluff, far away from enraged suitors and fathers.

Some stayed only a few days, just long enough for their mothers to make arrangements for safe haven with a relative or friend a distance away. Others missed their families so much that they returned home to face their fate. But several settled in for a few months, drawn by the warmth and compassion and respect they found. Clarissa felt overcome by sorrow and outrage whenever she considered what the girls had suffered to be among them. But she was continually grateful for Jaxon's foresight and generosity—and for the house with six more rooms to receive their growing community.

§

During the new moon in May, Johanna launched her series of stories in the cave about inspired and inspiring women of faith. Lisette moved next to Clarissa as soon as Johanna began to speak. Listening raptly, she clutched Clarissa's right hand tightly with both of hers.

Across the circle stood Aminah. Her head was wrapped in a *hijab* scarf that she had created that morning by cutting out a corner of her cloak. No longer a girl, Aminah smiled at Clarissa and she smiled back, warmly acknowledging Aminah's presence for the first time in the circle of women.

Clarissa was not the least bit surprised that Johanna began her stories with the five women who saved the life of Moses. With great artistry, Johanna wove the tales of Shiphrah, Puah, Jochebed, Miriam, and the pharaoh's daughter into a narrative tapestry celebrating these bold women. Johanna had asked Aminah to bestow a name on the anonymous daughter, and she chose Rehema, which, she explained, means "a compassionate woman of kind heart." As Johanna unfolded the saga for the students, they gasped, laughed, sighed, and cheered at appropriate points in the plot.

When she finished, Johanna declared, "The first acts of rebellion against unjust power in the Bible were carried out by women!" And then she added with a laugh, "And don't you think that pharaoh grew to regret letting the girls live?"

Clarissa stepped to the rock and called out Jochebed's name, then lit a candle in her honor and handed it to Lisette, who took it eagerly. Clarissa did the same for the other biblical women, handing a candle as she pronounced each name to a young woman who seemed especially moved by the story. When she named Rehema, she carried the candle to Aminah, who received it with a grateful smile.

Then Clarissa stepped back to the rock and proclaimed, "We give thanks for these mothers in the faith who reflected the light of God." The young women spread the light once more around the circle, reminding one another that they too were reflections of Divine Light.

§

Galorian was assigned a small room to sleep in, across the great piazza from the pope's Lateran Palace and its imposing basilica. His cell in the center of the city had only a tiny window, and he knew immediately that there was neither sunlight nor space enough for him to grow the seeds Brother Bernard had given him. He kept them in their packets and placed the box of insects on the floor in a corner, where they seemed not to mind their downgraded accommodation.

Upon his arrival, Galorian was handed a fine linen robe to replace the rough, dusty cassock in which he had arrived. He did his best to blend in with the cardinals and bishops who bustled around the stately buildings, adorning themselves in tall miters and flowing red robes embroidered with gold on Sundays and special occasions. Despite Bernard's proclamation, he doubted that his box of bugs could ever produce enough red dye to color all that finery.

In addition to containing the residence of Pope Innocent III, the palace had numerous rooms and offices dedicated to the work of the church. Galorian had a small desk in a room in the damp and windowless basement. He sat among rows of desks with other young men, all given to the labor of copying records from the lofty church councils that had convened in the fourth and fifth centuries to address great controversies about the nature of God and Jesus Christ. It was not as heady a task as Galorian had hoped for, but he tried to keep in mind that he had a role in preserving sacred history.

The young men worked long days in silence hunched over the documents. Their only break was a meal at midday in the refectory of the basilica. Then they engaged in lively conversation, often theological in nature. An opinionated and outspoken Italian Dominican monk named Eusebio, whose desk was behind Galorian's, soon emerged as Galorian's favorite among his comrades.

Galorian steeled himself every morning and evening to walk through the throng of clamoring beggars that crowded the huge piazza in front of the holy buildings. "I guess they know that churchmen are generous," he commented one day as the group of scribes ate their midday meal together.

Eusebio laughed cynically. "They are here to protest as much as to beg. It's the church that makes them poor." Galorian shot him a doubting look, as a few of the other scribes moved hastily back toward their work. Making no effort to hide his obvious contempt, Eusebio declared, "The priests practice simony, charging exorbitant sums to perform baptisms and funerals. The bishops practice usury, lending money at excessively high interest rates. And the pope practices taxation, overburdening the people mercilessly. The average peasant can't even begin to pay." The young monk swept his hand across the room, where colorful light streamed through elaborate stained-glass windows onto impressive marble-top tables. "But how else is the church going to finance its Crusades and all this luxury?"

That evening Galorian walked more slowly and deliberately through the crowd of beggars huddled in clumps around the piazza. He spied a young man off to himself, in a corner near the steps of the palace, and decided to approach him. The man was thin, dressed in rags, with a sparse beard growing on a gentle face.

Galorian reached out with a coin to place in the beggar's hand. The man in rags shook his head and held up his hand to refuse the gift. "God bless you," he said, locking his eyes on Galorian's. Galorian saw what looked like fire burning in those eyes. Then the beggar added, "Follow Jesus to simplicity, and no one will need to beg here." Galorian, stunned and troubled by the words, turned away quickly.

The next morning when he arrived in the basement of the palace, the desk behind his was empty. When he inquired as to the whereabouts of his friend, a cleric told him only, "Eusebio is no longer with us."

§

The warmer the weather, the farther Clarissa ventured on her walks. On a particularly clear day in June, she made her way down the path to the beach, passed by the cave, and kept walking. She was so taken by the radiance of the sun dancing off the waves that she almost missed the second cave. It was larger and deeper than their monthly ritual space. "Hello!" she called into the dark expanse when she discovered it, expecting the same echoed reply as before.

"Hello," came the response. The voice that answered was not her own. She peered inside and saw nothing but darkness. Then she glimpsed the shadow of a figure coming toward her. She felt a bolt of fear, but she didn't run away. As he came toward the light, she could see that the man was bent, leaning on a long stick. He was dressed from head to foot in white, and he carried a rattle—a gourd filled with pebbles—that he shook as he approached. He blinked several times as his eyes met the brightness of the day outside the cave.

He stopped several paces from Clarissa. "Where's the food?" he demanded as he looked her up and down suspiciously. She took a step toward him, and he backed up a step, shaking his rattle again.

"I didn't know you were here," she said and then introduced herself. He would not say his name, but he told her that nine people lived in the cave, three of them children. They depended on villagers to set food at the mouth of the cave for them. "But they don't come often enough," he said.

"I'll come back," said Clarissa. "with bread and cheese and vegetables from our garden."

"Bring onions!" the man shouted after her as she hurried home. She found Nerida in the kitchen. "We need to make up a basket," she declared, and Nerida helped her pack up a hearty supply of food, including four big onions.

The two women carried the basket to the cave's entrance. Clarissa called out again, and the bent man appeared and watched as they set it down. Behind him hovered a small child—*no more than three years old*, thought Clarissa—also completely covered in white. The boy's body was dangerously thin, and his eyes showed only a flicker of life. He stepped around to the man's side and reached out his arms toward Clarissa and Nerida.

Nerida turned away, tears streaming down her cheeks. Clarissa followed her, and they walked quickly toward home. "It's so unfair," choked Nerida between her tears. "That boy is no more a leper than you or I."

"I know," said Clarissa, taking Nerida by the hand. "But if one or both of his parents were declared lepers, they had only two hard choices—to abandon him, or to take him to the cave with them."

"What kind of a childhood is that?" wailed Nerida. Clarissa squeezed her hand and they walked in silence for a while. Then Nerida looked at Clarissa and said, "Now I understand how desperately you wanted to rescue Liliana."

Twenty-three

Galorian knew that he was unlikely ever to see Eusebio again. But he hoped to see the other young man who had captured his attention, to ask him to explain his words. For several days Galorian searched, but he never again saw the man with fire in his eyes in the piazza. He decided to take time as he came and went each day to seek out and listen to as many stories from the other beggars as he could. He harbored a hope of disproving Eusebio's denunciations of the church. "What happened to you?" he asked again and again. The people begging in the piazza were anxious to tell him.

"I called the priest to hear my father's deathbed confession and perform Last Rites," said a man with the rough and weathered hands of one who had spent a lifetime toiling in the soil to grow food. "Before I knew what was happening, the priest convinced my father to turn over his land to the church to pay for his burial. In the blink of an eye, I lost my inheritance and the land that fed my family."

Another man, with rheumy, bloodshot eyes set in a gaunt and pale face, added his sad tale. "My priest wanted to buy a church position in another town with more prestige and power. He started charging us even to receive the Mass. None of us could afford to be Christians and also feed our children."

Echoing Eusebio's indictment, a particularly angry and articulate young man summed up the church for Galorian this way: "The pope taxes the bishops, the bishops extort from the priests, and the priests rob the people."

Galorian had no words of solace or argument to offer. With each passing day, he found it more difficult to pass through the crowd of beggars in the piazza and take his place in the dank basement in front of Eusebio's empty desk. He continued to show up and do his work, but he did so with a heavy and troubled heart. The work was painstaking—and endless.

One night he sat alone, his head throbbing and his back aching. The other scribes had all retired to their rooms for the night. Galorian was intent on finishing a task of translation, but he could not stay focused on it. He yearned for the garden at Saint Catherine's, for the physical labor and the bright sun on his face. He thought of Aminah, wondering how she was faring in France with the nuns. Josselyn was never far from his heart, and he regularly marked the age of their daughter. *She would be two and a half now*, he thought that night, trying to picture how she would have looked and what she would have enjoyed at that age.

Galorian gave up on completing his task. He put aside the manuscript, walked down the hall, and started out the door. But then he turned back. He missed his late-night ventures through Saint Catherine's, and he decided to try to calm his spirit with a stroll through the Lateran Palace, allowing his curiosity to lead him down some of its unexplored corridors.

Unlike at the monastery, Galorian found most of the doors locked. He knew that the Holy of Holies, the pope's private chapel, was somewhere in the building. So was a special chapel that could be reached only by climbing up to it on one's knees. He had heard the stories from the other scribes, but he didn't know how to find these, and he assumed that they too would be locked to outsiders like him.

He walked down a hallway and soon realized that he had wandered onto the wing where the cardinals lived. Feeling like a trespasser, he turned to go. But a loud voice grabbed his attention. "You need to pay more!" shouted a woman behind the door nearest him. "We can barely afford to eat."

The door opened abruptly. Galorian got a peek inside an elegant room with a large and rumpled canopy bed, framed in dark blue brocade curtains. A cardinal he recognized was hastily throwing a purple velvet robe around himself. Galorian moved back into the shadows. The cardinal grabbed the disheveled woman around the arm and shoved her into the hallway. "Get out!" he said, shaking with anger but trying to keep his voice low. "And keep quiet . . . or you'll be sorry."

"*You'll* be sorry," said the woman, making no effort to speak softly, "when something terrible happens to your bastard son." The cardinal slammed the door, and the woman, cursing and sobbing, ran past Galorian, down the corridor and out of the palace.

§

The sun-drenched days of summer passed quickly on the bluff. Jaxon, the bees, and the owls made sure that music filled the air day and night. Clarissa found the courage to ask Jaxon if he would give her singing lessons. They met a few times in a clearing in the woods where she could practice without being heard by anyone else. But after their third session and her hundredth attempt—so it seemed—to sing a scale on pitch, she threw up her hands and declared in dismay, "A croaking frog!" Patient and full of encouragement, Jaxon was willing to keep up the lessons, but Clarissa decided to accept that she could no more change her voice than her raven-colored curls.

She took more frequent walks to the beach, often including Lisette and Liliana with her in the mornings when, to the girls' unending delight, the dolphins regularly greeted them. Clarissa and her sisters suspended classes for the summer, giving themselves and their students a break from inside learning and time to attend to the demands of food production. The abundant gifts of the community garden sustained them, the people living in the cave, and many of the villagers, who appeared regularly to help with tending and harvesting.

Either Clarissa or Nerida, and often both, visited the cave twice a week, exchanging a full basket of food for an empty one that they filled again. "It's not enough," declared Nerida to Clarissa on their walk home one morning.

"It's all we have to spare," Clarissa responded.

"I don't mean the amount," said Nerida. "I mean that I want to do more for the lepers than just leave food outside their cave."

Part of the answer came to her in a conversation with Sapientia. Though the old woman was just learning to read, she had spent her long life gaining knowledge of illnesses, healing herbs, and midwifery. Sapientia agreed to take on Nerida as an apprentice in exchange for her reading lessons, glad that all her knowledge would not die with her. Nerida spent many hours watching and learning from the wise woman.

On a mid-summer morning, as she and Clarissa were walking to the cave, Nerida shared the other part of her plan. "I want to make sure you feel all right about it," she said, "before I say anything to the people in the cave."

"I think it's a wonderful idea," said Clarissa.

When they got to the entrance of the cave, they shouted the usual "Hello." The bent man came as they set down the basket of food. Nerida asked to see the mother of the three children inside. He looked at her skeptically, but he shuffled back into the cave to get her.

The only part of the woman that wasn't covered in white cloth was her face, though even it was difficult to see. She kept her hands in front of it and stared at the ground. Clarissa and Nerida introduced themselves. When the mother looked up, they saw the festering skin lesions she was trying to hide. She told them her name was Sybille.

Nerida spilled her plan. Sybille said no. Nerida pleaded, but the woman was resolute. "Too risky for you and the child," she declared. Clarissa could see the deep disappointment on Nerida's face.

They turned to go. But before they left, Nerida said to Sybille, "There's something for you in the basket. It's chaulmoogra oil—from an evergreen tree. Rub it on your sores—and on those of anyone else who needs it. It will help."

Sybille nodded. She turned to go into the cave, and then looked back at Nerida. "All right," she said, "bring the child." And then she walked back into the dark expanse.

That evening after dinner, Nerida announced to her sisters, "I'm going to take Liliana to meet the children in the lepers' cave."

Lisette gasped. "But it's dangerous to mix with lepers! Why do you think they wear white robes and ring bells and shake rattles to warn people?"

"But the children aren't lepers," said Nerida gently.

"But won't Liliana get sick?" asked Lisette.

"Even if they *were* lepers, she wouldn't get sick," said Nerida, sharing some of her newfound knowledge. "Leprosy isn't contagious," she explained. "Just ignorance." Lisette looked sheepishly at the ground. "I didn't mean you," said Nerida apologetically. "I mean all the people who are in such a panic about it. Declaring their neighbors lepers and forcing good people to live in caves and forests like wild animals—for no good reason at all. It's madness."

A few days later, Clarissa overheard Nerida explaining to Liliana after breakfast that she would be meeting some children who dressed a little funny and lived in a cave. Liliana could barely contain her excitement about these unusual new friends. She and Nerida started off down the path toward the beach with a picnic lunch. At dinner that night, Nerida described the events of the day, with a weary Liliana asleep on her lap.

At the mouth of the cave, Nerida had called for Sybille. The woman appeared, and Nerida was pleased to see that her sores seemed less raw and inflamed. Clinging to their mother's white robe were three thin, wide-eyed children. Sybille introduced them as Giselle, Viviane, and Sylvain, and encouraged them to go with Nerida. They took a few tentative steps toward her, and then Liliana released her grip on Nerida's hand and ran toward them, almost bowling them over with her effusive hugs.

Sybille smiled and mouthed "Thank you" as Nerida led the small pack of children toward an isolated spot on the shore, where the waves were relatively calm and they were unlikely to be spotted. The receding water had hollowed out a tidal pool in the sand, where the shallow water was warm enough for the children to wade comfortably. For two hours they ate, splashed, and played, enjoying the warm sunshine and fresh air—and the antics of the dolphins that had come to entertain them.

Nerida made sure that their white robes were well dried in the sun before taking them back to the cave, where Sybille waited. The children chattered nonstop about their day at the beach as their mother ushered them back inside. "I'm going to take Giselle, Viviane, and Sylvain on an outing every time I visit the cave," a happy Nerida said to her awed sisters at dinner that night.

§

By late July, Q Cottage was filled to capacity, with Nerida and Liliana, Lisette, and eight other young women sharing its six rooms. Lisette, who had not spoken a word during her first week with the community, became a garrulous friend and advocate for the new arrivals, making sure they ate, helping them adjust to school, introducing them to the dolphins, and holding their hands when they needed to cry.

On the last day of August, the neighbor who had brought the gift of bees in spring arrived to show the women how to extract the honey from the hive. First he made a small pile of hay, surrounded it with a ring of earth, and set it on fire. While the smoke calmed the bees, he lifted the first wood frame off the stack. He held the long blade of his knife in the fire to heat it. Then he ran it over the dozens of wax caps that covered the honeycomb in the frame, as a rich gold liquid drained out and into the wood bucket at his feet.

Clarissa and her sisters kept some of the honey in jars, to have available for baking into, and spreading onto, their bread in the weeks ahead. But most of it they turned into mead, adding yeast and allowing it to ferment during the last month before the cold weather set in. Their first batch was a surprising success, and they looked forward to drinking the sweet, warm delicacy in the frigid days to come.

"I'd like to invite Viviane and Giselle to attend our school," announced Nerida at dinner one evening. "Sylvain is a boy and only three years old. But the girls are six and eight, and when we start our classes again, I think they should be in school."

Her words were met with silence. After a few moments, Johanna responded first. "It would be a risk for the school. A few of our students would leave. Some of their parents would insist on it."

Clarissa chimed in, "It would be more than a few."

The young women talked about it at length, weighing the possibility that they might lose the school if too many of their students disappeared. They hated the thought that they might have to give up teaching and their monthly rituals in the cave, as well as the good relationships with the villagers that they had so carefully nurtured.

But they all knew what they had to do. "It's wrong to keep innocent children away from learning," Johanna declared. "We all know how that feels." Clarissa, with reluctance, had to agree with her. "Jesus spent time among the lepers, listening and healing," continued Johanna. "How could we turn our backs on those precious girls?"

In the end it was Nerida herself who decided that it would be best for them not to include Giselle and Viviane in the school. After a few days of thought and prayer, she announced to her sisters, "I think it would be too hard on them. To see how the other girls live. To show up in their white robes and feel different." She sighed. "Maybe isolation is better than envy and embarrassment."

Clarissa nodded sympathetically. "I'm willing to add a school lesson whenever we visit their cave," she said. And so beginning that fall, they added reading lessons for the girls to their outings, teaching them on the beach until it grew too cold, and then sharing lessons by candlelight in a corner of the cave.

Clarissa and Johanna continued to take the older school students to the other cave for gatherings each month—what the young women called their "Moon Times." With eloquence, Johanna kept spilling her stories of biblical women. She introduced her eager listeners to Ruth and Naomi, whose love and loyalty to each other ensured their survival in a precarious time. She related the stories of Vashti, who refused to be exploited, and Esther, the queen who saved her people. She spoke of the wise judge Deborah and the renowned prophet Huldah.

When winter set in, the young women huddled more closely together in the ritual cave around a bonfire that Clarissa built in a hollow of the big rock. Shivering at times in the damp cold, they persevered in making their monthly pilgrimages, spreading warmth and light to one another. Johanna lifted up the sacrificial generosity of the widow of Zarephath, the cleverness of the prostitute Rahab, and the peacemaking wisdom of Abigail, whose gift of lavish food to an enemy prevented a war. She sang the praises of the faithful mothers Hannah, who gave her beloved son into God's service, and Rizpah, whose bold vigil on behalf of her murdered sons ended a famine and brought peace to the land.

The stories kept pouring out of Johanna, and Clarissa learned along with the other young women. *How could I have grown up in the church,* she wondered as she listened, *and never heard of these faithful women who changed history? And why didn't their heroic stories matter as much as the oft-told tales of men?*

Twenty-four

Lisette's baby was born on December twenty-first. Nerida caught him, with Sapientia guiding her and Clarissa assisting at her side. Clarissa held Lisette's hand throughout the nine-hour labor, reciting psalms, praying, and encouraging her.

When the baby boy appeared, Clarissa murmured thanks for a safe birth. And when he took his first breath and let out a healthy squall, she let her tears flow and cradled him close, as if she were never going to let him go. He was a glimmer of light on the darkest day of the year. Lisette named him Moses Jaxon.

Three days later, the women invited the villagers of Balnéaire to join them for a Christmas Eve that they promised would be unforgettable. A crowd packed into the Josselyn Center just before sunset, murmuring quietly and waiting expectantly as Jaxon serenaded them. When he stopped singing, a loud and insistent knock broke the silence.

Johanna ran to answer it, throwing open the double doors, as the villagers surged in close to see. There stood the donkey Reginald, minus his miter. Sitting atop him was Lisette, wrapped in a dark blue mantle that swaddled her still-distended belly. Standing next to them, holding onto Reginald's bridle, was Clovis, the rough boy in the Greek fisherman's cap whom Clarissa had shooed away from the school.

"My wife's going to have a baby. Right now!" he exclaimed. Clarissa could see that he had smeared some honey on his chin and attached a few pieces of lamb's wool there to create a fuller beard than the one that was just beginning to sprout on his face. "We need a room!" he demanded.

"As you can see," said Johanna dramatically, sweeping her hand across the crowd, "we're already full in here. There's no room for you." She paused a moment, and then added, "But we have a barn you can use."

"A barn?" said Clovis. "That's a terrible place to have a baby!"

"It's all we have," Johanna insisted. She walked out through the doorway and stepped onto the path, leading the couple, followed by the curious and enamored crowd. By the time the last of the villagers had crammed into the barn, Moses, swaddled in layers of cloth, was lying on a pile of hay in the sheep's feeding trough. Saint Catherine and her latest brood—who had apparently decided that winter that they were barn owls—peered down on the proceedings from their new home in the rafters.

Johanna began reading the miraculous story of Jesus's birth from the Gospel of Luke. When she got to "In that region, there were shepherds living in the fields, keeping watch over their flock by night," Jaxon led a parade of village boys into the barn. They wore long wool tunics and kept the community's small flock of sheep and lambs in line with long sticks. Once inside, they pushed and shoved one another, trying to get close to Moses. Jaxon had to intervene when two of them started a swordfight with their sticks over the baby's head. The sheep looked on curiously at the unusual bundle in their manger.

Clarissa, holding tight to Liliana's hand, could not take her eyes off of Moses, who was sleeping serenely in the hay. Gazing at his vulnerable innocence, Clarissa remembered that his biblical namesake had survived two death sentences from the pharaoh as an infant, and that the tyrannical King Herod had ordered the slaughter of all the babies around Bethlehem in the wake of Jesus's birth. It seemed a miracle to her that any children at all survived the rigors of birth and the evil designs of powerful men who were threatened by them. She felt a surge of gratitude and love for little Moses.

Nerida, standing next to her, whispered, "I have a surprise. Look up there, and soon you'll see." She pointed at the large opening in the ceiling above the rafters, through which hay was typically dropped from the hayloft above to the sheep on the barn floor. Johanna continued the reading: "Then an angel of the Lord stood before them, and the glory of the Lord shone around them. And suddenly there was with the angel a multitude of the heavenly host praising God."

Clarissa looked up and saw a pair of Jaxon's big shoes—the red and green ones with bells on the upturned toes—coming down through the opening. One of them fell off a small, dirty foot that was trying to keep it on. The shoes were followed by a white robe, and then a face plastered with sheer joy. Sylvain, with a rope tied around his waist, gripped a candle tightly as he was lowered through the opening. He wore a halo made of small gold bells looped over thin strips of bright yellow silk, which Clarissa recognized immediately had once been Jaxon's favorite shirt.

An unpleasant smell assaulted Clarissa's nostrils. She felt suddenly transported back to the barrel of dead fish that had carried her on her first channel crossing from England. She soon located the source. Attached across Sylvain's thin shoulders was a long stick draped with an old fishing net, into which had been stuck a few random owl feathers. The boy's wings reeked of dead herring. But he hovered proudly above the crowd, grinning. Upon seeing him, Liliana dropped Clarissa's hand and clapped, squealing with delight.

Soon Viviane was lowered next to her brother. Her wings were cock-eyed, and her halo had slipped below one eye. The candle she gripped illuminated a face etched with more fear than joy. Whoever was on the other end of Giselle's rope was in a hurry to let her down, and she fell through the opening laughing and swinging, knocking into her siblings—who tried to keep their angelic dignity and avoid setting each other on fire while trying to push her away. Even Viviane laughed then, and the enthralled crowd clapped and laughed along with her.

The villagers were used to a revolving cast of characters at the community, and no one questioned who these unusual angels were, or where they had come from. Clarissa noticed joyful tears coursing down Nerida's cheeks, and a few rolled down her own as well. She could barely contain the wonder of it all.

Johanna stepped up and announced a party back at the Josselyn Center. She started on the path, leading the villagers, who began filing out behind her. Clarissa turned and hugged Nerida. "Thank you," said Clarissa to her dear friend. "I can't imagine a bigger or better Christmas surprise." The words were barely out of her mouth when she heard gasps and shouts of "Look!" and "Oh my!" from the exiting crowd.

Expecting calamity, Clarissa rushed outside to see. She stopped, her mouth open wide in amazement. "No," she said softly, shaking her head. "No . . . it can't be." She stood and watched with the others, unable to believe what she was seeing.

The sun had set. A bright star hovered over the pasture. Three exotic and picturesque camels, silhouetted against a shimmering cobalt blue sky, were slowly making their way up the path from the village. The men perched on top of them, dressed in headdresses and robes, hummed gently as they climbed up to the bluff.

When they reached the top, the crowd of villagers, silenced by awe, parted to allow the camels to walk through them toward the barn. A few reached out to touch the shaggy creatures as they passed, or to pull on one of their green and red tassels, as if to make sure they were real. Clarissa, trembling, stepped forward as the camels knelt on the ground and the three men slid off them.

Asim bowed. Kafele and Madu, each holding an elegant wood box, knelt before her. Asim, smiling his toothless smile, said a few words as the two young men held out the boxes to Clarissa. She took them and tried to gather her wits and her budding grasp of Arabic. But the words Asim spoke were unfamiliar, not among those she had learned. She looked around for Aminah, who came and stood by her, steadying Clarissa with an arm around her shoulder. Aminah said softly, "He says 'We've brought frankincense and myrrh.'"

Clarissa felt the tears gathering in her eyes again. She remembered the words Aminah had taught in her very first Arabic lesson. She looked into Asim's eyes. "No gold?" Clarissa said in the language of her three friends from the desert, observing the surprise on their faces. Then she grinned, and they grinned back.

"No gold," repeated Asim, laughing.

Clarissa pried the lids off the boxes to release the pungent, sweet aromas they contained. Then she turned to face the crowd of villagers. "These are wise friends," she said. "They courageously guided Johanna and me safely through Egypt when we were on a holy pilgrimage, before we came here." She turned back to Asim, Kafele, and Madu. "Thank you," she said in Arabic, her voice breaking. "Thank you. Peace be with you. Welcome," she said, bowing to each of them.

The villagers began to chatter away then, clearly astounded that this Christmas miracle had visited them. They gave Clarissa and her sisters all the credit for orchestrating such a holy and magical night. They surrounded the three wise men from the East and ushered them toward the Josselyn Center to share in the celebration.

Clarissa watched as Sylvain ran up to Kafele and tugged on his robe, pointing at Quibilah. Kafele, smiling, reached down and scooped up the boy. Kafele carried him over and set him on top of his camel, whose bellowed response sent Sylvain into a fit of giggles.

Clarissa turned and thanked Aminah for her translation help. "I'm happy to give it," Aminah replied. "You've given so much to me."

The words prompted Clarissa. "Oh, I almost forgot," she said, "I have gold." She slipped the bracelet hidden under her left sleeve off her wrist and onto her friend's.

Aminah added her tears to the flood that flowed that night. "How did you find it—and get it back?" she asked, fingering the familiar Arabic letters.

"That's my secret," said Clarissa. Aminah gave her a grateful hug.

"Do you know my favorite part of the Christmas story?" Clarissa asked. Aminah shook her head. "It's when the angels appeared to the shepherds in the field and sang, 'Glory to God in the highest, and on earth, peace.'" They watched as Kafele handed Quibilah's reins to Sylvain. The boy, with halo and wings askew but still looking angelic, grinned from ear to ear as the beast lifted him high into the sky toward the brightly shining star.

"On earth, *salaam*," said Clarissa, as she put her arm around Aminah and began walking toward the Josselyn Center to join their friends.

§

Inside the center, they found Johanna and Nerida ladling up mead and spiced cider. The four friends touched mugs all around, with three of them offering warm Christmas toasts and wishes. Clarissa wanted more than anything in that moment to tell them all how much they meant to her. But though she was usually so good with words, she could not find any that night. She just smiled warmly at her sisters.

It was very late by the time all the villagers made their way home and the center was back in order. Aminah and Lisette, with Moses, had already retired to their rooms, too weary to stay awake to the end. Sylvain and Liliana had fallen asleep under a table, snoring softly and leaning against each other with their heads and shoulders touching. Nerida picked up Liliana, and Giselle carried Sylvain, with Viviane following them to Q Cottage, where they all found spaces on the beds and floor for the night.

Asim, Kafele, and Madu settled into the barn, insistent on sleeping there with Jaxon and all the animals. Clarissa worried that they would all suffer a long night of neighing and braying—punctuated with some bleating and bellowing. But she was unable to come up with another solution.

She and Johanna walked back to Manna House. Johanna went straight to her room and stretched out on her palette, and Clarissa flopped down next to her. Both exhausted and enervated by the events of the evening, Clarissa began to laugh. "What's funny?" asked Johanna.

Clarissa shook her head and rolled her eyes playfully. "Just picture it. Agnes Luc is hunched over her desk in her dark little office, frowning as usual, and a novice comes in and says, 'Sorry to interrupt, Mother, but three men on camels are at the gate.'" Clarissa, laughing too hard to say more, followed that with her best impression ever of the Mother Superior's sourest expression, punctuating it with several loud rattling wheezes.

"Or maybe," said Johanna, holding her side, which ached from the spasms of laughter that were overtaking her, "she looked up from her desk and saw Quibilah's face filling up her window, flapping his huge nostrils and smiling at her with his big yellow teeth." She added several gasping wheezes of her own, and they laughed until they were too exhausted to laugh any more.

Johanna tried to stifle a yawn as she asked, "How did you find Aminah's bracelet and get it back?"

"I know that the farmer Guilbert has the best lambs. And I also know that Aminah would have served only the best for the feast. I traded my mother's necklace for her bracelet."

"Oh, Clarissa," was all Johanna could manage to say in response, as the yawn overtook her. She closed her eyes and sighed, "What a night."

Clarissa squeezed her dear friend's hand and stood up. "I guess we meant it when we said it would be unforgettable," she said as she walked toward the door. Then she looked back and said with a smile, "We just didn't know *how* unforgettable."

§

They began Christmas morning early in the center, with Asim, Kafele, and Madu kneeling on their rugs, Aminah a short distance behind them on hers, and Clarissa, Johanna, and Nerida facing one another with their prayer books. After prayers, they all gathered around one of the large tables to share breakfast and hear more details of the great journey. A jar of honey, biscuits made with raisins and cardamom from Egypt, and mugs of lavender-and-lemon barley water spun around between them on the turning tabletop as Aminah translated the guests' story.

Kafele spoke first. "When our great-grandfather owned the family spice business, he kept Saint Catherine's Monastery and many families in the Sinai supplied," he began. "When Asim inherited it, he expanded the trade to include all of northeastern Egypt. Madu and I have had even greater ideas. For several years, we have wanted to see how it would go to sell our spices in Europe."

Madu picked up the story from his older brother. He looked at Clarissa and then Johanna. "Meeting you gave us the inspiration to try," he said. "We knew that Champagne, France, is the commercial center for Europe, and that many people buy spices for gifts and cooking before Christmas. And so we left on our journey in time to be there last week. We were more successful than we dreamed."

"We knew all along," said Kafele, "that we would stop on our way home to see you in the convent in Liège. We were surprised to discover that you were not there."

"But not as surprised as the Mother was to see that we *were*," added Madu, who furrowed his brow and puckered his lips in an impression of Agnes Luc that rivaled Clarissa's for accuracy and excellence. Clarissa and Johanna began to laugh again, and their three visitors laughed heartily along with them.

"We just kept saying your names over and over," said Kafele, "until she took out a piece of parchment and drew what we recognized was her attempt at a map."

"We took only a few wrong turns," said Asim, and they all laughed again.

Clarissa was flooded with disappointment when Kafele announced that they could stay only for the morning and had to begin their return trek that day. "It took time to backtrack here from Liège," he explained. "and so we must get on home."

"But we would not have come to your country without seeing you," chimed in Madu, "and we are glad we did." Clarissa tried to turn her disappointment into gratitude that their three friends had gone so far out of their way to make such a short visit.

"We must show you something before you go," said Johanna. She led them down the path in the opposite direction of the barn. She pointed to the wood sign that Jaxon had fashioned and hung on their newest building: "Q Cottage."

"It stands for Quibilah," said Johanna and Clarissa in unison. The three men smiled. Johanna explained that, true to its name, it was a peaceful house that offered shelter to young women who needed it.

"We are moved and amazed," said Kafele.

"But not as amazed as we were to see you," said Clarissa.

"We did not expect you to be surprised," gently chided Asim. "I told you we were coming this year."

Clarissa smiled at him. "No matter how long I live," she declared, "nothing will ever astonish me as much as seeing the three of you coming up our path on your camels on Christmas Eve." She believed this as strongly as Johanna had believed that the worst of their pilgrimage was over once they had crossed the Alps.

But life is full of surprises.

§

"Cardinal Vittorio has sent for you." Galorian looked up from his work and stared into the earnest face of the page carrying the message. *I've been found out*, he thought. *Someone saw me in the cardinals' residence, and now I'll be dismissed.*

Vittorio was not the cardinal upon whom he had intruded, but Galorian assumed that the powerful churchman would have found someone else to carry out the deed of his dismissal. He glumly followed the page out of the basement and up several flights of stairs to a large room on the top floor, feeling no love for his work but having no idea what he would do if he lost it.

"Take a seat," the cardinal commanded as he bustled into the room and sat in a chair behind a large marble-top desk. "You've come to our attention," the churchman began. Galorian nodded humbly and steeled himself for what he knew was coming. The cardinal smiled. Galorian was not expecting that. "As you may know, Europe is crawling with heretics. The Cathars are on the rise."

"The Cathars?"

"The most powerful and determined enemies of the church. These misguided souls believe in a divided universe—an invisible spiritual realm created by a good God, and a tangible material world made by an evil one. They live extremely ascetic lives, are opposed to war and marriage, consider Mary Magdalene a founder of the church, regard men and women as equals, and accuse our holy Roman Catholic Church of corruption, calling it 'The Church of Wolves.' We've tried for decades to remove them and their influence. But they have many followers, especially women, among an uneducated populace that is vulnerable to new ideas, no matter how heretical."

Galorian was intrigued and, based on the slice of information he had just heard about their beliefs, not altogether in disagreement with the Cathars. But he understood the seriousness of the threat of heresy and nodded.

"Pope Innocent the Third is looking for a few good men to assist in rooting out heresy in all corners," continued Cardinal Vittorio. "The Holy Father is committed to ending this plague upon the church." Galorian leaned in closer. "We're setting up a council to conduct hearings in response to charges of heresy. Father Alain at Saint Catherine's Monastery tells us that you are devout, fluent in three languages, and committed to the well-being of the church. It seems a waste to keep you in the basement working with manuscripts." Galorian nodded again, more vigorously, to show his agreement.

"You would have to travel. The Heresy Council will respond to charges all across Italy and eventually all of Christendom, observing and aiding our clerics in the field." Galorian's heart began beating wildly to a rhythm of hope, as he imagined himself out of that dismal basement and crisscrossing Europe on behalf of the church. *I've seen it at its worst*, he thought, *but this will be the church at its best, defending what is pure and true.*

"Will you join us in this effort to preserve the church?" asked Cardinal Vittorio.

Galorian was both honored and humbled by the request. He needed no time to think about it. "Yes," he said. "Yes, I will."

"Good," said the cardinal. "We'll start tomorrow."

Twenty-five

$\bigwedge$s 1206 dawned, Clarissa marked her seventeenth birthday and her third year in France. Her home in England was becoming a more distant memory with each passing year, and she had many things for which to be grateful in her present life. The increased goodwill between the community and the villagers created by Christmas Eve spilled over into the new year. The school continued to thrive, and Clarissa and Nerida kept up their visits and lessons with the children in the cave. Liliana, now six, grew more precocious and loving every day—and more like her mother in appearance and spirit.

Clarissa continued to treasure the monthly gatherings with her sisters in the ritual cave. Johanna kept up her inspiring stories of women from the Bible. She spoke of the anonymous women who touched, and were touched by, Jesus: the woman with a twelve-year flow of blood whose body Jesus declared holy, the bent-over woman he healed and called a daughter of God, and the woman caught in adultery to whom he extended mercy. Johanna told her rapt listeners about Jesus's encounters at a well with a Samaritan woman from an enemy race, to whom he revealed his mission, and with a Syro-Phoenician woman, whose bold persistence expanded his vision and ministry. She spoke of the courage of Priscilla and Phoebe, leaders in the early church, and the compassion of Dorcas and Lydia, widows who encouraged many disciples.

For the students, the year of learning about biblical women, which had begun just after the previous Easter, was coming to a close. They were lavish in their praise of Johanna for unearthing this buried treasure for them. Each in her own way had had her eyes and heart opened. In the stories of wisdom, dignity, and courage, the young women saw themselves—or at least the selves they hoped to be. And so did Clarissa.

For their last gathering before Easter, Johanna opened Revelation, the Bible's last book, and read:

"A great portent appeared in heaven: a woman clothed with the
sun, with the moon under her feet, and on her head a crown of
twelve stars. She was pregnant and was crying out in the agony
of giving birth. Then another portent appeared in heaven: a great
red dragon, with seven heads and ten horns, and seven diadems
on his heads. His tail swept down a third of the stars of heaven
and threw them to the earth. Then the dragon stood before the
woman so that he might devour her child. She gave birth to a
son. The dragon pursued the woman, but she was given the two
wings of the great eagle, so that she could fly from him into the
wilderness, to a place where she was nourished."

Johanna asked her spellbound hearers, "How do you know that you
are a woman 'clothed with the sun'? How do you reflect the light of God, and
what gifts do you bring to the world?"

The young women, so shy and overwhelmed in that space a year before, had grown in confidence and their trust of one another.

"I can read!" said one immediately.

"And write," chimed in another.

"I'm a good listener."

"I take care of the people around me."

"I see the beauty in the sun and the moon and the stars."

"I like to sing."

"And pray."

Johanna nodded and smiled as each spoke. Then she asked, "And what
is the dragon for you? When you think about your life now or in the future,
what makes you afraid?" The young women were more hesitant to answer.

"Marriage," one finally whispered into the silence.

"Having babies," said another, equally softly.

"My father," said one of the youngest, looking at the ground.

"Being beaten."

"Cooking and cleaning and keeping a house without any help."

"No time for myself."

"Forgetting what I learned here."

"Dying."

Johanna nodded with each response, several of which were watered
with tears. She offered a prayer that the young women would cling to their
strength and hope. Then she moved to the candle on the rock and lit her
own from it. Once more the group spread light around the cave. "You are
clothed with the sun!" Johanna proclaimed when each young woman held a
lit candle. "Go forth and reflect the light of God." As they began to file out,

she smiled and announced joyfully, "Next time we celebrate resurrection again."

§

Galorian began to dread his work with the Heresy Council as much as his time in the basement of the Lateran Palace. He traveled regularly throughout Italy, listening as church people accused their family members or neighbors of being heretics. Most of the accused gave desperate, bumbling defenses of themselves. But the effort was pointless, as no evidence was needed to convict them. The word of two witnesses was enough for a bishop to pronounce guilt and take away the accused's land and home and personal property.

In the wake of the Cathar revival, panic and hysteria had set in. Church people were prone to see heretics everywhere. And Galorian began to see the heretic tribunals for what they were: another scheme, in the name of God and under the guise of defending the faith, for the church to rob the people. As a representative of the church in Rome witnessing the work of local clerics, he did not need to speak during the proceedings. But he understood that his presence amounted to affirmation of, and cooperation with, the vile process.

On a morning in mid-March, with a brisk wind blowing and a bright sun doing its best to melt the last vestiges of winter, a curious crowd pressed into the Piazza of Santa Maria Maggiore, next to the bishop's palace in the heart of the charmingly picturesque town of Assisi. Galorian stood in front of the throng, beside the bishop. Behind them towered snow-covered Mount Subasio, and before them stood "the arrogant cloth merchant Pietro and his barely recognizable son," as the bishop had described them to Galorian.

"He rejects the church, and he rejects me!" shouted Pietro, pointing at his son, who kept his head bowed. "He opposes war in the name of our Lord. And he's wasted every penny I ever gave him."

When his father ran out of charges, the son gazed up at the bishop. Galorian almost cried out in astonishment. He recognized the young man. He was the one for whom Galorian had searched: the beggar from the piazza in Rome with fire in his eyes. But Galorian noted immediately that his eyes now looked dull, the flame extinguished.

The bishop turned to the accused for his defense. The young man said nothing. A murmur of surprise at his silence rippled through the crowd. The bishop made his pronouncement quickly, without even pretending to give careful consideration: the son must give up all his property and his right to his inheritance.

Without a word, the young man strode out of the piazza and disappeared into the bishop's palace. The crowd's surprise turned to shock when he returned a few minutes later absolutely naked, holding in his hand his roll of clothes. This he placed at the bishop's feet, along with the few coins he had.

"Listen, all of you," said the young man, scanning the crowd. "I return to the one who has been my father everything he gave to me. From this moment on, I call no one Father but God in heaven." Pietro stepped forward awkwardly, grabbed up the clothes, and stormed out of the piazza. The bishop moved over and threw his mantle around the son, who stood trembling with emotion and cold.

Galorian wasn't sure whether to pray or cheer. He watched as the young man walked out the nearest town gate, the image of him in the bishop's mantle growing smaller and smaller as he headed in the direction of the mountain. Galorian wasn't due back in Rome until late the following day, and he decided to follow. Or, more accurately, he didn't decide—his feet simply started moving toward Mount Subasio and the man who was climbing it.

Galorian took a slight detour to untie Thane from the tree where he had secured him. Riding up the path was tempting, and would have been easy. But, without fully understanding why, Galorian felt compelled to walk and lead his horse. The way was rough and steep. The higher he climbed, the more cutting the wind became. Patches of snow along the rocky path mounted into drifts as he rose higher and higher above Assisi.

Galorian noted that the deep snow slowed his pace just as the deep sand of the desert had done on his journey to Saint Catherine's. This, too, felt like a holy pilgrimage. Several times on the grueling ascent, he decided to turn back. But then, over the whine of the wind, he caught snatches of hymns wafting down from above him. And so he kept walking.

§

Night had closed in by the time Galorian reached the summit. He followed the light of a fire burning in a small cave, where he found the young man sitting before it as if in a trance. Galorian, spying on the ground the two sharp pieces of quartz that the man must have struck together to create a spark, thought it nothing short of a miracle that he had lit a fire in the damp cave. Galorian pondered whether he had made a mistake to follow him, wondering if he should slip out and head back down the mountain without announcing himself. But before he could decide, the young man's eyes opened and he saw Galorian and Thane in the shadows.

"I won't harm you," Galorian said as he approached.

"No one could harm me today," said the man. He took a good look as Galorian walked closer, into the light of the fire. "You were with the bishop."

"I was standing with him, yes," Galorian said. "I came from Rome."

The man nodded. "Would you like to sit?"

Galorian settled on a rock on the other side of the fire. As he peered at the young man, the story of Elijah raced through his mind. The biblical prophet who had railed against faithlessness and corruption escaped to a cave on top of Mount Sinai, where he encountered God—not in wind, or earthquake, or fire, but in sheer silence. When Elijah heard the silence, he wrapped his face in his mantle—as the bishop's mantle now wrapped the young man before him—and stood at the entrance of the cave to receive the call of God.

"You've made a long journey in the cold," said the young man.

"I don't mean to intrude. I've just . . . I've been trying to figure out what God wants me to do, and you seem to be on good terms with God. You seem to know the path."

The young man smiled. "It wasn't always so." They sat in silence for a few moments and then he said, "Tell me your story."

Galorian was grateful for the invitation, but reluctant to presume too much, so he tried to limit his telling to brief highlights. He spoke of his life as a knight, the horror of Constantinople and his rescue of Aminah, his time at Saint Catherine's and his work with the church in Rome. "We've met," he said when he was done, "in the piazza in Rome, by the steps of the Lateran Palace."

The young man stared intently at him. Then he nodded again.

"Will you tell me your story?" Galorian asked.

"It's a long one."

"I have time," said Galorian. The man smiled and began.

"My father spends much of his time in France, selling his cloth at the great textile fairs there and making lots of money. He was there when I was born twenty-five years ago. My mother gave me the name Giovanni, but when my father returned he changed it to Francesco, out of his love for all things French. He insisted that I learn French as a boy and promised to take me to France with him on one of his trips, but he never did. I have yet to see that wonderful country I'm named after.

"I lived a frivolous and extravagant life surrounded by rich friends. Then three years ago I joined the army. My father thought it would straighten me out and sober me up. But after a year as a prisoner of war, I returned to the same life, feeling that I was owed as much pleasure and extravagance as I could find after what I had suffered. Then a great fever overcame me. I came close to the point of death and began to see what a waste my life had become.

"I started walking long distances every day and was healed by the beauty of the earth: the cloud-draped hills in the morning, the sun-dappled slopes at midday, the rich colors of sunset spilling over pine forests and terraces filled with olive trees, the towering strength of this mountain. I began to see the emptiness of my life in contrast to the fullness and abundance that God has promised and given us.

"A year ago, a gallant knight of Assisi with whom I had been imprisoned was heading off to war in the south of Italy to fight on behalf of Pope Innocent the Third. I was thrilled at the prospect of joining at the side of this heroic friend for a good and holy cause. A purpose at last. I bought the finest armor and weapons and sat upon my horse with my page at my side, ready to do battle.

"As we started out for war, winding around the base of this mountain I had a vision. I heard Jesus speak to me from the cross. He looked down at me and said, 'I say to you, love your enemies.' I was stunned. How, I wondered, could I love people and make war against them at the same time?"

A chill raced through Galorian, as he recognized the words that had also launched him on his journey of transformation from knight to man of peace. He had not mustered the courage in recounting his own story to mention that he had been visited by a vision. He opened his mouth to speak, but Francesco was already continuing. "I turned back at once. My friends thought me a coward. My father thought worse. Not long after my return, I was busy with a customer in his textile shop when a poor man came in, begging in the name of God for charity. I turned him away sharply. But I regretted it at once. I ran out into the street after him and emptied my pockets into his hands.

"When they found out, my friends mocked me, and my father scolded me in a rage. But that beggar was the first person to open my eyes to truth. I began to see poor people everywhere. Poor not because of some moral deficiency or laziness, but because of war and illness and bad harvests; poor because they were exploited and underpaid and overtaxed. How could I continue to live in luxury and comfort without regard for them, while so many suffered so severely?

"I decided to make a pilgrimage to the heart of the church in Rome. I was surprised to see that beggars swarmed the piazza in front of the pope's palace and the great basilica. One man singled me out. I gave him my cloak in exchange for his rags. I stood there a whole day, fasting, with outstretched hands."

"That must have been the day we met."

"Yes," agreed Francesco. "That day I began to have a small understanding of what one must endure in such a circumstance. I knew in that moment that I was called to a life of simplicity—and that I needed Jesus to lead me to it. But I wasn't prepared for the jolt that was necessary to put me on the path.

"A few days later, I was on my horse, praying about how to pursue a life of absolute devotion to God. I turned a corner in the road and found myself face to face with a leper. I had always felt an overwhelming revulsion at the disease that visits festering sores and disfigured limbs on its pitiful victims. I recoiled in horror and turned my horse around.

"But immediately I knew the error of my response. I turned back, got off my horse, and gave the man all the money I had. Then I knelt and kissed his hand, as one would kiss the hand of a prince or a pope. That was my first moment of victory over weakness and fear.

"I took to wandering again, allowing the serenity and beauty of the earth to heal and encourage me. I frequented a cave, where I prayed daily and asked God for clarity and mercy. My favorite walk was over a stony path through a grove of olive trees and into a wide valley, where the sweet smells of rosemary and lavender perfume the air. Tucked behind a curtain of cypress and pine trees at the base of the valley is the Chapel of San Damiano.

"The chapel was served by a poor priest who could barely afford to feed himself, and it was falling into ruin. There was nothing inside but a simple stone altar and a crucifix. One day I was on my knees praying to Jesus, begging only to do the holy will of God. He called me by a new name and gave me a mission: 'Francis, go and repair my house.' I had in my possession only a few cloths from my father's trade. These I sold, along with my horse, and I gave the poor priest every bit of money from the sale to restore San Damiano and keep its lamps burning."

"I can guess that your father was less than pleased about that."

"Yes. My father, ashamed and enraged at the son I had become, collected a few neighbors and came to get me. But I heard their shouts as they were approaching and hid in a secret place that I had prepared for exactly such a moment. My father ransacked every inch of the chapel but returned to Assisi without me.

"I stayed in that secret place, fasting and praying, weeping and groaning for days, asking God to make the path plain. And then one day I understood that only a pitiful and cowardly follower of Christ would stay in hiding. I knew that it was time to confront my father.

"I went to the piazza in the heart of Assisi. I had become thin and pale, ragged and unrecognizable to my neighbors and friends. Children threw rocks and flung mud at me. They danced around me, howling, 'A madman! A madman!' My father heard the commotion and came out of his shop to witness the spectacle. Then he heard the name of his son—and then his own name—uttered. In a furious rage, he grabbed me, dragged me home and beat me, bound me and then locked me in a closet. I stayed alone and in the dark there for several days, until my dear mother found the courage to release me from that torture.

"I returned to San Damiano. When my father came after me again, I did not try to hide. I faced him and told him that I would no longer take orders from him; that I was now the servant of Christ. He announced his plan to disinherit me. When he returned to Assisi, he petitioned the bishop to convene the church tribunal in the piazza next to his palace, to pronounce sentence on me. A few hours ago, I gave back everything I still possessed that my father had given me, including the clothes on my back."

Galorian could feel the force of his heart beating. He understood more deeply in that moment why he had needed to shed his armor and all the trappings of his life as a knight. He saw with new vision that conversion to Christ involved giving up the assumptions of one's youth and the careful plans of adulthood, opening one's heart to the invitation of Jesus to go wherever he might lead, no matter how radical, or foreign, or frightening. Galorian needed to speak of it to his new friend, but Francis was just as excited to share the end of his own story.

"Never have I felt so free as I did in that moment," he said, smiling. "I ran and leapt through the snowdrifts up this mountain, crying and laughing, overcome with an unspeakable joy. At times I could not keep from singing. The forest around me, down to the valley, resounded with my hymns of praise. The cardinals and jays joined in. The birds and I sang until I made it to the top. And here I am."

When he finished, Francis gazed warmly at Galorian and smiled. "And here you are."

Galorian noticed then that the fire had been rekindled in the young man's eyes. Reflections both of the flames around which they sat, and of a soul burning with joy and hope, danced there with wild anticipation.

Galorian half expected a horse-drawn chariot of fire to sweep down and whisk Francis in a whirlwind up to heaven, as one had taken away Elijah. "Please let me inherit a double share of your spirit," the prophet's apprentice, Elisha, had pleaded before Elijah disappeared, and the request was honored. When Elijah was out of sight, Elisha picked up the prophet's mantle, carried it to the Jordan River, and struck the water, which parted miraculously to open a path. A chill shuddered through Galorian as he imagined it. He looked through the fire at Francis. *O God,* he prayed silently, *I would be content with half as much spirit as this young prophet has.*

Before Galorian got to *Amen,* Francis had moved over and thrown a corner of the bishop's mantle around his shoulders. "You're trembling," the young man said, focusing his burning eyes on Galorian. "Have no fear. The path will open before you. And God's wonders will never cease."

§

Young Lisette had the aid of many friends in raising her son, and little Moses the gift of many mothers. As soon as the last stretch of frigid weather passed, Lisette wove a small basket from the tall stalks of beach grass that grew in the dunes by the sea. Jaxon waterproofed it with pitch, concocted from the sap of a pine tree. When Moses fussed, Lisette swaddled him in layers of cloth and carried him to the beach. She set him afloat on the ocean and let the steady rhythm of the waves lull him to sleep, while dolphins gently swam around him and, she believed, through his dreams.

"I want Moses to be baptized," she announced one day to Clarissa and Johanna. She had not been raised in the church, and they had not wanted to pressure her and were delighted that she brought it up. "I want the two of you to do it. In the cave."

"But we're not priests," Clarissa protested.

"It's not the way the church does it," added Johanna.

But Lisette was insistent. That evening Johanna said to Clarissa, "If we believe what we've been sharing with the young women, then God will honor it. We should do it." Clarissa, surrendering her discomfort to Johanna's confidence, agreed.

Excitement was running high in the ritual cave as the women gathered for their second Easter vigil. Clarissa stood next to Johanna, who held Moses. Lisette proudly carried in the torch and lit the fire on the rock with the symbolic Light of God. Johanna proclaimed, "We gather tonight to keep the Easter vigil and to baptize Moses, beloved son of Lisette."

Clarissa offered a prayer for the life and soul of the child. Then she scooped up water in a scallop shell and poured it gently over his head, declaring, "Moses Jaxon, child of God, I baptize you in the name of the Father . . ." She took a second scoop and poured it. ". . . and of the Son . . ." And a third. ". . . and of the Holy Spirit."

Johanna asked the gathered group if they would surround and support Moses in his faith journey. They shouted vigorously in unison, "We will!"

Then Johanna lifted the child, resting peacefully in her upturned palms, high above her head. "Moses, you are a gift from God!" she declared, her eyes riveted on heaven, as the circle of women clapped their joyful affirmation.

They sang hymns and took turns reading the Scripture passages that carried them once more on the epic biblical journey from creation to crucifixion. When they finished, Johanna spoke again. "Judas betrayed Jesus, Peter denied him, and the rest of his disciples fell asleep in the garden on the night of his arrest, when he most needed their vigilance and companionship. As the tragic drama unfolded, the men kept their distance, huddled safely behind locked doors.

"But the women stood by him. They were there, watching and weeping and waiting, keeping vigil at the cross and carrying spices to his tomb. They were there because they were brave. And because the authorities weren't threatened by women. The women used their power of presence to make a statement about their loyalties and their hope. To courageously claim life in the midst of death."

Johanna read the resurrection story from the Gospel of John. The young women listened in rapt silence as they heard the account of Mary Magdalene's pre-dawn discovery of the empty tomb and her mistaking the risen Christ for the gardener. When he called her by name, she knew. "Go and tell my brothers," Jesus told her, and she ran to tell the disciples what she had seen. When Johanna finished reading, she placed the manuscript on the rock.

"As women, we are considered unreliable witnesses," she declared. "We are banned from offering testimony in court, and so were the women of Jesus's day. But after his death, Jesus appeared first to a woman. He instructed her to tell the good news to his male disciples, trusting her to spread the miraculous word. The first witness to the resurrection was a woman!" The circle in the cave murmured with excitement.

"What do we know about Mary Magdalene?" asked Johanna.

"She was a prostitute!" shouted a twelve-year-old, snickering.

"How do you know?" asked Johanna.

"The Bible says so," answered the girl proudly.

"Actually, it doesn't," said Johanna gently. "It took Mary Magdalene six hundred years to become a prostitute." A few giggles erupted in the circle. "She was an honored disciple—until some powerful men in the church became upset by the truth that Jesus had a close, beloved friend and follower who was a woman.

"In the sixth century," Johanna explained, "Pope Gregory the Great decided it was necessary to undermine the reputation of Mary Magdalene. In a homily, he intentionally confused her identity with two other women in the

Bible: the woman caught in adultery about to be stoned by a crowd, and the prostitute who anointed Jesus's feet with oil and wiped them with her hair.

"From that day on, Mary Magdalene has been portrayed as a disheveled, seductive 'fallen woman'—rather than the faithful and dignified disciple that she was." Johanna smiled. "But we know the truth. Mary Magdalene, cherished and trusted friend of Jesus, was the first witness to the resurrection."

That was the cue for Clarissa to call out "Christ is risen!"

The group responded passionately, "He is risen indeed!"

Clarissa offered a prayer of gratitude. And then she proclaimed, "We too have been called to be witnesses to the resurrection. Go forth to tell the story and be brave!" As the young women filed out to spread the good news around their village, the cave was abuzz with their animated talk.

Twenty-six

Galorian felt that he could have stayed forever on that mountaintop, drinking in the wisdom of Francis. But the man with fire in his eyes reminded him that they both had things to do. And so Galorian returned to Rome at the time he was expected and did his best to give himself to the anti-heresy crusade of the church.

On Easter Sunday, as the church hierarchs wearing their tall miters and ostentatiously lavish robes paraded in past its marble pillars and stained-glass windows, Galorian kept his eyes riveted on the front of the cathedral. There on an ornate gold cross hung Jesus, dressed in a robe to match theirs, wearing a shining crown embellished with bright gems. "It's wrong," Galorian whispered to himself, shaking his head. "It's all wrong."

The next day he was in the office of Cardinal Vittorio, asking to be released from his duties. The cardinal was not pleased, but he let Galorian go as soon as he located a replacement a week later. Galorian headed straight for Assisi and San Damiano, following Francis's directions over the stony path, through the olive grove, and into a vast valley. Tucked behind a row of cypress and pine trees, exactly as his new friend had described it, was the chapel.

Francis was there, barefoot and wearing a dusty brown robe, piling rocks where a crumbling wall was being rebuilt. When he saw Galorian, he walked toward him with his arms outstretched and gave him a warm embrace. Over his friend's shoulder, Galorian spied the chapel's crucifix. He let go of Francis and moved slowly toward it.

Galorian knelt beneath the simple wood cross. On it was nailed Jesus, all but naked, with bleeding wounds in his hands and feet, a cutting crown of thorns on his head. But his face—*Oh, that beautiful face*, thought Galorian—his face bore an expression of gentle, merciful, and inviting peace.

Francis stood behind Galorian and put his hands on the former knight's shoulders. Galorian turned to face him and whispered, "I'm home."

"Welcome, brother."

In the days that followed, the man on fire for Jesus shared with Galorian his vision while they worked side by side to rebuild the chapel. Hungry people and those made outcasts by leprosy appeared and found food and care there. Francis and Galorian sometimes ventured into town squares to share about their project, sing hymns, and beg for food or oil for the lamps of San Damiano. People thought them either madmen or miracle workers, and several of those of the latter opinion joined them in transforming the chapel.

Galorian was in awe of the many hours Francis spent lost in reverie as he wandered the countryside, praying for guidance and giving concrete shape to his hope. The young visionary recorded his dreams and his prayers. One evening he opened his diary and announced to the men who had gathered around him, "Brothers, hear our Rule of Life."

The brief rule he had devised—which he summarized as "to follow the teachings of our Lord Jesus Christ and to walk in his footsteps"—consisted entirely of Jesus's words from the Gospels: "If you wish to be perfect, go, sell your possessions, and give the money to the poor and follow me . . . Take nothing for your journey, no staff, nor bag, nor bread, nor money—not even an extra tunic . . . If any want to become my followers, let them deny themselves and take up their cross and follow me. For those who want to save their life will lose it, and those who lose their life for my sake will find it."

As Galorian listened, he changed his mind about "Love your enemies" being Jesus's most challenging words. *Is it possible*, he wondered, *to renounce all possessions? To live simply and trust that God will provide what is needed? To be willing to give up one's life for one's faith?*

Galorian had thought when he left for the Crusades that he was willing to make such a sacrifice. But now he wasn't so sure. A heroic death on the battlefield was one thing. But an unnoticed life of self-denial seemed like quite another.

§

Spring was announced at the community on the bluff that year with a flurry of wings and a fanfare of honking. An elegant pair of long-necked swans, brilliant white with bright orange bills edged in black, landed noisily on the pond and set about the task of making a nest on the bank. Fascinated,

Liliana checked on them every day, awaiting with as much patience as she could muster the hatching of four big, yellow eggs.

"You know something about everything," Clarissa said to Johanna with a wry smile one evening at dinner. "What do you know about swans?"

"I've been waiting for someone to ask," Johanna retorted, returning the smile and launching into spilling her knowledge of the wondrous creatures. "Since ancient times, the swan has been a symbol of the Holy Spirit and the soul. Swans are reminders of grace and beauty. Their long migratory journeys on strong wings inspire endurance. And because they mate for life, they are also signs of loyalty and permanence."

"We've been blessed then," said Clarissa.

"Yes," said Johanna. "Our pair of swans—and their offspring when they arrive—should help us to remember that, whatever comes, the Holy Spirit is hovering close, watching over us. And that we belong to God and each other."

A few weeks later, a loud and persistent trumpeting from the bank of the pond early one morning was the proud birth announcement. Liliana ran as fast as she could, dragging Clarissa by the hand. The four hatchling cygnets, covered in gray down, stepped and fell, stepped and fell, until their pinkish feet mastered the art of walking. Before long, they had white feathers and black feet and were swimming on the pond in a line behind their parents, serenading the community with a chorus of high-pitched squeaks and honks.

Clarissa noted that another year had passed without her and her sisters gaining enough economic security to carry any money to the convent in Liège. As the community grew, their needs continually outpaced their resources. She tried once more to stuff down her anxiety and her guilt, choosing to enjoy the blessings of another spring and to trust that all would be well.

Their flock of sheep had grown to seven ewes and two rams the year before, and sixteen more lambs joined them that spring. With great anticipation, Clarissa looked forward to their second annual Sheep Shearing Day. She knew it would be a festive celebration for the community and the villagers—though not nearly as dramatic as Christmas Eve had been.

It took place on a splendid day in early May. Villagers gathered on blankets near Nerida's new herb garden. A bright sun danced on a carpet of red poppies, which nodded in a gentle breeze in the field next to the pasture. Jaxon showed off a few new juggling tricks he had added to his repertoire.

Guilbert appeared with three of his best lambs, which turned on spits over a fire, next to tables piled high with the first fruits and vegetables of spring. The children, under the watchful eye of parents both human and swan, spent the morning chasing after the cygnets, which skittered around the pond, plunging in to paddle in its shallow water when grasping young hands got too close.

Clarissa thought that nothing could mar the perfect day. After lunch she sat down on a blanket next to Genevieve to watch the children play and chase one another among the poppies. Genevieve began to cry. "What is it?" Clarissa asked.

"He's calling me a leper," replied the young mother.

"Who is?"

"My brother-in-law." Slowly Genevieve spilled the story. After her coppersmith husband died in an accident, she inherited his property. The arrangement was unusual, Genevieve explained. Land and homes usually passed from fathers to sons, completely bypassing women. But in rare cases when no son was old enough to inherit, a widow could claim what had belonged to her late husband. "Keeping our home and land has made the difference between survival and starvation for me and the children," Genevieve said.

Her husband's brother resented a woman owning a portion of his family's holdings—especially since under the law Genevieve, like all married women, had been nothing more than part of her husband's property before he died. For more than a year, her brother-in-law had tried every legal avenue to take away Genevieve's inheritance, jeopardizing the well-being of her and her six young children. "He's failed so far," said Genevieve, "but now he's accusing me of being a leper."

Clarissa was shocked that anyone would stoop so low as to level such a condemning false accusation, especially against a family member. But she knew that such charges were becoming more and more popular as a way to steal property. All that was needed was the word of a witness and a corrupt judge to make the accusation stick. "We'll fight it, Genevieve," she said. "You're not alone in this."

That evening, when Clarissa and Johanna were back at Manna House recounting the day, Johanna reached into a pocket in her robe and handed Clarissa her mother's exquisite silver fleur-de-lis necklace with the bright lapis gem in the center. "How did you get it from Guilbert?" Clarissa wanted to know, moved and grateful to have it back.

Johanna said with a smile, "That's my secret."

§

The following week Felicite showed up on the doorstep. The small village in southern France from which she had fled was unknown to Clarissa and her sisters. The thin young woman with a disarming smile told them she had crossed the entire country from south to north on her own, running away from a forced marriage. She had done so at the same age that Clarissa had escaped hers.

Clarissa liked her immediately. She saw herself in the spirited girl, who was feisty and brave in the way that Clarissa liked to believe she had been at thirteen. She was delighted that Felicite and Aminah, who had been longing for some time for a peer her own age, became fast friends and confidants.

Felicite gave herself completely to the community. She was devoted to their times of prayer, helpful in the garden and kitchen, and dedicated to her studies. As Johanna began a year of leading the young women through the Psalms in the ritual cave in May, Felicite listened with focused attention to every word Johanna spoke, as if trying to impress each detail on her mind to remember it later. She lavished attention on the children and the other students in the school. And she was always the first to volunteer to carry someone to Balnéaire, or to go to pick up a needed item in Calais.

When Felicite moved into the empty room in Manna House, Clarissa had the feeling that their community was complete. Though, unlike religious orders of nuns and monks, they demanded no vows, in practice Clarissa and her sisters followed the traditional vows of poverty and chastity. But they did not promise permanence to one another. Clarissa knew that women would come and go—maybe even some to whom she was close. But she began to think of herself and Johanna, Nerida and Aminah, Lisette and now Felicite as the core that would last, welcoming and releasing others as the years unfolded.

Felicite accompanied Clarissa, Nerida, and Jaxon to Calais at the end of the month, fulfilling Clarissa's promise to stand by Genevieve. In a court of law there, Genevieve's brother-in-law pointed with disgust at the large birthmark on Genevieve's forehead, which had the shape of an egg and the red shade of a rose, with a distinct darker center the size of a marble. "It's leprosy, the mark of the Devil!" he shouted. "Beware—Lucifer's eye is staring right at us all!"

Clarissa was not allowed to testify in the court. But before the proceedings, she stated the obvious to anyone who would listen: Genevieve was a faith-filled woman, and labeling as leprosy the mark she had had from birth was cruel and absurd. Jaxon, wearing an ensemble of the most serious clothes he could dig up and borrow, tried to say the same from the witness stand. But he got rattled when the judge asked him, "Were you there when she was born?" Others who might have offered helpful testimony stayed away, fearful of being swept up in the tide of judicial capriciousness that was raging across France and throughout Europe.

Genevieve wailed as the judge pronounced the sentence: forfeiture of her inheritance rights and banishment to a leper colony. Seeing and hearing her distress, the two eldest of her young children ran and clung to her, crying. Clarissa, holding the youngest on her lap, was so appalled at the injustice that she picked up the child and jumped to her feet. Without pausing to consider the consequences, she shouted at the judge, "Your punishment is unfair! You know it's not leprosy!"

Had she been a man, she would likely have been slapped with a jail sentence for her outburst—or worse. But the judge ordered her thrown out of the courtroom. She hastily handed the two-year-old to Nerida, as two burly men took her by the arms and roughly escorted her outside. Minutes later, as she, Jaxon, Nerida, and Felicite began the ride home, she asked despairingly, "What are we going to do about Genevieve?"

After a little thought, the answer seemed obvious. They hatched a plan that would help not only Genevieve and her family but all the people living in the cave. Jaxon was eager to begin building. Sybille's husband Raulf, a kind man who had refused to abandon his wife when she was struck with leprosy, offered to help.

The community understood the risks of their effort, aware that for some of the villagers the idea of people with leprosy living near the school would be unthinkable. And so Jaxon and Raulf cleared a secluded spot in the forest beyond the pond, knowing that they might not be able to keep the building entirely hidden but hoping to give it some protection. They worked hard for many hours each day, felling trees and constructing the frame for the building with eight rooms to house Genevieve, her six children, and the nine inhabitants of the cave.

Soon after the frame was complete, Clarissa was startled awake in the middle of the night by Jaxon's voice. "Come quick!" he shouted. "Fire!" Clarissa bolted out of bed and joined her sisters, who were streaming to the clearing in the forest. Flames leapt high into the night sky from the crisscrossed limbs of the frame. Saint Catherine screeched from a branch high in a tree, and the swans cried mournfully from the pond.

Jaxon grabbed four buckets from the barn and began organizing everyone into a single line from the pond. Clarissa scooped up water and passed the buckets down the line to him as he tried to douse the fire. But there were neither enough buckets nor people to make much of an impact. She watched in despair and horror as the flames began to lick the trees. In a matter of minutes, she feared, they would catch fire, and nothing would stop the inferno from raging through the summer's dry limbs, into the hay pasture, and on to their homes.

Just as she began to believe that all would be lost, she heard a rumble on the path and looked over to see Johanna atop Magnus, leading a group of men from the village on horseback. In the drama, Clarissa had failed to notice that Johanna had run to the barn and galloped off on Magnus to Balnéaire. The men jumped off their horses. A group following Guilbert, waving hatchets and axes, began slashing trees around the fire, clearing a wide ring. The rest, toting buckets, followed Clovis and joined the line from the pond, picking up the pace and volume of the water brigade.

The men worked tirelessly in the blazing heat of the fire, their arms swinging and their faces shining with sweat. Clarissa was astounded at their energy and dedication to the task. The flames, finally reaching the cleared ring at the edge of the trees, died and settled into a smoldering pile of embers and ash. Clarissa stood between Jaxon and Johanna, gazing sadly at the devastation.

"I think the owl woke the swans, and they sounded the alarm," said Jaxon. "Without their racket alerting me, we wouldn't have known about the fire until it was too late."

Clarissa expressed her shock over the malicious act. "I feared that something like this might happen once people found out who was living in the house," she said. "But no one beyond us knew what we were building. Who would do this?"

Her question was met with silence. Then Johanna said solemnly, "It's clear that we have an enemy or two." She smiled then. "But the good news is that we learned tonight that we have many more friends." She sighed. "And the watchful protection of the Holy Spirit."

§

Clarissa, Johanna, Jaxon, and Raulf met the following morning to discuss whether to abandon the building. Johanna began. "I think we're all concerned that this might happen again—and next time there might be people in the house who would get hurt . . . or even lose their lives."

Clarissa was anxious to speak. "Yes. We don't know who our enemies are, how persistent they may be, or what they might have in store for us. I don't think it's fair to ask people to live with such uncertainty—and perhaps great danger."

Jaxon listened carefully and said only, "I'll do whatever you think is best."

Raulf pondered their words and then weighed in with his own. "We don't have a life in the cave," he said, his voice breaking a little as he spoke. "My children suffer in the cold and dark, without friends except the ones you bring." He cleared his throat. "If you're still willing, I think we should start again and build the house. And let the people decide if they want to live in it."

Johanna was swayed by Raulf's emotional plea. Though Clarissa still harbored deep fears about what might happen, she didn't voice them. Jaxon and Raulf headed straight for the clearing and began stacking the limbs that had been cut away from the fire the night before. By late morning, Guilbert and Clovis had joined them. Several other men from the village appeared in the following days to give an hour, or a day, to the reconstruction of the house. With their help, it was ready well before their original hopes for completion. Relieved that the work had proceeded without any more incidents, Clarissa wanted to believe that their enemies had given up once they saw that the fire had not weakened their determination.

In late summer, Genevieve and her children moved in. The young ones thrived with the attention of the women of the community and the entertainment of Jaxon. "The judge gave me a gift," Genevieve said one afternoon to Clarissa. "We're all happier here, surrounded by people."

The delight of everyone intensified when Sybille and Raulf, with Giselle, Viviane, and Sylvain, moved into the house.

Liliana loved her suddenly large extended family of sisters and brothers, and the adults were more than glad to create games and outings to keep them all happy. Nerida devoted several nights to making school clothes for Giselle and Viviane, who gratefully joined the other students when classes started up again. When Clarissa and her sisters decided that the cruel law forcing people with leprosy to wear white robes would not be enforced in their community, Genevieve joined Nerida in making clothes for all the adults as well. The sisters invited their newest community members to name their home, and they promised to ponder it.

The three other women from the cave moved into the house in early fall. Only the bent-over man who had never shared his name refused to join them. For three weeks Nerida continued to drop food baskets at the entrance of the cave for the old man. And then one afternoon he appeared on the doorstep of Manna House. He had his rattle, but he set it on the ground as the door opened. Clarissa reached out her right hand, and he slowly extended his own disfigured one, stating softly, "I'm Emmanuel."

Clarissa shook it warmly and said, "Welcome, Emmanuel." She walked with him to the still-unnamed house in the forest and helped him get settled there. She and the others soon understood why he had come. His breathing was raspy and labored, and many days he didn't have the strength to get out of bed. Clearly, Emmanuel was dying.

The young women of the community attended to him as they could. Nerida was a devoted presence, applying herbs from her garden to aid his breathing and heal his sores. Liliana accompanied her on every visit, bringing Emmanuel colorful leaves, acorns, pine cones, and other treasures she had found in the woods. He received each gift with a smile. Clarissa showed up every evening with a pot of onion broth—the only thing he would eat—and spooned sips of it into his parched mouth.

At the end, the community gathered around his bed, singing hymns, reciting psalms, and whispering prayers. Emmanuel died peacefully with a smile on his face, surrounded by love. Under Nerida's direction, the young women bathed and anointed his body in oil scented with lavender. Jaxon and Raulf made a simple pine box and dug a grave under the canopy of a towering oak.

The community came together that night in a circle, bathed in the light of torches. As they lowered Emmanuel's body into the ground, Sybille said, "He was kind. He came across as a gruff old man, but he was always kind to me. And he loved to tell stories to the children." She nodded to Sylvain, prompting the boy to step forward and toss a russet aster onto the coffin. The others followed, showering it with a cascade of fall flowers. While Jaxon spaded dirt to fill in the grave, they offered final prayers for Emmanuel's soul.

Then they walked to the Josselyn Center and brought out the first batch of that year's mead. When they were all gathered around one of the round tables, Sybille raised her glass and shouted, "To Emmanuel's Place!" The others echoed the toast. *At last,* thought Clarissa, *a name for the new house.* She loved that it honored their guest, as well as Jesus, who had been called at his birth by the same name, meaning "God is with us." She smiled.

People slowly trickled back to Emmanuel's Place, until only the young women of the community and Jaxon remained. "I want to make another toast," Clarissa announced, raising her glass to Nerida. "You're a midwife on both ends of life. You catch babies as they take their first breath, and you usher on those who are taking their last." Clarissa smiled warmly at her friend. "I believe that in the days and years to come, we'll need your extraordinary gifts more and more." A chorus of grateful "Amens" went up around the table.

The very next day Jaxon began erecting a frame for a small building in a clearing beyond Manna House and Q Cottage. "I want to get it done before the cold sets in," he explained to Clarissa.

"Are you finally getting around to building your own space so you can move out of the barn?" she asked.

"Oh, no," replied Jaxon. "You'll see."

§

Once again the minstrel-turned-troubadour had a prophetic eye. Within days of the building's completion, a family from Balnéaire showed up at the Josselyn Center, carrying their gravely ill child. "We heard you take care of dying people and pray for their souls," the father said, his sad eyes pleading. He handed over the child to Clarissa, who led them to the new house that Jaxon had designed for families in just such a circumstance.

Two days later, a sister and brother appeared with their dying mother and moved her into the house's other room. Clarissa was surprised at how quickly the word had spread. She welcomed this new ministry that was calling on the best gifts of the community and stretching them all in profound ways.

Once more they were in need of a name for a new house. Clarissa and Johanna, Aminah and Felicite, Lisette holding Moses, and Nerida with Liliana on her lap sat around the table in Manna House, drinking barley water infused with rosemary and lemon. Aminah spoke first. "There's so much hatred in the world. And so much cruelty. This is a place of mercy . . . where people can come and know that they will be accepted and loved. Like Emmanuel." She sighed and then added softly, "Like me."

Little more needed to be said. Clarissa and her sisters agreed to name their new house Mercy Manor, delighted that their smallest building was the one with the grandest name.

"We need a name for the whole thing," Felicite said then.

"What do you mean?" asked Johanna.

"We have all these names for all our houses, but who are we all together?"

They all liked the idea of naming their community and tried out a few possibilities, but nothing felt quite right. "It should have swans!" piped up Liliana. The others around the table exchanged glances and smiled at her. Clarissa assumed that Liliana hadn't been paying enough attention to even know what they were talking about. "Swans," Liliana repeated.

Johanna grinned. "You're right, Liliana!" She looked around the circle of her sisters and added, "I hate to come across as a know-it-all . . ."

"I hadn't noticed that," Clarissa interrupted before Johanna could say more.

Everyone laughed, as Johanna shot Clarissa a playful glare. "What I mean is, I know some things about swans that I didn't share before, and it's given me an idea. We already know that the swan is a symbol of the Holy Spirit and of permanence. Some people believe that if a woman about to give birth hears the song of a swan, her child will be specially blessed. And others consider swans the souls of departed loved ones or messengers announcing death." Clarissa remembered that Nerida had said the same to her about owls.

"Because of its long neck," continued Johanna, "the swan is considered a bridge between the worlds, an aide in making the transition from this world to the next. The Greek philosopher Socrates said that swans sing most beautifully just before they die. 'Swan song' means a final beautiful and glorious gesture before death."

Her sisters, always in awe of Johanna's knowledge, were riveted on her words. The passion rose in her voice as she continued. "I hope we can continue drawing inspiration from the swans, nurturing a community filled with music, beauty, and grace, trusting that God's Spirit is always hovering near. I want this to be a place of welcome where people can be born, live, and die well, ushered with compassion into this world or the next." Johanna smiled. "I propose that we name our community Swansong."

A murmur of approval surged around the table. "It's inspired!" exclaimed Clarissa, winking at Liliana and raising her glass of barley water in Johanna's direction. Waves of "Yes!" and "Amen!" filled the air.

The very next day, a dozen more swans landed on the pond in a great cacophony of noise. Liliana ran to tell Clarissa. "It's a swan party!" she shouted as they ran to see. Clarissa didn't have the heart to tell her niece that the party would soon be over and her beloved swan family would disappear along with the newcomers.

The next day they all took off, forming a large V, the drafts created by the beating wings of the elder geese aiding the young cygnets flying between them on their first long migratory journey. They honked loudly as they lifted high into the sky. Liliana stood on the bank of the pond, waving and calling "Goodbye," two rivers of tears streaming down her cheeks.

"If we're lucky," said Clarissa, stooping to face Liliana and pulling her cloak more tightly around her in the chilly air, "they'll come back to see us when it's warm again."

That night after dinner, Liliana got up from the table, walked into the vegetable storehouse, and returned with an enormous onion, almost the size of her head. She held it up and announced, "We're going to play The Onion Game."

"What's that?" and "I've never heard of it" and "How do you play?" all rose at the same time from the young women around the table.

"I'll tell you," Liliana announced proudly. "I made it up." She sighed a little-girl sigh. "It's too sad here. Emmanuel died. And the swans went away. And we need to make us happy again." She explained the rules of her game, promising a wonderful prize to the winner and "something really awful" for the loser.

Each person at the table took a turn guessing how many layers they thought the onion had. Liliana went first. "A hundred!" she said.

Based on Clarissa's many hours in the kitchen making batches of onion broth for Emmanuel, she knew that an onion that big typically had between twenty and thirty layers. "Two hundred!" she shouted.

Nerida guessed two hundred and fifty, and Lisette five hundred. By the time they got around to Johanna, she ventured "one thousand."

Liliana giggled as she removed the orange outer layer of the onion and proclaimed "one." Then she passed it on to Clarissa, who peeled the second layer and said "two." By its third pass around the table, Liliana was up on her knees, leaning in with excitement, and everyone was both crying from the teary effect of the onion and laughing with delight.

The onion had twenty-seven layers, and Nerida was the one left holding the tiny piece at its core. "You lose!" shouted Liliana. "You have to eat onion soup for a week!" Nerida scrunched up her face in mock disgust. "And I guessed closest! I win!" crowed Liliana triumphantly. Then she said "Oh no" and sighed again.

"What's wrong?" Nerida asked.

"The prize is a hug from me," groaned Liliana. "But how can I hug myself?"

"You can't!" said Nerida. She leapt up, quickly followed by the others, and they surrounded Liliana, hugging and tickling her until she begged them through fits of laughter to stop. When she caught her breath, with her arms looped around the shoulders of Clarissa and Nerida, she looked from face to face and announced with a broad smile, "I'm happy again."

Clarissa smiled back at her niece and said, "I think we have a new Swansong tradition."

§

A month later, the community and villagers gathered at the Josselyn Center for their other winter tradition. As before, the story of Jesus's birth unfolded with a colorful cast of characters and a pilgrimage to the barn. Playing the role of Mary, Liliana rode proudly at the front on Reginald, with a broad smile plastered on her face, waving at the crowd with both hands. When the procession took a sharp turn on the path, the large gourd Liliana had stuffed under her cloak to feign pregnancy shifted and knocked her off balance. As she slipped off Reginald with a cry of surprise, the gourd fell out at her feet. She lifted her cloak and replaced it, scolding loudly, "Get back in there, Jesus!"

A newborn from the village played the starring role in the manger—though he was overshadowed by Jaxon, dressed this year as one of the Three Wise Men in his green-and-black-diamond shirt over the green velvet gown that Clarissa had given to Nerida, with his purple wizard's hat on his head. A dozen young angels descended from the hayloft. Johanna shared about the people in the biblical accounts of Jesus's birth who were visited by angels, reading brief passages from the Gospels. She explained that Mary was "perplexed" when the angel Gabriel appeared to her. "'Do not be afraid, Mary,' Gabriel said to her, 'for you will conceive and bear a son.'"

Joseph, said Johanna, was upset when he found out that Mary, to whom he was engaged, was expecting a child. Unwilling to expose her to public disgrace, he planned to "dismiss her quietly." But an angel came to Joseph in a dream and said, "Do not be afraid to take Mary as your wife, for the child conceived in her is from the Holy Spirit. You are to name him Jesus, Emmanuel, 'God is with us.'"

When an angel appeared to the shepherds in a field, continued Johanna, "they were 'terrified.' And the angel said to them, 'Do not be afraid; for see—I am bringing you good news of great joy for all the people. You will find a child wrapped in bands of cloth and lying in a manger.'"

Johanna asked her listeners, "What do all these encounters have in common?"

"They're scary!" yelled Clovis, the second of the Three Wise Men, dressed far less colorfully than Jaxon but standing tall and proud with a full, natural beard.

"And what did the angel always say first?"

"Do not be afraid!" called out several of the villagers at once.

"Yes!" said Johanna. "Mary was terrified. But she said to the angel Gabriel, 'Here am I, the servant of the Lord.' She was willing to say yes to the astonishing call of God, to fulfill the role that was given to her." Johanna paused and then added, "Each of the people who received a heavenly visitation, no matter how scared, did what God asked of them."

She beamed a smile around to the gathered crowd. Then she proclaimed, "And so I hope that each of us will conquer our fears and be so bold and faithful in responding to God's call." The charge was one that

Clarissa needed to hear, especially in light of the growing demands on their community and the fire that had signaled that enemies were watching them. Though she was relieved that no more disasters had been launched against them, she could never quite release her dread that something was waiting just around the corner. She looked closely at Johanna's face as she pronounced the words, and Clarissa thought that her dear friend was trying to encourage and embolden herself as well.

The villagers began to file out of the barn. As Clarissa followed them back toward the Josselyn Center, she wished for the comfort and delight of a visit by real wise men from the East on camels. But she knew that no such surprise was in store for them that night.

Twenty-seven

"They're back!" squealed Liliana, running from house to house on a warm April day to spread the good news. The swans had returned, just as she had predicted at least once a week since their fall leave-taking that they would. Clarissa, who for five months had dreaded the disappointment that would visit Liliana if they didn't come back, crossed that petition off her prayer list and went to greet them.

A few weeks later they welcomed another quartet of cygnets. Liliana lavished most of her attention on one that had a stunted wing. Without a matched pair for balance, the poor thing wobbled when it walked and fell frequently, finding its stride only when it was old enough to take to the water. As compensation, it seemed, it had been blessed with the pinkest feet of the bunch. It was the only swan Liliana ever named, and nobody pointed out to her that before long she would have a bright white swan with black feet and an orange beak named Pinky.

When a few dozen lambs were born that spring, Clarissa thought of her father and gave thanks for his gift of three that had been the start of all this abundance. That year she stopped trying to count their flock, content to be grateful that it grew and thrived. Sheep Shearing Day of 1207 was a major production. The shearing, over in a couple hours the first year, now took all day, with several men working at once.

After lunch, Clarissa spent the early afternoon with a huddle of children, who were delighted to be petting the newborn lambs. She looked up and caught sight of two men walking up the path from Balnéaire. Each wore a monk's brown, hooded cassock and led a horse. The sight was not as strange as camels on the path, but it was curious nonetheless.

Upon spying the pasture, the horses stopped at the edge by the fence to eat some of the bright-green spring grass. The lamb that Clarissa held wriggled out of her grasp and scampered toward them. She began to chase after it. "I've got it!" shouted one of the monks. He ran and, with some effort, corralled the frisky young creature that was intent on eluding him. He lifted it and carried it back to Clarissa.

Their eyes locked as he placed the lamb into her outstretched arms and received her thanks. Clarissa knew at once that she had seen that face before, though she couldn't place where, and he didn't seem to recognize her. She took a moment and then remembered. He was now sober and thinner, but he was definitely the son of Pietro the Italian cloth merchant—whose soul she still prayed for occasionally, as promised, though it had seemed to her a hopeless petition.

"Francis," said the monk, extending his hand. Clarissa took it. She was about to say her name and mention their previous meeting in Italy, when his father had introduced him to her as Francesco. But the other monk had arrived at his side.

The sight was far more astonishing than Jaxon showing up unannounced, or the camels appearing on Christmas Eve—more shocking than anything Clarissa could have imagined. He had grown a trim, dark beard since she had last seen him, but she couldn't mistake those bright blue eyes. Clarissa's mouth dropped wide open. She and Galorian stared at each other and groped for words. Neither found them, but the look that passed between them spoke volumes.

"You know each other," said Francis, smiling. Galorian opened his mouth to explain, but he was distracted before he could get out a word. Aminah was charging toward him. When she reached him, she threw her arms around him.

"They definitely know each other," said Francis, casting a grin in Clarissa's direction. Clarissa was astounded to see that what he said was true. A multitude of questions crowded into her mind, but she was still at a loss for words.

§

Aminah took Galorian by the hand and, talking animatedly and nonstop, pulled him toward the sheep shearing party. He stopped only to ask if it would be all right to secure the horses in the fenced pasture. Clarissa, recognizing Thane then, said, "I'll take care of them." Gently stroking his neck, she led Galorian's beautiful steed through the gate into a sea of inviting grass, followed by Francis, who held the reins of his plodding horse.

Clarissa tried to sort through her feelings as she walked, wondering for a moment if she should be afraid of Galorian. He was, after all, what she had run away from. But he was also a living link to her memories of Josselyn. *Is he really a monk?* she wondered. The next thought was particularly troubling to her. *Or is this some sort of trick?* She decided to abandon the effort to figure out what she felt. It was just too complicated.

"I have a confession to make," she said to Francis as she closed the gate on the horses.

He gave her a surprised look. But then he said "Of course" and took on quite a serious demeanor as he prepared to take the role of confessor.

"I thought you were a totally lost cause," Clarissa said, and the monk's expression grew even more bewildered. Then she told him about their previous encounter in his father's cloth shop in Assisi—hiccups, drool, and all.

Francis groaned. And then he laughed. "So I have you to thank for my salvation," he said, grinning again warmly at her. "All those prayers."

They caught up with Aminah and Galorian at the back edge of the crowd. Clarissa anxiously scanned the faces for Johanna's but couldn't locate her. The rams were lined up, small black heads attached to fat balls of fluff, their wool discolored with dirt and loaded with burrs. Two men grabbed one young ram each by the horns—"conveniently outfitted with handles," one of them announced to the appreciative spectators—turned them on their sides, and began to shear.

In a matter of minutes the sheep were as skinny as fence rails, the bit of fluff still clinging to them now bright white as the rest fell away. While the men stuffed their fleeces into sacks, the two young rams struggled to their feet. They sized each other up for a moment. Then they faced off, horns down, and charged. "Ah, stupid sheep," said one of the shearers, trying to pull them apart. "They don't recognize each other anymore. They think they're strangers that need to be run off."

Aminah laughed. Galorian commented, "Fight first . . . It seems to be the default response for sheep and men alike, doesn't it?"

Clarissa was intrigued. She tried again to shake off the swirl of emotions that gripped her. All at the same time she felt moved by, envious of, and resentful about the obvious mutual affection between Galorian and Aminah. She wondered when she and Galorian would have an opportunity to talk.

When the shearing was finished, Francis, with a glint of mischievous merriment in his eyes, challenged Galorian to a round of water jousting. With the help of the shearers, they located the thick trunk of a fallen tree and rolled it into the water at the pond's edge. Francis and Galorian each picked up a large stick and stepped carefully onto the ends of the log, while the partiers gathered around to watch. A shearer gave the log a push toward the pond's center. Aminah raised her hand and then dropped it, the signal for the joust to begin.

Francis strode quickly toward Galorian, using his stick to keep his balance, while Galorian inched toward him. "I thought you were a knight!" taunted Francis, smiling broadly. The two whacked the centers of their sticks together a few times and tried to knock each other off the slippery log as it rolled in the water.

Clarissa, trying to keep one eye on the jousters, scanned the crowd again and spied Johanna watching Moses, who, like the recently hatched cygnets he was chasing on the bank of the pond, was learning to walk without falling. Clarissa rushed over to Johanna and said, "I'm glad I found you. You won't believe this." She nodded toward the two men jousting on the log. Just as Galorian lost his footing and fell into the pond with a big splash, Clarissa said, "That's the knight I was supposed to marry."

Johanna opened her eyes so wide that Clarissa thought they were going to pop right out of her head. Just then Moses took a tumble into the water and started crying for his mother. Johanna ran to him and picked him up. As she hurried away from the pond with him, she turned back to Clarissa and yelled, "I've got to find Lisette. We'll talk later!"

As soon as Galorian was off the log, at least a dozen boys shouted at once "My turn!" Francis stepped up to organize them as Galorian emerged from the pond. He stood beside Clarissa, his robe clinging and heavy, water dripping from his hair and beard. She grinned at him. "You're no longer a knight," she said.

He grinned back at her. "And you're no longer a girl." The blue of his eyes danced as he said it. Clarissa blushed, hoping he didn't notice.

§

The rest of that day seemed endless to her. She tried to hasten dinner, but the villagers took their time savoring it and hung around well past nightfall enjoying a large bonfire. When just the community and their two new guests remained, Nerida encouraged Liliana to say goodnight to everyone. The loving young girl happily went around the circle showering her many friends with kisses and hugs. She did the same to Francis, who embraced her warmly.

Though she had just met Galorian, Liliana wrapped her arms tightly around him and whispered, "I love you." He held her close, and then he smiled at the girl with flaxen hair and green doe eyes and said, "I love you, too." Their affectionate interaction both touched and unsettled Clarissa, who realized in that moment that she would have to tell Galorian Liliana's story.

Lisette stood up with Moses, who was too tired to do anything but wave goodnight to everyone, and followed Nerida back to Q Cottage to put the children to bed. Francis went off with Jaxon to get a juggling lesson. Aminah, who had clung to Galorian almost constantly since his arrival, leaned her head sleepily against his shoulder, while Felicite sat on the other side of the fire shooting him adoring glances.

Johanna got up, stretching and yawning dramatically, and announced, "Time for sleep." She squeezed Clarissa's hands, shook Aminah gently awake, and gave Felicite a hard stare. Aminah roused and followed Johanna to Manna House. Felicite stayed put, as if in a trance. Johanna turned back and called her name, and Felicite said grumpily, "I'm coming." And then only Clarissa and Galorian remained, sitting by the dying fire.

Clarissa had longed for this moment since she had laid eyes on Galorian hours before. But now that it had arrived, she was unsure what to say. And apparently so was he. "I don't know where to begin," said Galorian after a few moments, breaking the awkward silence between them.

"Nor do I," admitted Clarissa.

"You seem happy," he said, and Clarissa nodded. "You've found good sisters to share your life with here."

"Yes," she said. "And you?"

"I met Francis about a year ago. I was drawn to his spirit, as many brothers have been since. Our community in Italy is being replicated all across the country. Without intending to, Francis seems to have started a movement."

"Why are you in France?"

"I was about to ask the same of you," he said, smiling. "This is the country Francis is named for. He wanted to see it. And to grow the movement even farther. We're looking for a receptive spot in France to start a new community."

"And how did you decide to visit this particular spot?"

"I couldn't imagine visiting France without trying to see Aminah and find out how she's doing. Father Alain at Saint Catherine's Monastery in Egypt told me that a pair of Benedictine nuns took her to their convent in Liège."

So many thoughts and questions were racing through Clarissa's mind, but what she said was, "So you, too, have met the infamous Mother Agnes Luc."

"Yes," he laughed, puckering his lips into the dour and sour expression that was the abbess's trademark—as everyone who had ever met her seemed moved to do. "When I asked about Aminah, she didn't recognize the name. But when I said 'the Muslim girl who came from Egypt with two nuns,' she pulled out parchment and drew a simple map and said 'the coast,' pointing north. Then she dismissed me with a wave of her hand." Galorian dramatically mimicked the gesture of the abbess, adding a few noisy wheezes for accent.

Clarissa, laughing with him, was relieved to see that he was not an overly serious or pious monk. "She gets visitors looking for us about once a year," she said. "You and Francis are the most normal by far."

"That's saying something," Galorian remarked.

"Well," explained Clarissa, grinning, "the others included a minstrel with bells on his shoes, a donkey dressed like an archbishop, and a trio of dusty camels that bellowed all the way from Egypt." He laughed again, and she felt her heart fill with warmth, knowing that laughter came easily to him.

Clarissa wanted to know how long Galorian planned to stay, but she was afraid of being disappointed by the answer, so she didn't ask. She had so many questions. *How and where did you meet Aminah? When did you stop being a knight? Why? What took you to Saint Catherine's Monastery, and to Italy? How did you meet Francis? Do you miss England? What did you feel about your agreement with my father to marry me? Do you still think about it? Do you still think about Josselyn?* While the questions were swirling through her head, Galorian yawned and said, "Perhaps we should get some sleep."

"Of course," said Clarissa, trying to hide her disappointment. "You've had a very long day of travel and meeting people . . . and jousting." She smiled.

"Maybe we could talk tomorrow—beginning a little earlier in the day?" He smiled back, and she nodded.

Clarissa, with some embarrassment, pointed him toward the barn. "It's perfect," said Galorian graciously. "We've slept in far worse. Francis has built his movement on embracing poverty. He'll surely turn our time there into a spiritual lesson about sleeping among God's beloved animals in the sort of place where our Savior was born." He laughed again and said, "The man's a saint." And then he said goodnight.

Galorian headed in the direction of the barn as Clarissa made her way toward Manna House. After a few steps, she stopped, looked back toward him, and called his name. Galorian turned around and faced her. "I need you to know," she said, "that my running away didn't have anything to do with you."

He smiled once more. "I know," he said. "But thank you for saying it." She watched him walk down the path until he disappeared into the barn. Then she ran to Manna House to wake Johanna.

§

Everybody had an agenda for the next day. Francis and Galorian wanted to observe the school and visit Emmanuel's Place and Mercy Manor. Nerida wanted to show them her herb garden, and Jaxon wanted to sing to them. Liliana begged them to play with her and the swans. And Aminah just wanted to be wherever they were—as did Felicite, who had taken to batting her eyelashes at Galorian whenever he looked her way. Around the day's prayers and meals, the two gracious guests did it all and pleased everyone.

In the late afternoon, Clarissa grabbed a blanket and filled a basket with bread, cheese, figs, apples, two cups, and a bottle of mead. "I've put together a picnic supper," she said to Galorian, who had managed for just a moment to slip away from the attention of Aminah and Felicite. "We have a beach," she told him. "If we're lucky, we'll see dolphins."

He smiled at her, took the basket, and said, "Lead the way." They started down the narrow path. When they reached the shore, they walked side by side and talked about the day. Galorian expressed his admiration and gratitude for the work of Swansong. He asked about Clarissa's parents, and she had to share the sad news of Thea's death. "She had a loving and generous heart," responded Galorian, "and she was always good to me."

"She adored you," said Clarissa. "She was grateful and proud to have such a fine son-in-law." She remembered her mother describing him to her on the night she ran away as kind, brave, and handsome. "She thought you were kind . . . and brave," she said.

They kept walking until they arrived at the ritual cave. Clarissa led him inside, and they stood in silence for a while and listened to the echo of the waves. She didn't know quite how to describe to Galorian what happened there, but she wanted to try. "We bring our oldest students here every month," she began. "They call our gatherings our Moon Times."

Galorian smiled with understanding as Clarissa continued. "Johanna tells us the stories she knows about women of Scripture, and we share rituals that celebrate the faith, courage, and strength of womanhood." She stepped forward and picked up a burnt log from the top of the large rock in the center. "We pray around a bonfire on this rock. And then we spread the light to each other with candles. There are usually many tears."

Galorian stood in reverent silence for a few moments and then said, "What a terrible world we men have made for you." He shook his head sadly. "Thank you for sharing this holy place with me, Clarissa. I can only begin to imagine the impact you're having on those fortunate young women."

A strong tide was rushing in, the waves beginning to swirl around the rock and their feet. Clarissa led the way out of the cave and up to the cliff above it, her favorite spot for a view in all directions. They spread the blanket and settled in as Clarissa poured them each a cup of mead. Galorian broke off pieces of bread and cheese and handed some to her. Then they raised their cups to each other.

Clarissa tried to push back the tears that were gathering in her eyes. She looked away, moving her gaze to a circle of gulls that hovered high above them. "It's beautiful," said Galorian, taking a deep breath of the salty air. On the edge of the cliff stood a stately great blue heron. Down below them, sandpipers darted in and out of the waves.

"I love the birds," he sighed. He described to Clarissa his idyllic days in the castle mews with the hawks and falcons, and the antics of his cherished owl and merlin, when he was a young knight in training. Clarissa shared with him her unusual relationship with Saint Catherine the screech owl and the blessed warning of the swans on the night of the fire.

"I'm glad you have protectors," Galorian said. He kept his eyes fixed on hers. "I've worried about you, Clarissa. I've prayed that God would grant you safety and happiness. And I'm so very sorry for my part in your feeling you had to run away from your home."

Clarissa was still trying to keep her tears at bay. Before Galorian could say more, she asked him about his life, voicing several of the myriad questions that had plagued her for more than a day. She waited while he took them all in and gathered his thoughts.

"I lost my soul during the Crusades," he began, "and I found it again at Saint Catherine's Monastery." Clarissa had the feeling that he was sparing her the worst of the details as he told her about his discovery of Aminah in Constantinople and his decision to renounce his knighthood. He spoke about the word he received from God in a vision and his struggle to understand how to love his enemies. He described his sojourn at the monastery and his work in Rome, his conversation with Francis in the mountaintop cave and his hopes about starting a community of brothers in France.

By the time he finished, the evening breezes had begun to stir. The sun had collapsed into a distinct orange disk perched to their left on the western edge of the sea. The whole world seemed drenched in dazzling copper, the air itself vibrant with glowing color. Clarissa tried not to notice how bright Galorian's eyes looked in that light.

"And you?" He asked her to tell him how she had escaped, how she survived, how she came to be in France and at Saint Catherine's. "I want to know everything," he said. And so she told him about running away from home, meeting Nerida and Liliana at the Samhain celebration in the forest, encountering Jaxon and his donkey and lizard on the road, staying at the Benedictine abbey in Dover.

She explained that she and Johanna became close friends and decided to visit the sisters in Liège, where they cared for people with leprosy and learned French, and then to make a pilgrimage to Egypt when they discovered Saint Catherine of Alexandria. She told him about meeting Francis in his father's shop, and her proclamation that he wouldn't amount to much, which made Galorian laugh. She described in detail, with touches of hilarity, their trek across the desert on camels, and he laughed even harder. She mentioned meeting Aminah and told him she never could have imagined that he was the "kind knight" who had rescued her.

"You and I saw each other on the day you left the monastery with Aminah," he said. "As I recall, we even waved at each other."

"Yes," said Clarissa. "And we met once before then. In the mosque in the middle of the night."

"You were the nun who looked away and ran out the door when I was praying?"

Clarissa nodded. "I knew I was breaking a monastery rule, sneaking around at night. And the violation would have been greater if we had made eye contact."

Galorian broke off more bread and handed some to Clarissa. "It's sad that we made the same pilgrimage three years ago and were so close to each other, but didn't know."

"But we're here now," said Clarissa, smiling at him. She was still trying to sort out the questions and emotions that were ricocheting around her heart. She wondered if he was a vowed monk—or just a brother who liked to be around monks. *If he is a monk, am I relieved that he no longer considers marriage an option for his life? Or disappointed? And why does it matter? Certainly he wouldn't consider me. Not without feeling obligated by an agreement. And I have this community of sisters . . .* She realized the absurdity of the questions and tried to quiet them.

"Yes, we are," he said, smiling back. "Will you tell me the rest of your story?"

Clarissa described to Galorian her mystical vision in the Chapel of the Burning Bush at Saint Catherine's. She related her conversations with Mother Agnes Luc about the house on the coast, and the founding of Swansong. She talked for a long time, and yet she did not fulfill his request to tell him everything. The most tragic and troubling aspects of her saga she left unsaid. She wondered whether he had withheld as much from her as she had from him. Neither had yet spoken of Josselyn.

"You're living such a good and full life," Galorian said when she finished. "But you lost so much."

The tears began to spill down Clarissa's face then. "And so did you." Galorian moved closer and reached for her hand. "There's so much more I have to say," she told him. "But I don't know if you want to hear it."

"I want to hear whatever you need to tell me," he said, squeezing her hand gently.

"It's hard to know where to begin," said Clarissa, though she knew exactly where she had to start. She stared out at a distant point on the horizon as she spoke. "That night . . . the night Josselyn died, everything was so sad and confusing. I stayed at her side most of the day, holding her hand and praying. But then I got scared and moved away, just when she needed me most."

Clarissa pushed back a few more tears. "She was so brave." She turned to face him. "Josselyn was so very brave, Galorian." She looked down at the ground as she continued. "When the baby came, she was so small . . . and her color wasn't right. I picked her up. I prayed for her to live. But I didn't pray hard enough, Galorian. I was so scared." Afraid still to reveal the rest of that agonizing moment, Clarissa looked into his eyes again. "Can you ever forgive me?"

Lacing his fingers in hers and clasping her hand more tightly, Galorian returned her gaze. "There's nothing to forgive," he said. "Nothing that happened in that room was your fault." A wave of grateful relief washed over Clarissa. But Galorian didn't know the whole truth of that moment, and she had still harder things to share. She swallowed hard and continued.

"Did you know that Beatrix, the midwife, was murdered in the forest that night?" Galorian admitted that after the loss of Josselyn, he had been focused only on his fellow knights and their preparations for the next Crusade. Clarissa shared the details of the discovery of the midwife's body as gently as she could. Taking a deep breath, she said, "And here's why my father gave you a double dowry."

Tears slipped down Galorian's face as Clarissa told him about Father Augustus and Josselyn. "I loved her so much," Galorian said when Clarissa finished, "and she never told me."

Clarissa reached up and brushed a tear from his cheek. "I believe she wanted to protect you," she said. "To protect us all." Galorian put his arms around Clarissa and drew her close. She buried her head in his chest as they cried together softly.

"Thank you," she whispered.

"For what?" he asked, stroking her hair.

"For honoring her suffering. For not calling her 'damaged goods.' For loving her so much that that's all that matters." They sank into the comforting embrace for a while.

Then Clarissa felt Galorian's body tense, and she sensed that his sorrow was turning toward anger. He would have to feel it, she knew, to go to the depths of outrage over the violation of Josselyn, as she had. But there would be time for that. She had one more thing she needed to tell him.

She sat back and gazed into his eyes. "As terrible as it was," she said, "there's one very wonderful gift that came into the world because of it." Galorian eyed her curiously, and Clarissa smiled as she said, "Liliana is Josselyn's daughter."

The astonishment was clear on Galorian's face. Clarissa wondered if he had thought it mere coincidence that he and Liliana had so immediately and deeply captured each other's hearts. "Of course," said Galorian, crying and smiling at the same time. "She looks just like her."

"And she has Josselyn's loving spirit."

Galorian stared out at the sea, sitting with the wonder of the revelation. "It's amazing," he whispered. "The beauty and grace of Josselyn alive in her daughter."

Then he turned back to Clarissa. "And in you," he said. "You're a strong and brave and beautiful woman, Clarissa."

For the first time in her life, Clarissa believed the truth of those words. She held Galorian's gaze. "Sometimes," she said softly, "I wonder if I made a mistake running away."

They sat in silence, their eyes locked on each other, as a new and bewildering feeling overtook Clarissa. Galorian reached out and gently stroked her tear-stained face. Then he leaned in. She liked the sensation, the feel of his lips on hers. His tenderness flooded her with warmth and sent chills through her body at the same time. His kiss grew more passionate, and Clarissa matched its fervency. Her heart seemed to be melting along with her fears. She closed her eyes tightly, wishing the moment would last forever.

And then Galorian pulled back abruptly. "I'm so sorry," he said.

Clarissa opened her eyes, blinked, and reached a finger toward his lips. "It's all right."

"But I've taken a vow," said Galorian sheepishly.

"Oh . . . Of course you have," said Clarissa, sliding away from him slightly. "Then I'm sorry too . . . I mean I'm not sorry you've taken a vow . . . Well, I'm a little sorry." She felt her face flush and, thankful that twilight engulfed them, hoped again that Galorian didn't notice.

He laughed warmly. And then she did, too. "Who could ever have imagined this?" he said. He poured a second cup of mead for each of them, and Clarissa lost no time drinking hers. Then she poured herself a third. "To Josselyn," she said, as they touched their cups.

They watched in silence as night crept in. Clarissa pulled her sister's cross out from under her robe and removed it from around her neck. "She would want you to have this," she insisted, pressing it into Galorian's palm.

"Thank you," he said, gazing at the Crusader cross in his hand. "I made it a long time ago when I was a very different man. I wanted us both to live by this cross. I gave it to Josselyn to wear close to her heart, to have as a reminder of me when I left on the Crusade."

Clarissa pointed out the marks in the wood. "She was biting on it for comfort during her worst pain, just before she died."

Galorian moved close to Clarissa again. They sat with their arms entwined around each other on the cliff overlooking the sea. A point of white light appeared in the east, off to their right. In a matter of minutes, a large, bright orb rested on the horizon, casting a silver path on the water. And on that path were dolphins, leaping in silhouette against the full moon.

"Would you mind if I stay?" asked Galorian.

"Here with us?" asked Clarissa.

"It seems as good a spot as any."

Clarissa smiled.

Twenty-eight

The next day Galorian and Clarissa beamed grins in each other's direction during morning prayers. After the last "Amen," he asked her if they could watch the sunrise together at the beach. He held her hand as they walked, watching the gulls and sandpipers wake to a new day in the gradually growing light. "Thank you," he said, squeezing her hand. "I realized this morning that I still have a lot of questions."

Clarissa filled in the rest of the story, telling him about the circumstances of Liliana's birth and her arrival in Nerida's family, the black horse with the white cross on its right flank and the exposure of Father Augustus's crime by Zerah and Aldrich, Clarissa's rescue of Liliana at Nerida's wedding, the burning of Zerah's home and the dead sheep on the doorstep of the mansion. She told Galorian how angry and sad and afraid she felt having to flee from home again because of the death threats, and about her decision at the convent in Dover to escape to France with Johanna. Rolling her eyes, she described her channel crossing dressed like a foppish man in a stinking barrel of dead fish.

The telling took a long time, and the sun was fully up and warming the sand beneath their feet when Clarissa finished. Galorian thanked her again and said with admiration and awe, "You're even braver than I thought."

"There's one more thing I need to show you," Clarissa said as they started back up the steep path. When they got close to the community center, she told Galorian to close his eyes. She led him by the hand to the front and asked him to open them. There, hanging over the door, was Jaxon's sign: "Welcome to the Josselyn Center."

Galorian smiled. "I've been here a day and a half," he said, "and somehow I missed that." They stood side by side, arms around each other's waists, looking at the sign. "It's a beautiful tribute," said Galorian. "Josselyn would love this place, so full of life and faith and goodness."

"I still think about her every day," said Clarissa.

"So do I," said Galorian. "Each and every day."

§

Before lunch they had a conversation at Manna House with Francis, Johanna, and Nerida. Francis gave a brief history of the brothers in Italy, and Galorian explained that they were looking for a place to start a community in France. "I've discussed it with Clarissa," he said, "and we're wondering if you might be open to allowing us to try it here."

Galorian explained that Swansong was doing exactly what he and Francis felt called to do: teaching and feeding the hungry, caring for people suffering with leprosy and dying, sharing life in a community of compassion and prayer. "You're doing what Jesus commanded us to do in the Gospel of Matthew," said Galorian, "ministering to his hurting sisters and brothers, and therefore to him." Clarissa smiled to herself, remembering that passage of Scripture that had turned her life upside down when she discovered it in the scriptorium in the abbey in Dover. That seemed so long ago now. "I think there are many things we could learn from you," Galorian declared.

Francis spoke then. "We know you have enemies," he said. "The fire revealed that. There are people who want lepers to simply disappear and are against anything that is done for them. And there are a lot more people against women living together in freedom as you are, refusing to be wives owned by husbands or nuns controlled by the church."

"You've already proven that you're strong and brave," said Galorian, looking at Clarissa as he said it. "But there may be more trouble. In many places across Europe, monks are forming communities close to communities of women like yours, to send a message to the church that we respect your faith and ministry." He sighed. "I'm very sorry that the world is the way it is for women. If I can be a helpful ally, I'd like very much to be here."

Nerida responded first. "There are other communities of women like us?"

Before anyone could answer her, Johanna wondered aloud if having more men around would change the closeness they shared as women. But she added, "I know that Clarissa trusts you completely, Galorian, and I'm willing to try it. You may be right that we'll be glad for your protective presence someday."

Galorian clarified that the community of brothers would be distinct from Swansong. "We'll build our house out of sight of yours, and we'll stay out of your way when you want us to. I promise we won't meddle in your decisions or attempt to control what you're doing. You've already shown that you are more than capable of taking care of yourselves—and many others. I only want to learn from you and be helpful in any way I can."

Johanna turned to Francis. "Will you be part of the community, too?"

"No," he answered. "I love what's happening here, but my home is with my brothers in Italy." He looked from Clarissa to Johanna and then said with a grin, "Besides, I'm done dealing with cloth."

"Cloth?" they said in unison.

"Well," said Galorian, "it's only an idea." He brought out the jar and box he had carried in Thane's saddlebags from Saint Catherine's to Italy and then to France. He pulled out and held up the seed packets of woad and fennel, madder and safflower. "Brother Bernard, the gardener at Saint Catherine's, gave me these with instructions to plant them in a sunny spot. He told me, 'You'll grow a garden of dyes.'"

Galorian placed the packets back in the jar and opened the lid of the wooden box with the small holes in the top. Nerida peered inside and stepped away quickly, yelling "Bugs!" Galorian explained how the kermes insects produced red dye.

"During my year at the monastery, I learned everything I could about dyes," he explained. "And I just thought . . . Well, you have the wool, I have the dyes. I know it hasn't been easy for you to support everyone and every-thing you do, with your growing community and your generous hearts. I thought maybe we could work together in an enterprise that would help to keep it all going—and add some beauty to the world." He stopped and then added hastily, "But only if you want to."

Clarissa and Johanna both smiled. "When do we start?" asked Johanna.

§

Early the next morning they all gathered and said a sad farewell to Francis. "Come back and visit," Clarissa said to him.

"I'll be back to check up on him," said Francis, nodding toward Galo-rian and then grinning at Clarissa. His eyes sparkled again with the mischie-vous glint as he said, "And I need to give him another chance to beat me at water jousting." The two monks embraced warmly, and then Francis got on his horse and turned down the path toward Balnéaire.

Galorian wasted no time getting his dye seeds into the ground. Nerida helped him choose a level, sunny spot adjacent to her herb garden. Aminah and Felicite, who were beyond overjoyed that Galorian was staying, helped him open the furrows in the soil, and Liliana and Clarissa carefully planted the seeds. The kermes insects found a new home in the branches of an ever-green shrub at the edge of the dye garden.

Jaxon and Galorian went right to work building a small house in a clearing beyond Emmanuel's Place, which they finished quickly. Building a community of gentle and peaceful men required a good bit more time and effort. Galorian took the summer to meet villagers and spread the vision of Francis and his movement. Though Clovis had a hard time relinquishing his Greek fisherman's cap for a monk's cowl, he was the first to join up.

Jaxon announced that he wanted to be the second. When he voiced this intent, he was dressed in the colorful silk pantaloons and bright diamond-patterned shirt he had worn on his move to France. Galorian responded gently, "So you want to wear a brown monk's robe and pray seven times a day?"

Jaxon thought a moment and then said, "Well, now that you put it that way . . ."

"Why don't you just move into the house with us?" offered Galorian. "You practically built it yourself."

Jaxon pondered the invitation briefly, grinned, and said, "That sounds like a fine idea." And so he moved in with Galorian and Clovis to share the space they called Francis House, in honor of their inspiration in Italy.

§

On a warm, clear evening in June, Clarissa and Johanna stretched out in the pasture under a bright bowl of a moon that hung low in the sky, watching an assembly of fireflies blink in the trees. A choir of frogs serenaded them, the soprano hums echoing in the branches and the bass lines belching from the pond. "Do you remember Galorian mentioning other communities of women like us the day he told us he wanted to stay here?" Johanna asked.

"Yes," said Clarissa, sitting up. "I've thought about that more than once."

"Do you think we should go see where they are?"

"I want to. But I don't see how we could possibly get away now, with all the work in the garden and trying to get the cloth business up and running."

"Someday," said Johanna.

"Another trip," sighed Clarissa, leaning back with a smile.

"No camels," said Johanna, laughing.

It was a glorious summer. Galorian gave his Saturday mornings to Aminah, but he and Clarissa rode together on Thane and Magnus every weekday morning after prayers, often on the beach. Late every afternoon, the two of them and Liliana spent time together working in the garden, strolling hand in hand along the shore, or playing with the swans. Johanna joined them about twice a week. She and Galorian shared a love of Scripture and church history. Clarissa took delight in watching them exchange their knowledge and enjoy each other's company, learning from them both.

The gardens thrived, and the community earned enough money from the sale of their wool to invest in what they needed for their cloth-dying enterprise. Galorian built himself a simple dye shop. Jaxon carved a wood sign to hang over the door, changing one letter in a quote from the prophet Jeremiah: "You shall dye in peace."

Clarissa groaned when she saw it, and Galorian said, "If you think that's bad, look at this one." He pointed to the bench in front of his shop, which he had crafted by lashing together a few pine logs. On its back Jaxon had affixed an engraved plaque with a similarly altered verse, from the biblical book of Second Kings: "If we sit here, we shall also dye."

"But, truly, this is the worst," Galorian told her as he led her inside. Above the shelf on which he stored a few bottles of mead and wine was a sign quoting the prophet Isaiah: "Let us eat and drink, for tomorrow we dye."

Clarissa rolled her eyes at that one. But she was grateful to have touches of Jaxon's mirthful spirit and creative humor around the place. "Who knew," she commented, "that our troubadour paid such close attention to the Bible?"

Two more men from Balnéaire joined Galorian's budding community: Alfonse, a recent widower whose teenage daughters had been among the first students in the school for girls, and Damien, a young friend of Clovis. Galorian kept his promise not to interfere in the life of Swansong, but as the weeks passed, the two communities eased into a rhythm of spending regular time together, sharing prayer and work, meals and weekly communion. At the end of the summer, they dedicated Francis House and threw a big party, the highlight of which was Jaxon singing a song he wrote specially for the occasion while juggling three burning torches.

Clarissa had never felt so alive and at peace. During that magically idyllic season, everyone seemed settled and happy. She hoped it would last forever.

§

On a late afternoon in early September, Clarissa had Liliana by the hand. They walked past a vast array of leaves, roots, seeds, and insects spread out in the sun to dry, on their way to get Galorian for their daily outing. Clarissa noticed that Jaxon had added an altered quote from a psalm next to the door of the workshop: "When we look to the wise, they dye." She shook her head and smiled.

As they entered the shop, Liliana called Galorian's name, as she always did. Usually he dropped whatever he was doing and swept her up in his arms. But this time she got no response. Clarissa called then, too. Still no answer. They ducked around pungent vats of colorful dye, calling and searching.

Soon Galorian stumbled in from the back room. He tried to greet them, but his speech was slurred. He hiccupped a few times and then he slid to the floor in a corner. Clarissa quickly ushered Liliana outside and asked her to wait. Then she went back in to confront Galorian. She knelt in front of him, and he stared at her vacantly, in a stupor. "You're drunk!" she declared, appalled.

"Yes," said Galorian, snapping to attention with a witless grin on his face. "Let us eat and drink, for tomorrow we dye." Clarissa glared at him, and he said softly, "It's true."

"You're not making sense," snapped Clarissa.

"It's not what you think."

"That's what men always say," Clarissa shot back. She spied an empty wine bottle on a table in the back room, and another half full. "I can't believe it. I trusted you." She turned and stormed out of the workshop.

"Wait!" yelled Galorian. But she was already out the door.

Clarissa grabbed Liliana by the hand and led her toward the path to the beach. "Isn't Galorian coming?" Liliana asked.

"Not today," said Clarissa, trying unsuccessfully to keep her anger under control. Then she calmed her voice and said, "He's sick, Liliana. It'll be just us today." They took a long walk along the shore while Clarissa tried to calm her spirit to match her voice. Liliana skipped in and out of the waves, pocketing pretty shells that glistened in the water. Clarissa, preoccupied with her fury, watched her niece but didn't join in.

When they got back, Liliana announced at dinner, "I want to take the shells to Galorian. To make him feel better."

"That's very kind, Liliana," said Clarissa. "You can give him the shells tomorrow. I think he needs to be alone right now."

Just then Liliana shouted "Galorian!" Clarissa turned around to see that he had appeared in the doorway. Liliana ran to him. "Are you better?"

"Yes," he said, "much better." Clarissa had never seen him look so sheepish and embarrassed. He greeted the women at the table and, receiving

Liliana's shells with gratitude, apologized to her for missing their time to-gether. Then he looked at Clarissa and said, "Can we talk?"

Still harboring her anger, Clarissa hesitated. But then she nodded and followed him outside. They walked in silence to the pond and sat on a bench that Galorian had made to match the one in front of his workshop. He began to laugh.

"It's not funny!" fumed Clarissa, turning to face him. "I trusted you, Galorian, and you let me down."

"Can I explain?"

"This had better be good."

"So," Galorian began, "I learned a lot about growing dye plants at Saint Catherine's, and a little about using them to make paint pigments for icons. But I didn't learn anything about dyeing cloth." He hesitated. Then he said, "Since you caught me in the act, I guess I might as well just say it."

He cleared his throat self-consciously. "I found someone in the village who knows a lot about dyes for cloth. He told me that there are a few ways to 'fix' the color when the dye is fermenting in the vats. Salt works pretty well. Vinegar improves reds and purples. But the absolute best thing to use is ammonia." He shifted uncomfortably on the bench. "And the best way to get ammonia is to . . . well . . . drink a lot of wine . . . and then . . ."

Clarissa could see that he was struggling to find a way to say it deli-cately. "Pee in the dye?!" she said.

He began to laugh again. Clarissa joined him this time. Galorian put his head in his hands and laughed so hard he could barely speak. Then he looked up and managed to choke out, "He told me to drink two bottles. I'm sure he had no idea how rarely I've drunk wine." Another wave of laughter overtook him. "Or maybe he said two cups."

The two of them stayed on the bench, talking and laughing until dark-ness closed in around them. They watched the swans fold their long necks into their backs for their night's sleep. Then Clarissa took Galorian's hand and said, "I'm so glad you're here with us."

He squeezed her hand, smiled, and said, "So am I."

Three days later, when Jaxon showed up for dinner, his face and hands were dark blue. "Don't ask," he said, not even attempting to bring his usual lightheartedness to his predicament. Liliana stared, unable to take her eyes off of him. Galorian tried not to laugh out loud as he and Clarissa exchanged looks across the table.

Later when they were alone, Galorian explained. "He's looking forward to some colorful new clothes, and he wanted to help. So he drank a bottle of wine and then stood over one of the vats." Galorian grinned as he said, "The blue one," and Clarissa laughed. "He was a little tipsy and lost his balance."

"How long do you think he'll stay blue?"

Galorian shook his head. "I have no idea."

The next day, when Clarissa showed up at the dye shop with Liliana, she noticed that the sign by the door had been changed from "When we look to the wise, they dye" to an altered verse from Proverbs: "Fools dye for lack of sense."

§

That fall brought another complication in their life as a community, as Felicite's adoration of Galorian grew into an annoying obsession. More than once, when Clarissa and Galorian were walking on the beach, they turned around to find Felicite following them several paces behind. Whenever they spied her, she quickly ran toward the waves and pretended to be hunting for shells.

One morning as Clarissa and Galorian sat on the bench by the pond engrossed in conversation, they heard a sneeze a short distance away in the woods. "Felicite!" Clarissa called out. But the young woman refused to present herself. Clarissa heard her scamper off in the direction of Q Cottage.

"This is getting to be a serious problem," Galorian told Clarissa. "She hovers around my dye shop all the time." Clarissa noted to herself that the young woman who at one time had reminded her so much of herself could not keep away from the man that Clarissa had once abandoned everything to escape from. "She's a pest," said Galorian. Then he shook his head and said, "I'm sorry. That wasn't very Christian."

"You're forgiven for that."

"It's just that . . ." Galorian stopped, struggling over what to say and how to say it. "You need to know that she was waiting for me in my room one night last week."

"At Francis House?"

"Yes. And she was dressed . . . Well, let's just say that her intentions were clear."

"What did you do?"

"I told her to leave at once. I let her know that she was forbidden from being in my room—or anywhere in Francis House."

"And what did she do?"

Galorian hesitated again, obviously uncomfortable talking about it. "She grabbed onto me. I pried her away. And then I lost my temper." Clarissa had a hard time imagining it. She had never seen Galorian angry. "I said some very unkind things to her. I needed to make sure that I was being clear." He paused again. "She pouted and cried. And when I ignored her, she left."

"I have to speak with her," Clarissa said, furious at Felicite. Galorian didn't try to stop her. She left him on the bench and marched to Q Cottage. Wanting to save Felicite further embarrassment and more anger aimed at Galorian, Clarissa didn't reveal that he had told her about Felicite's visit to Francis House. Clarissa simply told her that, if she wanted to continue to be part of Swansong, she needed to keep more distance from him.

Felicite looked wounded and misunderstood. She said coldly, "Don't worry yourself about it, Clarissa. Why would I want to be near Galorian? I don't even like him. And I don't plan to be near him ever again." Clarissa did what she could to encourage Felicite to talk about what had happened between them and to share what she was feeling, hoping to avoid a rift in the heart of the community. But Felicite refused, excusing herself, walking into her room and slamming her door.

A few days later, Galorian told Clarissa that he was grateful for the change in Felicite. "She glares at me now when she sees me," he said. "But that's better than having her hovering around the dye shop or ambushing me in my room." Clarissa nodded, but the tension between Galorian and Felicite grieved her deeply.

"I hope someday Felicite and I can be friends," sighed Galorian. "But any effort or attention now on my part is likely to be misinterpreted. I think it's best for us just to stay apart for a while." Clarissa nodded again, feeling a great sorrow settle in her heart.

§

Felicite found more and more reasons to ride Magnus into Calais, inventing errands that sounded to Clarissa like veiled excuses to get away from Swansong as often as possible. On a late afternoon filled with gray clouds, Felicite returned from a brief visit to the city. Perched on the saddle behind her was a young woman who looked a few years older than she.

"This is Georgine," Felicite said to Clarissa and Johanna, who were talking in front of the community center. Felicite slid off the horse and then helped the young woman down. The gaunt newcomer appeared frightened, standing silently behind Felicite as she launched into relating the story that Georgine had apparently shared with her in Calais, or on their way back to Swansong. "When she was eight years old, her parents gave her away to a man to settle a debt. He treated her like a slave, beating her and abusing her in every way possible for over five years."

Georgine looked at the ground as Felicite continued unraveling the heart-wrenching tale. "When she finally ran away five years ago, the only thing she had that was worth anything was her body. So she's been selling it to men on the streets of Calais, for barely enough money to buy food to stay alive." She looked at Georgine sadly and added, "I found her on a street alone and crying."

Clarissa had never laid eyes on anyone who looked as broken in body and spirit as Georgine. When the young woman looked up from the ground, her hollowed face was unresponsive and her eyes stared vacantly. Johanna stepped forward to put her arm around her to welcome her, but Georgine shrank away from her. Clarissa went into the center to fetch some food. Then she helped Felicite get Georgine settled in an empty bed in Q Cottage.

"This is going to be a challenge," she said to Johanna when she returned. Johanna nodded somberly.

§

Clarissa met with Georgine every day before lunch, to see how she was doing and to listen to anything she wanted to share. Their first few meetings were spent almost entirely in silence. Clarissa wished that she could do something to relieve the young woman's suffering, but she felt helpless. She prayed fervently and often for Georgine. And she kept showing up each morning, hoping for a breakthrough.

When Georgine finally came to life, it was in the worst way Clarissa could imagine. She spewed her anger and pain everywhere. She refused to participate in any of the work of the community, and she was adamant about never being in the company of the men of Francis House. With spiteful venom, she criticized everyone and everything around her.

"This potato soup is cold!" she complained at dinner one night. "And it tastes horrible!" She dumped her bowl into the middle of the table, while the young women of Swansong watched, aghast. Lisette, the cook that night, bolted out of the room crying.

Clarissa and her sisters did their best to excuse Georgine's behavior. They understood that all the aggressive emotion erupted out of deep wells of rage and hurt and powerlessness, and that she was not to blame for what had been done to her. But it wasn't easy to live with. And so, after a week of suffering under the young woman's constant berating, Clarissa, Johanna, and Nerida met to determine whether they needed to ask Georgine to leave.

They went back and forth, feeling compassion for the young woman but longing for their life to be as it had been. Finally Nerida said, "Where else can she go? We can't just send her back to the streets." And so they decided to keep trying.

Clarissa had always believed that with enough love and prayer, any anguish could be healed. But her belief was sorely tested by Georgine. That fall she realized, with growing sorrow and a twinge of despair, that the presence of one person could dramatically alter a community's life and drain its energy. Clarissa imagined that if she had found Georgine on the street as Felicite had, she too would have been gracious enough to bring her to Swansong. But she couldn't help feeling resentment toward Felicite for forcing such a profound difficulty into their life.

One afternoon Clarissa was carrying an armload of gourds from the garden to the community center. Liliana was walking beside her, determined to carry one large gourd, when she stumbled on a rock. The gourd dropped to the ground and smashed. "You bad girl!" Clarissa heard a scolding voice shriek. "You're a very bad girl!" Georgine swooped on Liliana, grabbed her by the shoulders, and started shaking her hard.

Clarissa immediately pulled Liliana away from her. "Go!" she ordered Georgine, furious. "Go to your room." Georgine glared at her and left. Clarissa, repeating over and over "I'm so sorry," cradled Liliana as she calmed her fear and dried her tears.

That evening, as Clarissa sat on the bench by the pond with Galorian and related the terrible scene to him, she said, "I know she's just treating us the way she's been treated. And I'm trying to learn to live with that. But I can't bear her abusing Liliana." She rested her head on Galorian's shoulder. "I don't know what to do. She has nowhere else to go. And it would feel like such a failure to admit that our prayers and love for her aren't enough."

Galorian sat in silence with her in the confusion and anguish of it, and Clarissa was grateful that he didn't try to solve her dilemma or offer trite consolation. After a while, she said, "I have to think of Liliana. And of what's best for the community. How can we live together if we don't trust each other?" He nodded and smiled at her. "I'm going to try to accept what has to be done," Clarissa said, sighing.

She met again the next day with Johanna and Nerida. She expressed her fear of what might happen to their community if they allowed Georgine to stay. Johanna and Nerida reluctantly agreed with her conclusion. That afternoon she and Johanna shared the decision with Georgine, expecting a violent outburst or aggressive argument. But instead the young woman sat quiet and sullen, her eyes fixed on the floor. Her response broke Clarissa's heart. She wondered for a moment if they were doing the right thing; it would have been far easier to dismiss a raging Georgine.

But she took Georgine to the home of a woman who was part of the network that brought girls needing shelter to them. Though Clarissa thought it likely that Georgine would end up back on the streets or with an abusing man, she hoped for the best as she asked the woman if she would find a place for her. Remembering the dramatic transformation of intemperate Francesco into devout Francis, Clarissa prayed for such a miracle in Georgine's life.

She felt a pang of guilt as she rode away, knowing that she and her sisters had simply passed along their problem. But the relief that washed over her—and over the rest of the community when she got home—was enormous. Only Felicite protested Georgine's dismissal and abrupt departure.

§

The most joy Clarissa felt that fall was when she, Johanna, Nerida, and Liliana spent chilly September afternoons picking apples in their small orchard. As she observed Liliana, Clarissa recalled delightful hours of sneaking out to do the same with her mother, when she and Josselyn were young girls.

When the harvest was complete, Clarissa rolled a barrel to an isolated spot in the pine forest. She filled it with apples and poured boiling water to the top. Then she covered it tightly with a lid. For two days, morning and evening, she snuck out to the woods and stirred the contents. On the third day, she scooped out the apples one at a time, squeezing all the liquid from them into the barrel, and then replaced the lid once more.

The next day the migrating swans made a stop in the pond on their journey to a warmer climate. Liliana announced that the leave-taking of her swan friends wasn't as sad that year, since she knew they would be back again in the spring. On the day they took off, just before leaving, the pair that had spent the summer in the pond rubbed their long necks over Pinky for several minutes.

"Why are they doing that?" asked Liliana. Clarissa didn't know how to tell her. Before she could explain, the whole flock lifted up from the pond and soared into the sky, the exquisite wings of Pinky's parents and siblings carrying them at the back of the V as they joined the rest. Pinky ran along below them as fast and far as he could, flapping his mismatched wings, pitifully trying to follow. Then he collapsed in a heap, honking his bereft sadness.

"He can't fly!" wailed Liliana as tears filled her eyes. "How can they leave him? What's he going to do?" She walked to where Pinky lay and picked him up. She sat down at the edge of the pond and began rubbing him with her arm, as she had seen his parents do with their necks. He settled quietly into her lap as she stroked his back.

"Bring him," said Galorian after a few minutes. Liliana, clutching Pinky, followed him to his dye shop. He sorted through a collection of boxes that had carried supplies to him and picked out a crate that was slightly larger than Pinky. Then they walked to the barn and got some soft hay.

A few days later, Liliana spied the strip of leather that Jaxon had once used to tether Lizzie hanging on the wall, and she slipped it off its hook. Though Pinky would have followed her anywhere, twice a day she looped it around his neck and took him for a walk to the pond. The young swan thrived under Liliana's loving attention, keeping warm in his crate by the hearth in Galorian's dye shop.

Sorrow and a feeling of failure hovered over the community for days following Georgine's departure. Felicite sulked and kept her distance, not only from Galorian but from everyone else as well. Liliana, remarkably attuned to the mood around her, announced that it was time to play the second annual Onion Game. That year Lisette lost and, to no one's surprise, Liliana won again.

But even The Onion Game wasn't enough to lift spirits. Clarissa decided they needed another tradition. As October was coming to a close, she moved the gourds out of the Josselyn Center and into the woods, to the clearing next to the barrel of fermenting apple juice. She filled a tub with water and placed a pile of apples beside it. Then she laid the wood for a large bonfire. And before leaving, she found a private spot and placed an empty bucket there.

Late on the night of October's full moon, all the women from Manna House, Q Cottage, and Emmanuel's Place gathered in the clearing. "It's Samhain," announced Clarissa, smiling in Nerida's direction. Her friend beamed a smile back and then shared the history of the festival that had provided most of the few good memories she had from her childhood.

Keeping an eye on the bright moon as it traveled across the sky, the women sang and told stories around the bonfire. They prayed for departed family members and friends. Then Clarissa ladled out mugs of her sweet apple wine, and they toasted these dearly missed loved ones. They sang again and told more stories and took turns trying to fish apples out of the tub of water with their teeth, laughing at their efforts.

Just before dawn, Clarissa moved to the pile of gourds and invited her sisters to choose one. Each bore a frightening or funny face that had been carved by her with a delighted Liliana's help. One at a time, the women scooped up an ember from the dying fire. As they scattered for their rooms, they clutched their glowing gourds, reminders of the warmth that bound them together and would carry them through the long, cold days and nights of winter.

On her way back to Manna House, Clarissa took a detour to Galorian's dye shop. When he appeared, Clarissa presented him with a full bucket, declaring, "A contribution to your dyeing process." Galorian looked at her curiously, and she explained, "A lot of women drank a lot of my apple wine last night." He laughed and thanked her.

"I'd like to be more helpful, Galorian, to learn more about the dyes," she told him. "As Ruth said to Naomi, 'Where you go, I will go . . . Where you dye, I will dye.'" Galorian, mimicking Clarissa's response to Jaxon's bad dyeing jokes, rolled his eyes and laughed again.

"I'm serious, though, about learning the dyes," Clarissa said as she walked out the door. "And going wherever you go," she murmured under her breath out of his hearing.

She headed toward her bed, looking forward to some much-needed sleep. But when she arrived at Manna House, Johanna was waiting for her. "There's something you need to see," she said. They walked to the double doors of the Josselyn Center. Scrawled there in large letters with a black tarry substance were the words "Pagan Pervert Whores."

"Oh my," Clarissa said, taking a deep breath and clinging to Johanna, trying to stop the trembling that had overtaken her.

They called together the community to talk about the message on the doors. Johanna spoke first. "It's a tactic as old as the enemies of Mary Magdalene: try to undermine the reputation of strong and virtuous women by calling them prostitutes, questioning their faith, and accusing them of perversion. Whoever wrote on our doors did it all in just three words."

"It's curious how they used the words," commented Lisette. "Do they think we have sex with each other—and also sell it to men?"

"I don't think a lot of thought went into it," said Johanna.

"I'd give anything," sighed Clarissa, "to live in a world where men respect women . . . and everyone's belief is honored."

"And where all tender and devoted love is considered holy," said Johanna.

"And no woman ever feels forced to sell herself in order to survive," added Nerida.

Johanna confessed to her sisters, "I skipped a few of the stories of the women in the Bible. I wasn't sure our young students should hear them. But now I think they must."

By the time they finished their conversation, Galorian was already at work using some of his dye substances to remove the offending words from the center's doors. "I'm so sorry," he said to Clarissa as she approached to thank him. She settled into the embrace he offered, taking note of her growing gratitude for his presence.

Clarissa was fairly confident that the implied threat behind the words on the center's doors didn't have the power to rupture their community. But if the writer's intent was to sow misgivings and distrust, the shameful act had a measure of success. She and her sisters began to wonder who was behind it.

Only the women of Swansong had known beforehand about the Samhain celebration, and it took place at night in a very secluded spot in the forest. Questions swirled through Clarissa's mind. *Did a villager spy on us? Did Georgine have something to do with the words on the doors? Did Felicite tell her, or someone else, about our gathering?* That last question was particularly distressing to Clarissa. She found that she couldn't quiet the concerns she had about Felicite's distance and obviously wounded pride.

Only one question was more troubling to Clarissa: *Will there be more such warnings—or worse?* She felt anxiety creeping into her spirit. It ate away at the peaceful joy she had felt during the summer, threatening to take up residence in her soul. Even the delights of Christmas Eve in the barn and the community's shared Christmas Day feast didn't push away her growing worry.

Late on Christmas afternoon, she, Liliana, and Galorian got together as always. Liliana excitedly gave Galorian the simple basket that Clarissa had helped her weave out of cattail stalks. Clarissa handed him several bottles of her spiced apple wine. "One cup a day," she said, and he nodded and laughed.

Galorian, who had spent the fall experimenting with the colorful powders he had made from crushed plants and insects, gave Liliana a piece of bright purple cloth. On it he had embroidered a swan—with extremely pink feet. "It's Pinky!" shouted Liliana, delighted.

The cloth he presented to Clarissa was a rich green. Embroidered on it in gold thread were a cross and two scallop shells inside entwined oak leaves and lilies, the colors and symbols of her family's crest. "I haven't embroidered since I made a hood for my merlin Guinevere twenty years ago," said Galorian. "I'm sorry I don't have the talent to make a lion. But I wanted to give you something to remind you of home." Clarissa cherished the thoughtful and gorgeous gift, keeping to herself that England felt less and less like home.

As winter set in hard, and the relentless winds began to blow again, Clarissa tried to focus on the many things for which she was grateful: Galorian's closeness and Liliana's joy; her ever-deepening friendships with Johanna, Nerida, and her other sisters; their thriving school and ministries to people in need. But she couldn't help worrying about what 1208 would bring.

Twenty-nine

On January first, Clarissa's nineteenth birthday, Galorian handed her a bag of coins. "I've had a lot of success selling our dyed cloth in Calais," he explained. "We all worked together, and the profit belongs to everyone. Here's enough for a first payment on the property." He encouraged Clarissa to take Johanna and the money to Liège. She kissed him on the cheek in gratitude.

The timing was perfect. The school was still on its holiday break, and no garden clamored for their attention. On a snowy and bitterly cold morning, Clarissa and Johanna, wrapped tightly in their cloaks, started out on Magnus and Thane. "Give my best to Mother Agnes Luc!" Galorian called after them as they disappeared down the path.

The old abbess seemed pleased to see them, if only to get the money. Clarissa was effusive in offering her thanks to Agnes Luc for her generosity in allowing them to live on the property—and for directing their visitors to them. "Strange bunch," the abbess muttered in response. "But I expected that." She expressed no interest in their community on the coast, and neither Clarissa nor Johanna felt compelled to bring up the multiple building projects they had undertaken.

The other sisters were excited to see Clarissa and Johanna and to hear about their ventures. "There's a community like yours outside Liège," said Mathilde, now a vowed nun. After obtaining directions, Clarissa and Johanna went in search of women living as they did at Swansong. Not far from the city, they found five women living in a house, caring for people with leprosy. Like Clarissa and Johanna, they wore simple grayish-brown robes, but also wide-brimmed white headdresses. They supported themselves by brewing beer and baking bread to sell—the very enterprises that Clarissa had once mistakenly thought would earn money for her and her sisters. The women there were particularly renowned for their marigold-and-honey biscuits, which they baked and sold by the dozens every day.

"How did you get started?" Johanna wanted to know.

"We heard about two young women who left the Benedictine abbey in Liège," explained one of the sisters. "They didn't feel called to be cloistered nuns, but they wanted to be of service and live in a community with other women. And so they started their own. Somewhere on the coast near Calais." Clarissa and Johanna exchanged glances.

"As you know," another chimed in before they could speak, "it's almost impossible for women on our own to support ourselves in this world. But we decided that if they could do it, we could, too."

Clarissa couldn't help herself. "That's us!" she blurted out.

Everyone looked a little stunned. "So are you visiting all the communities you've inspired?" asked the first sister.

"*All* the communities?" said Clarissa and Johanna in unison.

The sister told them about two others that were nearby. Before heading back to the coast, Clarissa and Johanna visited a compound of fifteen women who ran a large school for girls, supported by the beautiful, delicate lace they made and sold. And then they stopped at a community of six that ministered to the dying, known for their exquisite sewing and embroidery. At both they shared the story of Swansong and were welcomed like saints. And at the latter they were bestowed with two wide, white headdresses in the style that all the women of the communities wore.

When they returned home a week after they left, the community was gathered for dinner in the Josselyn Center. After sharing hugs all around, everyone settled back onto the benches, spinning around to one another the marigold-and-honey biscuits the travelers had brought them. "Tell us about your trip," said Nerida, eying the headdresses Clarissa and Johanna wore.

Clarissa wanted to be more subtle, but she just burst right out with it. "We're a movement!" she exclaimed, her eyes sparkling and a grin spreading over her face. "We visited three communities like ours near Liège, and there are dozens more throughout France and beyond. Women everywhere are getting the same idea."

"They're calling us Beguines," chimed in Johanna.

"Be—what?" asked Lisette.

"Beguines," repeated Johanna.

"What does it mean?"

"Well, we don't know exactly," Clarissa replied. "But it's not a compliment."

"The sisters in Liège think it derives from the martyred priest Lambert le Bégue," said Johanna. "People are so anxious to give credit for us to a man. He inspired us with his love of Scripture, his simple translations, and his compassion for people in need. But he's hardly the founder of our women's movement."

She took a bite of biscuit and Clarissa jumped in. "Some people think it may come from the word *béguer*." Recognizing that it was an unusual term that Aminah and Nerida had probably not encountered in their vocabulary lessons, Clarissa explained. "It means to mumble or stammer. Apparently our critics say we do so when we pray, accusing us of practicing false devotion."

The sisters around the table were riveted on every word, fascinated that their way of life was shared by so many others and had generated such interest. "There's still another idea," said Johanna, "that the name comes from the word *beges*." It was a term familiar to all, applied to wool that was undyed and grayish-brown in color. "Some of our sisters in other communities believe that our detractors use it pejoratively because of our humble robes." She took another bite of the biscuit. "So be it," she said, sighing. "All the women we met wore robes like ours and headdresses like this." She pointed to the one she was wearing.

"The worst possibility," said Clarissa, laughing as she spoke, "is that they gave us a name that comes from the word *begun*." A few of the women at the table laughed with her. But others uttered responses like "terrible" and "disgusting" and "how insulting that they gave us a name that means 'dung.'"

"But," declared Clarissa, "I choose to believe that it comes from *benignitas*, because we believe in goodness and generosity. And I plan to claim the name Beguine proudly."

"Wait," said Lisette. "Who calls us Beguines?"

Clarissa laughed again. "All the people who think that women should be only wives or nuns."

§

Nerida made white headdresses matching those of Clarissa and Johanna for Felicite, Lisette, and herself, to wear as a sign of their commitment to their community and the Beguine movement. When they gathered in the cave with their students under the new moon in January, Johanna began her series of biblical stories that she had intentionally overlooked before. Clarissa worried that the truth of them was too heavy for the young students. But she knew that their lives would soon enough be burdened with the pain and suffering of womanhood, and so she supported Johanna's decision to tell the stories in the months before they gathered to celebrate the Easter vigil.

Johanna began with Hagar, enslaved by the powerful patriarch Abraham, forced to bear his child and then banished into exile. She related the story of plain-looking, unloved, desperate Leah, given away into an unhappy marriage through her father's deceit and trickery. She shared the tragedy of Dinah, raped on the road by a man who then staked a claim to marry her, and Tamar, a victim of incest who was cast out into lonely desolation.

Johanna told of the battered and burned wife of Samson, and the thirty-two thousand young women of Midian who were kidnapped as spoils of war and handed over to the men who conquered them. She shared the lonely tragedy of Jephthah's daughter, sacrificed on an altar by her own warrior father, and the unspeakable horror done to the Levite's concubine, raped all night by a mob of men and then dismembered.

As Johanna unveiled this world of vulnerability and violence against women, the tears flowed around the circle even more profusely than they had before. And so did the prayers. The young women in the cave began to understand more deeply that they faced a world in which they were the property of men, devoid of rights, subject to being overpowered by virtually any man at any time. And so they clung more tightly to one another.

Johanna had told Clarissa that she wanted their students to know what they were up against so that they could support and draw courage from each other. But she did not want to leave them trembling in terror and overcome with despair when she finished her stories. And so at the close of that year's Easter vigil, when they were leaning once more toward the brightness of dawn and the power of resurrection hope, she asked the circle gathered around the rock, "How do you imagine God? What do you see when you pray?"

"Light," said a few of the young women at once.

"Father," said several more in unison.

"Shepherd," offered one. "The Bible says so."

"It says refuge, too."

"And fortress!" shouted another.

"My rock and my salvation," said an eleven-year old proudly.

Johanna nodded at each response and then began to relate the biblical story of Job. She told them about this faithful man of God who was showered with calamity—losing his property, his livestock, and his ten children to thieves, fire, and a house collapse. "And, as if that weren't enough disaster and suffering," she said, "he was struck with a disease like leprosy that covered him from head to toe in loathsome sores. Job cursed the day he was born and angrily questioned the justice and goodness of God."

Johanna recited the words she had memorized long ago, God's response to Job, uttered from the heart of a whirlwind: "Where were you when

I laid the foundation of the earth? Who shut in the sea with doors when it burst out from the womb—when I made the clouds its garment? From whose womb did the ice come forth, and who has given birth to the frost of heaven?"

Johanna saw the looks of incredulity reflected in the firelight on the faces of her listeners. "Did you know," she asked, "that God has a womb?" Then she introduced them anew to God, who identified in the biblical book of Deuteronomy with a mother eagle that hovers over her young and carries them on her wings. She spoke of God claiming the role of a compassionate midwife in the Psalms, and a woman about to give birth in Isaiah: "I will cry out like a woman in labor, I will gasp and pant. As a mother comforts her child, so I will comfort you."

Johanna reminded them of where they began their biblical journey together two years before, with the words from Genesis at the very beginning of the Bible: "Then God said, 'Let us make humankind in our image, according to our likeness.' So God created humankind in God's image, male and female God created them."

Johanna posed the question, "How did the Holy One change from being a God with male and female essence at the beginning, to appearing a short time later only as Lord and Father?" She looked around the circle. "If you'll be patient with me, I want to share with you what I've learned."

She spoke first of the early church patriarchs' eagerness to embrace the Bible's second creation story—the one that portrayed Eve as a tainted temptress who was to blame for sin in the world, that relegated woman to a secondary and submissive role. "In this version," declared Johanna, "woman, rather than being created in the image of God, was a blighted and inferior 'helpmate' born of man—a stunning reversal of the laws of creation.

"If you believe that's true, then it follows that women can be declared less than human, considered possessions that can be controlled and violated. The Holy Scriptures can record the thoughts and actions of men and mostly ignore the voices, experience, and names of women." Clarissa could sense the anger rising in her friend's spirit as she spoke.

Johanna told her spellbound listeners that the second reason was related to their faith ancestors' obsession with idolatry, and their determination to be different from the pagan cultures around them. "When the Hebrew people were finally liberated from slavery in Egypt and moved through the wilderness to the Promised Land, they wanted to reject anything that looked like the surrounding Canaanite religion, with its many divinities—including its worship of fertility goddesses. The Hebrew people set out to worship the One, True, Male God.

"But if we are made in the image of God, as the Bible says we are, then God must look like us. God must be a Mother as well as a Father." She paused to let this sink in and then added, "Only a woman could have given birth to creation."

Clarissa was as wide-eyed as the young students around her. She shifted uncomfortably, feeling fear crawl into her throat. Troubling questions rampaged through her mind. *Does Johanna know what she's saying? Does she understand that she's uttering blasphemy? Can she imagine what kind of trouble we, and our school, will be in if word gets out to our enemies?*

The circle of women affirmed together once more that Christ was risen. Then Johanna sent them off with this proclamation: "We are sisters in Christ, all birthed in love from the same womb of God. Go forth to share that love with a world that desperately needs it, and to spread resurrection hope."

The young women were uncharacteristically silent as they filed out. Only Felicite spoke to Johanna. Smiling broadly, she said, "Very enlightening. Thank you."

Clarissa was seething by the time she left the cave. She tried to gather her courage, as she and Johanna walked back to Manna House without speaking to each other in the gradually growing light of dawn. When they arrived, Clarissa followed Johanna, who went into her room and sat on her palette. Standing in her doorway and shifting uncomfortably again, Clarissa declared, "We need to talk."

"I thought we might," said Johanna, in a tone that felt like ice to Clarissa.

Clarissa, with some hesitation, began to speak aloud the thoughts that had disturbed her in the cave. The pitch of her voice rose as she gained confidence, and she ended by practically shouting, "I think you went too far this time, Johanna. Way too far. You jeopardized everything we're building here. Just because you know everything doesn't mean you always have to say it!"

Johanna erupted in anger. "Sometimes I wonder, Clarissa, how you've survived this long away from your safe and happy home in England."

Clarissa was stunned. "You forget how much I gave up," she shot back. "And how much is at risk."

"And am I supposed to feel sorry for you because you gave up what I never had?"

"At least I made a choice," said Clarissa. "Nobody dumped me on a doorstep and made it for me. And I'm doing my best to live with it."

Johanna turned away. When she turned back, she said in her own defense, "You heard it, it's in the Bible." She shook her head and asked, "How is it that God can be a rock and a fortress, an earthquake and a whirlwind, a burning bush and a mysterious pillar of cloud or fire—but as a loving mother, God is too threatening?" She got up from her bed. "I need to get some sleep," she said to Clarissa, closing her door with a slam.

§

Clarissa didn't want to see Johanna the next day, so she kept away from morning prayers. She stayed in her room with her door closed, gazing restlessly out the window at the community center. When prayers ended, she watched Johanna and Galorian emerge and talk together outside the double doors. It was the time of day when Clarissa and Galorian always took their morning ride. But Clarissa didn't want to see him either, so she stayed put, out of sight. She was sure that Johanna was telling him how cruel she had been, and that Galorian was commiserating with Johanna in her hurt.

Clarissa sometimes felt like a child around the two of them, barely tutored in the vast knowledge they shared. That morning she began to picture a future in which Johanna and Galorian were best of friends, tolerating her like they would a little sister. Even worse, she imagined Galorian renouncing his vows and going off with Johanna to make a life together, leaving Clarissa to deal with the challenges of Swansong without them.

Embarrassed by her fears, she kept them to herself. Until that afternoon, when she could no longer live with herself. She went to find Galorian in his dye shop. "Will you hear my confession?" she asked, without even greeting him.

"I'm glad you're feeling better," he said with a smile. "Johanna told me you weren't feeling up to a ride this morning."

"Is that all she said?"

"About you? Yes."

"I did a terrible thing," said Clarissa. "And I need to make my confession. Will you hear it?"

Galorian hesitated a moment and then replied, "Only if you will hear mine when you're done."

Clarissa, deeply saddened by the rift she had created between herself and Johanna, unburdened her soul about their conversation the night before. "I didn't mean to hurt her," she said.

"Of course not," Galorian responded. Clarissa knelt before him, and with two fingers of his right hand he made the sign of the cross on her forehead. With the words "Clarissa, beloved daughter of God, you are forgiven," he offered her absolution.

"I need to go find her," she said, popping up and rushing toward the door. "God's not the only one who needs to forgive me."

"What about my confession?" Galorian called after her.

She turned around and said, "Next time."

He grinned. "I guess it can wait. I haven't committed a sin nearly as colossal as that one." Clarissa winced and then ran off to find Johanna.

"Can we talk?" she asked when she found Johanna in her room at Manna House. Johanna nodded. Clarissa sat down next to her on the bed. Looking into the eyes of her dear friend, she confessed, "I'm scared. With the fire and the threats . . . I'm worried about the community . . . and the school." She took a deep breath. "But you're right about God, and I'm sorry I didn't trust you. I'm sorry I'm so afraid. And I'm so very sorry about the mean things I said."

"We're all scared," said Johanna, taking Clarissa's hands in hers. "Of all the decisions I know that people have had to make, your running away from home is the bravest. I didn't mean to be so cruel." She sighed. "Sometimes I just get envious of the life . . . and the love . . . that you enjoyed and I missed out on."

"And I get envious of you, Johanna. For all the things you know. Your wisdom. Your way of telling stories. Your confidence. Your beauty inside and out."

Johanna held her friend's hands more tightly. "I like sharing what I know, and I can relate in an inviting way what I've learned." She sighed again. "But, Clarissa, you're the one with the creative heart. I've heard your prayers. It's such a shame that you don't reveal your eloquent, poetic spirit more. You let your fear get in the way and limit what you offer . . . and who you are."

Clarissa was a bit stunned by Johanna's words, but she was grateful for the honesty. She pondered both their affirmation and challenge before speaking again. "The worst part of me fears that you'll get bored with me. That you'll come to think of me as a daughter who no longer needs her mother—or, worse, as a pesky little sister." She hesitated for a moment and then decided to spill it all. "No. Actually, the worst part of me fears that you and Galorian will become best friends—or more—and leave young, scared, ignorant me behind."

"Oh, Clarissa." Johanna moved in closer and held her. "I hope the best part of you knows that will never happen. You're a bright and beautiful young woman who just needs the self-confidence to blossom. Galorian was right. You are strong and brave. You just need to believe it."

"I need you, Johanna. I wouldn't know how to go on without you," said Clarissa, leaning into the embrace. "Can you ever forgive me?"

"If you can forgive me," said her beloved friend, sitting back and gazing at Clarissa again. "I need you, too. And I can't imagine my life without you. We're in this together . . . Always." She placed her hand on Clarissa's cheek and added, "Maybe we can help each other be grateful for what is."

"Not fearing what will be," said Clarissa, nodding.

"Or regretting what was," said Johanna.

§

"Why don't I have a mama?"

Clarissa and Nerida knew that someday this question was coming. They had once asked Liliana what she remembered about her life before the manor, and she described wearing her new dress and carrying the basket filled with red berries for Nerida's wedding. They considered it a blessing that her memories started there. They hadn't told her that Thea and Aldrich were her grandparents, believing it would only confuse her. And they had decided not to say more to her about her past until she asked. They agreed that when she did, they would be honest with her.

Clarissa and Liliana were sitting on a blanket, watching children play with their parents and siblings, enjoying the fourth annual Sheep Shearing Day at Swansong. "You have a lot of mamas," said Clarissa.

"But why don't I have *a* mama?"

Clarissa looked into her niece's sad eyes. "That's a very good question, Liliana. Would it be all right with you if Nerida and I tell you the answer together tomorrow?"

"Tomorrow is a long way away," said Liliana, her lips beginning to pucker into a pout.

"All right then. How about tonight before bed?"

"All right."

Clarissa took her by the hand and they went to find Galorian, who was standing between his shop and bolts of dyed cloth he had spread out in front of it. Villagers were crowding around, touching and expressing their amazement at the beauty of the colorful wool and linen, cloth that until then had always been out of their reach. Galorian joyfully received bread and beer, chickens and vegetables and eggs in exchange for pieces of the cloth. One boy handed over a bullfrog he had caught in the pond in payment for a deep-blue wool weaving for his sick mother.

"What a gift you've given to the village," said Clarissa, admiring both Galorian's creativity and his generosity. "Now they will dress like kings and queens!" She left Liliana to help him and went in search of Nerida. They agreed that they would stick to their promise to be honest with Liliana—but also that there were some pieces of her story that she was still too young to hear.

That night, when Liliana was stretched out on her palette between them, Clarissa began. "Your mother's name was Josselyn. She was my sister, and I loved her very much. She was a very kind person, and she loved everyone, just like you do." She reached out and tenderly stroked her niece's blonde hair. "You look just like her, Liliana. She was beautiful just like you."

"What happened to her?" asked Liliana.

"She got sick and died, and everybody was very sad. But she loved you so much that, before she went to heaven, she made sure that you had Nerida to take good care of you."

"I love you just like you're my own daughter," said Nerida, squeezing Liliana's hand. "And now your Aunt Clarissa is like a mother to you, too. And you have many friends at Swansong who love you."

"Like Galorian," said Liliana.

Clarissa wanted to say something to her about Galorian, but she didn't know how to explain how it was that he had been married to her mother but was not her father. Liliana did not ask if she had a father. She seemed content to know about her mother.

"I miss my mama," said Liliana, tears rolling down her cheeks.

"I miss her, too," said Clarissa, holding her niece close.

The next day on their morning ride, Clarissa told Galorian about the conversation. When they returned, Galorian reached inside his robe and removed Josselyn's cross from around his neck. He pressed it into Clarissa's palm, as she had done when she gave it to him. "Liliana should have it. And you should be the one to give it to her."

When Clarissa placed it around Liliana's neck, telling her "This belonged to your mama," it hung almost to her waist. A big smile spread over Liliana's face. She threw her arms around Clarissa and said, "I love it forever."

§

The next warning to Swansong came in the form of a priest, who rode from Calais to make a surprise visit in June. The community was sharing lunch in the Josselyn Center when he barged in. "Who's in charge here?" he demanded to know.

"God's in charge," answered Johanna, getting up to greet him. Clarissa appreciated the truth and boldness of her friend's response but wondered if it sounded just a bit provocative. She looked around for Galorian, regretting that he was absent, likely still at work in his dye shop or the garden.

Father Lionel introduced himself and huffed his disapproval at Johanna. "Who's the leader of this group?"

"We don't have a leader," she said. "We all lead this community, with the guidance of the Holy Spirit."

"That's not what I've heard," retorted the priest.

"What have you heard?" Johanna asked. When he didn't respond, she said in her calmest and most inviting tone, "Would you like to join us for some porridge and bread?"

Father Lionel refused her offer. "What I've heard is this," he said angrily, his face turning red as he spoke. "You harbor prostitutes and enemies of Christ, you practice pagan rituals, and you reject God our Heavenly Father."

"And who told you these things?" asked Johanna calmly.

He ignored her question again. "This is a warning," he said, moving his hard gaze from person to person around the room. "You need to know that if you claim to be followers of Jesus Christ but continue to desecrate the church in these ways, there will be a price to pay." Before any questions or arguments could be voiced, he turned, stormed out, and took off on his horse.

A chorus of murmurs rose up around the tables. "It's all right," said Johanna. "We haven't done anything wrong." She led them in a prayer and encouraged everyone to return to their meal.

That afternoon Clarissa said to her, "I agree with you that we haven't done anything wrong. But it's troubling that he knew in such detail what goes on here."

"Yes," said Johanna. "But all we can do is live as faithfully and compassionately as we can—and trust the rest to God."

"It doesn't concern you that a representative of the church rode all the way from Calais to deliver a warning to us?"

"Of course it does," Johanna admitted. "But in the end, we're just a group of women on the margins of what counts as church in the minds of most people. Those who disagree with what goes on here ultimately know that bothering with us isn't worth their trouble." Clarissa, making an effort to live into the bravery that others seemed to see in her, tried to believe it.

Thirty

$\bigwedge$s another year came to a close and a new one was about to begin, Clarissa was grateful for the rituals that were touchstones of stability in her ever-changing world: the monthly Moon Times with her sisters in the cave, the Easter vigil and Sheep Shearing Day, the annual playing of The Onion Game, their Ramadan feast and Samhain celebration, Christmas Eve in the barn. And that year Galorian gave her the gift of another ritual to anchor her life. The day after she had shared with him her difficult conversation with Johanna, he got off Thane on their morning ride and knelt in the sand in front of her. "It's time for my confession," he announced.

From that day on, once a week Clarissa and Galorian shared with each other their deepest failures, hurts, and hopes. Clarissa's usually involved her fears and her struggle to discern and claim the fullness of life she believed God was calling her to. Galorian's often had to do with his impatience with his brothers, and increasingly with his estrangement from Felicite.

"How can I love my enemies if I can't even be charitable toward a sister in the community?" he wondered aloud one June morning. Then he added, "It's been long enough." He asked Clarissa if she would meet with him and Felicite, to help them listen to each other and work toward healing the chasm that separated them. Clarissa readily agreed and promised to devote herself to praying for a good outcome, knowing that reconciliation between Galorian and Felicite would be good for the entire community. But when she proposed the idea to Felicite, the young woman responded coldly, "Why would I want to talk to *him*?" She refused to participate in any conversation with Galorian, and none of Clarissa's repeated entreaties changed her mind.

When Clarissa reported Felicite's reaction to Galorian, he exploded in frustration, "She doesn't make it easy to love her, does she?" He sighed.

"I give up." He regretfully accepted that the rift would remain, while Clarissa tried to swallow the increasingly angry disappointment she felt toward Felicite.

As the weeks unfolded, Galorian both shared with Clarissa his heightened joy in his new life and confessed the depths to which he sometimes sank when he missed the adventure, valor, and renown that had marked his life as a knight. They both acknowledged their earnest desire to live in faithfulness and humility, in compassion and simplicity, free of the world's temptations of possessions and pride. They noted that his path required mostly surrendering ambition and control, and hers demanded gaining self-confidence and strength. Clarissa felt honored that Galorian trusted her with his heaviest thoughts and deepest longings, and in the spiritual bond that grew between them peace returned to her soul.

In late July of 1209, Galorian rode to Calais to pick up some supplies for his dye enterprise. When he returned, he asked to meet with Clarissa and Johanna. Clarissa had never seen him look so troubled and pale. "It's almost unspeakable," he said, groping for the words to describe what he had learned and needed to tell them. "Pope Innocent the Third has launched a new Crusade against heretics, and southern France is his first target. It started in Béziers, a stronghold of Catharism. On July twenty-first, Crusaders delivered an ultimatum to the Christians there: hand over all the city's heretics, or leave to avoid perishing with them. Mercifully, the Christians refused to turn over anyone and stood with their persecuted sisters and brothers in resistance.

"Before the siege a knight asked an abbot, a commander of the imminent assault, how the Crusaders were to tell Catholics apart from Cathars. The abbot said, 'Kill them all, and let God sort it out.' The next day the Crusaders stormed the city walls and carried out a bloody massacre by the sword, slaughtering twenty thousand people—young and old, men and women and children alike. No one was spared, not even the priests who took refuge with their people in the churches. The mob of raging invaders torched the cathedral, which collapsed on those who had sought safe haven inside, and then pillaged and burned the rest of the city."

Galorian trembled as he related the tragedy. Clarissa moved to stand by his side. Later that night, for the first time, he filled in for her the horrific details he had left out when he first told her about his life: the ghastly siege of Constantinople, the young knight's assault on Aminah, and Galorian's sword thrust that ended his life. Clarissa received it all, holding him close as he tried to purge the terrible memories.

Then Galorian knelt before her. "Will you hear my confession?" he asked. Clarissa nodded. "I share responsibility for what happened in Béziers," he declared, his voice breaking. "I left the work of the Heresy Council, but I didn't try to stop it."

He looked at the ground and then up at Clarissa again. She made the sign of the cross on his forehead. Pronouncing the blessing "Galorian, beloved son of God, you are forgiven," she offered him absolution. And then she spoke a prayer for the peace of his soul—and her own.

"Someone has to stop it," Galorian implored when she finished, his blue eyes riveted on hers. "Someone has to stop it," he repeated, "or soon we'll all be caught up in it."

§

That late summer and fall, amid all their other commitments, Swansong and Francis House dedicated themselves to one task. Young women still came seeking shelter and education, another baby was born under Nerida's watchful care, families brought their dying relatives to Mercy Manor, and the dye business and sheep flock, orchard and gardens, all demanded their attention. But anyone with an extra moment to spare went to work hauling rocks up from the beach to the spot on the bluff where Clarissa, Johanna, and Aminah had sat to watch the sun set on their very first evening on the coast. The women and men worked side by side, carrying and stacking rocks, making mortar, creating the strongest and most beautiful of the buildings on the property.

The work seemed to pull Felicite out of her sullenness, and though she still avoided Galorian completely, she participated with enthusiasm that almost matched what Clarissa had observed when she first joined the community. Clarissa began to regret that she had ever doubted Felicite's commitment to their life. Acknowledging the hurt and humiliation Felicite must undoubtedly have felt over Galorian's reaction to her, Clarissa prayed to be more understanding and to release every last vestige of her anger.

A Balnéaire artisan proudly donated Swansong's only glass window, a large, clear pane with a thin border of multicolored shards, for their chapel. "As beautiful as Chartres!" he exclaimed, wildly overstating the comparison to the stained-glass windows that would soon adorn the imposing cathedral under construction outside Paris. Galorian laid pine wood from the forest into the arched ceiling to resemble an ark, according to the description that Clarissa gave him of the Hanging Church in Cairo.

With her help, he also created an array of colorful paint pigments and crafted a translucent glaze out of ground eggshells mixed with water. As each inside wall was plastered, Lisette went to work with the paint. To everyone's surprise—most of all to Lisette herself—she revealed a previously undiscovered artistic gift. With Johanna's guidance, she created simple frescoes of biblical women and female saints. In the bottom right corner of each was the "signature" Lisette put on all her paintings: a pair of Beguines, dressed in their gray-brown robes and wide white headdresses, observing the depicted scene.

On one wall, Mary cradled the infant Jesus and Catherine of Alexandria held the torturing wheel that had failed to break her bones. On another, the judge Deborah and prophet Huldah consulted over a manuscript, while Ruth and Naomi shared an embrace. The large back wall portrayed the five women who saved Moses, standing together along the Nile River, between images of Jephthah's daughter on an altar and the dismembered Levite's concubine. In this chapel, anonymous women who had died alone in agony were honored alongside revered ancestors in the faith.

Everyone in the community took a turn stopping by to check the progress and express to Lisette their admiration for the primitive but beautiful paintings that were coming to life on the chapel walls. Clarissa lingered over one that was most unusual. In its center was a halo of light surrounding a series of elegantly flourished Arabic letters. Painted in its four corners were the Muslim symbol of crescent moon and star, a broken jug, a woven mat, and a brick. "I wanted to paint a Muslim saint for Aminah," said Lisette, coming to stand next to Clarissa.

Aminah overheard her and joined them. "I explained that we don't make images of our saints. But I was grateful that Lisette wanted to include one among the women in this holy place. So I told her about Rabia al Basri, whose story my mother told me many times." Aminah explained that the beloved eighth-century Muslim poet and mystic had introduced the concept of divine love in Islam. She had rejected many marriage offers to devote herself to prayer, and all that she owned was a broken jug, a prayer mat made of rushes, and a brick that she used for a pillow. "Lisette asked me to write Rabia's name on parchment in Arabic," continued Aminah, "and she copied it there on the wall."

The work had obviously been painstaking. Lisette was understandably proud, and Aminah deeply moved, by the achievement. "Amazing," said Clarissa, who thanked Lisette for both her talent and her thoughtfulness.

Late on the afternoon of November first, All Saints Day, the community members dedicated their Saint Mary Magdalene Chapel. The focal point at the front was Lisette's depiction of the beloved follower and friend of Jesus in all her dignity. Mary Magdalene stood gazing at a large, empty cross, which Galorian had fashioned from a fallen oak tree and fastened to the center of the wall. In simple letters beneath the saint, Lisette had painted "First Witness to the Resurrection."

On the other side of the cross was the large window, its colorful border radiant as the day's last rays of sun shone through it. Sitting on simple pine benches in their wondrous chapel perched atop a bluff, the community of awe-filled women and men sang hymns and offered prayers of gratitude that evening. Then they watched together as a blazing-red ball of sun dropped behind the cross and into the sea.

§

It took less than a week for Father Lionel to pay them another visit from Calais. He demanded to see the new chapel. "Of course," said Johanna in her usual, gracious tone. She led him up the path to the bluff, with Clarissa tagging along behind.

"Nothing but women," the priest muttered as he circled along the walls, scrutinizing Lisette's frescoes.

"But here's Jesus," said Johanna, pointing to the infant in Mary's arms. "Other churches honor one woman and many men. We just decided to reverse it," she explained matter-of-factly. Clarissa stood behind them, once more both awed and anxiety-ridden about Johanna's boldness.

When he got to the fresco honoring Rabia al Basri, Father Lionel stopped and shook his head disapprovingly. "Are these Muslim letters?"

Johanna decided not to correct his notion that Muslim was a language. "Yes," she said, unflinching. "And perhaps you've noticed that there are many Jews here, too. Deborah . . . Naomi . . . Miriam." She pointed them out on the walls as she named them. "Our Holy Mother Mary. And of course Jesus."

Father Lionel ignored her. Johanna began to tell him the story of the Muslim mystic Rabia, but he interrupted her. "I've already warned you once," he threatened. "The church will not tolerate heresy and blasphemy."

Johanna started to describe the beautiful mosque in the heart of a Christian monastery in Egypt, but Father Lionel was clearly not interested in hearing about that, either. He strode out of the chapel and down the path. He quickly mounted his horse, which kicked up a swirl of fallen leaves as it raced back to Calais.

§

That night Clarissa tossed and turned on her palette, her mind pursued by a mob of thoughts. Exactly seven years had passed since she had flung herself off the roof of her home and into the vast unknown. She had lost so much. But so many blessings had come her way. She tried to count and cling to these over the years, rather than to her grief, fears, and doubts. She wasn't always successful.

And now new vexations haunted her. *Will the church allow us to stay here? Or will we lose everything? How can it be that a small community of humble women is so threatening to men with power? Why can't my sisters and I just live undisturbed in the way we feel called to live? Is it fair for me to keep helping Johanna to lead them on what may become an even more dangerous path?*

Sleep, Clarissa realized, was not going to come that night. She got up from her palette, stepped out into the chilly air, and headed back up to the bluff. She sat in the deep quiet of the chapel for a while, trying to pray by the lamp that flickered on the altar. And then she went out and stood on what felt like the edge of the world.

Waves churned below her and broke loudly on the rocks. Clouds raced across the face of the full moon, which seemed to duck behind them and then peek out with alarming brightness. When the clouds finally blew away, the moon hung like a gleaming and constant beacon above her. But as Clarissa watched, an edge of its surface disappeared, as if someone had taken a bite from it. The bite grew, the moon being swallowed little by little.

Clarissa thought that she was being visited by another mystical vision. But soon she realized that what she was observing was quite real. Though she had never witnessed one, Johanna had once told her about the wonder of eclipses. Clarissa kept watching, spellbound, as the earth's shadow crawled across the face of the moon. When the two heavenly bodies were completely in line with the invisible sun, the moon glowed the color of blood. The sight took Clarissa's breath away.

And then, as she stood under the shadow of the eclipse, a vision did indeed visit her. Later, she remembered it this way:

> *I stood alone in the heart of a vast desert ringed by jagged mountains. Everything around me glimmered in the silvery glow of a full moon perched atop the highest peak. The moon crawled up the sky, and a piece of it disappeared, as if bitten away. As it climbed, the bite grew larger . . . and then larger still. When it was entirely swallowed, the moon blushed crimson.*
>
> *Stars blinked to life, strewn like diamonds across the blue-black expanse over my head. The brightest fell to earth and flared into a flame that danced in the distance. I walked toward the light,*

across a broad stretch of deep and drifted sand, and came upon a
rose bush. Its branches and blooms were ablaze, but the fire did
not harm or consume it.

As I watched, the bush sent out tendrils. These grew into massive, gnarled roots that snaked across the ground in all directions.
A voice in the center of the bush called my name. Then a single
flame separated from the blaze. It burst into a towering pillar of
fire that reached from the ground to heaven. When it began to
move through the wilderness, I followed.

It guided me through the sprawling tangle of roots and then
up the highest mountain, on a narrow path that was rocky and
steep. When I reached the crest, I saw Jesus. He walked toward
me through the pillar of fire, his arms outstretched, his face radiant. Flames blazed around him, licking the sky, but he emerged
unscathed. As he turned and swallowed the fire, the moon re-
emerged high above us, bright white and whole, bathing us in
shimmering light.

Jesus drew me close. The warmth of his embrace was so
peaceful and comforting that I wanted the moment to last forever.
But then a blazing ball of scarlet sun rose between two peaks, and
as night melted into morning he released me and pointed down
the side of the mountain. There, spread out before us, was a lush,
green valley. The city of Jerusalem gleamed like a gem in its midst,
reflecting the rose-gold radiance of sunrise. "You must go," Jesus
said, and I saw then that his heart was pierced with many wounds,
and light was streaming through them like rays from a lantern.

A small flame broke off from the sun. Reluctantly, I followed
as it led me off the mountain, through a maze of narrow city
streets, and into a cavernous room filled with people. A mighty
rush of wind blew through and fanned the flame of the sun into
great tongues of fire, which flew about the room and then came to
rest, one on each of us.

The voice of God declared:

"I will pour out my Spirit upon all flesh,
And your sons and daughters shall prophesy,
And your young ones shall see visions,
And your old ones shall dream dreams.
The sun shall be turned to darkness
And the moon to blood."

Immediately, day became like night. I heard a voice call with
urgency to me from beyond the walls. I ran outside to the street.
There I spied a woman clothed with the sun, standing on the

moon, with a crown of twelve stars on her head. She gleamed in the dazzling light of Creation, and I fell to my knees in awe.

She called to me again, and when I came close, I saw that she was crying out in the pain of childbirth. A red dragon, wearing seven crowns on its seven heads, breathing blasts of fire in seven directions, hovered behind her, ready to devour her child. But the woman turned her eyes to heaven and prayed, and help came. A great azure-blue falcon swooped down and lifted her on its wings, and the woman exclaimed with joy, "My child will live!"

Before she was swallowed up into the safety of heaven, she looked back and spoke to me. "Do not be afraid," she commanded. "Write. Write all that you have seen and heard. Give birth to the words, and you too will deliver hope into the world."

As she disappeared, she shed her robe of flaming sun, which fell to earth in a magnificent pillar of fire. The pillar moved in front of me, and I followed it. I asked where it was leading me. A voice spoke to me from the heart of the fire and said, "To freedom." And then I saw that my heart, pierced like the heart of Jesus, was leaking rays of light in seven directions.

Thirty-one

The very next day, Clarissa began to write. She took pieces of parchment and bound them together into a simple book. She left a sheet blank at the front. On the second, she recorded her vision. On the pages and in the days that followed, she wrote down her prayers and her reflections on the life of faith. Though she lacked Lisette's artistic flair, she illuminated her book with simple drawings that pleased her.

The book was her secret. She told no one about it—not even Johanna or Galorian. But slowly she began to fill its pages, usually late at night, sitting alone in the chapel on the bluff. And in the writing, she understood that she had been anointed into her calling by the woman clothed with the sun, from the Bible's book of Revelation.

As 1210 dawned, Johanna returned to leading their students through the Psalms in the ritual cave each month. When Liliana turned eleven in September, she joined her sisters. She had begun to ask on her eighth birthday what happened in the cave and when she could be part of it. Always, she had responded to the answer with a sigh of impatience. But her time had finally arrived, and with great excitement she found her place in the circle at the next new moon. Clarissa was amazed as she gazed from across the cave to see that her niece was on the cusp of womanhood.

The next evening the two of them sat with Nerida and Galorian by the pond. The adults in her life had decided that it was time for Liliana to know the whole truth of her story. Clarissa told her gently about Father Augustus and her mother's bravery. Nerida spoke about the family that took her in. And Galorian explained that when he was a knight, he was married to her mother, who was his dearest love. Then they all shared their favorite stories about Josselyn.

Liliana sat quietly as they spoke. When they finished, she said, "It's a lot to hear." Then she got up, said "Thank you," and gave them each a hug.

"Do you think she's all right?" Nerida asked as they watched Liliana head toward her favorite stretch of beach, below the bluff.

"She'll be fine," assured Clarissa. "I'll check on her when she gets back."

To everyone's relief, Father Lionel made no visits that year. And no one attempted to damage or destroy their chapel. The community received constant news of the ongoing persecution of people accused of heresy—the very charge that Father Lionel had raised when he saw the fresco dedicated to Rabia al Basri—and an entire year passed before Clarissa could surrender her fear that their beautiful worship space would be a target of the church's wrath. The resistance she felt to its escalating campaigns and threats found voice in the pages of her book. Through her writing, Clarissa discovered the courage that often eluded her in daily life.

§

Just when she had settled again into feeling that life was a joyful routine without surprises, another one visited. Never had she imagined Wilfred, to whom Nerida was still married according to the law, riding up their path. The years hadn't done much to mature him into a likeable person. Stiff and businesslike, he barely greeted Clarissa when he appeared at Manna House in late October, acting as if his presence at their coastal outpost wasn't a complete shock.

"Are you here to see Nerida?" Clarissa asked, expecting to do her best to keep him away from her.

"I'm here for you," he said coldly.

"How did you find us?"

"I overheard you describing this place on the coast of France to Nerida when your mother was dying." Clarissa was relieved that he wasn't among the visitors who had to go first to Liège to speak with Mother Agnes Luc—though she imagined that Wilfred and the abbess might have gotten along just fine.

"And why would you want me?"

Wilfred explained, with no emotion or sympathy, that her father was gravely ill. Despite being a woman, as his only living heir Clarissa would inherit the manor and estate outside Gladdington. "But I'm the one who's managed it all these years," Wilfred declared, "and I intend to fight you for it."

Clarissa was as stunned by his words as she was to realize that she had never given a thought about what would happen to the family property when her father died. For a brief moment, she allowed herself to imagine all the good Swansong could do with funds from the sale of the manor. But nothing about wading into that complicated commercial venture across the channel was appealing to her. She had not the slightest interest in returning to England, or in fighting with Wilfred.

"I don't intend to challenge you," she said. "Just show me what I need to sign."

"It's not that simple. You have to come back with me and arrange it all before the court."

"That's not possible. There's too much I'm needed for here."

"I won't go back without you," Wilfred said, his tone threatening, as he got back on his horse. "I'll be back for you in the morning." He rode off, never having asked about Nerida and Liliana. As she watched him ride away, Clarissa realized that neither had she asked him for the details about her father.

That evening she told Nerida, Johanna, and Galorian about Wilfred's visit. She wanted to make sure they agreed that it wasn't worth trying to profit from the turn of events. She was especially interested in Galorian's opinion, since he would have been the rightful heir if Josselyn had lived. Galorian didn't hesitate. "You should do whatever needs to be done to resolve it as quickly as possible and give Wilfred what he wants."

Nerida and Johanna nodded their assent. "It makes me sad, and angry, to see your home slip into his hands," Nerida said. "But I don't see any other choice." Clarissa realized that she too felt great sorrow when she imagined the place of her childhood memories—the home she had shared with her mother and Josselyn—taken by a man she didn't respect. But she had a new home and a new family now, and she was content to let it go.

"I'll go with you," Galorian said. Clarissa was surprised at the offer. "It's not safe for you to go back with him on your own," he declared. "What if his plan for taking over the manor is to do away with you on the way back to England?" That hardly seemed possible to Clarissa; but it wasn't impossible, either. "I haven't been back to England since I left for the Fourth Crusade," Galorian added. "I'd like to see the manor again, where I have so many good memories of Josselyn."

Clarissa felt her spirit shift dramatically—from dreading the trip to savoring the opportunity for time with Galorian on the road and in the place that meant so much to both of them. "All right," said Clarissa, smiling. "We'll go together."

§

Wilfred reappeared early the next morning. The three of them wasted no time getting on their horses and down the path toward Balnéaire. "I'm looking forward to this," Clarissa said to Galorian as they trotted away from the bluff.

"The journey?"

"Yes. But mostly to the look on my father's face when he sees us dressed in our religious robes . . . together."

The trip across the channel and on to Gladdington was uneventful, but Clarissa was grateful for Galorian's steady presence. They did not get to see Aldrich's reaction to their arrival at the manor. As soon as they appeared, Catrain rushed out, crying, to tell them that he had succumbed to his illness while Wilfred was away.

Clarissa felt relieved that she did not have to face her father. She shed a few tears along with Catrain. But she quickly recognized that they flowed from her realization that now the entire family she had known as a child was gone. "I'm an orphan," she lamented to Galorian.

That night the two of them broke out the bronze goblets and a bottle of mead. They sat in front of the fire in the dining room for hours, sharing memories of Josselyn and the manor. "She knew she was going to marry you the day King Richard made you a knight," Clarissa told Galorian.

He stared at her. "But she was only a child."

"Yes. But she knew."

In the middle of the night, Clarissa grabbed another bottle of mead and, taking Galorian by the hand, led him up the narrow staircase to the tower room. She showed him the route of her escape eight years before. Then they sat on the floor with a flickering candle between them. Clarissa told him the stories that Josselyn had told her when she was a very young girl, until the first light of dawn crept in the small window above them.

The legal arrangement for the inheritance was quickly taken care of in court later that morning. They'd been awake since early the previous morning, and Clarissa and Galorian agreed that it would be best for them to stay at the manor another night and get some rest before tackling the ride back to France. Clarissa was anxious for another evening of mead and conversation.

"I need to talk with you about something," she said to Galorian as they sat again by the fire in the dining room, under the unicorn tapestry. She wasn't quite sure how to share it, but she knew she had to. "I've been thinking about all that you've said about Jesus's command to love our enemies . . . About how hard it is. I think I've taken pride in the fact that Aminah is a Muslim, and Muslims are our enemies, and I love her, so I've followed his wishes." She sighed. "But Aminah was never my enemy. Since being back here, I know who my real enemy is." She drew a deep breath and said, "Do you think it would be a bad idea to try to visit Father Augustus?"

Galorian, stunned, didn't respond, and several silent moments passed. Then he said, "I have to confess, Clarissa, that you never stop surprising me. It would never have occurred to me to try to visit him."

"I don't even know if it's possible. But if there's one person alive that I need to forgive, it's him." She shook her head and looked at the ground. "I have such hatred for him in my heart. I can't even begin to show him Christian love unless I'm willing to forgive him."

All at once, it seemed, the travel and the night without sleep caught up to her, and Clarissa yawned self-consciously. She got up from her chair and stretched out on the thick wool fleece that was spread as a rug in front of the hearth. "I don't know if I can," she sighed. "But I think I need to try." Those were her last words before she slid into a deep sleep.

Galorian got up and threw a thick log onto the fire. The flames blazed and filled the room with a burst of orange light. He moved to the floor beside Clarissa. "You're amazing," he whispered as he kissed her forehead and then lay down beside her. The two of them spent that night warmed by the presence of each other and the fire, sleeping peacefully.

§

"I need to do this alone," Clarissa announced to Galorian as they shared a breakfast cooked for them by Catrain. "I know you need to find a way to forgive him too, but I have to do this myself." She knew it would be too easy to rely on Galorian to speak for her if he were there with her.

She could see the concern etched on his face. But he said, "I understand."

Getting access to the jail in Gladdington was easier than Clarissa had expected, and she went that afternoon. Galorian waited for her outside, pacing, as a shuffling guard led her to the former priest's cell. Strewn with filthy straw, it was dark and dank, narrow and not much longer than Augustus was tall. The stench inside was overpowering. Clarissa couldn't imagine surviving a week in that horrid place, and he had been locked up there for almost eight years.

As she slipped inside, she had to remind herself that she was there to forgive the man she had known as a pompous and violating priest, because that was not who she saw before her. He was gaunt, hunched in a corner, a man broken by his punishment and isolation. His ermine-trimmed velvet robe had been exchanged for a dirty cloak of coarse wool, cinched at his waist with a crude piece of rope.

He looked up and squinted at Clarissa when she walked in. She told him who she was. He turned away and stared at the wall, saying nothing for several moments. And then he asked, "Why are you here?"

"I came to forgive you," she said. He spat on the floor, and she stepped back, closer to the door.

"Why would you want to do that?" he asked bitterly.

Clarissa had anticipated the question. She had rehearsed her answer over and over in her mind. But facing him now, she lost her confidence to voice it. She shifted uncomfortably and decided to ask her own question. "Why did you go to the abbey in Dover?"

Augustus eyed her, and several more silent moments passed. Then he let out a derisive laugh. "To find you, of course. Your mother told me about the minstrel bringing her news of you. I sent Rowan, my assistant, to find him. With your mother's description, and a few questions asked around the square in Gladdington, Rowan had no trouble locating him."

"He does stand out in a crowd," Clarissa said to the ground. She was aware as the words flew out of her mouth that she was trying to quiet her pounding heart and nervous spirit with a light-hearted comment. It did nothing to break the thick tension in the cell, and she immediately regretted saying it.

Augustus ignored her and resumed his story. "Rowan learned that the minstrel was asking a lot of questions on your behalf. Without knowing it, he led Rowan right to the abbey and to you. It was easy for me to arrange an exchange of pulpits with Father Dudley. I just told him I wanted to see how the church was faring around the kingdom and spread some Christmas cheer."

When Clarissa thought about how Augustus had used her mother and Jaxon, she felt an intense anger rise up in her. But she did not interrupt again.

"I wanted to talk to the minstrel, to find out what he learned in Gladdington about the midwife's death. And to carry you home to your parents. When I talked with him after the Mass, I was convinced that he knew very little and my secret was safe. And I decided that letting you stay where you were, far from Gladdington with your curious questions, worked to my advantage."

"So you saw me at the abbey?"

"Of course," he said coldly.

"It's not the first time I tried to hide from you."

Augustus nodded. "It was you on the forest path that night." She wasn't sure if it was a question, or a statement of fact he had known for a long time, or a truth that was just then dawning on him. She decided not to ask.

"You were at the manor to baptize the baby."

"Yes. Your mother let me in. She happened to mention that the midwife was still there, resting. I waited for her to get up and leave. And then I followed her."

Clarissa's mind was racing as fast as her heart was beating. She realized in that moment how long she had wondered and how eager she was to know exactly what had happened on that forest path the night he murdered Beatrix. She knew this was her only chance to find out. But, facing him now, she decided that she would rather not know than give him the perverse pleasure of telling her. And she certainly didn't want to hear anything from him about his treatment of Josselyn.

She felt her resolve wavering as her fury grew. She knew she needed to say again why she was there—for her own sake as well as his. "I came to forgive you," she repeated.

He eyed her up and down. His tone was disdainful as he responded. "And I ask again, why would you want to do that?"

Clarissa wasn't sure that she still believed her answer, but she said what she had rehearsed and had come to this dungeon to say. "Jesus commands us to love our enemies. Ever since I found out that you raped my sister, you have been my enemy. I have hated you. But I have prayed more fervently to be able to release that hatred than I have for anything else. And now I'm ready, through the power of God in me, to forgive you."

"And do you think that means anything to me, coming from a mere girl like you?" hissed Augustus, turning again to stare at the wall.

"Maybe it doesn't," said Clarissa. "But it means something to me." She waited, but he did not turn back to face her. He offered no reaction at all to her costly pronouncement. She tried to accept that having said it was enough.

As the silence in the cell grew increasingly torturous, Clarissa berated herself for believing that he was a different person from the powerful priest he had once been. Broken as he was, he had still managed to crush her with his apathy and his arrogance. Disheartened, she nodded to the guard outside the barred door and said, "I'm done."

The guard opened the door to let her out. Before stepping through the doorway, Clarissa looked back. "You have a daughter," she said to the silent prisoner in the corner. "She's joyful and loving. Full of life." She saw Augustus stir and turn. "I thought you should know."

He looked up at her then, and she thought she caught the slightest glimmer of life in his eyes. As she headed again for the door, she heard him say softly, "My father raped my mother. He wanted to make sure she would marry him. She was ten years old." Clarissa slowly turned back. Augustus stared at the ground, speaking without emotion. "When I was a boy, he brought many mistresses to our home. Whores sometimes, too. I saw how it hurt my mother. When I was seven years old, she picked up a small millstone and walked out into the sea until she sank beneath the waves, disappearing forever."

He paused before continuing, and Clarissa moved in closer. "I became a priest because I didn't want to become like my father. But being a priest didn't protect me. Being a priest made it easier . . . All that Godly power . . . And so many opportunities to be alone with vulnerable young women." He gazed up at her. "I've had endless hours sitting in this miserable place to think about my life. I know what I witnessed and suffered as a boy doesn't excuse my turning out like my father. But I wanted someone to know." He took a deep breath. "I wanted *you* to know . . . And I regret hurting your sister."

Clarissa hesitated a moment. But then she knelt in the straw and raised her right hand to his forehead. She waited for him to flinch, or back away, but he did not. His eyes were moist with tears. She made the sign of the cross over him and proclaimed, "Augustus, beloved son of God, you are forgiven."

Before she stepped through the doorway, he said, "My daughter— what's her name?"

"Liliana," said Clarissa, with a smile.

"It's beautiful."

"Yes. And so is she."

When Clarissa got outside, she inhaled a large gulp of fresh air and threw herself into Galorian's arms. He asked her how she felt. She was quiet for a few moments, and then she said, "I don't think I know." They returned to the manor without saying more. Clarissa, exhausted, excused herself and went to lie down before supper.

That evening, she was ready to talk. She related in detail to Galorian all that had been exchanged between her and Augustus. "He's locked away in that horrible place, a prisoner of his crime. And when I dwell in my hatred toward him, I'm a prisoner of his crime, too." She released a heavy sigh. "By forgiving him, I've set myself free . . . even if I don't completely feel it yet. And I can only hope that the gift of forgiveness will bring him some freedom and peace, too."

The next morning, as they were getting ready to mount Magnus and Thane for their return to France, a messenger arrived at the manor with news. Father Augustus had been found dead earlier that same morning, hanging from the bars of his cell by the piece of rope that had circled his waist.

§

On their ride back to the east coast, Galorian did most of the talking. For a long time he had wrestled alone with his anger and his need to forgive Father Augustus. His inability to forgive Felicite had made forgiving the priest seem entirely out of his reach. And though he and Clarissa regularly shared their most intimate confessions and struggles, neither had mentioned Father Augustus until Clarissa brought him up at breakfast the day before.

After her visit to the jail, Galorian wanted only to listen. He didn't want to detract from her courage by sharing his weakness, or add to the burden of her ordeal by spilling his need. In months past, whenever he had considered talking with Clarissa about Father Augustus, he convinced himself it would only release a suppressed and savage fury. He never knew if he was trying to protect Clarissa, or himself.

But now, given Clarissa's brave act of forgiveness, and the death of the priest, and the distance that being on horseback imposed between them, he felt that he could speak to her about his struggle. His initial regret that he had lost his opportunity to confront Augustus melted into relief that the violating priest was dead. "I know I still have work to do in my heart to forgive him," Galorian admitted to Clarissa. "But for the first time since you told me what he did to Josselyn, I feel free of the oppressive weight of my anger." He thanked her for showing him how to let go.

When they reached Dover, Clarissa led him to the Benedictine abbey. Surprised and pleased to see her, Mary Peter welcomed them warmly, and, to Clarissa's delight, Scholastica joined them. Clarissa introduced Galorian as "the knight I ran away from." Mary Peter offered them beer and said, "Sit. We want to hear the whole story." And so Clarissa filled them in on what had happened in the years since she and Johanna had left the convent dressed in Jaxon's clothes.

"And how is Jaxon?" asked Scholastica.

"He was rather blue for a while," said Clarissa, and she and Galorian both laughed.

Galorian spilled the story, explaining, "It took almost a month before he looked like himself again."

"And what's the news here?" Clarissa asked.

Mary Peter reported that Zerah had lived happily for almost five years in the abbey. "And then she went on to spend eternity with her beloved twin sister, Beatrix." She added, "We lost Sister Mary Anthony last year."

Clarissa laughed again, realizing at once that it was an inappropriate response, but Mary Peter laughed with her. And then Clarissa told Galorian the story of arriving at the abbey with her turnip late at night and being let in by the nun who called Jaxon "the idiot with the ass and the lizard."

"Before her mind started leaving her," Mary Peter said, "Sister Mary Anthony was a generous and gentle gem. We're grateful she has found peaceful rest."

Clarissa and Galorian received all of the news, as well as affirmations of their community in France and its work, from the two nuns. Clarissa was glad for the opportunity to tell them, "Here is where I learned about prayer and hospitality and service. And about the power of community."

The visitors from France stayed much longer than they had anticipated. Scholastica left briefly and returned with food, and Mary Peter insisted that they spend the night. When they finished eating, she led Galorian to a cell in an isolated wing of the abbey and then ushered Clarissa to the one that had provided the first bed she had seen after her escape from home. "Your room," Mary Peter said, and Clarissa smiled. She fell asleep under the crucifix and the comforting, outstretched arms of Jesus.

§

Galorian and Clarissa crossed the channel the next morning. Clarissa decided not to tell her sisters about her encounter with Father Augustus, needing time to hold it in her heart and fearing it would upset Liliana. After greetings at Swansong, she headed straight down the path and walked along the shore to the ritual cave.

Inside, she paced and prayed. She pondered the power she possessed to be a vessel of God's love, and the unexpected consequences that could come from opening herself to that power. She wondered if she should feel guilty about Father Augustus's death by his own hand, but mostly she felt relief that he was free of his earthly agony and imprisonment. She hoped that she had helped to prepare him to come face to face in death with a merciful God who was quite unlike the one he had preached about in life.

Clarissa stayed all night alone in the cave, sitting on the rock as the tide swirled in around her and then back out to sea. In that sacred space, she received her second vision. When the community gathered the next morning for prayers before dawn, she felt moved to share it. These were the words she spoke:

I was in a cave, wrapped in absolute darkness. I saw a glimmer of light, and I began to move toward it. I fell out of the cave and slid into a meadow, its grass tall and lush, deep green and reflecting the bright gold of the sun. A stream, whose babbling water sounded like a hymn of praise, flowed through its center.

Surrounding the meadow was an orchard, which bore a tree of every variety on the earth. When I raised my hands, I could reach every fruit, from the lowest-hanging apple and pear to the highest dates and coconuts clustered atop tall palms. Behind the trees towered a ring of majestic blue mountains, a sanctuary for birds and gentle beasts. And I knew that I was in Paradise.

But the sun began to grow, and it swallowed up the sky. Its scorching rays burned up every tree, and shriveled every blade of grass, and dried up the stream. And I was in a vast wasteland, with nothing but sand and rock as far as I could see. The sun was blinding, and searing heat radiated in waves from the ground, and I did not know where to go to find relief.

I plodded forward, searching for something to slake my deadly thirst, my throat so parched that I could not swallow. In the distance I saw many children, sick and naked and crying for water, and I wanted to call to them and help them. But my tongue was like a stone in my mouth, and I could not speak. And I had nothing to give them.

I fell to my knees, and I began to weep, my body shuddering with sobs for the suffering of the children, and my powerlessness, and the endlessness of the desert. A drop at a time, my tears fell to the earth, where they collected in a pool. I looked up and saw the ragged children coming toward me. They knelt around me and began to scoop my tears from the pool, drinking feverishly, being revived by the nourishment. My tears of anguish became tears of joy, and they began to spill even more profusely out of my eyes and onto the ground. The pool grew to a stream, and the stream began to flow through the sand.

From atop a distant mountain came the voice of the prophet Isaiah, echoing like a thunderclap:

> *"Then the eyes of the blind shall be opened,*
> *And the ears of the deaf shall be unstopped;*
> *Then the lame shall leap like a deer;*
> *And the tongue of the speechless shall sing for joy.*
> *For waters shall break forth in the wilderness,*
> *And streams in the desert;*
> *The burning sand shall become a pool,*
> *And the thirsty ground springs of water."*

I looked around me and saw people everywhere, on their knees, weeping with compassion for the agony of the world. They were of all ages and human hues, women and children and men, dressed in the clothing of many nations and faiths. Their tears mingled together in the sand and formed more streams of water. These grew and grew, until they flowed into one great rushing river.

The children jumped in first, laughing, and then beckoned the adults to follow. One by one, the whole throng leapt into the water, as the heavens opened and poured forth more. A child, grinning, extended her hand to me. Surrendering to her invitation, I reached for it, and she pulled me into the great rushing river of humanity, as the rain baptized us in joy.

We bobbed in the water, singing and laughing, until the river carried us to a great sea. And in that sea, we felt like one great family, floating in the endless ocean of God's merciful, miraculous, magnificent love.

§

When Clarissa finished speaking, utter silence filled the chapel. She looked around the circle and saw faces reflected in the candlelight, but she could not read their expressions. *Are my sisters inspired . . . stunned . . . disturbed?* The candles guttered quietly. No one moved. And then Lisette, visibly upset, rose and ran out of the chapel.

Clarissa left the others and went to find Lisette, who was sitting on the bench by the pond. "It's the journey of faith, isn't it?" she said as Clarissa sat down next to her. Clarissa nodded, and Lisette continued, her gaze fixed on the pond. "You and I . . . we were born into a life with plenty of food, and comfort, and beautiful things. We had to have our eyes opened to see the hunger and want that afflicts most of the world." Clarissa nodded again, and Lisette spoke with more confidence. "But knowing it plunges us into a kind of wilderness, where nothing feels familiar . . . and we can't see the way ahead."

Lisette turned to look into Clarissa's eyes. "It was awful when I was attacked and my whole life changed. But I know it made me understand the truth of the world, and it helped me to see God." A single tear slid down her cheek. "And now I have dear Moses . . . and you and all my sisters . . . and the ones who are poor and sick and dying here. Now I know the joy that comes from seeing that my pain is part of their pain . . . part of all the world's pain."

Clarissa reached up and wiped away a trickle of tears from Lisette's face. "It's how we meet Jesus," she said. "In his poverty and suffering. He poured out his life and all of God's love on the cross for us—and for the world."

Lisette smiled. "And if enough of us who follow him are willing to pour out ourselves and God's love, too . . . if enough of us care and cry enough tears . . ."

She stopped, unable to say more, and Clarissa said, "then rivers of love will flow in every wasteland and wash away every pain."

They sat in silence until Lisette said, "But it's so hard."

"It's very hard. And it's very wonderful. It's how God changes us. And the world."

Lisette thought a moment and then said, "The Bible says the meek will inherit the earth. But all I see is the meek being robbed of the little they have and suffering terribly."

Clarissa took Lisette's hand. "That's only the way it looks. The world is being changed through the compassion and faithfulness of God's children. Even when we can't see it."

"But the journey of faith is so hard."

Clarissa smiled at her. "God will give you all the strength you need."

§

Johanna invited Clarissa on a walk after lunch on the day that she shared her vision with the community. As soon as they reached the beach, she said, "You have a divine gift, Clarissa. And we've all been blessed because you chose to share it."

"Do you think so?"

"I've always known so. You just needed to believe it yourself."

"It's frightening," Clarissa said.

"Most of the things that come from God are." They laughed together lightly. "Have there been other visions?"

"One."

"There will be more. God has chosen you to reveal truth to us."

"I'm writing them down, along with my prayers."

"Good. You should take as much time as you need to record the things that God is speaking to you. Someday you'll share them with others beyond us."

"I don't think so," said Clarissa.

"I know so."

Galorian too was sure that Clarissa's gift would inspire hearts in many places. He mixed up more pigments so that she could illuminate her book in color. Jaxon went to work making a leather cover for it. And the community welcomed Clarissa's visions whenever she shared them, feeling gloriously anointed with truth that they believed came directly from God.

The visions came when Clarissa sat alone in the chapel or on the edge of the bluff greeting the full moon, and when she was with her sisters in the cave during the new moon. The Holy Spirit visited her in the form of a swan, its wings shining iridescent in the moon's silver light or hovering in the shadows of the fire-lit cave, beckoning her to follow. Her spirit soared on the back of the swan to a dazzling place where the radiance of God filled every corner, including the recesses of her own heart. In that place of light, during the moments of her body's richest fertility and deepest emptiness, God met her in images and dreams, illuminating truth and filling her up with visions that were startling, and beautiful, and more precious to her than she believed her words could ever convey.

§

With the insistent encouragement of her friends, Clarissa devoted the next year to her book, allowing her gracious sisters to take extra shares of teaching and work in the garden to give her the time and freedom she needed to write. For hours each day, and often by candlelight throughout the night, she spilled words onto the blank pages.

She wrote letters addressed to younger disciples and to women living as she and her sisters did, sharing the wisdom she had gleaned about community and compassion, about forgiveness and faith. She created prayers and odes to God in the style of the courtly-love poetry that was beloved in medieval France. She recorded her reflections on the work of the church and the anti-heresy crusade. And she poured her many mystical visions, in all their resplendent detail, onto the sheaves of parchment.

Galorian, grinning broadly, showed up outside her door one early-summer afternoon with a most unusual gift. In his hands was a pottery head with puffed-out cheeks that had a vague resemblance to Mother Agnes Luc. Laughing, Clarissa looked at it and said, "What—?"

But before she could even voice the question, Galorian interrupted to explain. "I made it out of clay scooped from the bottom of the pond mixed with some of my dye powder." The top of the head contained many small but deep holes filled with dirt. "Just add a little water to it every day," he said with a smile. "It's my way of still getting your help with the dye plants . . . and keeping you from getting too serious with all this book writing."

Clarissa did as she was told. Soon sprouts of madder vine grew out of the Mother Superior's head, and before long her hair was trailing all over Clarissa's small writing desk. She was grateful for the gift that helped her to smile on even her longest writing days—and that reminded her of the joy Galorian brought into her life at a time of disquieting uncertainty.

The next time Clarissa visited him at his dye shop, Galorian showed her what else he was working on. Pointing to a clay head that was clearly intended to resemble Liliana's, he said, "This one will grow a crown of yellow-gold saffron crocuses." He lifted up another. "And this one's for Jaxon." The pottery head of a winking minstrel wore a hat with three points, which Galorian had painted yellow, green, and red and adorned with small bells. Its flat and jutting chin was filled with holes. "It will grow a beard of blue woad," he said with a grin, and Clarissa laughed. And then she had an unsettling thought: *Is the gift that looks like Agnes Luc Galorian's attempt to capture my own face?* She decided not to ask.

That year passed quickly. As 1211 came to a close, Clarissa spent the month of December in her room, emerging only to slip quietly into the back of the chapel for times of prayer and then leave again. Her friends left food outside her door and took away the empty plates. Nerida had perfected the art of baking honey-and-marigold biscuits, and she kept Clarissa well supplied with these and lavender-and-lemon barley water. For the entire month, Clarissa did not speak, as she tried to complete what she believed God had given her to do.

When she had filled the book, she turned back to the blank sheet she had left at the beginning. On the front of it she wrote *The Radiant Soul: Aflame with Love.* She held up the book and smiled, grateful for the title that she drew from her very first, fiery vision. Then she turned over the page and took a deep breath. *I must write it,* she said to herself, as she commenced to put down on the back of the title page the prologue that God had given her.

On January first of 1212, her twenty-third birthday, Clarissa handed the book to Johanna. "Whenever you find time to read it," she said, wanting to sound patient but hoping Johanna would find time soon. Her friend did not disappoint her. Johanna sat down with the book at once and went through it in her free moments, day and night, until she had read every word.

Then she walked to Clarissa's room. She stood just inside the doorway and cleared her throat, unsure about how to say what she had come to say. "You finished it?" Clarissa asked—a bit too eagerly, she thought after saying it.

Johanna nodded. Opening the book, she said, "I've been doing extra work and encouraging you for all these months, and *this* is what you were writing?" Clarissa thought she detected anger or disappointment in Johanna's voice; but perhaps, she told herself, it was just surprise at the volume of pages she had filled. Johanna began to read aloud the prologue:

"To the reader:

If you wish to grasp the truth illuminated here,
Open your heart and let faith guide you.

Catechist or cleric, pontiff or priest,
No matter how brilliant your intellect,
Understanding will elude you
If openness and humility are not your companions.

Abandon all arrogance.
Elevate your heart above your mind.
For love and faith conquer reason.
These are the noble mothers of understanding."

Johanna stopped reading and stared hard at her friend. "Oh, Clarissa. Do you really think it's a good idea to address our enemies so directly?" Before Clarissa could answer, Johanna started reading again where she had left off:

"If you burn with yearning
To be One with the Creator of All Life,
She will honor your desire.
If you seek the Holy One,
As a shivering pilgrim on a long journey seeks warmth,
Your longing will be satisfied.

Place your trust in love,
The fire that enkindles the heart and sets the world aflame.
Then your soul shall live forever in radiance,
Warmed in the tender embrace of the Holy One,
Reflecting in every dark corner the shining splendor of God."

Johanna closed the book and fixed her gaze again on Clarissa. "It will bring trouble," she said.

"But I've written what God—and you—have shared with me," Clarissa protested, "in the visions, and times of prayer, and your lessons in the cave. You're the one who told me I should write it all down . . . and share it with the world."

"The words are profound and full of truth," Johanna responded gently. "And I know they come from God. But I didn't expect you to take on the church like this . . . and on the first page! It's one thing to proclaim these truths in a cave . . . and quite another to write them permanently in a book for everyone to see."

Clarissa was unused to seeing fear in Johanna. She was stunned by the reversal of their usual roles, as surprised by Johanna's distress and concern as she was by her own strength and clarity. She didn't like upsetting her friend. "Then I won't share it."

"Of course you will," said Johanna. "You must." She paused, looked at the floor, and then at Clarissa again. "But you know it could mean the end of the community . . . or worse." She hesitated but then voiced the terror that was lodged in her heart. "The church is behind so much fear-mongering and hatred and persecution now." She said it softly. "Your book could get us all killed."

Clarissa wanted to dismiss her friend's words, but she believed that Johanna's response was only a slight overreaction. She was sure that she and her sisters had not heard the last of Father Lionel's threats. Almost every day now brought new reports of growing persecution, especially against those suspected of wavering from the church's teachings. In barely a whisper, she said, "Not all of us."

Johanna sank down onto the palette next to Clarissa and reached for her hand. Clarissa asked her, "Have you read the rest?"

Johanna nodded her head and sighed. And then, smiling warmly at her most cherished of friends, she said, "It's brilliant."

Thirty-two

The birds were starting to return, and the wildflowers poked through the dry grass of the meadow as warmth began moving back to the coast. Clarissa responded to a knock on the door at Manna House and found a tall boy standing on the stoop. "Are you the One?" he asked her.

"The one what?" asked Clarissa, taken aback by the question.

"The one who sees visions."

She hesitated. "Who are you?"

"My name is Stephan," the boy answered. "I'm a shepherd from the town of Cloyes. God sent me to you." Clarissa eyed the young man for a moment. Then she invited him in and ushered him to a seat at the table. She brought two cups of steaming barley water and sat across from him.

"What exactly did God say to you?" she asked.

"He told me to lead a Crusade of children to the Holy Land, to convert the Muslims to Christianity. And to come here first for your blessing."

Clarissa tried not to reveal the shock she felt. She looked the boy over more carefully. He was about the age she had been when she escaped from home, and she felt she could not simply dismiss him. *But children traveling to the Holy Land? To convert Muslims?* It was unthinkable.

Stephan interrupted her thoughts. "We will succeed where the adults have failed. Without war," he stated confidently. "Faith is stronger than weapons." And then, to give extra merit to his case, he added, "I have a letter for the king of France from Jesus himself."

Clarissa tried to form a response, but none came to her. She had only more questions. "Why did you come to me for a blessing?"

"Everyone knows that a woman here communicates with God in mysterious ways." Clarissa wondered who "everyone" was, surprised that such a notion would have spread as far as Cloyes, two days' journey at least. She had not shown her book to anyone beyond her closest friends, nor shared her visions beyond her community.

A debate went on in her soul. *Who am I to question the sacred visions and courage of another believer? But he's only a boy. But is his mission any more misguided than my escape from home at his age? Yet how could I possibly bless children to take on such a dangerous journey?*

She finally said to him, "I think you are brave, Stephan, but mistaken. I cannot give my blessing to this escapade. The Muslims do not need to be converted—even peacefully. What the world needs is for Christians and Muslims and Jews to respect each other's beliefs. Then we would have no need of war." She added gently, "Not everything we believe comes from God. Are you sure it was God who spoke to you?"

"Of course!" snapped Stephan. "I will lead this Children's Crusade with or without your blessing." He put down his cup and got up quickly. Before leaving, he looked sharply at Clarissa and declared, "And I will report far and wide that you are a fraud who does not know a vision from God when one is brought to your doorstep."

Clarissa watched as Stephan hastily untied his horse and led it down the path. He stopped at the garden, where Giselle was preparing a patch of soil for spring planting. Clarissa charged out of the house. "You must go now," she said firmly to Stephan when she reached them.

"But," said Giselle breathlessly, "there's a Children's Crusade. And Stephan has invited me to join it!"

"*Now*," repeated Clarissa, keeping her gaze fixed on the young shepherd until he got on his horse.

"You'll see," he said as he turned his horse toward the road. "When I lead a mighty parade of children to the sea, it will open before us, just like it did for Moses. And then we'll march right on to Jerusalem on dry land."

§

Clarissa's concern about the Children's Crusade was quickly distracted. In May of 1212 a German duke, having noted that the protective wall surrounding Liège had not yet been completed, launched an attack on the vulnerable city. As soon as Clarissa heard the tragic news, she remembered the day that Mother Agnes Luc had told her and her sisters that convents are primary targets for the plunder and violence of invaders. "They take special pleasure," the abbess had said in a chapel meeting one morning, "in violating those of us betrothed to Christ."

Johanna had leaned over to Clarissa that day and whispered, "And the priests always blame the nuns. They're sure it wouldn't happen if we didn't desire . . . or invite . . . or enjoy it."

Agnes Luc then added, unforgettably, "We know that the church has declared suicide unlawful and a sure path to the fires of hell. But it has made an exception for nuns who suffer 'the fate worse than death.'" The abbess was wheezing so violently that she could barely speak, but she managed to invite Johanna to share with the sisters what she knew about the subject.

Johanna stood and related some creative and startling acts of resistance by women from history. Clarissa's favorite was the Lombard women of Italy, who faced a summer invasion by the Avars, equestrian warriors from Eastern Europe. The women wrapped bands of cloth around themselves under their clothes and stuffed pieces of chicken flesh inside them. The raw pieces of meat putrefied in the heat and smelled so foul that the invaders could not endure the stench and left the women alone, cursing them as they left.

But most of the resistance was not so amusing. When Danish invaders were rampaging through Scotland, Saint Ebba, the abbess of a convent on an isolated stretch of coast on the North Sea, took a razor and cut off her nose and upper lip. Her obedient sisters followed her example. When the invaders arrived, they found the women repulsively disfigured and covered in blood. Such self-mutilation was considered the best defense against rape, and it worked. But the enraged invaders set the convent on fire, making martyrs of all the nuns.

Clarissa remembered all this as she and Johanna anxiously awaited news from Liège, keeping a community prayer vigil in their chapel day and night. She was worried about their Benedictine sisters and about the Beguines they had met, who were especially vulnerable as holy women without even the protection of cloister walls.

Within a few days they got word that, as the duke and his soldiers descended on the city, some of the Beguines had leapt into a river. Others jumped into the city's open sewer, preferring to drown in human waste than to be violated. But all of them, as well as the residents of the abbey, had survived unharmed. "Thanks be to God," proclaimed Johanna when they heard the good news.

Clarissa returned her attention to the Children's Crusade, trying to convince Giselle of its folly and dissuade her from participating. But Giselle, now fourteen and craving adventure after a life narrowed for so many years to a cave, had clearly fallen under the spell of Stephan's bold vision and charismatic charm. She was not alone. Word came that the young shepherd was traveling throughout France, inspiring throngs of youth with his preaching and purported miracles.

The campaign was opposed by Pope Innocent III and most of France's bishops, but parish priests and proud parents across the empire encouraged the youths' religious fervor and determination. The Children's Crusade left from the city of Vendôme at the end of June. Though Clarissa was strongly against it, Giselle was determined, and since Sybille could not be out in public, Clarissa felt she needed to be on hand when the young girl joined the throng headed to the Holy Land.

The spectacle they found in Vendôme confirmed her worst fears. Stephan, dressed from head to toe in silk finery, stood in a brightly festooned cart topped with a red canopy to shield him from the beating sun. "Look!" exclaimed Giselle, pointing and beaming excitedly when she caught sight of him. The young boys astride horses, and the poorer boys and girls on foot, seemed not to resent the comforts of the self-proclaimed prophet. In fact, they crowded around Stephan, treating him like a saint, requesting locks of his hair and swatches of his clothes, which they clutched like precious relics.

With a murmured prayer on her lips, Clarissa watched Giselle and the young throng follow Stephan toward the Mediterranean Sea. Weeks would pass before she would receive word of their fate. The knock came late at night at Manna House. Clarissa found Giselle, barely recognizable, on the stoop. Thin and ragged, she needed Clarissa's help to get inside. The Crusade was worse even than Clarissa had imagined, though Giselle was intent on telling of its great wonders first.

"Stephan was so brave," she said. "And he saw many holy visions that he shared with us on the way. Children all along our path just wanted to be near him and came along. Somebody said we were thirty thousand by the time we got to Lyon!" Giselle sighed. "But it was so miserably hot. And we had to beg for food and water. Almost nobody had any to share."

Summer was marked that year by unusually blazing heat and an intense drought. "Some of the children dropped out and turned around," continued Giselle. "A lot got too hungry and tired and just died at the side of the road. By the time we got to Marseilles, we were half as many as when we started."

She sighed again, more heavily this time. "And the sea didn't part like Stephan promised. We waited a few days, giving God plenty of time to do a miracle. But the sea just stayed put. More children went back home. Two merchants, who called themselves Hugh the Iron and William the Pig, saw the predicament of those of us who were left. They promised us free passage to the Holy Land, for the glory of God. We started out in seven boats. But we didn't go to the Holy Land."

Giselle began to cry. "We got as far as the island of Sardinia off the coast of Italy. We arrived in a big storm and one of the boats shipwrecked. Everybody on board died." She swallowed hard. "But they were the lucky ones. I overheard the men say they were taking the rest of us to Tunisia, where they were going to sell us into slavery. When they weren't looking, I ran away." Giselle continued between sobs. "I don't know what happened to the others. I don't want to know . . ." Clarissa tried not to imagine their fate—or what Giselle must have gone through to find her way back home.

§

Rumors flew after the Children's Crusade. Some of the villagers of Balnéaire, who had heard of Stephan's visit to Clarissa, blamed her for refusing to support it, thereby contributing to its demise. Others, knowing she had gone with Giselle to Vendôme for the launch, accused her of unwisely endorsing the disastrous campaign. What astonished Clarissa most was how many people seemed to be paying attention to what she said and did. *Perhaps Stephan did spread a negative report about me "far and wide,"* she thought.

People began that summer showing up at Swansong with odd requests. Would Clarissa pray that great wealth would come to one? Could she help another speak with a dead relative? Would she heal a sick child? Could she predict how the crops would do? Clarissa, explaining that she was not a miracle worker, offered counsel and prayers as she could. But most of her visitors went away unsatisfied.

When the crops failed that year in the withering drought, fingers began to point at her. "She's a witch," she overheard a woman say in the Josselyn Center.

"She refuses to help us," another chimed in. The understanding among most seemed to be that Clarissa had magical powers and special access to God but would not use them for the benefit of the villagers. Some believed that she had set loose the evil that was behind their misfortune.

The women of Swansong had to slaughter several of their lambs that summer when the grass dried up and the hay ran out. They shared the meat widely with hungry friends and got by themselves on a harshly austere diet, stretching what little they had as far as they could. Reminiscent of their first season on the coast, they ate a lot of gnarly carrots into that fall and winter, and not much else.

Some of their dearest friends from Balnéaire remained faithful and benefitted from their sacrificial generosity. But that fall attendance in the school was down to little more than half the number of students they had taught in the spring. Galorian's cloth business came to a standstill for lack of dye plants and customers.

Clarissa, Johanna, Nerida, and Galorian talked frequently through the difficult winter about how to respond to the rumors and to the hardship that had visited them. They were in agreement that Clarissa needed to live as quietly as possible for a while. And so she hid her book and kept her visions to herself, praying to know how and when to share the gift that God had given her.

§

Everyone gave thanks when the year ended, offering their prayers for better times in 1213. But winter hung on with bitter ferocity until late March, and only when it lifted did the community's spirits begin to rise as well. Only Clarissa seemed not to be buoyed by the return of spring. She was plagued by the feeling that for months—ever since the debacle of the Children's Crusade—she had not been living, but only going through the motions of life. Christmas Eve, usually her favorite night of the year, had seemed empty and lifeless to her, and so too did the monthly rituals in the cave. The things she loved most no longer brought her joy.

She still rode every morning with Galorian and spent as much time as possible with Johanna, Liliana, and Nerida. They all did their best to lighten her gloom, but Clarissa was unable to find consolation from either her dearest friends or in prayer. What comforted her most was taking long walks alone along the shore. Often she was greeted by the dolphins, whose delightful squeaks and perpetual smiles cheered her up, if only for a moment.

At night she frequently wandered through the forest, where her constant companion was Saint Catherine, whose plaintive screeches Clarissa found protective and reassuring. "You're my oldest friend," she said one night as her owl peered down at her from a pine branch. Saint Catherine flapped her wings, as if in grateful acknowledgment.

After a year-long absence, the rain returned on a May afternoon. Everyone left whatever they were doing and ran into the meadow, where they clasped hands and danced in a circle, showered by what felt like hope falling from heaven. Jaxon stood in the center and juggled rocks. Seven-year-old Moses leaned his head back and stood with his mouth wide open, laughing and catching the large raindrops. When the sun broke through a bank of clouds, a brilliant rainbow spanned the sky beyond the garden. "Look!" shouted Liliana, and everyone turned to admire it, placing arms around those next to them.

"The sign of God's protection and provision," declared Johanna. "A good omen." And indeed it was. The rain visited regularly again, and the garden soon came back to life. A new batch of lambs arrived healthy and strong, and Sheep Shearing Day was festive. All seemed to be well again. But still Clarissa felt plagued by an unrelenting weariness.

Late that summer she found comfort from an unexpected source. On one of her nightly ventures into the forest, she heard the haunting notes of a flute wafting among the trees. She followed the sound, as she had on the night she ran away from home and discovered the Samhain celebration. She parted a curtain of branches and gazed upon a young man sitting on a rock, absorbed in his music. She guessed him to be about eighteen years old. She listened and watched for several minutes. When he finished playing, she approached to thank him.

"I'm Philippe," he said, extending his hand. She took note of his charming smile and head of thick, blonde curls.

"I haven't seen you here before," Clarissa said after introducing herself.

"I live in a village between Balnéaire and Calais. My father and I just brought my mother to Mercy Manor. We heard it would be a good place for her."

"I'm sorry that your mother isn't well."

"The music comforts me," he said.

"It comforts me, too."

Philippe, who was an apprentice boat builder, made visits often with his father. The community admired how lovingly and attentively he cared for his mother, who was a kind-hearted woman known in her village for her devout faith and her care for people in need. In the evenings, Philippe and Jaxon played music together in the meadow, to everyone's delight. Soon a crowd was showing up with food and blankets, eating and listening, some dancing late into the night, serenaded by croaking frogs and honking swans and screeching owls under stars that blinked along with the fireflies. Clarissa found those magical evenings to be balm for her weary soul.

To no one's surprise, Felicite transferred her former obsession with Galorian to Philippe. Clarissa couldn't blame her for being attracted to the handsome young man with the creative spirit of a musician, the strong body of a craftsman, and the devoted heart of a saint. Philippe was kind to Felicite, but he usually found a way to steer them to other company—often Aminah, Lisette, and Liliana. Clarissa enjoyed watching the young people together, and she was particularly grateful to observe them including Liliana. It still amazed her that her niece, who seemed just yesterday to be three years old, was now a young woman of fourteen.

When the weather grew too cold to work on boats, Philippe spent even more of his time at Swansong, singing and playing his flute for his mother, helping to haul hay and water for the sheep, carving simple animals for

Moses out of pine wood. He particularly seemed to enjoy time with Moses, and the boy adored him. But so did everyone who met this extraordinary young man.

At dinner on Christmas Day, Liliana approached Clarissa. She was smiling giddily as she said, "I need to ask you something." They walked to a corner where they could be away from the crowd. Liliana blushed as she said, "Would it be all right with you if Philippe and I marry?" Her face lit up as she said, "He asked me last night, after everyone else left the Christmas Eve service."

Clarissa was astounded that she hadn't seen this coming. Of course she had noticed Liliana and Philippe enjoying each other's company—talking together, sharing meals and walks and an afternoon with the swans by the pond. But they both seemed to enjoy everyone's company. And, despite the many times that Clarissa had told her young students that marriage should be about love and not obedience or duty, she realized that even she hadn't fully believed that any of them would actually go against tradition and regulation and choose her own partner. Before she could respond, Liliana asked, "Does it disappoint you that I want to live with a man instead of being a Beguine?"

"O, my dear Liliana, I couldn't be happier!" exclaimed Clarissa, throwing her arms around her niece's neck. "He's such a fine man. We'll have a grand celebration."

"We want to marry next summer," said Liliana. She revealed all the plans that she and Philippe had already made sitting in the barn the night before. "Here's the best part. He asked me, 'Who will give you away?' I told him, 'No one will give me away, and that would be true even if I had a father. I am not a piece of property to be handed over to a husband.' And guess what he said? . . . 'You've been spending too much time with your Aunt Clarissa.'" She added quickly, "But he was smiling. He has so much respect for you. And he understands. He wants us to be equal partners in this marriage."

The already considerable admiration Clarissa had for Philippe rose even higher, and she found that she couldn't stop smiling.

Thirty-three

The wedding was set for June fifth, and preparations began as soon as Christmas festivities were over. Liliana wanted to wear the gown that Clarissa had given to Nerida to wear for her wedding. Clarissa and Nerida both felt honored by the request, but when the three of them looked it over, they all agreed that it was too worn for a wedding, and its green velvet definitely too heavy for a summer ceremony. "Destined now to be only a costume for Jaxon in the Christmas play," sighed Clarissa.

"It's a shame," said Liliana, fingering the intricate pattern on the bodice, "I love the pearls so much."

Nerida promised to make her a beautiful dress, and to enlist Genevieve's help in creating wedding attire for Clarissa, Johanna, and Galorian. Aminah offered to coordinate the wedding feast, and Lisette volunteered to work with her. Felicite grudgingly agreed to do what she could to help them. Jaxon set about writing a special song, and Galorian went to work with his dyes.

Though still ill and very weak, Philippe's mother, Celeste, who had seemed close to death when she arrived at Mercy Manor, had made some improvement under the tender care of the women of Swansong. In February she began making Philippe's wedding tunic. She told Clarissa that, as she sewed in her bed, she constantly prayed that she would live long enough to celebrate with her beloved son and the special young woman he had chosen to marry.

But by late April it was clear that Celeste was declining rapidly. Nerida shared at dinner one evening that she thought Philippe's mother didn't have long to live. "Then we must move up the wedding," Liliana said. "It would be too tragic for her and Philippe if she missed it."

Clarissa noticed the tears in Liliana's eyes and invited her to take a walk after the meal. "What's on your heart?" Clarissa asked her niece.

Liliana didn't answer for a while. "I love you so much," she said finally. "I love Nerida and all my sisters who have been like mothers to me." She stopped walking and gazed at Clarissa. "But it just makes me sad that my own mother won't be there on my wedding day."

"She will be," said Clarissa. "In spirit. " She took Liliana's hand. "I know it's not the same, and you have every right to your sorrow. But she'll be hovering close, beaming her joy and pride all over you."

On May first, villagers from Balnéaire and friends of Philippe from as far away as Calais packed into Saint Mary Magdalene Chapel. Aminah and Lisette had decorated the benches with sprigs of lily-of-the-valley, delighted to have discovered a spring flower beloved in France that both smelled like perfume and reflected the name of the bride. Jaxon sang and strummed love songs on his lute as they all waited for the wedding ceremony to begin.

Celeste was seated up front, and Philippe and his father walked in together from the side. Philippe's knee-length tunic with wide sleeves, so lovingly made by his mother, was a rich royal blue. Galorian had labored hard to perfect the color, and he was proud of the result.

When Jaxon switched his music to an instrumental number, Liliana appeared at the back of the chapel, standing between Nerida and Galorian. She looked breathtaking to Clarissa from where she stood at the front. Liliana wore a gown with full sleeves and a long, flowing skirt and train, in the same royal blue as Philippe's tunic. On the fitted bodice, in the rosette pattern she so loved, were scores of tiny pearls. Nerida had worked in secret day and night for almost a week to remove them from the green velvet dress and replicate the pattern with painstaking precision in time for the earlier-than-expected wedding.

Liliana wore her mother's cross around her neck. Her head was crowned with a garland of lily-of-the-valley, the delicate white bells of the flowers a perfect complement to the pearls on her gown. She carried a sachet of crushed lavender and rose petals, a special gift from Nerida, and a bouquet of white lilies, red poppies, and bright yellow buttercups picked from the meadow by Lisette.

Clarissa had a hard time taking her eyes off the stunning bride, but eventually they came to rest on Galorian. She hadn't seen him in anything but his plain brown monk's robe for five years, and her first thought was that he looked like a knight again. He wore his riding boots, gray leggings, and a cream-colored shirt under a dark burgundy, hip-length coat. Clarissa tried to push down the aching longing that rose up unexpectedly in her heart, and to focus on her role for the day.

Johanna stood at her side. They had shed their drab robes and head-dresses and were dressed similarly in ivory gowns, Johanna's with royal blue accent ribbons around the waist and sleeves, and Clarissa's with the same highlights in burgundy. They beamed smiles at Liliana, Nerida, and Galorian as the three walked down the aisle toward them. When they reached the front, Nerida hugged Liliana and took a seat beside Philippe's parents. Galorian kissed Liliana on the cheek and then moved next to Clarissa. Philippe came and stood beside Liliana, taking hold of her hand.

Johanna welcomed the family members and friends to the joyful occasion that had brought them all together. Galorian led the bride and groom through their vows as they promised to honor and cherish each other. Then he reached into his coat pocket and took out two silver rings. Crafted by Philippe, each resembled a swan, the wings forming the band, and a tiny pearl marking the eye on a profiled face in the center.

Liliana gasped when she saw the elegantly unique rings that would bind her and Philippe in eternal love. "As swans mate for life," said Philippe, gazing at her with adoring eyes and slipping her ring onto her finger, "so may we be loyal forever. And may we always remember that our marriage is guided and protected by the Holy Spirit." Liliana was too moved to speak as she slid Philippe's ring onto his hand and grasped it tightly.

Galorian placed his right hand on top of theirs, and then Clarissa added hers. She offered a prayer of blessing, trying to keep her emotions in check. As soon as she said "Amen," Galorian looked from Liliana to Philippe, smiled broadly, and proclaimed, "You are husband and wife. God bless this marriage!" He clapped, and the entire congregation rose and joined him.

Clarissa and Galorian stepped behind the altar. Clarissa raised the plate and Galorian the chalice, as he blessed the bread and wine. Together, standing side by side, they served the wedding congregation, beginning with Liliana and Philippe, as family and friends streamed forward to receive the Mass.

§

The party was held on Liliana's favorite stretch of beach below the bluff. Philippe lifted his frail mother and carried her down the steep path. Clarissa was moved by the poignant sight of a dying mother clinging to the neck of her newly married son, and she knew without a doubt that Liliana had been blessed with a rare husband. She walked in the other direction, to the edge of the pond, to sit for a while and try to corral her galloping emotions. Joy, grief, and confusion swirled through her in equal measure as she thought about Liliana, Josselyn, and Galorian. She knew it would take more time than she had to sort it all out, so she stood, wiped the tears from her eyes, and pulled herself together enough to join the party.

When she showed up on the beach, Aminah was ladling lamb stew into bowls, and loaves of bread loaded with honey and raisins were being passed around. Jaxon was juggling, and Philippe was playing his flute. Galorian, spying Clarissa, rushed over to stand next to her. Holding the burgundy sleeve of his coat next to the ribbons of the same color on her gown, he laughed and said, "We're a perfect match."

He told her that he had been looking all over for her and asked where she had gone. Dodging his question, she asked, "How can I get some of that good stew?" and hurried off to find a bowl.

When the feast had been consumed, Johanna clapped to get everyone's attention. She took Liliana and Philippe by the hand and led them to a small table. Then she invited everyone to bring forward their cakes. Dozens of sweet desserts were placed on the table, piled one on top of another in a precarious tower. "As you all know," said Johanna, "if Liliana and Philippe can kiss without knocking over the stack of cakes, they will have a long and happy marriage."

The bride and groom stood on opposite sides of the cake tower, shy and blushing. Clarissa was struck by the reflection of the setting sun shining gold on their hair, their skin glowing like burnished bronze in the light of the waning day. They leaned in and successfully kissed without knocking any cakes to the ground. The adoring crowd exploded with applause as the couple beamed smiles of gratitude.

Galorian stepped forward with the wedding cup filled with spiced wine. Clarissa, noting that he looked as radiant as the young couple, immediately recognized it as one of the bronze goblets embellished with rubies from her family's manor. Philippe held the cup up to Liliana's lips, and then she did the same for him.

Galorian came and stood by Clarissa again. "I hope you don't mind," he said. "I took two goblets when we were at the manor—my little rebellion against Wilfred getting it all . . . and a reminder of the sweetness of our visit there." He smiled at her and said, "I look forward to sharing more mead," and she managed to smile back.

Several toasts were made for the happiness of the new couple. Then Clarissa stepped up in front of the cake table and nodded to Aminah and Lisette. They came forward and unfolded a bed coverlet. Nerida had sewn it, and Galorian had dyed it saffron yellow. And everyone in the community had taken a turn embroidering a symbol on it. In the center Clarissa had created a flared cross that resembled the one that had been Josselyn's and now hung around Liliana's neck. Galorian sewed a reprise of Pinky the swan, and

Johanna made a lily-of-the-valley crown. Aminah added a crescent moon and star. Moses, who believed that a frog would have been the best wedding present ever, settled for allowing Lisette to help him embroider a bright green one in a corner.

Clarissa draped the stunning coverlet over the shoulders of the pleased bride and groom, and they kissed again. Then she declared, "May you produce many children under it!" At that, the laughing crowd launched a shower of seeds over Liliana and Phillippe, repeating the blessing. And, as if carefully orchestrated on cue, a dolphin couple and their young offspring sprang out of the sea in a dazzling, synchronized leap, squeaking their approval.

The amazed throng clapped again and then, led by the children, rushed forward to slice up and pass around the cakes. The spiced wine and mead began to flow freely. Several people congregated around a towering maypole that Galorian and Philippe had sunk into the sand, grabbing onto the brightly colored streaming ribbons that Galorian had dyed and dancing in a circle as Jaxon played.

Clarissa turned away from the festivities and walked up the narrow path up to the bluff, where she looked down on the partying crowd. She spied Liliana, beaming in the loving arms of her new husband. Clarissa shifted her gaze to the sky and said with a smile, "She's all right, Josselyn. I kept my promise to take care of your daughter, and Liliana is all right."

Then she walked toward her bed, feeling overwhelmed by a mixture of boundless joy and profound regret.

§

Johanna woke her a few hours later. Clarissa could hear remnants of music and laughter still wafting up from the beach. "It's Celeste," said Johanna. They hurried to Mercy Manor, where Philippe had carried his mother from the party. Philippe's father stood at the head of the bed, tenderly stroking Celeste's forehead. Mother and son held hands and gazed lovingly at each other.

"I'm so glad I didn't miss the wedding," Celeste murmured between labored breaths. "You're blessed to have Liliana to share your life." Liliana was sniffling in the corner, staring at the floor. She moved next to Philippe and took Celeste's other hand.

"She's so much like you," said Philippe, smiling from Liliana to his mother. "I know we'll be very happy."

"Yes," said Celeste, mustering the last of her strength to smile back at her beloved son. That was her final word.

Galorian moved to the side of the bed to perform Last Rites, offering gratitude for Celeste's life and asking for comfort for those who loved her. "Celeste, may Jesus Christ protect you and lead you to eternal life," he prayed as he made the sign of the cross on her forehead. Tears flowed freely in the room as Clarissa, Johanna, and Nerida recited a psalm. Liliana held Philippe as he wept on her shoulder.

The others left to give the family some time alone. "Can we walk?" Galorian asked Clarissa, who felt disheveled by her interrupted sleep and barely awake. But she noticed that Galorian, who had been up all night, appeared not much more put-together than she.

"All right," she said.

"You left the party."

"Yes."

"Are you all right?"

"Yes . . . no." Clarissa felt embarrassed, wondering what she should say, how much to share and how much to keep to herself. Galorian waited. "It's just that . . ." She hesitated. "I completely support your religious vocation as a monk. But sometimes I find it very hard to be just your friend, Galorian."

She had said it. She was glad—but a little concerned that her confession would push him away.

Rather than stepping back from her, Galorian smiled and drew her close. They lingered in the embrace. Then they walked again and arrived at the edge of the pond. "Sometimes," he said, sitting on the bench, "I wonder what would have happened if you and I had married all those years ago." Clarissa sat down next to him. "Knowing you now, I can imagine us being very happy."

Clarissa nodded. "Sometimes I feel such deep regret that I ran away."

Galorian smiled at her and took her hand. "What a life we might have had," he said. They sat in silence until Galorian spoke again. "But neither of us would be the people we are now if we had married then."

Clarissa nodded again. "I know that both of us find strength and purpose in our callings from God. I haven't taken a vow like you, but being a Beguine is what makes my life meaningful and true. I don't want to give that up. And I wouldn't want you to stop being a monk." She sighed and laughed. "But I have to say, seeing you in the back of the chapel in your riding boots and burgundy coat . . ."

He laughed then, too. "Do you have any idea how stunning you looked by the altar in that beautiful gown?"

Wrapped in each other's arms, they gently laughed together for a while, feeling the poignant irony of their situation, allowing the wondering and regret to linger between them.

Then Galorian turned to her and said, "I hope you don't ever feel like 'just my friend,' Clarissa. Our spiritual union, the depth of our mutual confession, our shared dreams and hopes . . . they're more precious to me than I can ever tell you. I can't imagine my life without you."

Clarissa sighed again and rested her head gently against his shoulder, as they watched the swans shake off the drowse of night and awaken to the dawn.

§

Liliana visited often from her new home with Philippe near Calais. As Clarissa observed the joy that resided in her niece, she pondered what would make her own joy complete. During a prayerful walk along the shore on a bright June morning, the answer came clearly to her. She understood the risks, but she knew that her spirit would not be at peace until she had spread more broadly the visions, lessons, and prayers that God had revealed to her. She needed to share her book beyond her circle of friends.

Jaxon built a simple room onto the side of Galorian's dye shop for a scriptorium. Johanna, Nerida, Aminah, and Felicite all offered to devote a few hours each week, around the demands of the garden and the school, to copying Clarissa's words onto sheets of parchment. Lisette illuminated these with beautiful illustrations using Galorian's latest hues, and Jaxon took on the duty of binding them together into books.

Copying a book was painstaking and time-consuming work, and by the end of the year, they had only two copies each, for a total of eight, to show for all their labor. Clarissa harbored a hope to visit the other Beguine communities in France and disseminate the books. She postponed her trip by six months, to the summer of 1215, when she had more copies to share.

She had assumed that she would invite Johanna to accompany her. But when the time came, Clarissa said to her, "You know I'd love to take this trip with you, but I think I need to invite Felicite. She works hard and gets very little credit or reward. And she's never quite recovered from Philippe's choice to marry Liliana." Thinking about how long she had clung to negative feelings about Felicite, Clarissa added, "And I don't feel that I've tried enough to know and understand her . . . to care for her as a sister like I should." Johanna swallowed whatever disappointment she felt and affirmed the generosity of Clarissa's choice.

Clarissa and Felicite rode first to Nivelles, where they visited a Beguine community with a large school. Among the pupils had been one named Ida, who ran away from a forced marriage at the age of nine carrying only her Psalter, which she had memorized by the time she arrived. The sisters of the community hosted a special meal and invited Clarissa to read excerpts from *The Radiant Soul: Aflame with Love.* She left a copy with them, which they promised to read aloud to one another daily.

Such was the welcome the two women from Swansong received wherever they went. Every Beguine community was anxious to share its stories and hungry for the spiritual wisdom Clarissa carried to them. She had an especially joyful reunion with the communities around Liège. She and Felicite ended their tour in Sint-Truiden, where a girl named Christina, the youngest of three orphaned sisters and the keeper of the household herds, had fallen ill and was given up for dead. When she made a miraculous recovery, she devoted her life to God and gathered a community of Beguines around her. They called her Christina the Astonishing.

When Clarissa went to pull the last copy of *The Radiant Soul* out of her bag, it was not there. She was both disappointed about not having one to read and leave for the sisters and also extremely puzzled. "Maybe we miscounted," said Felicite. But Clarissa was quite sure that the book had been there after their last stop. "Perhaps it fell out of the bag," Felicite offered.

They returned to Swansong both exhausted and exhilarated, bursting with stories to share with their sisters. "Our movement is strong," reported Clarissa to Johanna and Galorian when she met with them the next day. "We have sisters all across France doing good work. And now they're all praying for us." She smiled confidently. "Whatever comes, I know we'll have the strength and support we need to meet it."

Thirty-four

Innocent III had sent the invitation far and wide. The powerful pope wanted the Twelfth Ecumenical Council—an international gathering of dignitaries and theologians who convened to determine matters of church doctrine and practice—to be the largest and most significant in the church's history. On November 11, 1215, more than 1,300 cardinals, bishops, patriarchs, abbots, and priors—along with representatives of several kings and princes—converged on his Lateran Palace in Rome.

Francis was among those who received an invitation. He got word to Galorian that he wanted him to be one of the representatives of their movement, now called the Order of Friars Minor, or "lesser brothers"—known among the people as the Franciscans. The two of them had exchanged messages over the years when they could, sending news with anyone they knew embarking on the treacherous crossing of the Alps into the other's country. But they had not seen each other since their visit more than eight years before at Swansong.

Galorian was glad to respond affirmatively, anxious to return to Rome to greet his brother Francis. They embraced when they met as arranged near the palace before the ecclesial proceedings began. Francis introduced Amadeo, a young member of his community who accompanied him. "You're famous now," grinned Galorian to his old friend. "Receiving a personal invitation from the pope himself!"

Francis laughed. "As you know, I came here over six years ago with eleven of my Italian brothers, seeking permission to found a new religious order." Francis had sent Galorian news of the visit at the time, but he was clearly anxious to relate it face-to-face. "Pope Innocent agreed to meet with us but withheld his official consent. Then he had a dream." Francis laughed again. "He saw me holding up the cathedral"—he nodded at the Basilica of

Saint John Lateran across the piazza—"and he decided then to give us his endorsement."

Further greetings between the old friends were interrupted by the blare of a trumpet fanfare and the vigorous beating of drums, announcing the beginning of the Twelfth Ecumenical Council. Behind the parade of musicians came a slow-flowing river of brilliant red and dazzling white robes. The pointed miters on the heads of the cardinals and bishops bobbed like whitecaps on the sea. "I wonder if the pope remembers that *ecumenical* is Greek for 'the inhabited world,'" whispered Francis to Galorian, as they stood amid the enormous throng lining the street leading to the palace. "Nobody was invited to march in this parade except the churchly elites."

Galorian laughed. "Yes, but they believe they *are* the entire inhabited world."

Special lanterns were suspended on ropes throughout the streets and alleyways of Rome, shining brightly even in the daylight. Purple banners and pieces of cloth hung from the city's high towers and the windows of countless homes in honor of the grand occasion. A huddle of boys next to the three monks waved olive branches as the clerics passed by, shouting petitions.

Never before had Galorian seen such pageantry—not even at the launch of the Fourth Crusade.

Following the churchmen was a large, ancient icon, carried on the shoulders of two deacons. Painted on three tall, hinged panels, it bore the image of Jesus Christ sitting on a throne, his right hand raised in blessing. Galorian remembered from his time at the palace, indulging his love for church history and its antiquities, that Pope Innocent had secured the services of an artisan to add exquisite gems to Jesus's gold halo and to emboss the icon in silver.

Amadeo expressed his awe of the sacred work of art as it passed by. "It's one of the icons 'made without hands,'" explained Galorian. "Saint Luke began painting it, and it was miraculously finished by angels." He smiled at the young monk. "So the story goes."

Amadeo pointed and declared, "There's another."

"The most venerated in Christendom," said Galorian, catching a glimpse of the icon bearing a painted image of the Madonna and Child. Larger than a cathedral door, the thick cedar panel portrayed Mary in a gold-trimmed blue mantle, with a gold cross on her forehead. In her lap, the infant Jesus clutched a Gospel book.

"According to church legend," Galorian said, "after Jesus was crucified, his mother came into possession of a cedar table he had made in the workshop of his father, Joseph. When a group of devoted women of Jerusalem convinced Saint Luke to paint Mary's portrait, he used the top of the table. As he painted her image on it, the Mother of God shared stories about her son's life, and these became the heart of Luke's Gospel."

Appearing behind the icon was Pope Innocent himself, carried on the shoulders of four deacons in an ornate litter under an embroidered canopy of purple velvet. His right hand was raised in blessing, mirroring the gesture of Jesus in the first icon. Believers went to their knees as he passed, crossing themselves, some murmuring prayers, some weeping, others reaching out as if to touch him.

The procession took a turn toward the steps of the Lateran Palace. The pope and his cardinals, explained Galorian, were headed to the room in the pope's private chapel known as the Holy of Holies, where the Christ icon would be returned to its special altar. There the church leaders would kiss the feet of Jesus, share the Mass, and pray for a successful council.

The cardinals parted and lined the steps as Pope Innocent, aided by two deacons, descended from his litter and then walked up the open path between them. When he reached the top of the stairs, he turned to smile and make a final sign-of-the-cross blessing, as the crowd applauded. Then, gathering up his massive red robe, he ducked inside the open doorway and disappeared from view.

§

The following day, Pope Innocent III sat on a high dais, his robe like a waterfall that cascaded from his bejeweled, throne-like chair. Above him towered a ciborium, a domed gold structure with a cloth canopy signifying his holiness and authority. He called to order the Twelfth Ecumenical Council—which he preferred to call the Fourth Lateran Council, as it was the fourth to convene in his palace.

Galorian surveyed the gathered crowd from his humble bench shared with Francis and Amadeo in the back of the massive hall. He felt both honored to represent his Franciscan brothers at the occasion and entirely out of place in the suffocatingly pretentious atmosphere. As much gold was embroidered on the robes of the Church dignitaries as was inlaid in the ceiling. Galorian had a fleeting thought that perhaps he should feel ashamed of his ragged brown cassock amid their display of finery; but it was they, he quickly decided, who should be embarrassed by their ostentation.

His eyes wandered to the circular apse at his end of the great room. There he spied a large mosaic with three panels. The scene on the left showed Jesus handing a military banner—red and black, punctuated with gold Crusader crosses—to the Roman emperor Constantine the Great. Galorian wondered again, as he had many times, *How did the church stray so far? How could the followers of Jesus believe that he would bless the barbaric and misguided military adventures of the Roman Empire?* Looking around the hall, he added to his thoughts, *Or appreciate the showy display of haughty theologians?*

Galorian imagined himself standing up and making a passionate speech to the council, disrupting its business and pleading for a return to simple faith, holding up the example of Francis and begging the church to be faithful to its call. He would remind the stuffy hierarchs that while they sat there flashy and full, out of their sight the brothers and sisters of Jesus were starving and suffering, from one end of the empire to the other.

Galorian pictured all heads turned toward him: more than a thousand church leaders enthralled with his words, as if they had all just been sitting there waiting for someone to enlighten them with the truth and inspire them to change. But instead of rising and commanding their attention, Galorian sat silently and unobtrusively hunched on his bench at the back.

Over the days that the council convened, he listened in quiet agreement as pronouncements were made from the dais condemning the drunkenness of priests and prohibiting them from dueling. He silently applauded the banning of priests' participation in the practice of Trial by Ordeal. This horror of a judicial procedure was based on the premise that God would intervene with a miracle on behalf of innocent persons charged with crimes, while those who were guilty would suffer or die.

The Ordeal by Fire required the accused to walk barefoot over red-hot blades. A person charged with robbery or murder had to submit to the Ordeal by Water, reaching in to remove a stone from a cauldron of boiling water, oil, or lead. The wounds incurred would be bandaged and then examined three days later by a priest. If they had healed, the victim was pronounced innocent. If they festered, the poor soul was declared guilty and exiled or executed.

Galorian was relieved to see the barbaric practice ended by the council, but other decrees were troubling to him. Over the course of the assembly, Pope Innocent presented seventy-one of them. None generated any controversy, or even discussion. What became clear to Galorian was that the Fourth Lateran Council had been convened only to add a religious stamp of authority to the pope's personal opinions and campaigns.

Galorian squirmed when a Fifth Crusade was announced, to be launched on June 1, 1217, with Pope Innocent's presence and blessing. He silently lamented as a series of grievously shameful decrees were read: prohibiting Jews and Muslims from holding public office; requiring them to wear special dress distinguishing them from Christians; and ordering them to stay off the streets and out of the public eye during Christian holy days.

Among all the decrees, two particularly grasped Galorian's attention. He took careful notes so that he could relate all the details on his return home. The first forbade the founding of new religious orders, "lest too great a diversity lead to grave confusion in the church." Any orders founded without papal approval were "forbidden and dissolved."

The second was a frontal attack on heresy: "We condemn all heretics under whatever names they may be known, for while they have different faces they are nevertheless bound to each other by their tails. Let them be abandoned and punished." Priests determined by church authorities to be heretics were to be defrocked and exiled, their property confiscated. All "pestilential people" who defended heretics were to be excommunicated from the church.

The decree called for "scrupulous vigilance" by all bishops to cleanse the church of "the ferment of heretical wickedness and depravity." Each was mandated to make the rounds of his diocese at least twice a year, calling neighborhoods together and compelling everyone to swear that they would make known to the bishop any individuals they knew to be heretics. Anyone who refused to swear this oath was to be considered and treated as a heretic.

When he heard the decrees read, Galorian thought of Clarissa and Swansong. He knew of no way to interpret them as anything other than a direct assault on Beguines and other communities living out their faith apart from traditional church patterns and authorization. The irony was that Clarissa and her sisters lived in exactly the same way as faithful Franciscans . . . but as women, without the pope's blessing.

§

Galorian once again imagined himself rising from his bench, loudly confronting and exposing the evil forces at work in the council. But instead he continued to sit—until he could bear to do so no longer. He slipped out quietly. He knew where he needed to go: to the steps that could only be climbed on one's knees.

When he had worked at the palace, Galorian was curious about the Holy Stairs, but he had never seen them. There were twenty-eight of them, made of marble. They were believed to be the stairs that had led up to the praetorium of Pontius Pilate in Jerusalem, where Jesus was condemned to death. Saint Helena, mother of Emperor Constantine the Great, brought them to Rome in the fourth century.

At the base of the long marble stairway, Galorian looked to the top and took a deep breath. According to church doctrine, anyone who successfully climbed the steps was guaranteed complete forgiveness of sins and exemption from all punishment. A very low ceiling forced a penitent to his knees. Painted on its dark wood were plump cherubs trying out their wings, floating and tumbling freely. Galorian knelt and began to climb.

On the first of the twenty-eight steps, he prayed that God would give him a willing spirit for the sacred task before him. On the second, he asked that his eyes would be opened to see truth. On the third, he pleaded for a heart soft enough to receive it. By the fourth stair, Galorian was overcome with distraction by his cumbersome cassock, which did not move smoothly under his knees. He felt an enormous weight pressing down upon his shoulders. He was stunned at how difficult it was to lift his body a few inches. The cherubs playing above his head seemed to him a taunt rather than a comfort.

He understood what he needed to do. With each painstaking step, he confessed a sin that he knew was part of the burden he carried: judgment toward the church, impatience with his brothers, anger at Felicite, regret over his losses, pride. He tried to ignore the throbbing pain in his knees. He felt the weight falling away with each step, his burden slowly lifting.

When he was about halfway up the stairway, Galorian glimpsed up and saw Jesus standing at the top. His hands were bound in front of him, as they would have been in Pilate's praetorium when his death sentence was pronounced. Galorian thought of the overwhelming weakness and failure of Jesus's disciples: the betrayal by Judas, the denials of Peter, the doubt of Thomas, the fearful sleep of the others who could not stay awake even to keep vigil with him on the night of his arrest. Galorian did not want to be among the followers who failed in the moment of trial. But he knew in his bones the depth of their fear.

As he gazed up, he saw the face of Jesus transformed into Clarissa's. She stood there above Galorian, her hands bound. He gasped when he saw her, and he tried to crawl quickly toward her. But he could take only one slow, painstaking step at a time. He prayed for wisdom, for courage, for the strength to stand by her. He had valiantly faced enemies on the battlefield, and bravely accepted the death of his wife and child. But he did not know how to prepare for what he dreaded was coming. He pleaded to be released from his fear.

When he reached the top, the figure standing there was Jesus again. Galorian untied the rope that bound his hands and Jesus stretched out his arms. Galorian fell into his loving embrace, the tears spilling from his eyes onto the marble floor.

In a moment the vision was gone and Galorian was alone, kneeling and weeping. "O Merciful God," he prayed with all the fervency flooding his heart, "if my reward is release from all punishment, give this blessing to Clarissa instead. Punish me, but spare her . . . Please."

§

Galorian had been right in Rome about the decrees of the Fourth Lateran Council being targeted at Beguines. A few sympathizers rallied to their support. In the most dramatic effort, Father John of Liroux, a priest from Liège connected to the women's communities there, attempted to secure papal support for Beguines everywhere. He died while crossing the Alps on his way to Rome.

In late January of 1216, just two months after the close of the council, Father Lionel appeared at Swansong again. Offering no greeting or explanation, he charged into Manna House and grabbed Clarissa's copy of *The Radiant Soul: Aflame with Love* off the table next to her palette. While she sat dumbfounded, feeling more violated and angry than afraid, the priest strode up the bluff path to the chapel, followed closely by Johanna. There, over her protests, he seized the copy that lay on the altar. "You'll be hearing from the bishop!" Father Lionel warned as he rode off with the confiscated books.

Clarissa, Johanna, and Galorian met that evening to discuss what to do. All that could be done, they agreed, was to wait and see what happened next.

"He knew exactly where the books were," Clarissa said.

"Yes," said Johanna. And then she added, "But they were in the places someone would expect to find them."

Clarissa had not told them about the missing book on her tour of the Beguine communities. But as a disturbing clarity began to dawn on her that night, she decided that she must. She ended her telling by saying, "I think Felicite must have taken it and passed it on to Father Lionel."

Johanna, visibly upset, spoke as one who also was beginning to put together the pieces in her mind. "I've always wondered why she goes so often to Calais. And she focuses so intently on everything I share in the ritual cave, as if trying to remember every word." Johanna shook her head angrily. "I guess she's had a lot to report."

Galorian looked at Clarissa and added his observations. "Think of how many times she's followed us, hiding sometimes and listening in on our conversations. And people in the village seem to know far more about us than they should."

They sat for a few moments in a troubled silence. And then Johanna asked, "Do you think she brought Georgine here to disrupt our life?" Clarissa felt her anger rising as she pondered that possibility.

"We need to be fair," said Galorian. "We could be wrong."

"Even if we're right," said Johanna, "we need to be fair."

Galorian nodded and added, "Another lesson in loving our enemies."

Clarissa knew that her friends spoke truth, but she snapped, "I don't know if I can ever forgive her. Such betrayal." She shook her head. "What should we do?"

"We must talk with her," said Johanna. "You and I, if you're willing." Clarissa nodded, but she dreaded the thought.

They spoke with Felicite the following morning. "We believe you've acted as an informer against the community," accused Johanna, making no effort at preliminaries and clearly trying to keep her anger under control.

"Why, I never—" protested Felicite. "I can't believe that you would think so."

Johanna repeated the charge, enumerating the evidence. Felicite's face fell. "Why?" asked Johanna.

A tense silence enveloped them as Clarissa and Johanna waited. "I needed the money," Felicite finally admitted.

"We've shared everything we have with you," said Johanna, no longer trying to mask her outrage. "Why did you think you needed money?" Felicite shrugged her shoulders and remained silent.

"Who paid you?" asked Clarissa.

Felicite hesitated, but then she said, "Bishop Renard in Calais."

Clarissa was furious—at Felicite's betrayal, at the bishop's manipulation of one so vulnerable, and at her own inability for almost a decade to see the true character of the young woman she had once believed was like a younger version of herself. Johanna interrupted her silent fuming. "Do you have someplace you can go?" she asked Felicite.

"Yes," Felicite answered softly as she stared at the floor.

Clarissa was unconvinced, but she believed the young woman was so anxious to get out of their presence that she would have said whatever she thought they wanted to hear. "Good," declared Clarissa. "You need to gather your things and leave by this afternoon. Jaxon will take you wherever you want to go, as far as Calais." As Felicite stood up and walked toward the door, Clarissa asked, "Are you really from southern France?"

Felicite turned back to face her. "No. I grew up in a village near Calais."

"And there was no forced marriage?"

"No."

"And Georgine?" asked Johanna.

"She's my older sister," Felicite admitted. She stared at the floor again. "Everything I told you about her is true. One day she was just gone. I was five, and she was eight, when our father sold her to a horrible man in Calais. After she escaped, she sold herself over and over to survive."

Felicite sighed and then sat back down to tell the rest of the story. "My parents are very poor. When my father started talking about selling me . . . I knew that girls who get sold aren't just servants. The bishop saved me. He knew how desperate my family was, and he offered to pay my father if I moved here and reported on what I saw and heard."

Clarissa noted the sadness in Felicite's eyes as she continued. "Every time I went to Calais to report to the bishop's assistant, I looked for Georgine. One day I found her standing on a street. I hadn't seen her in over nine years. She looked different . . . older . . . like a broken doll. But sisters always know each other. We both cried for joy. And the hug she gave me is the best thing I ever got in my life.

"I told her about the bishop's money and tried to convince her that it was safe to go back home. But she was too mad at our father. She told me she could never forgive him. It was Bishop Renard's idea to pay her to break up our . . . to break up your community by being difficult and demanding." Felicite smiled for the first time during their conversation as she said, "She's good at that."

"Will you go back home now?" asked Johanna.

Felicite's smile evaporated. "No. My parents won't want me if I'm not making them money." She stood up and looked at Clarissa. "If you will tell me, I'd like to know where you took Georgine. Whoever helped her may know where she is now. I want to try to find her and see if we can figure out how to take care of each other." She wiped a tear from her eye as she said, "I don't ever want to lose her again." Then she walked out of the room to gather her few possessions.

Clarissa and Johanna sat for a while with nothing to say. "It's so very sad," said Clarissa finally, breaking the crushing silence. Then she sighed, "And now I have to go tell Aminah the truth about her best friend."

Thirty-five

The report from Bishop Renard was not long in coming. Father Lionel delivered it on a Friday when the community was gathered for lunch. He tried to take Clarissa outside, but she refused to go, declaring, "Whatever you have to say, I want my sisters to hear it."

The priest relayed the bishop's judgment to her: "You have ignored the authority of the church and written blasphemy. You are ordered to appear in the Place D'Armes in Calais tomorrow evening at sunset."

"And what will happen to me there?" asked Clarissa, trying to keep her voice calm and even.

"Nothing will happen to you if you swear never again to write or speak about the heretical ideas in your book."

"And if I don't?" Clarissa asked, attempting to sound more confident than she felt.

"You'll find out tomorrow night," snapped the priest. Without any further word of explanation, he got on his horse and rode off.

"You shouldn't go," Nerida pleaded.

"I have to," said Clarissa. "It will be worse for me—for all of us—if I don't."

"I'm going with you," said Galorian. And both Nerida and Johanna insisted that they too would accompany her to Calais.

Her friends offered to stay close to her that night, but Clarissa needed to be alone. She spent the night in prayer, trying to keep the terror at bay and to trust that God would make clear what she needed to do. Late the next afternoon, Galorian and Clarissa rode to Calais on Thane, followed by Johanna and Nerida on Magnus. Clarissa, shivering in the frigid air, leaned against Galorian for both warmth and comfort.

When they arrived at the Place D'Armes, a crowd was already gathered and waiting in the large plaza. The Tour de Guet, a tall and newly built watchtower, loomed at the edge of the square over the proceedings. Atop it was a dovecote, with many openings for birds to build their nests. Saint Catherine took up position there, her noisy arrival scattering all the pigeons and doves in a fright.

In the center of the plaza was a tall stack of kindling. Piled on top of it were copies of *The Radiant Soul: Aflame with Love*. Clarissa assumed that, when Felicite had carried the copy she stole to the bishop, she reported on all the Beguine communities they had visited on their tour. Then, Clarissa guessed, someone from the bishop's office retraced their steps and seized all the books.

Bishop Renard, a beefy man with multiple chins, dressed in a formal robe and miter, stood by the pile of books. He lifted a copy high in the air, repeating the words of Father Lionel's warning. Pointing at Clarissa, he proclaimed, "This woman, a so-called Beguine, has ignored the authority of the church and written blasphemy. Tonight we burn all copies of her heretical book." He threw the copy back onto the pile.

A young man handed the bishop a torch. He set it to the kindling, which flared into a roaring blaze, quickly engulfing the books. So intense was the fire's heat, Clarissa had to take a step back. She watched, numb, as months of work by her sisters went up in flames.

Then Bishop Renard looked directly at her and warned, "If you keep spreading this heresy, you will be next." The threat was unmistakable. Clarissa felt her knees buckle, and Galorian and Johanna, who were on either side of her, grabbed hold of her arms to keep her upright. Then they ushered her toward Thane and helped her up on his back. She leaned even more closely into Galorian on the cold ride home.

§

When they arrived, Clarissa and her friends decided to warm themselves around the fire in the hearth of the community center. No one knew what to say. Galorian passed out mugs of mead. Clarissa took a few sips and then set hers down. Finally, breaking the tense silence, she looked from Johanna to Nerida and said, "I'm so sorry that all your work was destroyed."

"You've suffered the greatest loss," Johanna said. "You must think about yourself, Clarissa. What are you going to do?"

Clarissa, weary and dismayed, said, "Right now I'm going to go to bed." Noticing the concern and disappointment on all their faces, she thanked her friends for their support and said, "I just need a little time to rest and figure things out."

She headed toward Manna House but then turned and walked up the bluff path to the chapel. There she fell on her knees in front of the cross and prayed to Mary Magdalene: "Help me, beloved sister, to remember that crucifixion wasn't the last word. You were the first to see with your own eyes the power of life over death. Help me to believe it now . . . *Please.*"

On her way back to her room, Clarissa stopped in the barn. She went right to the hollow in a beam where Saint Catherine, now off hunting mice, had made her home for several years. Clarissa reached up, lifted the owl's nest, and felt around for the book wrapped in a piece of thick wool. Then she carried the only remaining copy of *The Radiant Soul: Aflame with Love* back to Manna House.

§

Clarissa hid the book under her palette and kept it a secret from her friends for three months. They regularly expressed their concern, asking her what she planned to do in response to the bishop's threat. But when she had no answer for them, they eventually understood that it would be best not to ask again and to wait until Clarissa was ready to bring it up herself. She prayed daily that God would open a path and give her the wisdom to see it.

It was while she was in the cave celebrating the Easter vigil with her sisters, standing in the light of the fiery presence of God and hearing again the resurrection story, that clarity came to her. That year Johanna chose to relate to the young women the legend of the phoenix, a sacred and stunning creature of Greek mythology. As always, they were all wide-eyed and mesmerized as Johanna spoke.

"The phoenix is a grand, breathtaking bird, brilliantly colored with shimmering red and gold feathers that radiate the rays of the sun," Johanna began. "Her blue eyes shine like sapphires, and her head is circled in a fiery halo. Every dawn she bathes in water and sings an enchanting song—so beautiful that the sun god Helios stops his chariot every morning to listen.

"The phoenix flies above the deserts of Arabia, feeding on the oil of the balsam tree and the resiny gum of frankincense. Only one phoenix lives at a time. Every five hundred years—when she has become old and weak, and her eyes have grown dim and clouded, and her wings are scarcely able to lift her from the earth—she weaves a nest of cinnamon bark high in a towering palm tree at the top of a mountain. She lines the nest with myrrh and other aromatic herbs that she gathers from the sun-warmed hills and settles into it with a sigh.

"With a single clap of her wings, the phoenix ignites a spark in the nest, which bursts into flame. So eager is the bird for rebirth, she meets her death with joy. Like the swan, she sings a melodious hymn—the most beautiful of her life—as she surrenders herself to the consuming fire. As she burns, fragrance rises like incense into the desert air, until all that remains in the nest is a pile of silvery gray ashes.

"Suddenly, the ashes begin to tremble. Out of them arises the phoenix reborn, young and powerful. The cinnamon-bark nest is both pyre and cradle as the new life emerges and grows. Energy surges through her body, lights the fire in her eyes and the halo around her head. The phoenix, restored to her former glory and splendor, as large and dazzling as she once had been, unfolds her massive wings and greets the sun.

"She molds a large egg out of myrrh, hollows it out, and places the ashes inside. Then she carries the egg in her claws to Heliopolis in Egypt, the City of the Sun. As the phoenix flies, throngs of other birds follow her—eagles and hawks, falcons and swans, sparrows and doves—darkening the sky with their numbers, too many to count. And the phoenix, which was present at the birth of the world and throughout all of history, deposits the egg on the altar of the great Egyptian temple and soars into her new life."

Everyone in the cave was stunned into silence when Johanna finished relating the story. She stood by the fire on the rock, bathed in its dancing light, and said, "You can understand why early Christians adopted the phoenix as a symbol of immortality and resurrection. We, like the phoenix, are always being reborn in the power of Jesus Christ."

As she spoke these words, the Holy Spirit appeared to Clarissa once more as a swan. It flew into the cave carrying a book in its beak, circling above her. And as it left, it multiplied into dozens of birds, flying out and in all directions, each one carrying a book.

That evening Clarissa took out the copy of *The Radiant Soul* that she had kept hidden and showed it to Johanna and Galorian. "We have to make more copies and spread them as quickly and widely as possible," she said. "If you're willing."

"But, Clarissa, the bishop . . ." Galorian began, unable to finish the sentence. "We can find a place for you to hide. You could disappear for a while in Dover . . . or Assisi . . . or even Saint Catherine's Monastery. I know Sister Mary Peter, or Brother Francis, or Father Alain would protect you."

"I don't want to be apart from you," Clarissa said, looking into his troubled eyes. Then, resting her gaze on Johanna's anguished face, she added, "Or from you . . . or any of my sisters."

"Just for a little while," Galorian pleaded. "Until the heat of the heresy crusade dies down."

"I'm not ashamed of what I believe," Clarissa declared. "And Jesus didn't go into hiding. He rode openly into Jerusalem before the crowds, knowing what awaited him there, and accepted his fate."

"But, Clarissa, you're not Jesus Christ."

"But aren't we all called to live as he lived? To speak truth and live by courage?"

"But you heard the bishop," said Galorian. "They'll do to you what they did to Jesus . . . what they did to your books."

Clarissa looked again at Johanna, who had remained silent as she and Galorian had exchanged words. "It can't possibly be a coincidence that you chose to tell the story of the phoenix this Easter. I know it's a resurrection story. But weren't you also trying to tell me that my book can have a second life?"

Johanna nodded. "I'm so very glad that a copy still exists. It's too brilliant . . . and eloquent . . . and holy to let it die in a heap of ashes in the square in Calais. It's a gift from God." She smiled tenderly at Clarissa. "But maybe Galorian is right. Maybe you could disappear for just a little while."

"I won't blame you if you don't want to help me make and spread more copies," Clarissa said. "The greatest risk is mine, but I can't promise that anyone involved with this will be safe. I just know that this is the gift God wants me to share with the world." She sighed heavily. "So many people suffer from hatred and injustice, and they have no option to disappear. How could I take that choice when they can't? Sharing my book is my way of standing with them, reminding them that they are not alone and that a merciful God hears their prayers and carries their pain."

Clarissa stood up then. "It's been a very long day," she said. She looked at her two dearest friends. "I'm not afraid." She wanted them to believe it, but she knew it wasn't true. Her knees knocked together under her robe as she said it, and she thought she was going to faint as she turned to leave them. She knew how much she depended on them, how much she needed them. But she also understood that—ultimately, in the end—she would have to face alone whatever was to come.

The following afternoon Galorian invited her to a meeting that also included Johanna, Nerida, Lisette, and Jaxon. "We've decided," announced Galorian, "that the money and wool we'll get next month from shearing our large flock of sheep will be more than enough to buy or trade for the food we'll need."

"We're not going to plant the garden this year," piped up Nerida. "Except for Galorian's dyes and my healing herbs."

"We want to devote every moment we have to making more copies of *The Radiant Soul*," said Johanna. "It's our most important work now."

Clarissa, speechless, stood up and made her way around the tight circle, hugging them all.

§

At the end of August, Johanna came to Clarissa's room and announced, "I have a surprise." Clarissa, curious, followed her friend to the Josselyn Center. She was astonished to see the family from Calais that had carried her and Johanna across France on the first leg of their pilgrimage to Saint Catherine's Monastery. "Natania!" she shouted with her arms outstretched, and the woman she hadn't seen in a decade immediately stepped forward and embraced her.

The boys Levi and Yosef had grown into young men. In addition to the long robe and pointed hat that they and their father Malakai were forced to wear, every member of the family now also had a bright yellow oval badge sewed onto their clothing in the center of their chest, marking them as Jews. "They destroyed our bakery and burned our books," said Malakai. "They took our home, our wagon, all our possessions. For no reason other than that we are Jews and they need to finance their Fifth Crusade against the Muslims."

Clarissa was both comforted and alarmed that she was not alone in experiencing persecution in the aftermath of the church's pronouncements at the Fourth Lateran Council. "We want to get to our relatives near the Italian border and then go on to Jerusalem," explained Malakai. "But until we can, we have nowhere to stay."

"Then you must stay here," said Clarissa. She shot a look at Johanna to make sure that she concurred. Johanna nodded. "How did you know we were here?" Clarissa asked Malakai.

"We didn't. We only heard in our shop in Calais about a community of Christian women here who care for all people. Not until we arrived did we recognize one of the young women we had carried across France many years ago." He smiled at Johanna.

A little shuffling was required to make room for the family, but it was done rather easily. Moses had let it be known since his tenth birthday in December that he was ready to live among men. Lisette reluctantly gave her approval, Galorian made the case with his brothers, and Francis House was happy to receive the boy.

With Liliana and Felicite both gone, and no one needing refuge from a forced marriage at that particular moment, Q Cottage had empty rooms. Clarissa, Johanna, and Aminah moved in with Nerida and Lisette, keeping one room empty and available in the event that a young woman might appear needing temporary shelter. Malakai and his family took over Manna House.

The day after their arrival, Clarissa cut from a piece of white linen a dozen ovals—the width of a finger and the height of half a palm, according to the description Galorian had said the church council in Rome had mandated. With his help in the dye shop, the two of them appeared at dinner that evening wearing yellow ovals sewed onto their robes, over their hearts. Clarissa invited anyone in the community who felt moved to join them to pick up one of the badges they had made.

"You really are trying to get us all killed, aren't you?" Johanna said to her after the meal.

"The badges the Jews are forced to wear are cruel," declared Clarissa. "They're an official stamp of separation and discrimination, a sign that Jews are a scourge in the eyes of the church. They'll only lead to more hatred and violence. We can't ask our Jewish friends to bear the risk of not wearing them, but we can protest the badges' power by joining them." She sighed heavily. "Silence is the same as cooperation, and if we don't resist this outrage, we're as guilty as the barbarians who designed the loathsome things."

"This may be your worst idea yet," said Johanna, as she picked up one of the yellow ovals and held it over her heart. "May I borrow a needle and some thread?"

§

Natania wept with grateful surprise when she saw the entire community wearing yellow badges at breakfast the next morning. Malakai decided that day that Levi, their younger son, would go to the border to make arrangements with the relatives, and Clarissa offered Magnus for the journey.

The family didn't expect to stay long at Swansong, but it turned out to be long enough for Aminah and Yosef to fall in love. The devout young man with a joyful spirit was gracious and kind—and the best baker in the family. His loving attention pulled Aminah out of the sad space into which she had sunk after Felicite's abrupt and difficult departure.

Aminah, proudly claiming Clarissa and Galorian as her parents, invited them to a meeting with Yosef's. Malakai and Natania were opposed to the match, but their older son had already rejected several other potential brides, and they could see that Aminah made him happy. They were full of questions. How would Yosef and Aminah worship God together? Would the wedding be Jewish or Muslim? How would the children be raised?

Clarissa understood the need to raise such concerns. But to her, only one question really mattered: Where, in the prevailing climate of hatred and separation, could such a young couple find acceptance and safety? She didn't know how to hold the delight she felt alongside the tremendous fear that overcame her whenever she tried to picture their future.

Aminah, Clarissa, and Galorian talked late into the night after the meeting with Yosef and his parents. They grappled honestly with the challenges of such a union. Finally, Aminah looked at Clarissa and said, "You're the one who taught me, against everything I had ever been told, that love is what matters in a marriage. Yosef and I love each other, and that will have to be enough."

Clarissa nodded at her and smiled. And then the three of them waded into the difficult topic of where the couple should live. Even before Yosef had appeared, Clarissa had been concerned about Aminah's safety at Swansong. Muslims were targeted along with Jews by the Fourth Lateran Council. The only reason they weren't forced to wear badges was because their dress, including Aminah's *hijab*, already distinguished their faith—or, as church officials would have it, their status as infidels lacking faith. Clarissa believed it was only a matter of time before Aminah would feel the weight of persecution, especially with another Crusade officially announced.

"I'd miss you all if I left," Aminah said. "But sometimes I miss my home. I don't even know if I still have uncles and aunts and cousins in Constantinople . . . or if they all died in the massacre. I know you'd try to protect Yosef and me here. But what if you can't?" She sighed. "But where else in the world would people accept us the way you do here?" It went like that, back and forth, for several minutes.

Finally, Clarissa said, "God will be with you, Aminah, wherever you are. And no decision now has to be permanent. You can always leave later— or come back if you go now."

Aminah nodded. And then she said, "I'd like to go with Yosef's family to Jerusalem. I know that Muslims, Jews, and Christians don't always get along, but it's a place where they live together. And it's not too far from Constantinople. Yosef will do whatever we and his parents think is best, but I know it's what he wants."

Clarissa felt an immediate sadness overwhelm her, but it was followed with a wave of peace. She grinned at Aminah. "What a life you will have!" she said as she threw her arms around her young friend. Galorian got up and embraced them both.

§

There wasn't time for extensive planning. Aminah and Yosef decided to have a simple wedding with rituals from both their faiths as soon as Levi returned. Nerida once again sewed day and night to create a beautiful wedding gown, and Galorian went right to work making the *chuppah*, the wedding canopy of Jewish tradition. When it was finished, he spent a day boiling a mountain of grapes in one of his large dye vats until he had an impressive stash of grape molasses.

Two days before the ceremony, he concocted the henna paste that Aminah requested, mixing crushed leaves with water and some of the molasses to thicken it. Keeping a tradition that Muslim brides had observed for centuries, Aminah sat quietly as Lisette painted the paste in an intricate pattern of flowers on the tops of her hands and feet. A day later, she removed it and allowed the orange color left behind to darken to reddish-brown.

The next day members of the community and Yosef's family gathered on the beach just before sunset. Aminah, looking elegant atop Thane, captured all eyes as she rode from down the beach to the wedding site. She was radiant in a cream-colored dress, her dark hair and eyes shining beneath a cascading veil, the henna accents on her hands and bare feet glowing in the fiery light of the setting sun.

Yosef's olive-toned face gleamed, and his gray eyes danced with hope and delight, as he reached out his hand to help his bride off the horse. He led her under the *chuppah*. Held up with four poles stuck in the sand, the white silk canopy was a symbol of the openness and hospitality they hoped to nurture in their new home—wherever it might be—and of the sheltering presence of God.

Readings from the Qur'an were interspersed with the traditional seven Jewish blessings known as *Sheva Brachot*. Every honored family member or guest who read a part held up one of the ruby-studded bronze goblets Galorian had taken from the manor, and then passed it on to the next person to speak. The goblet was filled with *jellab*, a sweet beverage made of grape molasses mixed with rose water, raisins, and honey. Galorian had worked hard to perfect the drink typically consumed during Ramadan feasts. When all the blessings were finished, he held the goblet to Yosef's lips to drink, and then Natania did the same for Aminah.

The evening breezes began to waft off the sea, setting the edges of the canopy fluttering. The bride and groom exchanged gold rings and spoke their promises to each other. Then Yosef picked up a cup, dropped it on the ground, and tried to crush it with his right foot, as he had witnessed countless times at Jewish weddings. But the cup only buried itself in the sand. Malakai rushed forward with a piece of driftwood he had spied and slipped it under the cup. Laughing, Yosef tried again.

As the cup broke, the guests, who had been coached beforehand, shouted "*Mazel tov!*" and "*Jazakallah!*" Yosef put his arm around Aminah, and the young couple gratefully received the shower of congratulations and good wishes. As at Liliana and Philippe's wedding, Clarissa was riveted on the beautiful grace of the bride and groom, who clung tightly to each other and could not stop smiling.

The centerpiece of the feast that followed was bread that Yosef and his family had baked. It was in the form of Jewish *challah* bread, but the three ropes of dough that had been braided into each loaf were three different shades: pale wheat, brown barley, and dark rye. "They're like us," announced Malakai proudly. "Different colors and different faiths, all woven together. My family and I mixed each loaf with the prayer that Jews, Muslims, and Christians would someday live together in such beautiful harmony."

The community had pulled off in record time making another beautiful bed coverlet. Aminah and Yosef gratefully received the lovingly embroidered gift as Clarissa draped it over their shoulders.

This time Clarissa stayed to enjoy the party. She was particularly glad that Liliana and Philippe had come from Calais to celebrate the day. When they were ready to return home, Liliana said to Clarissa, "I have some news." Grinning, she blushed as she announced, "We're going to have a child."

Clarissa embraced Liliana and Philippe in a wide hug. "I'm so happy for you!" she exclaimed, moved by this exciting new development. And then she sent them on their way with wishes for safe travel home.

That night Johanna and Galorian tried again to convince Clarissa to leave for a while. "Tomorrow you could get a ride with Aminah and her new family," said Johanna. "You could go as far as Italy, or on to Jerusalem, or Saint Catherine's if you wanted. It's as if God has handed you an escape plan."

"Please, Clarissa," begged Galorian. "We can spread your book around without you here. Please think about living quietly for a while somewhere safe . . . Anywhere but here."

Clarissa was moved by their concern and thought carefully about how to respond. "But don't you see? If I leave, it could be the end of everything we've built here. Our enemies would come after the two of you if they can't find me. They have ways—horrible, unspeakable ways—of getting information out of people. How could I live knowing that you might suffer because of me?"

Johanna and Galorian sat in silence. "And I couldn't possibly leave now. Liliana is going to have a child. She'll need me. And I want to be here to welcome that precious new life." Johanna and Galorian expressed their delight at the news. And then they sighed together in resignation over Clarissa's decision to stay.

Early the next morning, the community gathered to say goodbye to Aminah, Yosef, and his family. Aminah clung to Galorian, too overcome to put into words her feelings about leaving him. Then she hugged Clarissa and Johanna, thanking them for giving her a home when she needed one.

"This will always be your home," Clarissa said, moving next to Galorian and trying to keep tears from spilling from her eyes. Aminah, allowing hers to flow freely, smiled and slowly turned from them. Then she climbed onto the wagon that Levi had borrowed from the relatives she was about to meet.

Seated beside her new husband, Aminah waved to Galorian, as she had when she left Saint Catherine's Monastery in the company of Clarissa and Johanna years before. She kept it up until the wagon disappeared from view.

"O God, Allah, Adonai," whispered Clarissa when they were gone. "Please, I beg you, protect them."

Thirty-six

That fall Liliana visited frequently, and Clarissa was reminded with deep poignancy of the joyful season of anticipation that she and Josselyn had shared while awaiting the birth of her and Galorian's child. With every visit, Liliana looked more like her mother to Clarissa. She tried to live in the delight of the moment, fighting off the terror that overwhelmed her whenever memories came to her of everything that could go wrong. She prayed often to Josselyn, asking for the protection of the angels for Liliana and her child.

Johanna and Clarissa, glad to be under one roof with their sisters, decided to stay at Q Cottage when Yosef and his family left. In September they invited another family to move into Manna House. As with the residents of Emmanuel's Place, Simone, Ansel, and their four children had been cast out of their home when Ansel was discovered to have leprosy.

Little Fernand, the young couple's three-year-old son, reminded Clarissa of Sylvain when he first came with his family to Swansong. He was shy at first, but then happily boisterous as he grew comfortable and realized that the sheep, frogs, swans, dolphins, and humans around him were all there to entertain him. He tagged along behind Sylvain, now thirteen, wherever he went, and Sylvain seemed happy to have the boy as his shadow. Fernand claimed he would grow up to be a troubadour like Jaxon, and he entertained them all that fall with his attempts at singing and juggling.

In October, Jacques of Vitry, a renowned cardinal, preacher, and friend to Beguines, succeeded where John of Liroux had failed. Pope Honorius III—successor to Innocent, who had died in July—told the cardinal on his visit to Rome to pass along this blessing: "Religious women, not only in the diocese of Liège but also in France and the empire, are permitted to live in the same house and to incite each other toward the good by mutual exhortation." Though Jacques carried the papal approval back to the Beguines in

France, it was oral, informal, and never officially recorded—with little effect against the gathering anti-heresy storm.

That month Clarissa, with Johanna at her side, returned to the communities she had visited with Felicite, to replace the copies of *The Radiant Soul* that had been seized. "It may be risky to have it," she warned at each stop. "If you'd rather not take it, I understand." Not one of the Beguine communities refused the book. And in fact the hunger to read it seemed to have grown since it had landed Clarissa in the center of a heated church controversy.

In Courtrai, an elderly Beguine told Clarissa and Johanna that the bishop in their diocese had called all his clerics to the cathedral to receive a warning and a task related to Beguines. "Whatever it takes, bring those women under control!" the bishop had yelled, according to a Franciscan who reported on the meeting. The bishop had sent the clerics off, saying, "We can't have this disobedience. Soon women everywhere will be rebelling against their husbands and my priests, and there will be no end of it. I want it stopped. Now!"

The old woman took Clarissa's hands in hers and looked up into her eyes. "Bless you, my child," she said. "May God grant you all the strength and courage you need."

§

On Christmas Eve, Liliana, very great with child, sat on Reginald. Clarissa smiled as she remembered the last time her niece had played the role of Mary and needed a gourd to appear pregnant. Sylvain led the donkey and the procession of villagers to the barn. Fernand, though hardly a newborn and barely able to fit into the sheep's manger, had insisted on being the Baby Jesus. A parade of shepherds herded in the lambs, and three boys dressed as kings carried the gifts of frankincense and myrrh. It was still Clarissa's favorite night of the year.

Johanna read from the Gospel of Luke the description of Mary's visit with her cousin Elizabeth, when both were miraculously pregnant. It was among Clarissa's most beloved stories. She listened in rapt joy as she heard once more about young Mary, still trembling with the news that she would give birth to the Son of God, running to find solace in the arms of the elderly Elizabeth. At Mary's greeting, Elizabeth's child "leaped in her womb." Then Mary sang the song known in the church as the Magnificat:

> "My soul magnifies you, O God,
> and my spirit rejoices in my Savior,

For you have looked with favor
on the lowliness of your servant.
You have scattered the proud in the thoughts of their hearts.
You have brought down the powerful from their thrones,
and lifted up the lowly.
You have filled the hungry with good things,
and sent the rich away empty."

Clarissa smiled as Johanna spoke with her usual eloquence to a circle of spellbound listeners. "Long before Jesus preached the compassion and justice that got him into trouble with the authorities and led to his death," declared Johanna, "his mother understood the radical social upheaval that was coming. She knew everything was going to be turned upside down. The starving and the sick, the persecuted and the poor, the lepers and the lame, were going to rise up and say to the kings, 'Move over. Your turn is up. This is our throne now.'

"The miraculous shift was already beginning with Mary. A young woman living in a world run by powerful men, a Jew in a land under Roman military occupation, a peasant on the run who had to give birth in a barn—this is the one God chose. God anointed this young, poor, powerless Jewish woman—unworthy by every measure in the world's eyes—and said to her, 'You are worthy to bear my Son.'

"And so tonight God says to each of us, 'You are worthy of this extraordinary gift.' God sent Jesus into the world, not because we are damned and worthless, as many in the church will tell you, but because we are precious and beloved. God tells us through the birth of Jesus, 'This is how much I love you. I'm giving you my only son.' Just as Elizabeth's child danced in her womb, so should our hearts quicken, and our spirits lift, and our limbs leap at the knowledge that this gift is given to *us*! We are created in the image of God by love, and we are worthy of this gift, this treasure, this blessedness."

Clarissa would always remember the next moments, replaying them in her mind many times in the days and nights that followed. She noticed the candlelight reflected in the tears in Liliana's eyes. She caught the wink Galorian sent her from among the shepherds. She heard Johanna announce that angels proclaimed the good news of Jesus's birth.

She watched a dozen children dressed in white robes, with halos and wings askew, descend to the barn floor. The last to come down was Fernand. He had popped out of the manger and run up into the hayloft, apparently no longer content to be the savior of the world when he saw the opportunity to fly. Clarissa was overwhelmed by the same joyful awe she had felt when she was utterly surprised by three-year-old Sylvain, coming down from the rafters wearing his leper's robe and Jaxon's upturned shoes.

As soon as Fernand's feet touched the ground, four men dressed in black clothes and half masks, wielding swords and clubs, stormed into the barn on horses. Gasps rippled through the gathered crowd. Galorian immediately stepped away from the shepherds and ran to position himself in front of Clarissa.

The tallest of the men shouted out her name. Clarissa slipped around Galorian to face him. "I am the one you've come for," she said, relieved that no tremor weakened her voice and betrayed the terror she felt.

"By order of the Inquisitor of Calais," declared the man in a gruffly official tone, "you are under arrest for heresy." He pulled out a rope and began tying it around her wrists. Galorian lunged forward to try to stop him.

Clarissa intervened with a look, aimed at the fury she observed in Galorian's eyes. She was grateful for his protective response, but she knew that resistance was futile and would likely endanger her friends. "It's all right," she said to him as she held out her hands in front of her.

When she was bound, one of the men came toward her to pick her up and set her on the horse they had brought to take her. "Let him," said Clarissa, nodding at Galorian. She could see that the anger in his eyes had melted into anguish, and she knew that the last thing he wanted to do was lift her onto the horse that would take her away and into the jaws of the anti-heresy dragon that was devouring victims all across the empire. But she also knew that he would understand why it was better for him to do it than to allow one of them to grab her.

As Galorian gently raised her onto the horse, he whispered, "I'll find you."

Clarissa locked her eyes on his. "I know." The tall man tied the rope that bound her wrists around the saddle's pommel to secure her. Before they took her away, Clarissa looked from Johanna to Nerida to Lisette. She smiled at Liliana, who was wiping tears from her cheeks, and nodded at Jaxon, who moments before had been happily playing his lute but now had a look of terror on his face.

"Anyone who tries to follow us," said the man on the lead horse, "will be arrested for defending a heretic."

"I'll be all right," Clarissa said to the shocked onlookers, trying to convince herself as the men led her away. "Please, stay here and be safe." Most of the people in the barn, paralyzed by fright, needed no such instruction. Only one observer of the arrest refused to pay attention to her.

§

They rode slowly at first, down the path toward Balnéaire. And then they picked up the pace as they turned toward Calais. Clarissa was in the middle of them, with two men in front of her and two behind. One held the rein of the horse that carried her. As on the night that the bishop burned her books, the air was bitterly cold and the horses breathed heavily. But this time Clarissa did not have her friends alongside her, or Galorian to lean into for warmth and comfort. She was scared, but she felt remarkably calm.

They put her in a tiny cell with only a pile of straw, a bucket, and a rough blanket. An open window, up near the ceiling and covered with a grate, let in the winter air. Clarissa shivered under her cloak, but she could not bring herself to wrap the filthy blanket around her. She knew she would be warmer if she managed to cover the window with it. But she couldn't bear the thought of being totally shut off from the outside world and she craved fresh air, no matter how cold.

She burrowed into the straw and thought immediately of Father Augustus, finding it impossible to believe that he had survived in a similarly wretched dungeon for almost eight years. And then a shriek startled her. She stood immediately and looked up toward the window. "Saint Catherine, you bad owl," she whispered. "You didn't listen to me." Catherine was perched on the other side of the window, trying in vain to squeeze herself through a narrow opening in the bars of the grate.

Clarissa peered past her owl and saw a few stars sparkling in the night sky, one brighter than all the others. She smiled as she thought of her three friends from Egypt arriving on their camels on this very night a decade before. She returned her gaze to Saint Catherine. The presence of her screech owl comforted her. "I'm glad you've come," she said, smiling. "You're still my oldest friend."

Clarissa alternately sat and paced, reaching up to the window from time to time to let Catherine know she was still glad to have the companionship. She tried to pray, but words escaped her. She pictured the faces of her friends, imagining them sitting together in the Josselyn Center around the fire drinking mead, trying to decide what to do. She hated that she had put this worry into their lives.

She finally piled some straw in a corner and sat, trying to quiet her spirit. And on that first night of her imprisonment, when nothing was clear and everything seemed frightening, she was transported into a vision that she experienced this way:

I was standing on a mountaintop, and Jesus came to me. His precious face was warmed by a smile and radiant in the early-morning sun. I asked him, "What must I do?"

He looked at me tenderly and said, "You shall love your God with all your heart, and with all your soul, and with all your mind, and with all your strength."

"But how?"

He took my hand and led me down the mountain on a steep path. It was rocky and hard to follow at first, but as we descended the way grew easier. Flowers appeared along the path's edges, and then lush bushes. A vast and verdant valley, crisscrossed with streams, came into view, and Jesus said to me, "This is the land flowing with milk and honey."

A woman, tall and strong, wearing a long robe of many bright colors, with skin the hue of ebony and dark hair flowing to her waist, walked toward me. When she got close, I could see that she was nursing a child. She sat down on a bed of grass, gathering me into her lap and holding me next to the baby, who cooed happily.

Jesus moved behind us, placing one hand on my shoulder and the other on the woman's. He said to me, "God is your Mother, always sustaining you with the milk of compassion. She is your heart."

Then a swan alighted on the ground in front of us. Balanced on its beak was a glass bowl, and the bowl was filled with golden honey, glistening in the light of the sun. Jesus offered thanks to the swan and took the bowl. He dipped a finger in the honey and then placed it on my lips. "The Holy Spirit is the world's sweetness," he said. "She is your soul."

I looked around, anxious to see what wonder would appear next. Then Jesus stepped in front of me with a scroll of rolled parchment. He opened it, and I saw written there the commandments and parables that he taught when he walked the earth. "I am the Word," he said, "imprinting God's light and truth on the world. And, when you need wisdom, I am your mind."

I was silenced by awe for a moment. And then I remembered Jesus's first words to me. "And what about strength?" I asked.

Jesus smiled. "The three of us, bound together in love, are your strength."

Bathed in the peace of the vision, Clarissa dozed lightly. She was startled awake by a call from Saint Catherine and noticed a hint of light outside the window. The call sounded again—oddly, and at the wrong time of day for an owl. Clarissa, suddenly realizing that it was not Catherine trying to get her attention, leapt off the straw. "Nerida, I'm here," she whispered.

"Thank God. I've been walking up and down this wall, calling like an owl below all the windows."

"I'm here, too," said Johanna.

"And me," Galorian said.

Clarissa, relieved to hear the voices of her friends, longed to see their faces.

As if reading her thoughts, Johanna said, "They won't let us see you. Not until after the trial."

"We can't stay long, or they'll discover us," Nerida said. "We just didn't want you to be all alone on Christmas Day."

"And we needed to know that you're all right," added Johanna.

"I am," Clarissa said.

"I'll find out what I can," promised Galorian, "and come back tonight when it's safer." She saw his hand reaching toward the bars, and she reached hers up to touch it. Then Johanna and Nerida added their hands for a moment, and they were gone.

§

Once, around the middle of the day, the trap in the thick cell door slid open and a piece of hard bread and bowl of thin gruel were pushed through. Clarissa could not make herself eat them. She thought of the trap in the front door at the abbey in Dover, and Sister Mary Anthony staring at her through it on the night that Clarissa had arrived holding her turnip. She managed to smile.

Saint Catherine had left with her friends, and the lonely day dragged on. She got through it buoyed by the hope of Galorian's visit that night. She expected to see him as soon as the light disappeared outside, but several hours of darkness passed before he came. She released her disappointment when she realized that it was far safer for him to come in the middle of the night.

When he whispered her name, she got up and stood below the window. "I'm here, Galorian."

"Are you all right?"

"Yes," she said. "And you and the others?"

"We're worried about you, but we're all right, too. Everyone sends their love. They're keeping a prayer vigil day and night in the chapel for you."

Clarissa was moved by her sisters' gesture of spiritual solidarity. "Tell me what you've learned. What can I expect?"

Galorian hesitated, but he knew that it was best to tell her, even though the news wasn't good. "You'll appear before the Inquisitor of Calais, Bishop Renard, and a council of men they've picked for the trial." Clarissa groaned quietly. "They need two witnesses to convict you, and they don't have to tell you who they are. You're not entitled to legal counsel, because it's considered a crime to defend a heretic. Your sentence will be lighter if you confess your guilt. They save the worst for those who refuse to bow to their authority."

Clarissa knew the worst. Saint Catherine's wheel and torture devices like it. Hanging people by their wrists for days at a time. Threatening to hurt the loved ones of the accused. That's the one she couldn't bear.

"I'm going to do everything I can, Clarissa. I plan to get word to Francis, to Rome, to anyone who might be able to intervene and help."

"When will the trial be?"

Galorian hesitated again. "I don't know. They could have it tomorrow—or keep you here for months." Clarissa reached up and grabbed the bars of the window to keep herself upright. Galorian wrapped his hands around hers. The two of them stood like that until, fearing the dawn that would reveal his presence, Clarissa sent him away.

Thirty-seven

Clarissa was greatly relieved when her trial was set for the following week. She felt that she could endure her imprisonment as long as she could see its end. On a cold Tuesday morning, her hands bound again in front of her, she stood alone before Inquisitor Laurent of Calais, Bishop Renard, and their chosen council of five men. The frowning church officials sat in a row on a dais behind an imposing table, dressed in the grand red robes embroidered with gold that signified religious authority.

Laurent, a Dominican theologian and scholar with a cascade of chins to rival the bishop's, opened the proceedings with introductory formalities. He explained his duty to root out "heretical depravity." He described the Beguines as "an aberrant and abominable sect of mad and malignant pseudo-women." Then he nodded at the bishop, who stepped forward and yanked the yellow oval off of Clarissa's simple, soiled robe, leaving only a few remnants of cloth.

She did not react. She was determined not to give these powerful men the satisfaction of seeing her cower in their presence. She longed to have Johanna and Galorian standing at her side, or watching behind her, offering support. But the rules of the Inquisition demanded that Clarissa face her prosecutors on her own. She never felt so alone—not even the night she had flung herself off the roof and escaped from home.

Laurent pronounced the council's verdict: "This Inquisition finds the accused guilty of heresy. Two witnesses have testified against her, with these charges. She harbors Muslims, Jews, and pagans, the enemies of Christ. She consorts with prostitutes and leads young women down the path of carnal lust and perversion with orgies and pagan rituals in caves." Clarissa didn't need to have her accusers identified. Felicite had clearly done her damage, and Father Lionel would certainly have added his own observations.

"But more damning than the words of the witnesses are those of the accused herself," continued the inquisitor. "Evidence of heresy is provided by her own hand." He held up a copy of *The Radiant Soul: Aflame with Love* and then enumerated the list of her crimes. "She writes in simple vernacular French, with the intent of deceiving our simplest citizens. She rudely addresses the leaders of the church, including our honorable pope, accusing them of arrogance. She dismisses the value of reason. She refuses to acknowledge the prevalence of sin and the truth of God's judgment."

He held the book higher in the air. "And furthermore," he declared, "she insists on referring to God as Creator and Mother, rejecting God our Lord and Father. She persists in spreading her lies and influencing women to reject the authority of the church. And she usurps the priesthood, performing baptisms and profaning the Holy Mass!" The inquisitor took his seat and leaned toward Clarissa, his eyes brimming with fury and condescension. "Do you wish to speak in your defense?"

Clarissa, unflinching, returned his stare. "Only to say that I am guilty," she declared. "Guilty of Jesus's command to love our enemies and shelter those in need. Guilty of valuing love over reason. Guilty of praying to a merciful God who is Lord and Father, but so much more. In summary, I am guilty of the Gospel." A murmur surged through the panel of men who were there to judge her. The bishop called for order.

"And one more thing," said Clarissa, capturing their attention again. "My Beguine sisters and I did not participate in pagan rituals in a cave, but Christian ones. Our only pagan ritual took place in the forest."

The inquisitor's jowly face flushed with rage. "I declare you an unrepentant heretic!" he thundered. "You are condemned to die at the stake by fire." Then he calmed his voice. "You can save your life if you recant of your heresy." He leaned toward her. "While you're rotting away in that cell, you think about that."

One of the men from the council stepped forward with a yellow cross, the symbol for heretics who refused to repent and change their ways. Clarissa stood still as he roughly stitched it onto her robe, over the place where the yellow oval had been. Then the inquisitor turned to the guards who had moved to flank her and commanded, "Take her away."

§

Clarissa turned twenty-eight alone in her cell. The night she ran away from home, she was almost fourteen. She had spent half her life in France, she realized. *It's been a good life*, she thought, *filled with many blessings.* She hated to have to lose it.

Liliana and Philippe came in the middle of that night, bringing birthday wishes. Liliana pushed a piece of shrewsbury cake, sweet and fragrant with hints of rosewater and nutmeg, through the bars of the window. It was like a little slice of heaven to Clarissa.

Trying to voice a question, Liliana could barely speak through her tears. Philippe came to her aid. "What she's wondering is if you'll recant so that you can be here for the baby."

Clarissa paused, believing that the words she was about to say were the hardest she would ever have to utter. "There's nothing I want more in this world, Liliana, than to hold and love that precious child." She swallowed hard. "But I cannot turn back now from what I believe."

She heard her niece whisper, "I know." And then Liliana said, "It's just that . . ." She couldn't continue.

"I know how terribly painful this is, Liliana," said Clarissa, struggling through her own tears. "If I thought I could do anything to stop it and be with you, I would." She reached her hands up to the bars. "You don't have to come back," she said, allowing her love for her niece to override her own heartbreaking desire. "I know it's hard. And risky for you. Please, think of yourself and the baby." She whispered, "You don't have to be here for me to know that you love me."

Liliana touched her hands to Clarissa's, and Clarissa clasped them tightly. Liliana told her that she and Philippe planned to move into Clarissa's empty room in Q Cottage so that Nerida could catch the baby. It was news that warmed Clarissa's shattered heart.

Galorian, Johanna, and Nerida also came later that night. Clarissa had insisted that they not visit her more than once a week; she hated the thought that they might get caught and suffer on her behalf. Her rapidly thinning body was grateful for the food they slipped to her, especially Nerida's birthday gift of marigold-and-honey biscuits.

They also brought news. "Aminah is happy in Jerusalem and expecting a child," said Johanna, and Clarissa smiled.

"Felicite and Georgine want to move back into the community," added Nerida. That piece of information shocked Clarissa. "They showed up one night, and Felicite cried and asked for forgiveness. She told us they want to work to atone for the damage they did."

"What did you tell them?" asked Clarissa.

"That we would give it serious thought and prayer," Johanna said.

"What are you going to do?"

Nerida answered Clarissa's question with another. "How could we live with the person who betrayed you and put you here in this horrible place?"

"How could we ever trust her?" Johanna asked.

"Or Georgine," added Nerida. Clarissa's mind flashed on several of the spiteful things Georgine had said and done while she was with them, and then Nerida spoke again. "It seems too risky to open ourselves again to her hateful behavior."

"But you must," Clarissa said. And then she added quickly, "I'm sorry. It's not my decision to make. And I certainly understand your feelings."

"We want to know what you think," Johanna said.

"I think we have to believe that no soul is beyond redemption," said Clarissa, her voice passionate with conviction. "I think we have to believe that even the worst of us can find her way back to grace, through the power of forgiving love." She paused. "But I know it's asking a lot of you to be the means of that grace, welcoming and forgiving and trusting Felicite and Georgine."

"Maybe we can start small," Nerida offered. "Invite them for prayers and a meal. Let them work alongside us for a while. See if the change is genuine." Clarissa smiled. "And, with time," said Nerida, "maybe we can be their home again."

"I'll pray about it," Clarissa promised. "I have lots of time to pray." Then she asked, "How's Jaxon? I've been worried about him."

"You being here is hard on him," said Galorian, "but he's all right."

"And the children?"

"They miss you and don't understand why you're gone," answered Nerida. "We haven't figured out yet what to tell them—other than to say that you need to be away for a while."

When they had spilled all the news, Galorian took out the bread he had brought and blessed it. He tore a piece from the loaf and passed it up to Clarissa, who grasped it between the grate's bars. Then he served bread to her visitors outside the wall. He poured the wine into one of the goblets from the manor and blessed it, realizing too late that it would not fit between the bars. He apologized to Clarissa and served the others. "Merciful God," he prayed when they had finished, "give our sister Clarissa courage and strength. And may she always remember your undying love—and ours. Amen."

After his prayer, they offered tear-laden goodbyes and promised to return in a week.

Clarissa felt her spirit flag as she heard their footsteps receding. And then Nerida was back at the window. Her tone was desperate as she pleaded, "Please, Clarissa, recant and save yourself!"

Johanna had followed her. She stepped to the window and said, "We wouldn't blame you."

"We need you," Nerida added.

Clarissa spoke calmly. "What good would my life be if I gave up now on what I believe?" And then she added, "God gives me strength."

§

Late one night a guard entered Clarissa's cell. She could tell by the look in his eye what he intended to do to her. She thought about her sisters in Liège throwing themselves into the sewer to avoid being raped. But, to her constant dismay and discomfort in her new surroundings, there was no sewer. Only a bucket that rarely got emptied.

When the guard stepped toward her, she did not flinch or cower in the corner, as he likely expected her to do. She stepped toward him with her right hand raised. Making the sign of the cross over him, she said, "May the all-knowing, all-seeing God bless you." Stunned, he stared at her for a moment. Then he turned around and skulked out the door, as she fell onto the straw trembling.

The inquisitor left Clarissa in her dismal cell for a month. And then a guard came and hauled her back before him. "Have you decided to recant?" a stern Laurent asked her.

"I cannot turn my back on the truth," she answered, "even to save my life."

"Perhaps you don't understand what you're facing," huffed the inquisitor. "The executioners like to bind the condemned high on the stake. That way you are a spectacle that can be clearly seen by everyone, a warning about what happens to those who resist the authority of the church. And they prefer to have the damned roast slowly above the flames rather than burn quickly down in them."

Laurent let her ponder that image of prolonged agony for a moment and then said, "I'll give you one more chance." He glared at her as he threatened, "We have ways of extracting confessions." Then he ordered the guard to take her back to her cell.

As the days crawled by, Clarissa realized how much she wanted to live. But she was not afraid of dying. She was afraid of suffering. Terrified of it. She tried not to think about the inquisitor's threat, but eventually her thoughts always returned to it. Sometimes at night, the tormented screams of those in the cells around her who had been dragged to the torture chamber reminded her. She tried to draw courage and strength from the witness

of Saint Catherine, who had faced and overcome the designs of her tortur-
ers. But only for a while, she remembered all too quickly.

The next time Galorian visited, she asked him, "Will you hear my
confession?"

"Yes," came the answer from the other side of the wall.

"I want to be fearless, as Jesus was . . . to accept whatever I must. But I
want to live. And I'm afraid. God forgive me for my weakness and my fear."

"Clarissa, beloved daughter of God, you are forgiven," pronounced
Galorian, as he had so many times before. This time his voice broke as he
made the sign of the cross toward the bars. Then he added, "Remember that
even Jesus, on the night that he was arrested and facing death, prayed in the
garden to God, 'If you are willing, remove this cup from me.'"

"Yes," said Clarissa. "And then he prayed, 'Yet not my will, but yours
be done.'"

§

*I'd rather be crossing the Sinai desert in a wool habit on a bellowing camel un-
der a blazing sun*, Clarissa thought one afternoon when she felt she couldn't
bear another minute in her cell. Her captors allowed her nothing to read,
and certainly not anything with which to write. Her days were hour upon
hour of grueling monotony. The nights were worse, filled with potential ter-
rors. In the middle of a particularly restless one, Clarissa heard a quiet song
being hummed on the other side of the wall. "Jaxon," she whispered.

"It's me."

Clarissa, imagining how difficult it must have been for him to summon the courage to visit her, assumed he had to be on a mission. "And have
you, too, come to convince me to recant?"

He didn't answer her question. "I have a gift for you," he said. It was just
the right size to fit through the bars of the window—a small, hard, black,
wrinkled, misshapen ball. "Do you recognize it?" Clarissa turned it over in
her hands a few times and then laughed. "It froze the winter you gave it to
me," Jaxon explained. "And then I set it out in the sun to warm it up."

The turnip had shrunk and shriveled almost beyond recognition, but
it had retained enough of its former self that Clarissa could tell what it was.
As she held it, she recalled the Samhain celebration around the welcoming
fire in the forest, and the old man who gave it to her on that night that she
met Liliana and Nerida, and the community that drew comfort and strength
from each other and the embers they carried home. She thought of the day
Lizzie had startled her awake and Jaxon called the turnip her friend. She

remembered giving it to Johanna as a reminder of warmth and light when she left the Dover abbey, and then passing it on to Jaxon. As she turned it over in her hand, she even imagined with gratitude the wrinkled faces of Sister Mary Anthony and Mother Agnes Luc. And she pictured the joyful fall days when she and Josselyn had gathered apples in the orchard and spread them in the sun to dry.

"The life has gone out of it," said Jaxon, "but it still has the power to remind us of what's important and good." As she held it and let the memories spill over her, she knew that he spoke truth. He cleared his throat. "That's all I came to say." Clarissa heard his footsteps moving away from the window.

"Wait . . . Stay," she said. She realized that it had been a very, very long time since she and Jaxon had shared an actual conversation, something other than simple talk about how the animals were faring or what to build next. "Tell me about your life, Jaxon. How did you become a minstrel?"

She heard him sigh as he slid down the outside wall and sat against it. She pictured him in his red-blue-and-yellow striped silk pantaloons and green-and-black diamond-patterned shirt, though he was actually wearing dark pants and his frayed brown coat. "I loved music and juggling and riddles when I was a boy," he began. "My father wanted me to be a soldier. But I never did understand what all the killing was about."

He sighed again and continued. "I had a gentle and kind friend who loved poetry. His father had named him, oddly enough, Manley." Jaxon laughed. "We became extremely close . . . inseparable . . . bound by a deep admiration and love. And so our angry and powerful fathers decided that we needed to be parted. Over my dear mother's protests, mine gave me a beating—to toughen me up, he said—and then sent me off to a soldiers' camp when I was thirteen. I escaped. Like you.

"Before the nuns in Dover took me in, I lived on the streets for a few years. The only way I could afford to eat was to juggle and sing and receive the coins of appreciative patrons. I was hungry a lot—until I got Lizzie."

"Did you ever see Manley again?"

"No," said Jaxon sadly. "I looked all over England for him, but I never found him." He sighed once more. "I still think about him. And about my mother. I never saw her again, either." They sat in silence for a while, and Clarissa wished she could be beside him. "What about you?" Jaxon asked. "How did you come to care so much about people?"

Clarissa pondered her answer and then shared with Jaxon what she had never voiced to anyone before. "Josselyn was beautiful and graceful. She sang like a lark and prayed like a saint. She was creative with stories, talented with needlework, and good with children. She was the perfect daughter and wife. And the perfect sister." Clarissa released a sigh that mirrored Jaxon's. "Except that sometimes it was very hard to live with her."

She laughed lightly. "People always talked about how special she was. I always felt awkward and plain around her. My father told me more than once that I would never be a worthwhile wife." Her thoughts wandered for a moment toward difficult memories, but she forced them back.

"One Sunday, when I was about ten or eleven, I noticed for the first time the poor children huddled behind the screen at the back of the cathedral. I wouldn't have been able to explain it back then, but I think something deep inside me understood what it felt like to be hidden . . . cast aside . . . unworthy. That's when I started putting sweets up my sleeves before church every Sunday and dropping them for the children on my way out."

"There's nothing good about perfection," Jaxon declared. "Far better to be human. To suffer enough to grow a selfless heart."

That night Clarissa and Jaxon talked about every topic that came to them. "I'm practicing my scales and singing when I get bored in my cell," Clarissa told him. "Which is most of the time. Maybe my jailers will set me free as an act of mercy toward the other prisoners, who already suffer enough torture." They both laughed uneasily at her attempt at a joke.

Their conversation through the grate was the longest they had ever shared—and the longest Clarissa had had with anyone in years. Through the hours of that night, they said a great deal to each other. But the most important feelings between them still remained unspoken, simply understood between them, as they always had been.

Clarissa noticed the slight lightening of the sky beyond the window. "You must go, Jaxon, before someone finds you," she said to her dear troubadour. "Thank you for coming . . . and for staying."

She heard him get up. He reached up to squeeze her hand through the window. Clarissa laughed again. "What's funny?" he asked her.

"I was just thinking that this isn't the first time I thought I was going to die by fire. I was sure my life was over at thirteen the minute I woke up on the road face to face with Lizzie."

Jaxon managed another laugh in response. And then he said "Goodbye." In all their partings over the years, he had never before uttered the word that he had always found too sad to say. "Remember what I said about the turnip," Clarissa heard him whisper.

"Goodbye, my friend," she said. She listened as his footsteps got fainter and fainter and then disappeared. She could not see the tears that streamed down his face.

§

Clarissa expected Felicite to appear outside her window late some night to ask for forgiveness, but she did not. Clarissa wavered between feeling compassion toward Felicite and giving in to an intense and gnawing rage about her betrayal, which would not let her rest. Though Felicite had not requested it, Clarissa wrestled in her heart to forgive her. She was surprised to discover that it had been easier to forgive Father Augustus, whom she had always considered an enemy, than Felicite, who she had once believed was a friend.

Some days Clarissa thought she would go mad, weary of her relentless thoughts and desperate to move and breathe fresh air. Despite the food her friends snuck to her through the bars once a week, she watched helplessly as her body grew thinner and thinner. *They won't have to kill me*, she thought. *I'll waste away to nothing before they have the chance.* The cold had settled into her bones, and she shivered uncontrollably much of the time. She did not know when her agony would end.

Even prayer didn't comfort her or assuage her anger. God seemed silent and distant. She missed the people she loved and the life she had. And she ached to accompany Liliana as she awaited the birth of her child. That was the hardest sacrifice of all.

Clarissa began to wonder if her refusal to recant was simply stubbornness—or maybe a misguided bid for attention. She thought that perhaps she could change her path and still find a way to live faithfully. *Why not just lie to the inquisitor? Save myself and make my friends and Liliana overjoyed. Get away from this horror and take up a quiet, unnoticed life of prayer and service with the ones I love. Surely God would understand.*

Doubt was a tormentor far worse than her captors.

When Holy Week arrived in late March, Clarissa hoped it would break open her spirit and bring her peace. She imagined living more deeply than she ever had before into the poignant events that always touched her so profoundly at this time of year: Judas's betrayal, Peter's denials, Jesus's anguished prayer for a different ending, his arrest and torture and crucifixion. But alone in her cell, facing the inevitability of her own death, the tragedy of it all felt like more than she could bear.

She thought about the girl with leprosy she had held outside the convent gate in Liège. "Why has God abandoned me?" was the question on the girl's lips as she took her last breaths. Clarissa remembered that it was Jesus's as well. In tortured anguish on the cross, he had moaned, "My God, my God, why have you forsaken me?" Now it was Clarissa's lament, too.

When her friends visited on Easter, Galorian painfully shared with her that there would be no intervention in her case from Rome. Even Francis had not been able to get the pope's attention to counter the mounting hysteria that surrounded the Inquisition and tame the anti-heresy dragon that had been unleashed on the empire. Galorian solemnly passed Clarissa the bread of the Easter Mass. He had brought a cup rather than a goblet for the wine this time, but when he tried to hand it to her, it too didn't fit through the bars. As he apologized again, Clarissa felt more excluded than she knew she should have, and wondered if she still believed in resurrection. She did not tell him so.

A month later, another menacing guard entered Clarissa's cell. Spewing vulgar taunts, he announced, "I'm going to make you recant!" He slapped her hard on her left cheek. Then he pushed her to the ground and kicked her several times in the ribs. The blows were so intense, Clarissa was sure he had broken one or two of them. Threatening "I'll be back," he left her doubled over in agony.

That night, wracked with pain, feeling utterly alone, totally bereft, and desperately powerless, Clarissa sobbed herself to sleep. In her last moments of wakefulness, she felt clarity come to her. She knew that could not endure another day of this suffocating torment. At the earliest opportunity, she would say and do whatever was necessary to get free of this hell in which she felt trapped. The decision gave her just enough peace to fall asleep.

When she awoke at morning's light, she felt cleansed by the night's tears. She lay calmly on the straw. Her mind wandered back a decade and a half to her second night with the Benedictine sisters in Dover, when she had wept her way through the psalm during Compline with Mary Peter at her side. *How many times have I heard that ancient prayer since?* she wondered. *Enough to have its words etched forever in my heart.* She voiced aloud the psalm of comfort:

"Answer me when I call,
O God of my right!
You gave me room when I was in distress.
Be gracious to me, and hear my prayer.
I will both lie down and sleep in peace;
For you alone make me lie down in safety."

She sighed, and a slight smile made its way to her face as her mind skipped forward a few years to the journey she and Johanna had made to Saint Catherine's Monastery. She recalled crouching next to her dear friend behind the protection of Quibilah during the sandstorm. She remembered Johanna quietly reciting her favorite psalm: ". . . Yea, though I walk through the valley of the shadow of death, I fear no evil; for you are with me . . ."

She recalled how she had struggled with her first Ramadan fast years before. Now she was being forced against her will into fasting far more intense. She realized then that she could either waste away to nothing at the hands of her enemies—or surrender to utter emptiness in order to fall into the loving arms and fullness of God. She understood that if she were willing to open herself spiritually to her imposed fast, she would discover the rare and precious deepening that comes when all else is stripped away and nothing but God remains. *It's what the ancient wanderers in the desert learned*, she reminded herself. *When their guiding pillar of fire disappeared, they found the Spirit of God that burned within their own souls and followed its truth.*

She was able to pray again then. She felt her heart opening, her strength returning. "They may break my bones," she whispered aloud to herself, "but I refuse to let them break my spirit." She stood up, walked to the window, and saw the growing light of the morning sun. Gazing at the sky, she said, "They grind up those they cannot grind down, but they will not make me hate them or rob me of my faith." As she sat in the straw, she added "or my resolve."

The guard's assault turned out to be a gift in disguise. Despite the Inquisition's seemingly random irrationality, it stuck to its rules. And one of its rules was that a person under its authority could be tortured only once. The inquisitor determined that the guard's attack qualified as torture, and Clarissa's captors were forbidden from doing worse to her.

In early May, they dragged her back before Inquisitor Laurent. He gave her one last opportunity to recant of her "pestiferous book full of damnable lies." She hesitated for just a moment, knowing that this was her very last chance to save her life.

"With the help and strength of God, I must follow the truth," she said, her voice clear. "No matter what the cost."

The inquisitor flew into a rage again and spewed a gush of spiteful words, accusing her of being "obstinate, stubborn, recalcitrant, contrary, and mulish." He set her date of execution for the following week. On Pentecost Sunday.

Thirty-eight

T hree nights before Clarissa was scheduled to die, in the middle of the night, Saint Catherine screeched and landed on the windowsill. "You're back," said Clarissa, smiling. The owl flapped her wings wildly. Clarissa remembered then what Nerida had told her about owls the first time they had parted: they are an omen not only of death but of new life. "The baby's coming!" gasped Clarissa, picturing Liliana in her room in Q Cottage, attended by Nerida. She prayed without end that night that all would go well and mother and child would be safe.

No one else came to see Clarissa that night, or the following one. She was sure that something had gone terribly wrong—that, like her mother, Liliana had died in childbirth. Tormented with this terror, she did not sleep at all those two nights.

The following night she felt a particularly sharp sorrow. The rules of the Inquisition allowed the condemned a face-to-face visit with family members on the eve of execution, but Clarissa had no parents, no siblings, no children, no spouse. She had pleaded with her guard for time with her community of sisters, explaining that they were her family. But the young man, fearful of the trouble he would face if he bent the rules, denied her request and refused to pass it on to anyone in authority who might have approved it.

In the middle of her final night in her cell, feeling abysmally alone, Clarissa heard Johanna whisper her name outside the window. Without even greeting her, Clarissa said, "Tell me about the baby. Is Liliana all right?" Johanna didn't answer. Clarissa felt an enormous grief engulf her. But a few moments later she saw, lifted up to the barred window, a tiny child wrapped in wool, asleep and shining in the moonlight.

"Her name is . . ." Liliana could not say it.

"Clarissa," whispered five voices at once. That's when Clarissa realized that her friends had come together to see her one last time. She recognized Johanna's gentle hands holding up her great-niece. How she wished she could cradle that precious child, watch her grow, tell her the fascinating tales that her grandmother had spun around sputtering candles in the tower room of the manor. Clarissa reached up through the bars and touched her namesake's soft forehead.

"This is like Moses's baptism," Lisette observed. "When you lifted him up in the air inside the cave, Johanna."

"Will you baptize her, Clarissa?" Liliana asked.

Tears gathered in Clarissa's eyes in response to her niece's poignant request. "Is there water?" No one had expected a baptism, and there was no water.

"Did you bring a cup for the communion wine?" Clarissa asked Galorian, who told her yes and added, "And it's small this time."

He passed the cup through the bars of the grate. Clarissa held it against her unbruised right cheek and allowed a stream of her tears to spill into it. She handed it back through the window. "Pass it around," she said to her friends, "to collect your tears." A mixture of sorrow and joy was pouring from all eyes, especially Liliana's, and Clarissa's request was easy to fulfill.

Galorian handed the cup back to her, as Liliana and Philippe together held little Clarissa, now awake and calm, up to the window. "Does she have a middle name?" Clarissa asked, and the young couple said together "Celeste." Three times Clarissa dipped her hand into the cup of tears and then reached through the bars and touched her great-niece's forehead. "Clarissa Celeste, I baptize you in the name of the Creator . . . and of the Savior . . . and of the Holy Spirit." Then, drawing from the biblical stories that Johanna had planted so tenderly in her heart, she offered a prayer of blessing:

> "Clarissa, may God bless you with the loving resourcefulness of Jochebed, the clever courage of Shiphrah and Puah, and the trusting loyalty of Ruth. May God grant you the wisdom of Deborah, the prophetic power of Huldah, and the peacemaking spirit of Abigail.
>
> Like Mary the Mother of God, may you always recognize and welcome an angel when you see one. Like Elizabeth, may you discover deep joy and faithful friendship on your life's journey. And like Mary Magdalene, may you always be a true, strong, and dedicated witness to the power of resurrection.
>
> Clarissa, you are a beloved daughter created in the image of God, who breathed holy life into you. It was for you that God created the world and all its wonders. May the Holy One bless

you and keep you, and may you be drenched inside and out with God's gentle grace and tender mercy. Always and forever. Amen."

There was nothing but silence and more tears for several moments. Then Liliana reached up and slipped her mother's cross through the bars. "You need this now more than I do," she said. Clarissa thought to protest the precious gift that she knew the next day would be lost in the ashes, but she wanted the comfort of her sister's cross, so lovingly made by Galorian, around her neck at the end. "I love you more than I can tell you," she said to her niece, and Liliana repeated the words back to her.

Little Clarissa began to fuss. "We'll go, so that her cries don't alert the guards," said Philippe. "We pray for you constantly."

"Thank you, Philippe," Clarissa said, "for being the kind of husband and father Liliana and Clarissa deserve. I love you all." And then they were gone.

Clarissa thanked Nerida for giving her the gift of Liliana, for caring for, nurturing, and guiding her niece on the way to becoming the magnificent young woman she was. "Your friendship has enriched my soul, my dear sister."

She spoke next to Lisette, encouraging her to help Liliana to be a good mother, as she was for Moses. "You're the youngest of us. Keep alive the vision of the journey of faith and spread it far and wide. And stay strong, my sister and friend."

Clarissa also had instructions for Johanna. "Keep telling the stories. Keep nurturing women to be true to their faith and their strength." Her voice cracked with emotion. "Oh, dear Johanna, what would my life have been without you? I can't ever thank you enough." There was so much more she wanted to say, but she could not.

And then, wondering how she would ever say goodbye to him, she turned to her last friend. All she could utter was a question. "Galorian, are you prepared to perform Last Rites?"

He hesitated and then whispered, "Yes."

"Will you hear my final confession?"

"Yes."

"I've carried this secret for over half my life, and now I must tell it. I didn't give you the whole story the night we caught each other up on our lives." She paused, wondering if she could finally speak it. "It *is* my fault that your daughter died, Galorian. Moments after she was born, I held her. With my words, I pleaded for her to live. But in my heart, I prayed with all my strength for her to die."

Clarissa swallowed hard before continuing. "I didn't want her to live. Not without a mother. Not in a world that is so hostile and difficult, where a child so precious would be judged of so little worth. 'Only a girl.' I wanted to save her from a lifetime of feeling as scared and powerless as I did." The crushing sorrow of being unable to see or touch Galorian felt unbearable, and she hated the wall between them. She wanted to tear it down, stone by stone.

Galorian, with a tremor of emotion, repeated what he had said to her when they shared their stories on the cliff after so many years apart. "It's not your fault. None of it is your fault, Clarissa. And whatever you did in your life that needs forgiving is forgiven." He reached up to the bars and made the sign of the cross, offering the final blessing from the Order of Last Rites: "Clarissa, may Jesus Christ protect you and lead you to eternal life."

He blessed and broke the bread. He said a prayer as he poured the wine into the cup to mingle with the tears there. Clarissa and her friends shared communion across the wall in silence laced with sorrow.

When they finished, Clarissa thanked Galorian. And then she said, "And thank you, my dear sisters. Because of you, I don't believe anymore what I believed the night I lost Josselyn and her baby. If I held that child now, I would know that she can thrive in this world under the care of many mothers, and that no child is ever 'only a girl.' Alone it may seem that way, but I know now that together we are powerful and strong."

When she finished speaking, she looked up at the window and was astonished to see Lisette's smiling face shining in the moonlight beyond the bars. "Jaxon is making a new sign for The Clarissa and Josselyn Center," she announced. "We love you." Lisette reached her hand down through the bars into the dark cell as Clarissa extended hers, and then she disappeared.

A few moments later, Nerida's face appeared. She too squeezed Clarissa's outstretched hand. "And Lisette is already painting your fresco in the chapel—next to Saint Catherine's. We'll miss you terribly, Clarissa."

Johanna was next to hover beyond the window. "My beloved sister, I will always remember your faith. And your courage. And your strength. You will live in my heart forever . . ." She stopped. And then she said, "Damn! You know how I feel. I just want to bellow and roar and cry with a . . ." Clarissa spoke it with her: "gurgleburblegrumblerumble." The two dear friends laughed together through their tears. When Johanna grasped her hand, Clarissa thought she couldn't bear to let it go. But soon Johanna was gone as well.

There was a bit of commotion on the other side of the wall then. Johanna explained, "Galorian lifted each of us, but it will take all three of us to lift him." Clarissa understood that they were taking a risk to let her see their faces, and she was enormously grateful for the gift. She was relieved that it was too dark in her cell for them to see hers clearly.

"We're going to build a prayer room in your honor, on your favorite spot on the beach," Galorian told her when her sisters had hoisted him up to the window. He swayed unsteadily, and they both knew that their time to speak was short. "I won't forget you," he said, gripping her hand tightly. She noticed the moonlight reflected in the pools of tears in his eyes. "Ever."

"I'll carry you with me," said Clarissa. And then his face too disappeared.

Clarissa sighed deeply. And then she asked her friends, "Will you indulge me . . ?" She wanted to say "in some final words," but she could not utter the phrase. She decided that, under the circumstances, they would let her say whatever she wanted. And so she spilled what was on her heart, the words she wanted to leave with them.

"Unjust powers have always tried to silence the truth," she began. "But they have never succeeded. Always . . . without fail . . . clusters of faithful believers rise up to keep the witness alive. To keep hope burning in hearts that are open."

She wished that she could see their faces again. "No one can destroy the truth. It resides not in just one of us, but in the fullness of us together. Whatever happens, who I am . . . who we are . . . will never be lost." She struggled to keep her voice even and strong, to finish saying what she felt with such hope-drenched conviction. "I'll live on in each of you. And in every woman who finds her voice. And every person who refuses to believe the lie that power and violence and possessions are truth. And every community that chooses to live for the common good." She sighed again. "A thousand years from now, the world will still know what we believed and did."

She stopped then, feeling weary and spent. "Goodbye, my friends," she said. "I thank God for you and love you with all my heart." Speaking all at once, they returned her love, promised their prayers, and encouraged her to be strong. "Now go," she said, as she sank into the straw, unable to stop a deluge of tears.

§

After Clarissa's friends left her, the woman clothed with the sun appeared again to her, flooding her cell with bright light. As Clarissa gazed at the vision, she saw the woman's face change into her own. She saw herself standing on the moon, under a crown of stars, radiating the dazzling light of the sun. A monstrous red dragon appeared beside her. Its seven scaly heads bore the faces of Inquisitor Laurent, Bishop Renard, and the five men of the heresy council. Its jaws were massive. It roared and breathed fire at her, sweeping stars from the sky with its tail.

Clarissa saw herself clutching a copy of *The Radiant Soul: Aflame with Love* over her heart. She knew in that moment that she had fulfilled the purpose for which God had given her life. She had birthed the book that reflected her understanding of truth as God had revealed it to her.

Then a great bird entered the vision from the sky, floating high above her, its plumage so blinding as it reflected the sun's rays that Clarissa could not discern its color or shape. "Be a falcon," she pleaded in a whisper. "An azure-blue falcon to swoop down and carry me away from this danger to a safe place."

But as the bird descended toward her in the vision, she saw that it was not a falcon but a phoenix. Its wings glistened red and gold as it lifted her— one wing love, the other grace. As she and the bird flew into the sky, they were like one magnificent creature, wrapped in light, reflecting the splendor of the sun. They soared higher and higher, until Clarissa spied in front of her a towering palm tree on the top of a mountain peak.

As the phoenix folded its wings and came to rest in the branches of the tree with Clarissa on its back, she looked down at the desert below her and beheld a huddle of people in robes. She saw Saint Catherine, holding the wheel of her torture. She recognized Theodora of Alexandria disguised as a man, and Daniel the Stylite standing on his pillar, surrounded by other desert mothers and fathers and an array of saints and martyrs of the church. In the center of them stood Jesus, his eyes lifted and arms outstretched toward her.

As Clarissa surveyed the faithful assembly, she wondered, *Must some give up everything to save faith from the clutches of power? Must some die so that others can live in freedom?* She reached out to stroke the neck of the phoenix for assurance and noticed for the first time the pieces of cinnamon bark in the great bird's beak.

It was then that Clarissa understood that her salvation would come not through escape, but by sacrifice. Never had she yearned so fervently to be wrong. Lodged in her heart was the tiniest sliver of hope for a different outcome, but she did not trust it. She relinquished her will to the searing furnace of God's love and the refining fire of grace.

§

Clarissa stood at the back of a huge throng, at the edge of the Place D'Armes, her hands bound once more in front of her. A path had been cleared through the spectators to the stake, which was flanked by two burning torches. She guessed it to be about two hundred paces, but it seemed endless to her. Before and behind her were the four guards who had arrested her, dressed in their black garb and masks, carrying two ropes, two swords, a mace, and an ax.

A drum began a slow, steady beat, and the five of them walked in time with it down the long aisle. As the stake loomed close, Clarissa saw the bundles of branches placed around it. She noted that, this time, no books were piled up for burning.

When they reached the front, the guards lifted her and tied her to the stake high off the ground. Clarissa felt the girl's bell, her mother's necklace, and Josselyn's cross pressing into the flesh over her heart as two guards tightened a rope around her shoulders. The other two bound her knees. She tried to ignore the stabbing pain in her side, beneath her wounded ribs.

As soon as she was secured, hovering alone above the crowd that had come to watch her die, the thought came to her that leaving her earthly life at sunset was both sad and beautiful. Since the earliest days of her childhood, that moment in each day when the sun slipped off the edge of the earth and the sky flamed into color had always been her favorite. She felt an unexpected sensation of gratitude that she was tied to the stake facing west, toward the sunset and home.

She scanned the crowd and saw Johanna, Nerida, and Lisette up front, not far from her. She was relieved that she did not see Liliana. She was not surprised that Jaxon was not with them, but she looked around anxiously for Galorian.

Standing at the opposite end of the aisle, at the back of the throng, was Inquisitor Laurent, dressed in a gleaming white robe embellished with gold embroidery, holding a shiny gold scepter in his raised right hand. He began walking through the crowd toward a pulpit that had been placed a few paces from Clarissa. But commotion at the back stopped him.

Clarissa spied three more white robes, quite unlike the inquisitor's. Genevieve, Sybille, and Raulf had followed the requirement of the law and put on the robes they had abandoned wearing at Swansong. Raulf carried Emmanuel's rattle, holding it exactly as Laurent held his gold scepter. As they pushed past the inquisitor, Clarissa marveled at her friends' boldness. Spectators stepped back, some murmuring, others shouting "Lepers!" But her friends kept coming toward her, looking to Clarissa like a small band of angels as they floated down the aisle to join her loved ones at the front.

The inquisitor resumed his walk. Clarissa thought about the signifi-cance of the day. At Pentecost the Holy Spirit appeared as rushing wind and tongues of flame over the heads of the gathered believers. She tried to draw comfort from that vision—and to claim the power of that moment when the church was born through wind and fire—as the setting sun slipped out of sight and the sky erupted in color.

§

Around a corner behind the throng, Galorian sat atop Thane. The night before, he had slipped into the Mary Magdalene Chapel and knelt at the altar, praying for wisdom and strength. In the dark, he removed his monk's robe and put on the leggings, shirt, coat, and riding boots he had worn at Liliana's wedding. He set out that morning for Calais before dawn, choosing not to risk telling anyone his plan.

He was hidden from Clarissa's sight, but he had a clear view of her. Even from the distance that separated them he could see the thinness of her body under her robe and the bruise under her left eye. *Oh, my dear Clarissa, what have they done to you?*

Thane, impatient to run, stomped and snorted, his nostrils flaring. Ga-lorian, too, felt anxious to make his move, but he understood that his rescue needed to be carefully timed. He had to act when all eyes were focused on the inquisitor. He knew that he could reach Clarissa in a matter of seconds and that surprise was his greatest advantage. But he had only a moment to free her before the guards would react and flames would engulf the stake.

Galorian's heart beat to the rhythm of the drum, as it had during the spectacular launch of the Fourth Crusade. He had abandoned his sword in an alley in Constantinople and never picked up another. But he still knew how to ride like a knight. And the knife in his sweating palm would cut the ropes that bound Clarissa.

He watched as a full moon crowned in the east, a bright semicircle behind and below Clarissa, whose feet seemed to touch it. Her face glowed in the day's last brilliant stabs of orange light. Above her, high in a sky dark-ening to a deep shimmering blue, a few stars blinked on. The sight took his breath away.

A strong wind began to stir as the inquisitor moved behind the pulpit, exhorting the onlookers against the sin of heresy and announcing the In-quisition's decision to hand over the condemned to the secular authorities for punishment. Galorian saw Clarissa raise her bound hands and make the sign of the cross, blessing the crowd that had come to witness her execution.

What he could not see was that the blessing was intended for one person in particular. When Clarissa's hands dropped, Galorian spurred Thane, who rounded the back of the crowd and charged down the aisle.

All eyes turned to focus on the rider and horse whose hooves clattered on the cobblestone square. Johanna, overwhelmed by both shock and hope, called out, "Save her, Galorian! Please save her!"

Galorian rode full tilt toward the stake. Suddenly he spied Felicite in front of Clarissa, kneeling in the aisle in an apparent last-minute act of contrition and plea for forgiveness. In one horrible instant, he realized that saving Clarissa would mean trampling Felicite. He shouted to the young woman on her knees to get out of his way as he kept charging. Felicite, paralyzed with terror by the horse bearing down on her, remained frozen in place.

Galorian saw one of the guards lunge for a torch. He cried out again to Felicite. And then, just steps away from her, he pulled up on the reins. Thane reared high into the air, so that Galorian was face to face with Clarissa when the torch touched the branches. She nodded and smiled at him, and he felt his heart melt in despair.

Clarissa looked away from him and up toward the stars then, and Galorian heard her murmur, "Mother, forgive them, for they know not what they do." Felicite scrambled out of the way and disappeared into the crowd. Galorian leapt off Thane and raced toward the pile of wood as the dry tinder burst into a fiery blaze.

"Hail Mary, full of grace . . ." whispered Clarissa as the flames licked her feet. Galorian staggered back from the intense heat. The prayer kept tumbling from Clarissa's lips.

". . . blessed art thou amongst women . . ."

Genevieve, Sybille, and Raulf were on their knees, honoring the young woman who had shown them such profound acceptance and compassion.

". . . and blessed is the fruit of your womb."

Lisette reached her arms up toward Clarissa and cried out her name.

"Holy Mary, Mother of God, pray for us . . ."

Nerida clasped her hands together and brought them to her lips.

". . . now and at the hour of our death."

Johanna, convulsed with grief, sobbed openly.

"Amen."

Overwhelmed with the anguish of his failure and loss, Galorian fell to his knees alongside the others. "My dearest love," he murmured.

The flames burned through the rope that bound Clarissa's hands. She raised her arms and spread them out beside her. And then she began to sing.

Her wordless song was as primal, and clear, and exquisite as the ancient hymns of the birds at the dawn of Creation.

All eyes were riveted on her, all ears attuned to the sacred, surreal sound drifting from the stake. And then, one by one, the throng of spectators joined Clarissa's friends on their knees, many bowing their heads in reverence and awe as the magnificent melody wafted over them and reverberated throughout the square.

From the parapet of Calais's tall watchtower, the shrill shriek of a screech owl pierced the velvet veil of the night. Saint Catherine spread her wings and lifted into the sky. Clarissa's soul flickered and then followed, rising with the owl. As it flew toward the beckoning spirit of her beloved Josselyn, drawn by the welcoming embrace of Jesus, it flared for a brief instant like the sun. And then it soared to join the stars in the heavens.

In that moment, Clarissa's body blazed into a pillar of fire, its fierce and dazzling brilliance lighting up the night.

CPSIA information can be obtained
at www.ICGtesting.com
Printed in the USA
LVHW051714030621
689279LV00008B/761